C000121494

UNHAPPENINGS

EDWARD AUBRY

Copyright © 2014 by Edward Aubry

All rights reserved.

No part of this book may be reproduced in any form or by any electronic or mechanical means, including information storage and retrieval systems, without written permission from the author, except for the use of brief quotations in a book review.

CONTENTS

[PART 1]
NIGEL

[1]

November 2081

The first time my life unhappened was Beth Richmond. I was fourteen. She was fifteen. There was a kiss involved. It wasn't a particularly noteworthy kiss, just one of those high school kisses that are more about learning how to feel than actually feeling. I doubt it would have led to anything like a relationship, even the ephemeral kind so common to that age. Still, a kiss is a kiss, and it was memorable enough.

She didn't show up for school the next day. I was either too nervous—or too immature—to call her. It wouldn't have mattered. She didn't show the day after that either. As casually as I could, I asked around to see if she was sick.

No one had any idea who she was.

Understand, this wasn't a girl who showed up one day and then disappeared. I had known Beth since sixth grade. Most of my friends knew her too, so I was troubled by how they reacted to my inquiries. They began with polite confusion, and then rapidly degenerated to cruel jokes about my imaginary girlfriend. Over the next few days, I learned that none of my teachers had ever heard of her, and there was no record of her ever having been enrolled at my school. While the fruity taste of her lip gloss was still fresh in my mind, not a single other person had any memory of her at all. Torn between my need to understand what had happened, and my need not to be seen as insane, I quietly let it drop.

I think that was the first time my life unhappened. In truth, it's only the earliest example of which I am certain. It may have unhappened any number of times before that, in ways too subtle for me to perceive, or at times when I would have been too young to understand. Of the two people who would be able to tell me about earlier examples I may have missed, one has retroactively ceased to exist, and the other has yet to be born. That's not to say I don't see them from time to time anyway, but neither of them are speaking to me lately.

I want to say what happened to Beth Richmond was the first step on my path to becoming an applied hyperphysicist, and that it inspired my work with time travel, but that probably represents a causality loop. Regardless, that was the day I first became aware of the non-deterministic nature of the universe, and that the past is every bit as flexible as the future.

More to the point, that was the day I realized no one was aware of it but me.

[2]

March 2085

Over the next few years, my life was a series of minor unhappenings. Most had no serious impact on me. I had a red bicycle that one day suddenly became—and had always been—blue. A TV show I had enjoyed for years was never produced. My cat one day was always a dog, with the same name. I found I could train myself to ignore these sudden and bizarre discrepancies, and thus simulate being a normal teen.

These events were usually spread out, separated most times by stretches of several months. Sometimes they came rapid fire. I went through four cars the week after I got my license. They were all gifts from my parents, or rather, they were all the same gift. I was the only one who noticed it varying.

Similarly, I went through four physics teachers my senior year of high school. One would disappear, leaving no legacy or memory in the community, to be replaced by a brand new one everyone had seemingly known for years. Every time it happened, my grade took a sudden, retroactive, and sharp decline. It would take me weeks to pull it back up to anything close to an A, only to have it snatched away again. Unlike most other unhappenings, this was no mere inconvenience. That fall, I had been accepted through early decision to MIT for physics.

I persevered. What choice did I have? Still, the underlying frustration was often difficult to endure. Each successive teacher had a progressively diminished opinion of me, at a time in my life when I was most in need of a sympathetic mentor. It was during this period that I began to cultivate a deliberately detached personality, my only available defense against the constant barrage of rugs being pulled out from under me. I look back on those days now and see them as the phase of my life when I taught myself how not to feel joy, and convinced myself that the world was devoid of wonder. Delight and adventure would be for other people, never for me. Sometimes I reflect on how things would have played out if I had not willingly dropped my emotions into that abyss, but drop them I did. At every shift in reality, I became a colder student, turning further inward, driven to succeed against ever-increasing obstacles.

On the third teacher, those obstacles became insurmountable.

In early March, the class was assigned to write a 3,000 word paper analyzing any historically significant development in theoretical physics. I chose string theory, which was a bit of a gamble. Two months earlier, an experimental probe orbiting Pluto, whose purpose in part was to observe and measure an as yet unproven aspect of string theory, was accidentally destroyed in its test flight. An international team of scientists was still sifting through the debris, and very little information regarding their findings had yet made its way back to Earth. Depending on how soon that information was released, any observations or conjectures in my paper could immediately prove insightful or preposterous. I chose to explore a minority view, linking string theory to technologically attainable time travel.

Two weeks after the due date, Mr. Lewis, physics teacher number three, returned graded papers to everyone but me. As everyone else was scrolling through his comments on their tablets, I vainly attempted to find the file.

He walked to my desk and said quietly, "Nigel, can you stick around for a few minutes after class?" After a moment of awkward silence, he added, "It's nothing bad."

I nodded, and the bell rang. My classmates filed out. I approached Mr. Lewis at his desk. Even seated, he was absurdly tall, and I was instinctually intimidated by him. The previous teacher, Ms. Oswald, had been significantly less physically imposing. My paper lay in front of him, open on his tablet, no markups on it.

"Pull up a chair," he said.

Apprehensively, I did so.

"Nigel, I think we should publish this."

It took me a moment to compose a response to that statement. In the little amount of time he had been my teacher, he never seemed even remotely impressed with my work.

"What do you mean?" I finally asked.

"It's not perfect," he said. "It's solid high school writing, and I still need you to polish it, but your take on this topic is absolutely brand new. I have never seen this level of insight in a high school paper before. I took the liberty of running it by two other physicists, and they agree that it's worth exploring."

He paused there. I didn't know what he expected me to say.

"It was a guess," I admitted.

He grinned, in a way that straddled the border between delightful and sinister. "I know, but it's an amazing guess. We have a win-win situation here. If we submit this to a peer reviewed journal, we have nothing. I propose that we shop it to the non-academic science sites. If your guess is a dead end, we still have an entertaining article. If your guess has merit, we have a lock on it. No one will ever be able to explore it without citing this paper."

His repeated use of the word 'we' did not thrill me, but there was no denying that this represented an opportunity I had not conceived of before this moment. Cautiously, I asked, "How do we do that?"

His smile became friendlier. "Let's do this right. I know some people, so I'll make a few calls. I'd also like to have a conference with your parents before we move on this. We should do this soon, though. The quicker we get it out there, the better."

I nodded. The hugeness of it began to set in. I was about to become a published theoretical physicist at age seventeen. The rest of my day was spectacular. Mr. Lewis called my father at work and we all went out to dinner that evening. Plans were solidified. I barely slept that night.

Then it unhappened.

The very next day, physics began with Mr. Lewis sending back papers. They were the same papers I had seen him returning to students just the day before. Once again, everyone received a file but me. A troubling déjà vu set in, cemented by Mr. Lewis quietly telling me, "Nigel, I need to see you after class." This time it was not a request, and it did not include a reassurance.

A bell rang. The rest of the class filed out. Mr. Lewis sat at his desk, my paper open on the tablet in front of him. He did not offer me a chair.

"Mostly," he began, "I am insulted by this."

Any other student in my position would have been confused by that, but I was so used to having the rug pulled out from under me, all I could do was wait for it with a sick feeling of inevitability in the pit of my stomach.

"Do you think I'm stupid?" he asked. "Did you think I wouldn't recognize this?"

I said nothing. I looked down at the paper in front of him. It was mine. Next to it lay a hard-copy printout of the same exact paper, dated two years earlier, authored by someone else. I was numb. Not stunned, simply heartbroken. I stood there and listened to Mr. Lewis pass judgment on me, describe disciplinary actions to be taken, and detail phone calls he had already made to MIT and my parents. I stood there and took it. I had no choice. When he finally dismissed me, I left his classroom silently broken, throat tight, eyes moist.

A woman sitting on a bench in the hall frowned at me as I passed through the door. I had never seen her before. She appeared to be in her twenties, and I thought for a moment she must have been another new teacher, but she wore a denim jacket that was both unprofessional and hopelessly out of style. Her long, straight, blonde hair was pulled back in a ponytail, and for a moment it seemed remarkably familiar to me, like I should know her. Then her frown softened. She put her finger to her lips, and shooed me away with a flip of her head. Still sullen, I walked away, but looked back just in time to see her quietly enter Mr. Lewis's room and shut the door behind her.

The day after that, I came to school expecting to be called before the principal. That did not happen. With dread, I went to physics. A short man wearing a bow tie announced that he had finally graded our papers and transmitted them. As I sat, reading a file that had finally been sent to my own tablet, he walked by my desk. "Nice work," he said crisply.

The paper was identical to the one I had now seen twice in this very room, in two totally different lights. I now saw it in a third. Above the header on the cover page was the number 92, bold and red. No publication, no punishment.

After school, as I waited outside for my ride, I saw a woman across the street with long blonde hair, wearing a denim jacket. She smiled at me, put her finger to her lips, and briskly walked away.

[3]

January 2085

As with so many dramatic advances in human history, time travel was discovered by accident.

On January 4, 2085, a probe orbiting Pluto was briefly accelerated to approximately three hundredths the speed of light. It had been fitted with an experimental engine, which in turn was powered by an experimental fusion reactor. The name of the probe was Hermes 4, but not many people called it that anymore. In addition to testing the equipment itself, the purpose of the test flight was to measure the effects of propelling an object to fractionally relativistic speeds. Time dilation was a well-established principle, and the general expectation was that the measurable results would perfectly comply with predictions. A trend in physics at that time was the conjecture that great enough acceleration might serve—even if only for a tiny fraction of a second—to partially uncoil some or all of the elusive hidden extra dimensions on which string theory still hinged. A variety of methods were proposed to measure this effect, all of which were implemented on the day of the test flight. Because this aspect of the test most appealed to the media, and because of the eventual result of the experiment, the probe forever came to be known by the nickname, "Slinky." The probe itself was not expected to survive the acceleration it was meant to undergo. It did not, but for reasons distinctly other than predicted.

While the engine was still spinning up, and 2.7 seconds before it was fired, an object blipped into existence literally from nowhere, collided with one of the radiator fins mounted to the engine, and rebounded at an angle that ultimately brought it to rest on the surface of Charon. There was insufficient time to abort the flight. With one radiator fin damaged, waste heat accumulated in the probe at an unanticipated rate. 9.1 seconds into the test flight, and approximately 11 seconds short of the most conservative prediction of its life expectancy, the probe broke apart. The fusion generator detached and traveled a considerable distance into the Kuiper belt before exploding.

A large fragment of the probe was thrown backward in the direction of its original orbital position. Then, in front of thousands of real time observers, and recorded on hundreds of cameras, it blipped out of existence.

In the wake of the accident, a search was conducted for the object that collided with the probe. It was recovered from its crater on Charon, and went on to become the single most studied object in the history of science, and the most puzzling. By every possible method of scrutiny, it was determined to be the same fragment of the probe that had vanished in front of countless witnesses and cameras.

In short, a piece of the probe traveled back through time, and caused an accident that resulted in the piece of the probe traveling back through time to cause the accident.

That was the day hyperphysics was born.

As I said, this happened during my senior year in high school. It would be a full year before the realization of time travel became public. As information began to trickle in about the experiment, the accident, and its world-changing implications, and while everyone else was scrambling to make sense of it, I had the opposite reaction. My life had finally begun to make sense.

[4]

2082 - 2085

I n the fall of my tenth grade year, I met Mindy Decker. We were in the same calculus class. I didn't really get to know her until about November. We had gotten together with several other kids to study for an exam. There was some obvious chemistry. After that, I started contriving reasons to spend time with her. So did she. We dated for about two weeks, just long enough for me to fall for her, hard.

One day she was missing from calculus. I briefly panicked, flashing back to Beth Richmond, until I saw Mindy in the cafeteria at lunch. I sat with her, as always, and asked her where she had been.

She had no idea who I was.

To call that a horrible moment would downplay its effect on me. I attempted to pass the whole thing off as a case of mistaken identity, and pretended to be embarrassed, to mask my pain. After fleeing, I considered starting over with her. Partly from a grim recognition that recovering from that first impression would be challenging, and partly from cowardice, I decided against.

When I was in eleventh grade, and she was in ninth, Leslie Dietrich joined the math team. She had one of the keenest minds I have ever seen in action, and with the added edge she brought to competitions, we made it to the state championship that year. She also had a crush on me that everyone but me on the team found very amusing.

At first, I kept her at arm's length, making it clear I really only wanted to be friends. I felt our age difference left anything else out of the question. She was also a bit small for her age, and I was already taller than most of my peers. The longer I got to know her, however, the less it seemed to matter. She had an outspoken maturity that belied her youth, and she was easily my intellectual superior. Just as I was about to relent, and had worked up the nerve to ask her out, she beat me to it.

Over the next two months we were inseparable. My friends all adored her. I got to know her brother, who was a year older than I, and we became close friends. More than one of my teachers referred to us as a cute couple within my earshot. It was one of the most joyous periods of my adolescence.

One day, in a van on a way to an important meet, Leslie was sitting between me and Stan Rosen, one of my best friends. I wish I could remember what we were talking about. All I do remember is at some point I made a joke to Leslie that was overtly flirtatious. She got uncomfortable. Stan accused me of hitting on his girlfriend. I tried—and failed—to laugh it off.

My entire relationship with Leslie unhappened to me, and happened to Stan, all in one, smooth, agonizing motion. It cost me my friendship with him, not out of some kind of jealous confrontation, but simply out of my depression over it. I withdrew from my entire social circle after hearing them ask me what had gotten into me one too many times. Ultimately, I quit the team without explanation. Neither Leslie nor Stan expressed any misgiving over that decision.

At the end of that school year, at a time in my life when I felt more alone than I could ever recall, Carrie Wolfe spontaneously kissed me. We had been friends, on and off, for years. I had no idea she ever had feelings for me, and she admitted she hadn't realized it either. We had both had difficult years, for different reasons, and we sort of stumbled upon each other in our times of need.

Carrie was my first summer romance. As far as she—or anyone else—knew, she was also my first girlfriend. It got very serious, very quickly. We started planning a future together, applying to all the same colleges as a precaution against becoming separated when high school ended. Our parents had all known each other since we were children, and were all pleased with this turn of events.

In October, we had our first major fight, and broke up for an entire week.

In December, we lost our virginities together.

In April, I asked her to marry me. We agreed to a five-year engagement, long enough for us each to earn at least one college degree.

Our plan was to keep this betrothal secret from everyone for those five years, but we each told one person, and after about two days, that was that. Our parents expressed the proper level of concern, but generally supported us.

One Sunday morning in late May, the day after our senior prom, one of the most glorious nights of my entire life, I called Carrie's house and asked her mother if I could speak to her. She hung up on me without comment.

It took me three days to find out that Carrie Wolfe had died in a car accident when she was twelve years old. My subsequent mental breakdown terrified my family, and what few friends I still had left. That I would fall apart six years after an event I had apparently been fully aware of at the time without ill effect baffled everyone. I ended up hospitalized and missed my own graduation ceremony. Eventually, more from a unique sense of understanding my situation than anything else, I pulled myself up from my despair, and soldiered on to MIT.

I did not have any girlfriends in college.

[5]

2085

My freshman year was peppered with more unhappenings than almost any other time in my life, before or since. Sometimes they came so quickly I began to think if I were observant enough, I would actually be able to see the changes in real time. That never worked out to be the case, though. Invariably, the people in my life whose memories of me fluctuated never had that experience in my presence. There were times when I discovered a classmate was unaware of a conversation from only an hour before, or I would first meet someone I had evidently already known for some time, but those shifts always took place outside my own frame of reference. In this sense, while my life was hideously inconsistent, it appeared, even to me, to be in perfect continuity.

This phenomenon, among others, pushed me further and further toward my studies of time travel theory. It was, at least at that time, the only plausible avenue of explanation. As disorienting—and occasionally devastating—as these disturbances were for me personally, their nature fascinated me. Was the fact I could never perceive the changes directly a property of the event, or of my own consciousness? Were the occurrences random, or were the patterns I sometimes seemed to observe indicative of some underlying structure?

Of one thing alone I was absolutely certain: no one but me ever shared this experience.

Part of that certainty came from presumption, bordering on conceit. The ways in which my life was routinely tortured and gutted were so personal it was virtually impossible for me to conceal the effects they had on me. My family, my friends, my professors, and often total strangers made frequent remarks that I seemed off. Which, indeed, I was. So, if my own pain was that obvious to everyone I encountered, another's pain for similar reasons would have to be obvious to me. I looked for it everywhere I went. Every human contact included a quest for signs of this trauma. No one ever had it. No one ever even understood it.

Another part of that certainty came from arduous research. As a boy, I was naturally inclined to ask my friends, from time to time, if they had ever seen signs such as I had. It was always easy enough to do with subtlety. Never broach the subject in the presence of more than one other person. Only discuss it with individuals who could be trusted completely. Describe the phenomenon as some queer variation of déjà vu. I learned to ask the questions in ways that prevented me from being seen as insane, but I never found the answers I so eagerly sought.

And yes, part of that certainty came from exploring the possibility it was, in fact, madness. I scoured the literature on abnormal psychology, hunting for some sign I had an identifiable disorder. I did find some cases of perceptual disconnection that approximated what I felt, and I did occasionally take on those labels to see how well they would fit my mind. Always, however, there were too many other indicators that persuaded me that I did not have these particular disorders. Some other aspect of my psyche was too functional to comfortably fit whatever diagnosis I chose to explore. So, either I was the only person to be experiencing these retroactive life changes, or I was the only person with this particular mental illness. Either way, I was unique.

I did, of course, go down this road of investigation with the aid of psychotherapy. However, on more than one occasion, I found myself showing up for an appointment with a psychologist who had never heard of me. In other aspects of my life, that sort of awkward moment was a familiar embarrassment; in this context it represented a risk that might have broader consequences. On the third try, I gave up.

So, I firmly established the fact this undoing and redoing of my personal history was an experience linked solely to me.

I was, of course, quite mistaken. Obvious now in hindsight. Whatever hindsight even means anymore.

[6]

January 2087

One day, halfway through my second year at MIT, something unhappened to me twice. Or, perhaps more accurately, two completely different things unhappened simultaneously. They effectively neutralized each other, and I would not even have been aware of them if I hadn't almost been arrested for one of them.

I was in the library when the police came for me. Sitting alone, as always, and engrossed in my reading, I honestly didn't see or hear them until I heard one of them speak my name.

"Nigel Walden?" A loner by choice, I wasn't used to being sought out, much less by a stern looking man in a uniform. I can only imagine the expression on my face as I looked up. Standing beside me were two police officers, one male, one female. For a fraction of a moment, I allowed myself to perceive them as campus security, but the guns on their hips snapped that image into proper focus. Behind the woman stood a man about her height, rotund, with a comb over that drew far too much attention to his hair loss. This was Dr. Ainsley, a professor I had the previous year. His lips, barely visible through his excessive mustache, were pursed, and his eyes narrowed. Broadening my field of awareness, I could see dozens of students, most strangers, taking an interest. One caught my eye for a moment. She wore a charcoal beret, and in the fraction of a second it took me to realize that I recognized her but couldn't quite place her, she ducked into the stacks out of my line of sight.

Her identity immediately dropped to the bottom of my list of priorities as I refocused my attention on the trouble I was apparently in.

As I said, I have no idea what my face looked like in that moment. I do remember the look on the face before me, and whatever shock I was feeling was somehow mirrored there. His mouth hung open, an unfinished idea (probably involving my rights) perched on his tongue. He turned to his partner, whose expression went from bored to confused, then he looked at me again. Dr. Ainsley continued to stare daggers.

The male officer addressed Dr. Ainsley. "This is him?" There was an edge of impatience to his voice.

"That is he," said Dr. Ainsley with slow deliberation.

The officer looked at me again. His shock morphed into a frown. Confusion, laced with irritation. "You're sure?" he asked, maintaining eye contact with me.

"Quite sure."

Still looking at me, he pulled a tablet from a holster on the hip opposite his gun. He began to manipulate the screen. "What time did you say the break-in occurred?"

Dr. Ainsley audibly sighed. "1:15."

"1:15 a.m.," confirmed the officer.

"Yes, of course a.m.!" blurted Dr. Ainsley.

The officer turned on the professor and held the tablet about ten centimeters from his eyes. Ainsley lurched back startled, then slowly leaned forward, squinting at the screen. After a few seconds, he asked, "What am I seeing?"

"Security feed. From four angles. That's a convenience store about five klicks from here." He paused. "Please note the time stamp."

Ainsley's jaw dropped. "Surely," he sputtered. "Surely that can be faked."

The officer took back his tablet. The thump of his finger tapping the screen in rapid sequence was the loudest sound in the broad chamber where I sat. He held it out again. "The five witnesses I count will probably say otherwise. These three I have already IDed by facial rec, and this one," he said, leaning in closer, and gritting his teeth, "is me."

Ainsley opened his mouth, shut it, opened it, seethed, spun on his heel and stormed from the building. The female officer watched him go, then, wide eyed, shrugged for some sort of explanation. Her partner put his hand up gently to ward her off for the moment.

He crouched down next to where I still sat and said, "Mr. Walden, I apologize for troubling you." Then, more quietly, almost a whisper, "And it's nice to see you sober for once. Try to keep your nose clean, okay?"

I nodded dumbly.

"Good man," he said, patting my back. Then they walked out, two dozen silent stares following them.

At that moment, I was certainly the least confused person in the building, and even I had no idea what was really going on. But this much was clear: at some point in my recent past, I had been in two places simultaneously.

At some point in my near future, I was going to travel through time.

April 2087

I have never been especially fashion conscious. With respect to my own appearance, I have always preferred to keep everything simple, tidy, and generally unnoticeable. Add to that natural inclination the fact that for my entire time as an undergrad I actively shunned the company of women, lest I grow fond of one and end up inadvertently and retroactively causing her death. As such, I invested absolutely no energy in what it meant to be visually interesting. Similarly, I took no notice of what women wore, how they styled their hair, or anything else even remotely connected to how they chose to present themselves to the world at large. So, it is no trivial feat of observation for me to state with confidence that in 2087, nobody—and I mean *nobody*—wore a beret.

It's not something that would ever have occurred to me had I not been confronted with it, but much like a background noise that is undetectable until it stops, that one charcoal beret threw the global absence of any of its ilk into sharp relief. And, once seen, it could not be unseen.

From that moment in the library, not a day passed that I did not catch sight of that beret somewhere on campus. It was always from a distance, and never for any length of time. At no point did I consider that suspicious; there were, after all, undoubtedly many students whom I encountered every day without a second thought. The fact this one wore a beacon on her head made her obvious, but nothing more. I never made any attempt to engage her, nor did I have any such desire. But I always noticed her. Apart from that one time in the library, when an entire floor of students and staff couldn't help but notice my brush with the law, I had no reason to suspect she ever noticed me. All else being equal, simply as a matter of her own safety, it was for the best.

And so, when I inevitably encountered her, it was with no small degree of apprehension.

It was a lovely spring afternoon, several months after my first glimpse of that beret. I was outside, enjoying the sun and the breeze, my head buried in a novel.

"Hi," she said.

Again, not a lot of people interacted with me socially, so it took a moment to register that someone wanted my attention. I bookmarked my tablet, and looked up. There she stood. I was seated on the ground, against a tree, so right away I felt at a disadvantage. She looked at me, neither smiling nor frowning, and apparently unable to sustain eye contact for more than a second or so.

I weighed my potential responses. It was not unusual for complete strangers to approach me and talk to me like they had known me for their entire lives, which, from their frames of reference, was in fact true. This girl could be trying to introduce herself for reasons not yet clear, or she could be a classmate come by to ask why I missed a study session, or she could be my roommate. There was no way to know. My safest course in these situations was a meticulously practiced neutrality.

"Hi," I said.

There was a pause, whose awkwardness value was not yet measurable. Finally, she said, "You... don't know me."

True, to be sure, but curiously unhelpful. Was she clarifying this was our first encounter, or expressing disappointment that I did not recall her? Impossible to say. Given my penchant for revisionist disasters, she could easily be a day I spent innocently in my room, unhappened into an ill-advised one night stand I wouldn't even have the benefit of remembering. Up close, I could see, at last, how young she was. College age, perhaps, but if so, only barely. Visions of an irate father intruded on my peaceful day. As I tried to compose a cautious but probing response to that, she forged ahead.

"Um...?" she began.

"Nigel," I said, guessing she was trying to remember my name. It was a shot in the dark, but it seemed like a safe way of moving this discussion in a less confusing direction. It backfired.

"I know," she said. Then her eyes flew wide as she caught herself. They were blue, striking, and inexplicably familiar. "I mean... I know... that you're Nigel." Apparently realizing this explanation did not count as a recovery, she winced. More possibilities began to shape in my head, not the least of which was that I had a stalker who had finally worked up the nerve to approach me.

"Okay," I said. I powered off my tablet and set it on the grass beside me. "Why don't we start over?"

"That's not funny!" she snapped. She immediately clapped her hand over her mouth, appearing shocked all over again. After a beat, she said, in a weak voice, "This was a mistake. I... I'm sorry."

Then she ran. In her haste to flee, she stumbled and fell. I heard a cry, and then she picked herself up and tore away.

I closed my eyes and rubbed my temples. There was no clear avenue now. If this represented some sort of unhappening, following her might make it worse, but letting her go might be an even greater danger. If this wasn't an unhappening, pursuing her would just draw attention to me, which was always my last resort. I counted to ten in my head and opened my eyes, preparing to stand. Directly in front of me, I could see her bleeding knee. I looked up into her eyes. She held my gaze with a new steadiness, in an obvious and difficult act of courage.

"Things happen to you," she said. "And then they don't."

To anyone else, this surely would have been gibberish. To me, those words were the end of a nightmare, or so I thought. "You too?" I asked. She nodded, and as she crouched down to bring her eyes level with mine, she wiped away a tear.

"How long?" I asked.

"Most of my life," she said. "You?"

"Ever since I was fourteen. Maybe earlier." This girl had been going through the same disorienting reality reboots that I had, but for substantially longer, apparently. Setting aside my cascade of relief that I finally had someone to talk to about this, it was also likely she understood it better than I did, especially given that she sought me out. "Is this going to unhappen?" I asked.

She shook her head. "It can't. You and I share variable frames of reference. We can't lose this."

So many things went through my head at that moment. "I don't know what that means," I said. She pursed her lips, in an expression I read to mean no simple explanation was forthcoming. But it didn't matter. She knew what it meant, and that was enough to sustain me for the time being. "Who are you?" I asked.

At that, she finally smiled, and it was delightful. "You can't ask me that one," she said. "Not yet." And suddenly, I did know who she was. I had been fixating on the beret. I should have been picturing her in a denim jacket.

"Are you…" I began, and then realized I hardly knew how to form the question. This was the woman who had appeared when a paper I wrote in physics class was nearly published, and then nearly got me expelled, all in one horrific unhappening. I saw her twice, and then never again. But that woman was easily five years older than I was, and this girl was quite a bit younger. "Did you intervene with my physics teacher when I was in high school?" I asked awkwardly.

She grinned at that. "Huh," she said. "I honestly have no idea."

And then it gelled. None of that had happened to her yet. This young girl would grow up to be—on at least one occasion—my time traveling savior. But not now. Now, she was just a girl, whose life had been riddled with inconsistencies, just as mine had been. I had already deduced time travel was my eventual destiny. Clearly, some day, it would be hers as well.

And she already knew it.

[8]

April 2087

I skipped the rest of my classes that day. We got a pizza. For the first time in six years, I had found someone with whom I could be honest about what my life had become. She didn't think I was a nut job, she didn't find me confusing, and she understood exactly how it felt to be me. It was so invigorating that none of the restrictions she put on what she was willing to share in return bothered me—and those restrictions were intense.

"If you don't give me some kind of name to work with, I'm just going to call you Blondie."

"No you're not," she said.

I took a bite. The pepperoni didn't bite back quite hard enough, so I added some pepper flakes. "No," I agreed. "I'm not. I'm going to call you Gray Beret. Or Hey You."

She slurped the bottom of her soda. Rattled the ice. "Nope," she said, standing. "You're going to find my name on your own, and it's going to be a good one, but not today." She went to refill her drink, giving me a moment to reflect on her oblique prophesy. I wondered how much she already knew of her own future, and mine, and how much of this name mystery was real. My honest impression at that moment was she was just using it as an excuse to seem more exotic. When she returned, she pulled another slice onto her plate without comment, and then looked at me patiently instead of eating.

"All right, Susan," I said. She smiled faintly, shook her head ever so slightly, but did not interrupt. "Why does my life keep unhappening?"

She thought about this for a moment, then around a mouthful of pizza, she said, "You think I'm your fairy godmother, or your guardian angel or something. I'm not. I'm just a fellow traveler. You and I exist on the same level, and a lot of your questions are my questions too."

"But you know things I don't."

She nodded. "Mm hmm. Not as much as you think, but yeah. And more than I can tell you," she added with a slight pout.

"I'm getting that. I don't suppose you can tell me why that is."

"I wish I could. It's nothing bad, if that's what you're thinking. You're not in any kind of weird danger or anything. It's just..." She fidgeted with a plastic fork, spearing a pepperoni and twirling it into a small gob of cheese. "Some stuff will make more sense to you if you work it out on your own."

"That's a dodge," I said.

"You betcha."

I laughed. Calling her out wasn't going to get me anywhere. "All right, let's take it from the top. What can you tell me?"

She shrugged. "What do you want to know? Ask me little things. Yes or no."

I drummed my fingers on the table. "Is this a real thing? Is the world really changing all the time, and nobody notices but me?"

"You're not nuts, if that's what you're asking."

"That's what I'm asking. Is there anyone else? Anyone besides you and me?"

She considered this, and I tried to read whether she was considering the answer, or just deciding if she was going to tell me. "Yeah," she said.

"Lots of people?"

"That I don't know," she said.

"Are you a student here?" Her eyebrows went up, indicating the question had its desired effect; it threw her.

"No," she said.

"You don't look old enough."

"That's not why," she said quickly. "Um, that's... Don't ask me stuff about me, okay?"

I leaned back in my seat and sighed. "Throw me a bone here, Penelope. You're the first person I've really been able to talk to for a very long time, and you're not saying anything."

"Penelope," she said. "I like that one. Call me that."

"Did I find your name?" I asked. "That seems too easy."

"No, but I like it. It'll do for a while." She took another bite, and continued to talk while chewing. "You don't want to know about me, anyway. You want to know about the other thing. And I can tell you about that; I just have to be sure to tell it right. You know?"

"Not really."

"Try this: You say I'm the first person you can talk to, so talk. You go first. Tell me about yourself. Tell me about what changes, and what you do when it happens."

I thought about this. Apart from my aborted psycho-therapy sessions, I had never opened up about the most important part of what it meant to be me. "It's usually little stuff," I began. "Conversations that I know I had but no one else did. Stuff I'm supposed to do but don't know about. Objects that appear, or disappear, or turn into other things. When it's that kind of unhappening, it's just embarrassing. People think I'm a flake, that I forget everything, that I'm unreliable. That's why I don't socialize much."

"That's an easy fix."

I perked up. "I'm sorry, what did you just say?"

She sipped her drink. "I said you can fix that." She waved away what must have been obvious on my face. "I don't mean you can stop it from happening; I mean you don't have to be embarrassed. There are tricks I can teach you."

"Is that why you're here?" I asked.

"Partly," she admitted. "From now on, you're on the attention deficit spectrum."

I shook my head. "Is that a real thing?"

"Oh yeah," she said. "It's very real. You don't have it, but it's real. It's a disorder. Um," she added, "I hope that's okay."

"Tell me how this helps me."

"Right. Well, it's basically an underactive frontal lobe issue. The diagnosis is about a hundred years old, and they used to treat it with stimulants. In 2087 it's treated mostly as a low-grade perceptual dissociation, and they don't always medicate for it, depending on where you fall on the spectrum. So, no pills, don't worry about that. I can teach you the management tools deficit spectrum people use. Basically, you're going to mimic what a person does who has clinically chronic and severe issues remembering things and staying organized. You're going to use these tricks in an obvious way, and work it into conversations over and over again. You will be making a show of how much work it is for you to remember all the stuff that you don't actually have any trouble remembering. Everyone will come to know you as an extremely high-functioning ADD. When your life does unhappen, the little stuff I mean, it will look like you slipped. Your friends will step up with reminders and favors because they think they're helping you catch up."

"I don't have any friends."

"You will," she said, and for the first time since Carrie Wolfe, I remembered what optimism feels like.

"It sounds manipulative."

She slurped the bottom of her drink again. "It totally is. And it works like a charm."

"My God," I said quietly. "I don't know what to say."

"Well, you should probably say thank you, but wait until I train you and it works first. Welcome to survival, Nigel." Then her smile faded to something more contemplative. "Now," she said, "tell me about the bad ones."

[9]

May 2087

The first time I used one of the tricks Penelope taught me and made me practice until I got it right, I couldn't help but wonder what circle of Hell was reserved for people who pretended to have disabilities. To be fair, I rationalized it with the secret understanding that I did have a disability, just not one that was diagnosable, or even remotely explainable.

It was a weekday, a few weeks after my lessons with Penelope began. I was in one of the campus eateries, sipping a coffee, nibbling a croissant, and scouring the Net on my tablet for any plausible reference to time travel. Very little of the information on the Slinky Probe accident was declassified at that time, so I found myself spending an absurd amount of my downtime getting to know the crackpots and fringe conspiracy theorists. As of that point, I had yet to come across a credible report from anyone who had actually traveled through time, but as I knew it to be my destiny, I assumed it would only be a matter of patience before I made a connection.

I was not so absorbed that I missed another student joining me at my table. He put down a tray with a chicken salad sandwich and a soft drink, and sat directly across from me.

"Excuse me," he said politely.

I scrutinized him. On his narrow face sat thin glasses with wide frames, and his black hair stood in a flattop crew cut. Over a long-sleeved, peach-colored shirt, he wore a burgundy plaid vest, buttoned up. I had no idea whether to consider that pretentious, but I made a mental note of it. The next few moments would be critical. I did not recognize him, but from years of experience I knew how meaningless that was. Penelope had taught me a slew of visual and verbal cues to watch for to determine if any given person was supposed to be known to me. This new arrival was making steady eye contact. That meant a probable first introduction; a more familiar person would more likely be splitting his focus between me and his food. No clue was a guarantee, however. I offered a greeting in practiced neutrality. "Hello."

"You're in my combinatorics class, aren't you?" he asked. Bingo.

"With Dr. Carter?"

He nodded. "Yeah. I thought I recognized you. My name's Pete. Some of this stuff is starting to go over my head, and I'm looking to start a study group. You want in?"

I stared at him for a second, then formed opposing L's with my thumbs and forefingers and framed his face with them. "Pete," I said. "Pete. Your name is Pete. 'Are you in my combinatorics class?' Pete. Pete wears a burgundy vest. 'I'm looking to start a study group. Do you want in?' Your name is Pete." I dropped my hands and made a show of relaxing my face. "Sorry about that. I'm Nigel."

Pete's face took on a look of surprise, but where I expected to find discomfort, I saw fascination. "That's a mnemonic trick. My cousin does it all the time. You're bonding a semantic memory to an episodic memory, right?"

I had rehearsed this explanation so many times that it threw me off balance hearing it from someone else the very first time I tried to use it. I rolled with it, and laughed. "Yeah, something like that," I said. "Your cousin does that too?"

He nodded. "She has an attention disorder. She does it every time she hears a new name. Is that what you have? Does it work?"

I shrugged, secretly grateful that he had fed me a cue to one of my rehearsed lines. "Most of the time," I said. "Not always."

"Then you're better off than she is," he said. "I love her, but she's kind of a disaster." He bit his lip. "Oh. Sorry. I didn't mean—"

I waved away his concern. "Don't. I've had years to get used to it," I lied.

"Well, you must be doing okay with it. Heck, you made it into MIT. My cousin barely made it out of high school."

I shrugged. "I'm told I am highly functional. It doesn't always feel that way. I'll tell you right now, though, don't be surprised if I can't remember your name the next time I see you. Or I might remember it for five years and then suddenly lose it. It doesn't always stick." Another lie. There was no way I was ever going to forget that this person was named Pete. However, there was always a chance that I could encounter someone else in his presence whose name I was supposed to know, and whom subjectively I had never met. I had now planted a suggestion in Pete's head that could protect me later. Penelope had been drilling me on this for weeks, but feeling it play out in real time was a very new experience. I could already tell it was working, and I was already connecting with another student.

For the first time since preadolescence, I began to reclaim a social life.

[10]

November 2087

My first trip through time was in no way like what I expected.

It was an early November evening. I was walking back from Pete's dorm, where I had spent the past few hours with him, two of his friends, and at least four beers. It was dark and just beginning to rain, and neither of those things dimmed my joy in the slightest. What had started as a study session on the topic of exponential generating functions gradually rolled into a discussion of music, a debate on the comparative merits of Hamlet and Macbeth, and no small amount of observations about our female acquaintances. I was intoxicated, as much by the experience as the alcohol. I had enjoyed myself in the company of peers, none of whom thought I was crazy. And, even if it all unhappened right then and there, I believed I had the tools to recover.

My reaction time thus diminished, by the time I felt the hand on my shoulder, it was already spinning me around. I caught sight of the old man's face, just before the slippery sidewalk and my own tipsiness sent me backwards, landing hard in a puddle.

"Nigel!" he shouted. It was a hoarse, weathered voice I did not recognize. "It is Nigel, yes?"

I had neither the wherewithal nor the inclination to play out my mnemonic charade. "What do you want?" I said, scrambling backward in an unsuccessful bid to stand. He grabbed my hand, and pulled me up, his strength belying his aged countenance. I stood, wet, trying to make out his features in the half-light of the campus streetlamps. All I could see was gray stubble, wrinkles and pain. He squinted at me.

"No," he grumbled. "No, this was a mistake. You're a boy. Christ, look at you! You'll never pull this off."

My heart began to race, as genuine fear began to take hold. For anyone else, this would be a difficult situation on its own terms. For me, the chronic uncertainty of what might be true about my own past at any given moment, combined with a creeping feeling of recognition, made me silently beg my metabolism to burn off those beers quickly. I was in no condition to plan my way out of this encounter. The rain chose that moment to open up full throttle. Perhaps in reaction to that, or perhaps for some other reason, my assailant shoved me, and I returned to my puddle. As I twisted and flopped to regain my footing, or find some way to crawl away at top speed, there was a flash of lightning. Dangers were accruing more quickly than I could compensate for them. As I got to my feet and prepared to bolt, hoping I wouldn't slip again, I wobbled in a complete circle.

He was gone.

It was dark enough, and I was disoriented enough, that he could have easily made his way out of my field of vision without any particular ninja skills. As I stood there, slowly scanning my surroundings for any pending ambush, I reflected on that face. The more I did so, the more I wanted to reject the nagging apprehension that the face threatening me was nothing more than a stubbled, wrinkled, haggard mirror.

I waited for the thunder. It never came.

November 2087

My other first trip through time happened the next day.

I had overslept. Although not exactly hung over, I was certainly not feeling my best. It had been a fitful night's sleep, punctuated with a series of dreams about meeting myself. In some of them, I was the tipsy bewildered student, in some, the broken old man. I woke frequently, each time marked with the dreadful transition from telling myself it was only a dream to remembering it really wasn't. When my alarm sounded at 8:00, I worked it seamlessly into my current nightmare, and slept straight through it. The only thing finally able to rouse me was the banging on my dorm room door.

I woke with a start and a headache. "Time," I growled.

"10:47," replied the clock with a hint of judgment. That nuance was an optional setting. It seemed much more amusing when I selected it than it did in practice.

There was more door banging. I clutched my head. The time meant I had already slept through most of my first class, and that I probably wouldn't have enough time to make myself presentable and eat before the next one. Depending on who was at the door, that might be moot anyway.

I stumbled out of bed and opened the door. Standing there was a woman about ten years older than I, with a long blonde ponytail, wearing a denim jacket. Apart from being obviously and significantly older, this was the spitting image of the girl who had been giving me lessons on how to pass for someone whose life was not constantly, retroactively changing. I considered the possibility that this was another variation of the dream I had been sweating through all night, but I knew full well I was awake.

"Penelope?"

She laughed with delight. "Penelope! Wow, that takes me back!" She smiled, and allowed that smile to stretch right to the edge of an awkward moment. "Are you going to let me in?"

I stood aside, and she floated into the room, planting herself in my desk chair. Another pause blossomed awkwardly.

"Are you going to put some pants on?"

Crap. It was more or less clear what was happening here, especially after my experience with my older self the very day before, but it came at me so quickly I had no idea how to form the questions I had to ask. In light of that, the fact that I was still in my underwear had escaped me as insignificant. I nearly tripped getting to my dresser, and nearly fell over pulling on a pair of slacks.

"Relax," she said. "We're not in a hurry."

Zip. "Not in a hurry for what?"

I turned around to see her rearranging the supplies on my desk into neat, but functionless, rows. "The usual. We have to run a fix."

"What's a fix?"

She looked up at me as I fumbled into a shirt, a curious smile on her face. Then the smile faded to something less amused, between surprise and trepidation.

"Oh," she said. "Oh. No way." She stood slowly, then reached for my left hand. Turning it over she traced a line from my wrist to the crook of my elbow, with noticeable pressure. She stared at the invisible line she had drawn, and her jaw dropped, just a bit. "No way," she whispered.

She pulled something the size of a coin from her pocket, which promptly snapped out to an object that looked like a pen. As she waved this object over my forearm to no apparent result, her entire demeanor became more reserved.

"It's not here," she said calmly. The pen object collapsed back into a coin, and went back in her pocket. "We need to talk," she said. "You may want to sit down."

I pulled the covers taut on my bed, and sat down. This was more for her benefit than mine. She pulled up my desk chair and sat facing me with deep concern in her eyes.

"Nigel," she began formally, "this may be difficult for you to accept at first, but…" She paused, evidently collecting her thoughts. "I've come here from your future."

"That part is kind of obvious."

She pulled back. "Oh," she said, with some combination of confusion and disappointment. "Well then, how much do you know?"

I shrugged. "That's pretty much it, I think. A younger version of you is a recent friend of mine. I recognized you right away. No offense, but you don't look her age anymore."

"None taken. The time travel doesn't surprise you?"

I shook my head. "My life keeps unhappening. You know that, right? I've known some version of this was coming for years. And…" I stopped, unsure how to describe the evening before. "You're not my first visitor."

Her eyebrows rose at this. "Who?"

"Me, I think."

"Oh." She sat for a moment in a silence I could not read. "What did he say?"

"I'm not sure. It was raining, and he wasn't exactly coherent." Describing a moment from my life that was disturbing, and likely inevitable, was not easy. "He said I was too young. A boy."

She nodded, as something seemed to fall into place. "Well, he's not wrong on that count. That was his first trip. You won't see him again for a few years, unless something changes before then." She shook her head. "I'm sorry he got to you before I did."

"Tell me everything." The words were out before I could find a better way to ask.

She screwed her mouth to the side. "No," she said flatly. She took my hand again and traced my forearm. "I've gotten so used to not having to explain anything, I forgot there would eventually come a time when you didn't know." She reached into her jacket, and unzipped an inner pocket. "And I've been carrying this for so long, I forgot that someday I would have to give it to you." She opened her palm. In it sat an oblong silver bead, about a centimeter long. There were lines etched into it, so fine they might have been drawn with a pin. She looked into her hand at this object, and for a moment she appeared frozen by it. Then she closed her hand around it. "Are you sure?" she asked quietly.

"Sure about what?" I asked.

Still looking at her closed hand, she put a finger to her lips and said, "Shhh." I gave her a moment of silence, after which she said, "Okay. I know."

That was when I realized she was having some sort of discussion with herself. It was impossible to tell if that should make me uncomfortable.

Then she looked at me and her entire demeanor changed. She gently pulled my arm forward, and pressed the silver bead into a spot on the invisible line she had drawn twice. Instead of looking there, she stared straight into my eyes. That was when I noticed how firm her grip had become.

There was a pinch, then a burn. Then, with a searing stab, the bead disappeared into a centimeter long incision in my arm.

"Ow!" I cried as she planted her other arm on my shoulder and threw her weight into it. I could feel the bead tunneling into my muscle. The agony was intense, but oddly brief. The spot surrounding the wound was already starting to numb. I looked at the hole in my arm, and saw a thin trail of clear liquid ooze out of it, pushing away the blood. The liquid hardened, and the edges of the incision pulled themselves tightly together. Deep inside my arm, I felt a dull, painless scratching. "What is it doing?" I managed to gasp.

Still staring me in the eyes, she said, "Bonding itself to your ulna." There was another stab of pain, and I cried out. At that she let me go, and I clamped my hand over the already sealed opening.

"It's well into the bone now," she said. "The anesthetic will wear off in about thirty minutes. I'm sorry, but you're going to be pretty sore for a few days."

"What did you just do to me?" I felt a tear escape my left eye and tried to ignore it.

She covered her mouth with her hand and looked away for a moment. When she met my gaze again, she did so with a look of profound sadness.

"I just made you a time traveler."

[12]

January 2087

We were suddenly in an alley, standing in snow, well after dark. Penelope had given me just enough time to finish getting dressed before grabbing my arm without warning and turning the world inside out.

"What...?" This was all I had time to say before the dry heaves began.

"The nausea will pass," she said. "After a few more trips, your body will adjust and you won't feel it anymore."

This was little comfort as my stomach tried to empty itself of food I had not yet eaten. That's how I thought of it at the time, mourning my lost opportunity for breakfast. I later learned that the nausea in early trips was literally that very thing; my body somehow understood that there was a significant chronological gap between my last meal and my current position in time, even though that gap was, in this case, well in reverse. It was reacting the only way it knew how, by assuming anything I hadn't been able to digest in that span must be toxic. It would be quite a while before I learned all the nuanced physiological consequences of time travel.

"Here," said Penelope, handing me a hip flask. "Rinse and spit."

I took a swig without thinking, instantly replacing the taste of bile with that of whiskey. I spat. "Gah! That's not helping!"

"It isn't meant to." She took the flask and sipped from it. After swishing the alcohol in her mouth for a few seconds, she sprayed my shirt with it.

I held my arms out, and looked down at myself, soaking wet and reeking.

"Oh," I said. "Fantastic."

I looked at Penelope. She tucked the flask into a pocket without making eye contact. I scanned my surroundings. Nothing was familiar. The absence of sunlight at what was—only seconds before—ten in the morning, could only mean we had jumped in time. Of course I knew it was possible, and of course I knew it would happen to me sooner or later. The only aspect of this event I found in any way shocking was the sheer anti-climactic nature of it.

"Where are we?" I asked. "When are we?"

Penelope looked, as if to get her bearings.

"Still in Boston," she said. "I hope. The spatial displacement component is rarely as precise as it should be. And about ten months prior to our point of departure."

So. My first step through time was backward, by a trivial amount. No jaunt through history, no extraordinary visit to the future. Back one year and around the block.

Penelope pulled out a small tablet and drew her finger across it. "This is good. We're within two clicks of the target, and thirty-five minutes early." She pocketed the device, and met my eyes for the first time since the jump. "Listen, I know this a lot for you to take in. I will explain what I can as we go, but for now I need you to trust me and follow directions. Don't ask a lot of questions. I promise I will bring you up to speed on the big picture, but I… I'm just not ready, okay?"

I looked around myself, and considered my options. For the first time since meeting her younger version, I found myself questioning if I should trust her, and wondering why that hadn't occurred to me before. Her demeanor had been so jaunty and carefree when she strolled into my room, and now her face was etched with a trouble I could not fathom. She had been caught off guard. That was all. She missed the detail of which moment in my life she was traveling to, and she wasn't prepared for me not knowing the ropes. This was easy enough to accept, and yes, there was just something about her that made me want to believe her.

"Okay," I said.

She nodded. It was humorless and businesslike. "There's a mini-mart a short walk from here. We are going to go there, behave very conspicuously for about ten minutes, and leave. With me so far?"

"I think so."

"Good. I need you to act like you've been drinking. That's why you smell like scotch. Sorry about that, by the way." There was no sorrow in her voice.

"No problem."

"When we get there, follow my lead. I'm your date, someone you just met, and a little bit too wild for you. You're tipsy, and I'm flat out drunk." She looked over her shoulder, then turned and started walking down the alley toward the street, gesturing me to follow. I did.

"You'll want to act a little bit impatient with me, and embarrassed by me. I'll try to make that easy."

I nodded. "Are we? Dating?"

I meant it partly as a joke, and partly as a probe. Younger Penelope still hadn't told me any solid details about who she was. Maybe Older Penelope would. It didn't seem likely we were a couple in any time, but I needed to start somewhere. I expected a reaction either way. A coy hint, perhaps, or a revolted denial? Instead, she didn't even look at me.

"No," she said. "And please don't go there again."

That left me with even less information than if I simply hadn't asked at all, and I felt some level of indefinable awkwardness with no clue how to correct for it.

"Sorry," I said, in no way sure what I was sorry for.

"Leave it alone," she said.

A few minutes later we arrived at a Cumberland Farms.

"Follow my lead," Penelope reiterated, then threw the door open, giggling maniacally. It was in no way clear what kind of lead that was, or how it should be appropriately followed. By the time I got inside, Penelope was already running up and down the tiny aisles, shouting, "Wheeeeeeee!"

Her suggestion that I feign embarrassment was quite unnecessary. I looked around furtively, trying to imagine something I might want to buy, to lend some degree of authenticity to the proceedings. I managed to be looking in just the wrong direction when Penelope crashed into me.

"Nigel!" she shouted directly into my face. "Buy me an ice cream!"

I pushed her off of me. Remembering I was supposed to be buzzed, I shook my head and pretended to steady myself holding her shoulders. She started giggling again. The few people in the store were now all staring at us, some of them having moved to a better vantage point to do so.

"Oh!" shouted Penelope, slamming herself into the counter, and bumping into a man who was attempting to buy a pack of cigarettes. "Nigel! Nigel! Buy me a scratch ticket!"

I waited for the man ahead of us to flee with his smokes, then said, in my best attempt to appear like I was trying not to slur my speech, "One scratch ticket, please."

"Which game?" asked the clerk with an expression somewhere between irritation, amusement, and nervousness.

"A big one!" said Penelope. One swipe of my card and fifty dollars later, she was furiously scratching away with her fingernail. "Oops!" she said, gouging a hole in the paper.

I turned around to see just how many people were watching this freak show, and locked eyes with another customer, still standing in the doorway.

"You!" he said. It took me a moment to place him, because he was out of uniform. It was the officer who nearly arrested me at the library. Then I realized that hadn't happened yet. This was the scene he showed Dr. Ainsley on his tablet. My alibi. And yet, apparently, this still wasn't the first time we met. How many such retroactive encounters still lay ahead of me?

He shook his head in disgust. "Show some better judgment for once, will you?"

That was the moment Penelope crashed to the floor, still giggling. I picked her up, and held her steady as I walked her to the door. We collectively staggered around the corner to the back of the store. Then we were in my dorm room again, an hour before noon, and ten months later.

"Nice work," she said. "We just supplied you with an iron clad alibi for the break-in."

"I know," I said, trying not to give in to the sudden and profound queasiness. "I've already used it."

"All right then. Take care."

"Wait!" I held up my hands. "This is a lot to process. Can you... can you stick around? Can we talk? My whole world just changed. I've been waiting years for this. Please don't go without telling me what this is all about."

"I'm not ready," she said, frowning. "I didn't know this was going to be your first time. I should have seen it coming, but keeping track of this is harder than you can possibly know. Give me some time. I will be back. I promise. Soon enough you'll know." She paused. "And you're not going to like it."

I watched her stand there in a fragile state of indecision, and threw out the only question I thought she might answer. "Can you tell me about the break-in?"

She thought for a moment. "Ainsley's lab. Two hundred grams of palladium and seven terabytes of data."

"I stole that?"

"You will." There was a flash of light, and she was gone.

[13]

November 2087

Time travel paradox is a quaint, but hopelessly irrelevant concept. Every trip to the past changes it. The changes are instantaneous, retroactive by their very nature, and permanent. Any apparent contradiction is simply and elegantly overwritten by the new continuity. Time, it turns out, protects herself, much the way the earth will inflict quakes on the surface in order to relieve pressure deep below. Thought experiments like the grandfather paradox, once believed to be the cornerstone of time travel theory, have no power in time travel application. If a man travels back in time and murders his grandfather, thus preventing his own birth, the universe simply carries on with the grandfather dead, the time traveler forever unborn, and it does so without a care in the world as to how that murder was possible in the first place. No one will ever be aware that history has changed, and no one will ever be aware that he was supposed to have offspring, and grand-offspring. No one, that is, except the time traveler. That person, who should now never have existed, continues to exist anyway. And again, the universe just shrugs it off, insisting—and rightly so—that it owes no one any explanation for its conduct.

Mind you, the time traveler does experience consequences for his actions, but I'm getting ahead of myself.

It would be several days after that encounter with Penelope's future self before I saw young Penelope again. During that time, I made my best attempt to carry on with life as usual. I was used to keeping secrets, after all. In that respect, it was easy enough for me to get through my daily routines without any noticeable change of behavior. But no amount of pretending otherwise could lessen the impact of that one event. I had traveled through time. For real. I would never see the world the same way again.

It took about a day for the initial rush to wear off, at which point I had become mired in questions. Whereas I imagine most people would find themselves in a philosophical or scientific crisis in my position, I found that my own reflections—and fears—ranged from the pragmatic to the mundane. I barely knew Penelope, even in her present day, youthful incarnation. She wouldn't even tell me her true name. And yet, I trusted a future version of her, apparently without question.

As the reality of that began to take hold, I found myself increasingly wary. Worse, there was now some object, obviously of a technology not yet existent in my time, housed inside a bone in my arm. I could not feel it and I could barely even see the scar, but the knowledge that it was there spun into an escalating fear of it. The notion that time travel was somehow my destiny had at first allowed me to accept this implant with bizarre ease, but having had some time to reflect on that, I felt like a reckless fool. I had no idea what this device did, if indeed it did anything. Maybe it was a time machine, or maybe Penelope was the one doing all the time travel mechanics, and what she put inside me was a surveillance device. Or a bomb.

I spent two days in a distracted haze, scanning for a gray beret everywhere I went. My classes were a blur, when I even bothered to attend them. I had so effectively constructed my disability alibi that what little concern my friends voiced over this change in behavior were polite inquiries to see if I needed any help getting back on track.

On the third day, Penelope—young Penelope—found me. We had no set schedule for our meetings; three or four times a week she would simply appear at a generally convenient time, and give me a survival lesson, or just milk me for information about my life in the guise of a friendly chat. So, when she encountered me in the middle of the day, on campus between classes, it was with a comfortable, bubbly wave. My greeting was a bit less enthusiastic.

"We need to talk."

Her smile dropped, and for a fraction of second, she became that future version of herself. It was the same expression she wore when she planted that bead in my arm.

"Am I in trouble?" Not exactly a question I had anticipated.

"Probably not," I said. Then I corrected, "Probably not yet."

She furrowed her brow. "What is this about?"

Whatever statement I had been rehearsing for two days disappeared from my head. Planning to tell her everything, perhaps even to confront her on how much she already knew, suddenly seemed like a spectacularly bad idea. I chose one detail and ran with it. "I had a visit a few days ago, from a future version of you."

Until that moment, Penelope and I had successfully avoided any direct mention of time travel, theoretical or otherwise. In my heart, I had known for years—ever since I first heard of the Slinky Probe accident— that my situation had to be the result of someone or something repeatedly traveling to my past and changing it. Knowing it and trusting another person to believe it, even someone who clearly shared my exceedingly rare experiences, were two very different things. It seemed to take Penelope a moment to absorb the full meaning of my words. When she did, her expression softened to something between awe and fear. In that instant, the teenager reemerged in her eyes.

"Me?" she said quietly. Then, almost a whisper, and with a touch of a squeak, "From the future?"

I nodded.

She was silent then, and looked away. Up. At her shoes. Anywhere but my eyes. I watched her work through her complicated emotional cascade, and for the first time realized this was brand new territory for her. I had somehow imagined that she had already had a similar experience. My own future self had visited me once, after all, but seeing her grapple like this clarified for me that she was indeed essentially a child, quite out of her frame of reference. I tried to imagine how it would have felt if I had been confronted with this at eighteen, or sixteen, or however old this girl was, and seeing that mental image, I found myself regretting having been so blunt. As I tried to formulate a hopelessly inadequate apology, she finally screwed up the courage to look me in the eye.

"What's..." she said, and the fear came back, almost destroying the moment. She took a deep breath and pushed through it.

"What's she like?"

December 2087

After learning that at some point in the future, her adult self was going to travel through time to see me, probably repeatedly, Penelope became curiously distant from me. She still met with me every few days, but it became less social, and more businesslike. It didn't take much time—or advanced detective skills—to figure out the reason for the abrupt change in demeanor. Penelope was now living in fear of the possibility that her future version had told me things her present version did not want me to know.

Obviously, Penelope had been keeping things from me (her refusal to give me her real name was strong supporting evidence of this). For the most part, I had chalked that up to her maturity level and a need to feel important. I humored it because she was already giving me so much beneficial information I hardly saw the advantage to pushing my luck there. Her new reticence around me did little to change that perception. Future Penelope had told me almost nothing of value. That was one of the first things I told Young Penelope, but clearly she was either not convinced or not taking any chances.

Over coffee one day, her standoffishness took a particularly interesting turn. We were discussing my progress as a social being. It had been several months since Penelope first taught me simple tricks to blend in. My friendship with Pete had expanded to inclusion in his social circle. It was the first time in years I had felt truly comfortable around other people. It was also the first time I had spent long enough in anyone's company to discover I didn't like some of them, and that was as rewarding as any aspect of the experience. Learning how to manage myself around people I found irritating was a skill that had atrophied since high school, and it felt wonderful to put it back into practice.

Now that I was starting to trust other people, Penelope and I talked about the next steps, including how safe it would be to broach with my closer friends the true nature of my existence. The better I got to know Pete, the more I felt he might be both smart enough and stable enough to understand my plight for what it was. There was risk there, including the very real possibility that doing so might precede an unhappening that would retroactively collapse my entire social network. I still had no idea what the underlying cause of my problem was, and if Penelope did, she wasn't saying. Instead, we simply mapped out a recovery plan, should I happen to need one.

While we organized how I would word my revelation, and what type of opportune moment I could contrive to drop it, I mentioned the possibility of telling another person as well. A woman named Sandy was in two of my classes, and I had gotten to know her pretty well around the same time I was being inducted into Pete's clique. When I mentioned this to Penelope, her reaction was unexpected.

"Oh," she said. "Um. Maybe." She stopped there, and the awkwardness of the pause surprised me.

"Is that a bad idea?" I probed.

"I don't… This isn't because you're attracted to her, is it?"

These words came out in such a rush I almost didn't process them. This was a topic that had never come up in our talks, primarily because I was, by that point, so thoroughly convinced that any woman who got involved with me would pay for it with her life. In any case, the answer to Penelope's question was no. Sandy and I had some things in common, and I had a great deal of respect for her, but there was never any sexual tension there. It would have been easy to dispel Penelope's concern, but the fact of it intrigued me. It harkened back to Future Penelope's revolted reaction to my question about whether we were in a relationship that hadn't started yet. This new question made me wonder if there was a story connected to whatever she felt she needed to hide from me. I believed her when she said that we would never be a couple, besides which, Young Penelope couldn't possibly know what lay in store for either of us, any more than I did. And yet, this now smacked of an unexpected loose thread, and I couldn't help but tug it.

"Would that be a problem?" I asked, with an exaggeratedly feigned innocence.

"No," she said quickly. Then, "Maybe. I don't know." She rubbed her face, clearly trying to regain her bearings. "Probably not," she said finally. "But don't tell her anyway. Let's stick to the plan. We don't even know what will happen when you talk to Pete. For now, let's not complicate anything." She waited a beat, then added, "Please?"

I nodded. "Yeah, that's probably right," I said, and while I was being honest about my intent to hold off on saying anything to Sandy, I filed away my certainty that something about this circumstance was the nerve Future Penelope had exposed in her younger self. There was something about my eventual relationship with a woman—perhaps Sandy, perhaps someone else, surely not Penelope—that she desperately wanted me not to know.

[15]

January 2088

After my third attempt to tell Pete about my problem, I gave up. The first time he was amazing about it. Asked me all kinds of questions, took everything I said at its face. We spent an entire afternoon talking, at the end of which he told me he had never felt more touched than he did to know that I trusted him with something that big and risky.

By the time I saw him that evening, the whole thing had unhappened. Thankfully, there was no awful moment of discovery that I would need to explain my way out of. I had become so accustomed to Penelope's tricks for entering any conversation without exposing myself, and so used to people utterly transforming between times I saw them, all I needed was a quick probe to learn Pete knew nothing.

I tried twice more over the course of that week. The second time was a fiasco. He accused me of trying to play him for a fool, and wanted to know if I was on drugs. I had made the mistake of broaching the topic too quickly, because I already knew (or thought I did) what his reaction would be. He avoided me for two days, then reverted to a blank slate on the matter. Having learned from that, I was substantially more cautious on my third try. That one went very well, until I realized that he was humoring me, first out of amusement, and eventually out of compassion. He begged me to seek professional help. I backpedalled by informing him (honestly) that I had already tried that to no avail. When that final confession unhappened, I resigned.

Sandy was a different story, many times worse. It took me weeks to work up the courage to go to her, but I never got the chance. One day, to my profound surprise and discomfort, she confessed her feelings for me. Given that our friendship had always seemed entirely platonic from my end of it, my initial assumption was that this was some sort of super awkward unhappening of it. However, the more that story played out, the more details she revealed about events exactly as I recalled them. This crush had always been there, and I missed it. At first I tried to stay friends with her, with the clear understanding that I wanted nothing more. The longer we tried that, the more she began to fall apart. It finally got to the point where she would not leave me alone, her communications with me alternating between desperate pleas for a chance, and threats.

It is with no great pride that I admit when she ultimately, inevitably, retroactively vanished, I was not sorry to see her go. I hoped her unhappening was not some dire or dreadful fate, but not enough to investigate.

For the next two years, I settled into a comfortable social life. My friendship with Pete—all of my friendships, in fact—never progressed beyond surface camaraderie. Nothing else seemed worth the bother. I never again shared my tale with another peer. I never allowed anyone to get overly close and learn who and what I really was.

And I never, ever dated.

May 2088

The second time—from my perspective—that Future Penelope visited me (or third, counting her mysterious appearance when I was in high school) was about six months after our Cumberland Farms outing. In our previous meeting she looked about thirty. This time I guessed her for mid twenties. Once again, we were to "run a fix." She gave no indication of awareness that this sort of thing was new to me, and I gave her no reason to believe it was. We traveled back in time about four years, and visited a florist in a small city in New Hampshire. Our objective was to stall a woman who had come there to pick up flowers for a hospitalized friend. We only had to keep her there an additional seven minutes, which proved remarkably easy. We arrived just before she did, and Penelope had prepared a barrage of extensive and picayune questions to occupy the manager. My job was to engage the only other employee there, with an imaginary conflict regarding a previous purchase that never happened. She deferred to her boss, who then became tangled between our two distractions. The woman—the only real customer—patiently waited for us to resolve our issues. When the seven minutes were up, I stormed out, and Penelope bought an orchid that she left in the dumpster behind the store before we returned.

Our next fix was three months after that, for me, and at least a couple of years earlier for her. We traveled thirty years into the past, to a dog track, where we persuaded a bettor to drop two thousand dollars on a dog that finished fourth. By the time his money was lost, we were long gone.

She whisked me away a total of fifteen times during my years as an undergrad. There was never any explanation given for our objectives, nor any clear consequence of them. I learned not to ask questions, because it was pointless. The purpose of the device in my arm was not clear, although it certainly did something. On our longer trips, I sometimes thought I could feel it tingling.

But with or without any sense of what we were really doing, absolutely nothing could beat the thrill.

All the while this was happening, I was also continuing my association with Young Penelope. She learned not to ask questions as well, which struck me as an extraordinary measure of self control. There were times her future version appeared to me at an age that couldn't have been more than five years older than she was now. At the time, I imagined that telling her about that would have been hazardous somehow. More to the point, I knew that her career as a time traveler was bound to begin very soon, and I didn't want to somehow interfere with that by warning her about it.

During her fifteenth visit, that concern became moot. After traveling more than fifty years into the past to steal someone's taxi, we returned to my apartment. I made a joke about her looking exhausted after such a hard day's work, and she laughed. Then she said, "You try jumping back a total of a hundred and forty years, and tell me it wouldn't wipe you out."

I didn't laugh. Penelope gasped.

"Oh, shit," she said. "This is when you find out, isn't it?"

[17]

December 2088

I only saw Penelope—Young Penelope—twice after that. Things between us ended very badly. So much so, in fact, that I had a great deal of difficulty reconciling it with how well her older version got along with me.

Our penultimate encounter happened on a cold December afternoon, just before sunset. I was walking home from a quick trip to the store when she accosted me on the sidewalk, as was her way. For two years, the only way I had ever seen her was by her own initiative. Given that I viewed her less a friend than a co-conspirator, it always seemed appropriate to me that we had no normal social interaction. We never exchanged phone numbers or emails. None of my other friends had any idea she existed. I certainly had no idea where she lived. All of this seemed entirely reasonable to me, in a bizarre, adolescent, fantasy-of-being-in-a-spy-movie way. The obvious, true explanation for all of this evaded me through sheer willful self-misdirection. I was now furious with myself, not only for being so naïve in the first place, but for allowing it to continue as long as it did.

That day, I heard her voice from behind me. "Hey, Nigel," she said. I looked over my shoulder without returning the greeting, but did pause long enough for her to catch up to me. "What are you up to?" she asked, with rehearsed innocence.

"How old are you?" I asked her. If this non sequitur fazed her, she showed no sign. Instead, she gave me a coy, mysterious smile.

"How old do you think I am?"

We had played this game before, but not for a long time now. I learned early on that questions about her background were pointless. In two years she hadn't even given me her real name. Her question was meaningless bait.

"Eighteen," I said.

Her smile faded. This was not going to be a game. "Yeah," she said. "That's right."

The revelation so quickly given was unexpected, but I forged on. "What year were you born?"

She frowned. "Do the math. I just told you—"

"You're eighteen. Got it. What year were you born?"

The pause that followed was painfully silent, and couldn't have been anywhere near as long as it felt. "2070," she said quietly.

I laughed. "You can't even pretend to answer that naturally, can you? Two years to rehearse that answer, and you still flubbed it." We had stopped walking at that point. Penelope's smile was gone, and she wasn't making eye contact. "What year were you born?"

"I said—"

"I heard you. What year were you born?"

This pause was longer, and quite a bit more painful. Her older self told me she had traveled a hundred and forty years into the past when for me it had been a little more than fifty. That left at least eighty years, minus the twenty-something years old she appeared to be at the time. Rounding, I guessed, "2150?"

"That's... close enough," she said quietly.

Hearing her admission out loud was far less satisfying than I expected. And far more troubling.

"Plus 18 makes 2168," I said. "I'm a hundred years old in your time. Am I still alive?" I meant it as a dig, but its impact as a real question hit me once it was out of my mouth, and I braced myself for the answer.

"Um," she said. "It's kind of..." She trailed off, and while I mentally juggled all the reasons she might not be able to answer that question truthfully, she said, "Yeah. You're alive."

Wow. "I guess that's something," I said. "So what does that make you? My great-granddaughter?"

"It's not like that," she said.

"Well, what is it like?"

She still wouldn't look at me, and her face took on a pained look that might mean she was about to cry, or punch me in the face. Impossible to predict.

"You wouldn't understand."

With those words, she backed away from me, then turned and ran. I watched her flee, secure in the knowledge that she would find me again, having already done so many times in her own future. Still, something about this new understanding felt even less resolved than before, and perhaps irresolvable. As she shrank out of sight in the fading twilight, it began to snow.

[18]

February 2089

For several weeks after that encounter, I spent each day expecting a visit from Penelope, although never certain which version I expected more. I did the best I could to carry on with my normal life—at that point I was only a few months away from graduation—but the distraction began to mount, and my schoolwork began to suffer. This was not the first time I had found myself underperforming at school, but it was the first time I could remember that struggle happening in real time, and not as the result of an unhappening. I grappled with the possibility that whatever relationship I had forged with this woman, at whatever various points in her own time, might actually have come to an abrupt halt in my own frame of reference. The thought troubled me in ways both obvious and inexplicable. My primary ostensible concern was the plethora of questions that would now go forever unanswered by her. Underlying that was a sick feeling that a part of myself had been torn away with her.

When she did finally break silence, I didn't recognize her. She caught up with me in a shoe store, trying on a pair of hiking boots. It was a whimsical purchase, meant as part of a random reinvention of myself. Honestly, I half-expected the shoes to disappear after I got them home, and perhaps even hoped they would.

"Nigel?" I heard the voice as I was tying the second lace, and for a moment could not place it. I looked up into her eyes, and another moment elapsed before her face resolved into familiarity. Her blonde hair was quite a bit shorter than usual, and riddled with streaks of silver. A quiet smile with a hint of exhaustion spread out, and carried with it a collection of lines I had never seen before. This woman was fifty years old if she was a day.

"Penelope?"

She shook her head. "Once," she said. "Not today."

I looked at my shoes. "Should I take these off, or pay for them? Are we going somewhere?" I hoped my eagerness was less apparent than it felt.

"Either," she said. "And no. I'm just here to talk." She paused there. "Do you know when I was born?"

I nodded. "Circa 2150."

"How long have you known?"

I shrugged, thinking back. "Two months? About?"

She sighed, audibly. "I didn't think I would get this close."

She let that hang, long enough that I felt compelled to take charge, something new for me around her. I stood.

"I'm going to pay for these. You want to go grab a cup of coffee?" She nodded. The stiff leather of the shoes strained against my feet in ways that did not say proper fit. I ignored it. "You okay?" She nodded again, quite unconvincingly. I abandoned my own shoes to pay for these uncomfortable ones. The five hundred forty dollars it cost me to wear them out seemed a reasonable sacrifice.

We walked in silence a block and a half to a café. Over a latte and a chai, I prompted her. "I haven't seen you in a while," I said.

"I haven't seen you in eight years," she replied.

Unexpected, but unsurprising. "Why now?" I asked simply.

"Because I owe you some apologies, and I don't think..." She stopped there, and turned away. I gave her a moment, as she regained her composure by focusing on her latte. She blew on it, sipped it, and said into it, "Do you know how difficult time travel is?"

"Sort of," I admitted. "I've only done it a couple dozen times, but it does take the wind of me most days."

"That's not what I mean," she said. "Yes, it is taxing, physically, emotionally. I'm asking how much you know about the mechanics."

"Nothing. You never told me. I never asked. I assumed I would find out when I was ready, to protect the space-time continuum or something."

She laughed softly at that. "Space-Time takes care of herself just fine. That was always just about keeping you innocent. That part of your life is over, I'm sorry to say." She looked up. "Time travel is technologically, mechanically, extremely difficult. Setting up the field is child's play. Riding it is another thing entirely. Have you ever wondered why my visits to you were always non-sequential from your point of view? Or why my ages varied to the tune of about fifteen years? Aiming a time travel field is a desperately imprecise science. Do you want to guess what the margin of error is for a typical jump?"

I thought back on what little she had revealed to me in our travels about how closely she had made her goals. "Three days?" I considered the guess to be conservative.

She took another sip. "Seven years," she said. "Ish," she added with a slight smile that almost seemed genuine. "Mind you, that's a typical jump. Ours were anything but that."

"Is this stuff I'm supposed to know?"

"Doesn't really matter," she said. "I'm only telling you because I'm glad I got here when I did. I'm sorry I didn't tell you I was from the future. I mean, when I was Penelope."

"I know what you mean. You're apologizing for something you did, what, thirty years ago?"

"At least. I still wanted you to hear it. That time I saw you and knew I had accidentally let it slip... I tried for months to get back to that point in time, to tell you how sorry I was, but I couldn't. I was shut out. But now... Nigel, you will see me again after this point, many, many times. Most of those times we will be allies, close friends even. And most of them will be good times. But I... I think this is the last time I see you. And I just want to say I'm sorry. I'm sorry for a lot of the things that are about to start coming your way, and I'm sorry for what happened eight years ago. I wasn't well then, Nigel. Not well at all. It's been very difficult to own that. And I'm better now. Much better. But then... Just... When the thing from my eight years ago finally plays out for you, whatever you are thinking at the time, whatever you are feeling at that moment, try to remember..."

She looked down. A single tear dropped into her coffee. After a beat, she took another sip from it. Quietly, she said, "Try to remember that someday after that, I came back here to tell you how sorry I am." She stood, and as she walked past my seat she put her hand on my shoulder to stop me from getting up, or following her. "How sorry I am," she repeated, "and how much I love you."

She kissed me on the forehead, and drifted out the door.

[19]

June 2089

Penelope's words of warning and apology haunted me, and her timing was dreadful. I was just finishing out the last few weeks of my undergrad career. With some carefully honed tools for maintaining a real social life under my belt, and feeling like I had some kind of handle on the unhappenings that had plagued my life for years, I looked forward to striking out into the world with a reasonable facsimile of normality. Not to be, apparently.

I did what I could to maintain stability in my schoolwork, and withdrew a bit from my friends. Whatever crisis loomed for me, I already knew I would outlive it to at least my one hundredth birthday, but there was no telling what could yet happen—or unhappen—to the people around me.

It was about a week before I graduated that I got my first taste of what she meant by the things that were about to start coming my way.

It was late in the evening, and I had just eaten dinner with Pete. He and I had begun to drift apart. That was entirely intentional on my part, but he had no way of knowing that. This get-together was something of an olive branch from him, and I humored it. In truth, that was a friendship I had come to value deeply. The fact that I was passively ending it was entirely for Pete's protection, and I was sorry to see it go.

As we left the restaurant, Pete told me he needed to walk back to one of the physics labs to check on an experiment he was running for Dr. Ainsley. I had managed to avoid that professor entirely since his attempted arrest of me years earlier. Pete knew all about that, as did everyone who was a student at that time, but he assured me Ainsley would be nowhere near the building, so I went with him. When we got there, he asked me to wait outside.

"I'm not supposed to let anyone near the equipment," he said. "It's some sort of weird classified thing."

"Really? He trusts you with top secret research?"

Pete laughed. "He absolutely does not. Honestly, I don't even have a clue what this is all about. Twice a day I take some readings and answer a few observational questions, which usually amounts to recording the same exact numbers over and over again, and noting that nothing has changed. Part of me thinks this isn't even a physics experiment, and that I'm really a subject in a psych study on pointless activity. This is how I earn my stipend, so I don't ask a lot of questions. Whatever it is, he has told me absolutely nothing, and sworn me to secrecy about it. If he knew I was telling you even this much—especially because it's you, by the way— he'd probably have me drawn and quartered. Stay put. I'll be right back."

As I waited for Pete outside the building, I began to feel a tingle in my left arm. It was the same sensation I felt during some of my travels through time with Penelope, and once or twice I felt it just prior to her arrival. I had come to think of the implant as my trick knee that can always tell when a storm is coming. I paced nervously, wondering if she was about to appear and if I would finally have to introduce her—or explain her—to Pete. But she didn't come. The tingling carried on, and began to take on a pulse-like quality, which was new. I started to rub my arm, as a reflex.

"Are you okay?" asked Pete. I jumped, a bit startled, and realized I had been scanning the area so intently and nervously for any sign of Penelope that I had completely forgotten about him.

"My arm hurts," I said honestly. If he was asking whether I was all right, he must already have seen me rubbing it anyway.

"Did you do something to it?" he asked, and as he spoke, in simple curiosity he took a step toward me and leaned in to look for an injury.

The tingling suddenly shifted to stabbing pain, and I yelped. Pete jumped back, clearly surprised and concerned, and the pain stopped.

The sensation wasn't coming from Penelope; it was coming from Pete.

Whatever covert experiment Ainsley was running with Pete as his lackey was generating the same field around him that Penelope always carried with her. The futuristic technology I had been using for two years was no longer so futuristic. It was to be the eventual product of research and development going on in real time in my own school.

Time travel was starting to happen.

[20]

June 2089

And then I graduated.

I finished in the top quarter of my class, which I thought was pretty impressive under the conditions in which I had spent my four years of study. My parents took me and about a dozen members of my extended family out to a very expensive restaurant, where I ordered a whole lobster. It was a pretty good day.

My diploma was framed within the next week. Lacking a proper office in which to hang it, I chose to display it on the wall of the living room in my parents' house. It was a genuine source of pride to read the words "Bachelor of Science in Physics." Every morning before breakfast I would head into the library, and read the entire document, whispering the words softly to myself.

And every day, in recognition of the fact that—very much against my expectations—it was still there, I would finish by whispering, "At least for now."

June 2089

My diploma turned out to be permanent. Unfortunately, it was about the only thing from that part of my life that was.

During my senior year, I applied to, and was accepted into, a Masters program at Cornell. I wasn't due to start until the fall semester, so I spent much of the summer relaxing, and planning to relocate. My displacement—physical this time—was a refreshingly simple ordeal, and preparing for it made me feel pleasantly normal for a change. Toward the end of July, my father carefully broached the topic of how long it was going to take me to start looking for a job. To anyone else preparing to move out of state for graduate school in a month, such a suggestion would be confusing. To me, it was all too clear. A search through my correspondence from that year soon turned up the rejection letter from Cornell in my saved e-mails, along with similar letters from several other universities.

It was surely an act of remarkable restraint that my father's inquiries about my future plans were as kind as they were. The conversations we must have had about my universal rejections from graduate schools were probably awful for both of us, and I was at least partially grateful not to have actually experienced them. Dad was always deeply invested in my prospects as a physicist. His own field had been computer science, and he had been fortunate enough to be exactly the right age to ride the cascade of developments in artificial intelligence that transpired in the 2060s. Had he graduated two years earlier or later he would have missed what was a very narrow window of unprecedented opportunity in his specialty. While he never wished for me to follow directly in his footsteps, I was his only child, and the possibility that I would follow science of some sort was a point of personal delight for him. I know he often saw me as a younger version of himself. We even looked strikingly similar. Same skinny build, same unmanageable hair (although unlike him I did ultimately get to keep mine), we even had the same taste in eyeglasses, at a time when those had gone nearly extinct. When I finally asked for optic surgery, it nearly broke his heart. I can only imagine how he must have crashed at my apparent washing out of a career in science.

With grad school suddenly no longer an option, I did indeed begin to look for work. This proved significantly daunting. My intent was always to pursue a PhD and spend the rest of my life steeped in research, exactly as my father had hoped, preferably in time travel applications. I never had a plan B.

How short-sighted of me.

Fortunately, my parents were people of means, and there was no real urgency for me to be employed, at least from a survival perspective. Nevertheless, it was unacceptable to them, and to myself, for me to begin a career as a layabout. My first choice was to put my physics degree to work, especially as I was now planning to start the grad school application process all over again, and I wanted to be able to build experience to make myself a more desirable candidate. Partly on the strength of my background, but largely as a result of my father's connections, I was able to get a job as a research assistant, which he found encouraging. That lasted for nine days. On day ten I woke to discover that I had been working for three weeks as a tech support person for a communications firm. The next few days were an embarrassing sequence of incidents in which I needed to be retrained on very simple matters. Eventually, I settled into the work.

That job lasted for ten weeks. Then, abruptly, I was a substitute teacher at a private high school. Seven weeks after that, I discovered that I really worked as the electronics manager at Sears. A few weeks after that I was unemployed, and had always been. A few more weeks along and I was suddenly, retroactively, a cashier in a grocery store. The unhappenings continued in cycles of four to eight weeks, and each was progressively more discouraging than the last, as my new jobs drew me further and further away from science.

This went on for over two and a half years.

[22]

February 2092

The spate of unhappenings I experienced after graduation had a very different character than anything I had seen previously. Many of my losses over the years had been profound, and there were occasional, if brief, patterns. My experience with girls in high school was the most obvious example of this, as was my rotating panel of physics teachers, but both of those were sporadic, even at the time. This crisis of new and surprising occupations every few weeks—sometimes switching in shifts of only a few days—was the longest sustained obstacle in my life to that point. The fact that it was so consistent, and prolonged, coupled with the specific timing that the barrage began immediately after my school days had come to an apparent end, made it impossible for me to continue denying the inescapable. This was no mere obstacle; it was a sustained attack.

Penelope, in every age at which I encountered her, always refused to tell me the cause of our unhappenings. Sometimes she claimed she didn't know, other times she simply dodged the question. All she ever shared freely was that she and I shared that experience, along with at least one other person, possibly more. Eventually I learned to stop asking, but the more times she spirited me away to "run a fix," the more convinced I became that we were engaging in some sort of covert, time travel combat. I wondered how many of my own unhappenings were "fixes" being run by some unseen foe.

More than once I wondered if that foe might not be Penelope.

Adding to that nagging thought, I received no visits from her during this stretch of my life. The oldest version of her I had yet encountered assured me we would meet again, many times, but I had seen no sign of her since that day. I could not bring myself to believe that she had been playing me for nefarious purposes this whole time, but it would have been very gratifying to see some evidence of that.

It became clear that I was not going to be allowed to pursue my PhD when every attempt I made to submit applications to schools was immediately undone. It was equally clear that I was not destined for any sort of rewarding employment, or a career in any type of science. The jobs through which I was rotated were all menial, or middle management in companies that held nothing of interest to me, and that was when I had a job at all. I spent a fair portion of those days unemployed, to various degrees of parental disappointment. All of this combined to weigh me down with a despair that my dream of becoming 'Dr. Walden' and spearheading the research that would lead to time travel was not to be. It was a terrible conceit on my part, but I had spent the previous five years certain that my destiny was to be the sole scientific mind to be credited with the most significant discovery in human history. It turned out that my true destiny was to be a bystander.

Then I met myself for the second time, and everything changed again.

It was during one of my stretches between jobs. I told my parents I was going out to look for work, then camped out at the public library. Soon enough, I would be assigned a random job that I might even be able to maintain long enough to see a paycheck. Until then, any genuine job hunt would be an absolute waste of time. Usually I would bypass the terminals on the main floor, and hide out in the print collection. Apart from the librarian who worked there, no one ever took an interest in it, leaving it peaceful, pleasant and private. That was where he found me.

"What are you doing here?" I heard myself say. In the light of day, and out of the rain, I could better see his face. It had the same gray stubble I had seen in drunken closeup, and I could now see his hair, long, completely gray, and not particularly kempt. It was impossible for me to know if he was wearing the same clothing as the last time we met, but his hair looked like it was just drying out. The weather outside was sunny and very cold. Five years ago we had an awful encounter that was probably an hour ago for him. He seemed less crazed now, but I wouldn't say that reassured me.

"Hiding from your parents," I countered.

He froze, a confused frown on his face. Whatever conversation he thought we were going to have, it wasn't that one.

"No," he said, "I mean why aren't you at Cornell? I was just there. They said you never enrolled." He took a moment to look around the room, perhaps to confirm we were alone, perhaps just to get his bearings, then pulled up a chair. "You know who I am," he said. It was difficult to tell if he meant it as a question.

"I've had five years to work it out," I told him. My exploits with Penelope sat poised on my tongue as clarification of my understanding of time travel, but something held me back. By all rights, I should have been able to trust him, but I couldn't let go of the fact that Penelope had always been kind to me, and that my only encounter with this version of me ended with him pushing me into a puddle. He nodded thoughtfully, and did not further pursue that topic. For a brief instant, my stomach lurched as I realized I had just successfully, and literally, lied to myself.

"Cornell?" he repeated. "What happened there?"

I shrugged. "Didn't get in," I said. "Didn't get in anywhere."

His frown deepened. "That's... that's not possible." He stood, visibly rattled, and walked to a window, carefully scrutinizing every object he passed on the way. After staring out onto the library courtyard for a few moments, he said, "I have no memory of this."

"The library?"

He turned and met my eyes. "This event. This conversation. I don't think it ever happened to me. How can that be?"

Of all the excellent reasons I had right then to feel uncomfortable, the one that trumped all else was the notion that this man—this version of me —had traveled through time what was probably dozens of years, at least twice, and somehow expected me to have answers for him. There were so many things I wanted to ask him—any reasonable person would beg for an opportunity like this—and yet somehow, horribly, I was the one with upper hand.

"Lots of things happen that I don't remember. And lots of things I do remember unhappen," I said, "but you know that."

He stared. Not good. "I don't understand what you mean. I don't understand any of this. Is this even the same timeline?" He clutched his head. "This is never going to work." My earlier assessment that he was less crazed started to unravel.

"Why are you here?" I asked, in a desperate attempt to push this in a coherent direction.

He buried his face in his hands. After a very long, very audible sigh, he looked up and began to speak in a tone so even it barely seemed natural.

"I came back here to tell you about the Time Travel Project. I did not anticipate that you had already deduced its existence from my earlier visit. That was incautious of me, but what's done is done."

He paused there, and it was all I could do to keep myself from screaming at him. The only constant fact in my life had ever been that what is done is never, with any certainty, done.

He soldiered on. "In fact, it may be fortuitous that you are already aware of it. That will save me a lot of work persuading you. Because here it is, Nigel: I need you." He let that hang between us.

"In what way could you possibly need me?" Those words were out of my mouth before I fully processed how confrontational they were. This entire encounter was beginning to play out as a darker version of my association with Penelope. The thought that I might be put in a place where I would be expected to choose sides was too horrific to contemplate at that moment. To my profound relief and confusion, his next words put me in a much different place than that.

"I need to you to help me correct the flaws in the process. Time travel was my brainchild. Every facet, every functional aspect of the theory, every path to application, was mine, and it doesn't work." He choked on that last word.

"But… You're here." Again, I withheld that I was an experienced traveler already.

He shook his head. "There are bugs. Bad bugs. It doesn't work the way it is supposed to, and we are deep into it now. If we don't find ways around the gaps and flaws in the process… A lot of people are going to die, Nigel."

"Die? What are you talking about?"

"I can't give you specifics. Not yet. I'm sorry, but I need your help before it's too late."

Setting aside what 'too late' could possibly mean in this context, none of this made any sense.

"Why me?" I asked.

"Because you already have the background to begin forming the theory. I know you do, because this is when I started pulling it together. Right now, your insights are pure. They are not dulled by age, or cynicism, or politics. I need to go back to formula on this. I need to go back to you. Given the resources that I never had the first time around, and the benefit of my own mistakes…" He rocked his head, looking for the words. "You're the only hope I have left."

I was speechless. There was no way I could have this conversation extemporaneously. Evidently, he already understood that.

As he stood to leave, he said, "Don't answer now. I am going to give you two months to think this over, and then I will be back. Think of questions for me during that time. Good questions. Lots of questions." He walked to the door without further discussion. Just before he closed it behind himself, he looked back and said, "I know you can do this, Nigel. And I also know you want this, more than anything else in the world. Think about it." Then he was gone.

So much weighed on me at that moment, but nothing as severely as the fact that I had just lied to myself, repeatedly. Nothing, that is, but the certainty that while I was lying to myself, myself had been lying to me.

[23]

February 2092

From there, I had two months to consider the most important question of my life. Of course, it wasn't at all the question I was supposed to be considering. That question, as to whether I wanted to circumvent every scrap of common sense about how the universe was supposed to work and throw myself into time travel research to make possible something that I had already been doing for years, was easy. Oh my goodness, yes, I wanted to do that. The more pressing question I would need to consider was how I could possibly trust the man who had made me that offer, despite the fact, or especially because, that man was me.

Everything about his manner suggested that everything he told me was a clumsy fabrication. Unfortunately, I had no guess as to his true intentions. Perhaps I could play along just to get access to the research he was asking me to assist. Logically, there was no chance he could be planning to harm me in any way. That was comforting, apart from the abundance of evidence that time travel did not operate in any manner that could be remotely considered logically consistent. I would never be able to gauge the true danger I would be placing myself in. The only issue was the level of recklessness I was prepared to exercise.

I pondered all of this on my way home that afternoon. By the time I got to my parents' house, I realized I had completely forgotten to prepare my fictional job search report. My hesitation to go inside and face them with nothing to show for my day lasted only as long as it took me to remember that in a few days, or weeks at the outside, none of this would have happened anyway. Lying about looking for work would be exactly as useless as actually looking for work. Work would find me soon enough. For today, I would feign depression about my circumstance to buy some sympathy. If that didn't work, plan B was to simply not care what they thought, and patiently wait for them to never have thought it.

With that level of indifference, I entered my home, and found my mother talking to Penelope in the living room.

It is difficult to convey on just how many levels this sight caught me off guard. For starters, Penelope had consistently kept her own existence as secret as possible from everyone I knew. To see her casually chatting with my mother flew in the face of years of surreptitious behavior. I had only a split second before my mother greeted me and inevitably attempted to engage both Penelope and me in conversation, in which to determine (or wildly guess) exactly which version of Penelope this was. From the smile on her face, she clearly expected me to be happy to see her. I struggled to recall the last encounters I had with her, in various stages, and could not place one in which we had parted comfortably. From my frame of reference, working backward, I had seen her at fiftyish, deeply sad and apologetic; eighteen, furious and defensive; and early twenties, severely embarrassed. My best guess under pressure was that this was the eighteen version.

"Nigel!" said my mother. "You have a visitor."

"I can see that," I said, with my best attempt at a natural smile. "What have you two been talking about?"

"You, of course."

I laughed politely. My mother gave me a look of serious intrigue. Unlike my father, she had never been particularly invested in my career choice. All she ever wanted was for me to be happy. If physics did that, then she supported my choice. But that's where her interest in science began and ended. She was a medieval history professor, and had little use in her own life for any idea that was less than eight hundred years old. One such idea, of course, was that every human needed companionship. Like everyone else, she was oblivious to my failed high school romances. From her perspective, I had never shown an interest in—or at least any success with—girls. On more than one occasion, she asked me very frankly if I had any luck with boys. She needed me not to be lonely. The fact that this young woman suddenly materialized must have been nothing less than a long-awaited miracle to her.

There were so very many things that could go wrong in the next few moments. My top priority was to end the small talk and get Penelope out of there where we could talk without fear of dragging my parents into a world they had no idea existed. My father might have had some hope of understanding what my situation had really been all these years, but there were few people in the world less like me than my own mother. I didn't even really look like her. She was all curly red hair and freckles, framing the roundest face in the world. My possible changeling status was a running gag in my family for longer than it could ever have actually been funny. If I hadn't been such a perfect duplicate of my father's sharper features, it might even have been cause for investigation. Honestly, this virtual stranger in my living room looked more like my mother than I did. Given that she and I were practically from different worlds, I couldn't even hope to predict how she would react to the truth.

"You'll have to help me out," my mother went on. "This young lady says she won't tell me her name until you introduce her."

Good grief. Setting aside my irritation over the fact that Penelope had persuaded my mother to play that game—it would have been child's play to take advantage of Mom's need to have any sort of girl in my life whatsoever—that simply confused the issue for me further. I had no idea what her name was, of course, and without the clue of what name I was calling her at the moment, I had one fewer way to place her. In every encounter with her youngest version, I had always called her Penelope. In every other encounter, I had called her variations of "Hey You." Our explicit agreement was that I not concern myself with her name, and that someday I would simply happen across it. It never quite made sense to me. Cornered now, I chose an alternative.

"Her name is Una."

Una's face held steady in an expression probably intended to convey glee, but was easy for me to see as surprise. I interpreted that to mean I had never called her this before. Given my immediate resolve to call her this for the foreseeable future, that would mean until this moment she had been Penelope. Eighteen then, or near enough. Like so many of my management tools, this was a complete guess.

Una got up and put her jacket on. "It was lovely meeting you, Mrs. Walden," she said with a cheery grin. "Thank you for letting me wait here."

My mother got up as well, and gave Una a hug. "It was my pleasure. When do you think you'll be back?" It took me a second to realize that was directed at me, but Una caught it.

"I'll try not to keep him out past curfew," she said to my mother. Another round of polite laughter. Una took my hand and led me out of

70

the house. My mother raised the eyebrow of we-have-much-to-discuss-young-man, and waved us both goodbye.

With the door closed behind us, and the two of us walking to I had no idea where, I asked, "What on Earth did you tell her?"

She countered with, "Me? What about you? What's with Una?"

That made me laugh for real. "Can I assume I still haven't found your name?"

"You have not. And I much prefer Penelope."

"Well," I said, "now you are Una. Unless you'd like to come clean with me." Pause. "I thought not. Oh, and by the way, what are you doing here, and where the hell have you been for the last three years?"

"Three years?" She seemed genuinely surprised by this. "You haven't seen me for three years? Not even some future version of me?"

"Not a sign. I was beginning to wonder if you had given up on me."

"Never," she said. We walked in silence for a bit.

"You could have told me you were from my future, you know. When you first met me."

"I'm not sorry about that, if that's where you're going."

"You will be," I said.

She huffed. "You can't possibly know that."

"Actually, I know it for a fact."

"Oh," she said. Making the connection, she pouted. "Well, I'm not sorry now."

"Fair enough. That's not where I was going anyway. Are you going to tell me why you're here?"

She shrugged. "I didn't like the way we parted. I thought if maybe I gave you a while to cool off, we would be okay again."

"Well, that much worked. We're fine. How long ago was that for you?"

"Yesterday," she said. "Why Una?"

"Yesterday? Wow. Yesterday." I finally released my first impression of this girl as a contemporary of mine. Time travel was second nature to her already, and perhaps had been her whole life. "I'm calling you Una to remind myself that no matter how many versions of you I get to know, there's really only one of you. Someday I'm going to reconcile all the different points of your life and figure out who you really are."

She laughed. "Good luck with that."

"Can I ask your advice on something?" I said.

"Me? Is that a thing you do? Ask my advice?"

The question sounded sarcastic to me at first, until I realized she was sincerely trying to get a feel for what her relationship with me was going to be as she got older. I almost never shared with her anything that her future selves did or said. "Sometimes," I said. "I got a visit today from future me. He wants me to help him with some bugs he is having on the Time Travel Project."

Una got very quiet.

"Am I asking the wrong thing? If I'm not supposed to know this stuff, I don't want to put you in a bad position. But I figure if I'm not supposed to know it, I wouldn't be traveling back in time to tell myself stuff. Mind you, I kind of have the sense that Future Me isn't quite playing with a full deck. That's troubling in a couple ways, and I'd rather not dwell on it, but I'm just trying to figure out how safe this is going to be."

Una's silence continued to stretch. Looking away from me, she said, "Don't."

This was turning very uncomfortable. "Don't? Don't help him?" Una seemed afraid. I tried to think of a way to backtrack.

"Don't," she repeated. "Don't... Don't ask me about this. You can't ask me about this."

"Hey," I said. "I'm sorry. I don't want to compromise you, or whatever this would do. Forget I asked. I'll figure it out on my own."

She shook her head. "No, you won't, but I can't help you with this. It's... I'm too close to it. You'll understand some day. Just, please don't make me choose."

"Choose?"

She shook her head.

"Okay, I'm sorry." Whatever Una knew, it was something vital, something I absolutely had to know, but I wasn't going to get it out of her, and I was afraid if I tried I would lose her for another three years. Pathetically, I tried to change the subject. "How did you convince my mother to let you in without telling her your name? She's not usually that trusting."

Una smiled a bit at that. "Do you seriously think this is the first time I have met your parents?"

"Too much to hope you'll explain that?"

"Not happening." She smiled, but it was heavy, and masking a pain she clearly hadn't expected to be confronted with today. "I should get going." She surprised me by giving me a hug, something she had never done before. Or had done many times before. Impossible to know.

"Don't be a stranger, okay?"

"I won't," she promised.

I never saw that version of Penelope again.

[24]

February 2092

Somewhere in my head was the secret to time travel. If Future Me was telling the truth about that much, at least, then my dream was no conceit after all. Part of me knew that would be exactly the sort of thing someone would tell me to lure me in. The rest of me told that part to kindly shut up.

Given the proper resources, I could make it work. I did not have those resources, at least not exactly. I did have one thing, though. I had a functioning example of the technology bonded to my left ulna.

The prospect of digging it out to inspect it did not appeal. But with only two months to go, I needed answers, and that was the only place I knew where to start. What I really needed was access to a medical scanner and a technician who wouldn't ask a lot of questions. That was not going to happen. However, I did have access to something that might accomplish approximately the same purpose.

My father's work was designing multi-processor industrial robots. Specifically, he was a Restrictable Intelligence engineer. His job was to traverse that narrow band between non-intelligent and artificially intelligent machines. Too dumb, and the robots can't do their work. Too smart, and they won't want to. Dad helped develop the Crawford-Walden Processor, which is meant to be both fully integrated and remotely reprogrammable. Part of that system incorporated a CWP scanner, which could both diagnose and reorient the robots' multiple brains without the need to physically remove them, which was often a prohibitively complicated procedure. Presumably, whatever the device in my arm was, it had to have some sort of processor. A diagnostic scan might give me a starting point in figuring out what it was.

A proper CWP scan would have to be conducted at the manufacturing facility. Even if I could convince the dozen or so people who would need to authorize it—including my father—it would end up entailing every one of them knowing what I was looking at. My own reluctance to dig it out of my arm might not be shared by all of them.

However, Dad kept a couple of early prototypes from his lab. They were technically obsolete, useless for any application to current CWP models, and a form of technology that had already been cracked by dozens of other companies. Security being a non-issue, he was allowed to keep them in a trophy case in his office. He was also allowed to bring one of them home, to satisfy the curiosity of his son who had a sudden and renewed passion for science and wanted to study it. The prospect of getting me fired up to go back to school was more than enough incentive to bring me one, which he did the same day I asked for it.

It took me two days of tinkering with it in my room to figure out how to have it scan through soft tissue without risk of injury, something it was certainly never designed for. I got some fantastic images of the interior of the module, revealing a nanoscopically complex structure. I also got a plethora of data regarding its functionality, as the scanner attempted to guess how and why a CWP would behave the way this device did. Several treatment solutions were presented to correct what it saw as aberrations, and I of course rejected them all.

Unfortunately, the scanner was not equipped to tell me anything that I was able to connect to time travel theory. The only hard piece of analysis it was able to provide was both entirely foreseeable, and regrettably troubling.

Too Smart.

[25]

April 2092/May 2115

With one week to go before I had to make my choice, I got another visit from Una. She looked about thirty this time. "I'm calling you Una now," I informed her.

"I'm still Una? I thought we were past that one."

It was a Saturday, early Spring. Una found me alone at the park. "Maybe you are," I said, "but it's still novel for me. I only just named you that a couple months ago. You seemed annoyed with it at the time."

"I got over it. Take my hand."

I took her hand. My left arm tingled. The world flashed, and when my eyes readjusted, and my gag reflex obeyed my mental command to settle down, we were still in a park, but clearly not the same park. There were maybe a dozen other people there—children playing on the swings, a young woman walking a dog, a couple with a stroller—but no one appeared to notice our arrival.

"What year is this?" I asked.

"2115."

She said this without looking at me. She was staring at something, but I couldn't tell what. Given that this was my first ever trip into my own future, I was a little put off by the anti-climactic nature of the revelation.

"Do you know why I'm here?" she asked.

I didn't. The last time I had seen her at this approximate stage was the time she let slip that her year of origin was many decades into my future.

75

"Do you mean here in 2115? Are we running a fix? It's been a long time. I miss that."

"I don't mean the year. Sometimes I come here when I need to think, that's all. And sorry, no, not a fix. When I need you for a fix, I pick you up from college. You were a lot more susceptible to suggestion at that age. Any time I need a sidekick, I set the destination for September of your senior year. Plus or minus one year lands me in your last two years at MIT, and away we go. I'm sure I'll have more reasons to do that down the road. How many fixes did you run with me, total?"

I counted mentally. "Fifteen? I'm not sure."

"I've only done nine of those. So yeah, I'll see you there again, but from your frame of reference, that job is over."

"Wait, I thought the margin of error for a jump was seven years, not one."

She perked up a bit at that. "It's different when it's you," she said. "The longer you travel, the easier it is to find you. You're already at the point where I can catch up to you to within days. But even back then, you're right, the error was a lot smaller than it would be for a standard jump. How did you know about the seven years?"

"An older you. Sometimes you tell me things. Usually not so much. You're being uncharacteristically honest today," I said.

She shrugged. "Not at all. I'm plenty honest with you most times. It's just easier for both of us if you don't know anything when you're that young. Anyway, no, that's not why I'm here."

I looked away from her. "This is about Future Me. His offer."

She nodded. "You have a few days yet, am I right?"

"A week," I said. "Are you here to give me advice this time? Because my most recent conversation with you about this ended with you panicking and begging to stay out of it."

"Advice, no," she said. "I can't be part of this decision."

"Why not? How is this different from anything else you've had me do?"

"It's bigger," she said. "And I'm too closely tied to it. Influencing you would be... I don't know. 'Unethical' is nowhere near severe enough a word for it, but that's as close as I can get." She put her hand on my shoulder. "Here's some of that honesty you're not used to hearing from me yet: whatever you decide, you're going to regret it. I'm so sorry. I can't advise you because your choice is going to affect me even more than it will affect you."

"Oh, good lord," I said. "Did you really come back to this point in time just to make this harder on me?"

"No. I came back here to make sure your decision is as informed as possible. I want you to ask me questions. I want you to have as much information as you can possibly get. Because when you finally regret what you do…" She paused here, perhaps looking for the right words. "I want you to be able to forgive yourself."

"Great." I rolled that all around in my head, while Una watched me, for probably a full minute. "Future Me said a lot of people are going to die if I don't help him," I said. "Was he telling me the truth?"

Una took a moment to compose her answer before speaking it. "No," she said. "He was not telling the truth, but he wasn't wrong either. People are going to die." As she said this, her gaze drifted away from me again.

I thought about this for a moment, wondering if she meant people would die either way. It seemed like a pretty important detail for her to be vague about it. "He visited me once before," I said. "When I was a sophomore. Said I was too young or something. What can you tell me about that?"

This got her attention in a way I hadn't expected. "I don't know," she said carefully. "Was… Are you absolutely certain it was him?"

"Yes. He and I even talked about that briefly this time."

She frowned. "I don't know anything about that. I'm not even sure I know what to do with that information."

"Really? We talked about this right after it happened."

"Not yet we haven't," she said, and then it gelled for me that she was younger now than she was when she first made me a traveler. She probably had the silver bead in her pocket right now, still waiting for the day she would plant it in my arm.

"Sorry," I said. "That's my past, your future. So, you don't know why he would have considered asking for my help that early?"

"No," she said. For a moment it looked like she was going to speculate, but then she chose silence. I wasn't going to get anything else from that angle of inquiry, but it wasn't my priority right then anyway. I made a mental note to come back to that discussion at some point, and chose to ask her a much more important question.

"If I make the wrong choice, are you going to die?"

That brought her back. She gave me a very sad smile. "No. I won't die."

"Then I don't think I want to know anything else," I said.

Her smile faded into a look of worry. "Are you sure?"

I nodded. "I get how big this is. And I appreciate what you're trying to do here, but I don't think it's going to make a difference. Knowing that I'm going to regret this either way is strangely liberating, so thank you for that. At this point I just want to hear what Future Me has to say about a couple of things, but I think I already know what I'm going to do."

With that, Una took me home. Expecting to regret my choice made it easier to make, if not more wisely. But I definitely missed the point of her visit that day, because what I didn't expect was how much I would regret not asking her at least one more question.

[26]

April 2092

Early in the morning, two months to the day after Future Nigel made his offer, I went back to the print collection room again and waited. He hadn't specified that he would meet me there, but it seemed the logical place to wait for him. At about one in the afternoon, he poked his head in the door.

"I wasn't sure you would come back here," he said. "I was about to try your parents' house."

"Really? I'm sorry I missed that, then. What were you planning to tell them? I'm sure Mom's reaction would have been something for the record books."

He stared at me, that same distant look in his eyes I had seen now twice before. The last time I saw him, I suspected it was the same day for him as our first encounter five years before that. This time I was sure. His clothing was exactly the same, and his hair was still damp from five year old rain. "I guess I didn't really think that one through," he admitted.

"Not a problem," I said. "I wouldn't have been home anyway. You happened to catch me during a week that I have an actual job. Playing hooky today, of course. Probably getting fired. Not that any of that matters."

None of that seemed to penetrate. "Have you considered my request?" he asked.

"You wanted me to ask you questions," I reminded him. "Are you ready for them?"

"Of course."

"Okay then," I said, and felt my heart begin to race. "Here's the only question I have: What is this really about?"

"Um," he said. "I told you—"

"Something that's obviously not true. You said time travel doesn't work properly. Then you said you'd be back in two months. It's two months later, here you are, and you never even left the building. You jumped two months forward with negligible error. My best theoretical estimates of jump error should be plus or minus seven years, and you brushed that off like it was nothing." The seven years comment clearly hit him hard. He had no way of knowing it was inside information, but if he wanted to think I was that smart, let him. "So I want to know, since you've obviously mastered the thing you say doesn't work, what is it you really want from me?"

Future Me came fully into the room, sat down, and put his hands flat on the table in front of me. Even braced, they were clearly shaking. "I need you to help me, and the best way for you to do that is to help with the time travel research."

I stared into his eyes, looking for some sort of tell. "Even though you clearly don't really need my physics insights."

"That's not..." he began to say, but evidently remembered whom he was trying to deceive. "Yes," he said. "Even though that."

"I'll do it," I said.

His look of surprise was expected. "Why?"

"Because you are a train wreck," I said. "You are an absolute disaster. I've only talked to you for ten minutes total, and I already know you are a mess that has no idea how to clean itself up." I leaned in closer, and he recoiled slightly. Whether this was in fear of me or whatever had already brought him to this state was impossible to tell. "I will do this because there is no way I will ever let myself become you."

At those words, he closed his eyes, and slowly smiled.

"Thank you," he whispered.

"Don't thank me yet. Thank me if it works. Show me everything you have, and I will get started on whatever it is I am supposed to do. Do you have any of it with you?" He did not appear to have brought any equipment with him, and any data storage he might be carrying would surely not be compatible with contemporary machines, so I expected him to leave at that point, and return shortly with materials and notes for me to peruse. Instead, a look of confusion retook his face.

"No," he said. "You're coming with me."

I ran those words over in my head a few times. "Wait, what? I can't do that! You never said anything about coming with you!"

"I'm sure I did," he said. The general note of desperation was creeping back into his voice. I had not anticipated this, but now it suddenly held great appeal. A short jaunt into the future, perhaps several jaunts. If I played this right, it would be an adventure beyond my already remarkable experiences.

"For how long?"

"Not long," he said.

"And you can bring me right back here when I'm done?"

"Yes."

"I mean right here. This room. This moment."

"Yes."

As every scrap of common sense and wisdom in my soul bellowed at me to abandon this idea, he pulled a device out of his coat pocket and handed it to me. It was roughly bar-shaped, about twenty centimeters long, and covered in buckles. "Strap this onto your arm." I stared at it. Its descendant already lived in a bone in my left arm. I weighed the pros and cons of revealing this, and ultimately hoped they simply wouldn't interfere with each other.

In a flash, we were gone.

[PART 2]
GRAHAM

January 2144

2144 was surprisingly not all that different from 2092. Clothing styles had changed, but not in a way I could readily articulate, nor in a way that was any more out of sync with my own appearance than I was used to. Cars still didn't fly. There was no evidence of a robot insurrection, or an epidemic of cyborg implants. No devastating world wars, no zombie apocalypse. The most dramatic differences were the invisible ones. Peak oil production had come and gone, and the world had adapted to other energy sources that did the same work and filled the coffers of the same companies. Medical advancements had extended life expectancy beyond a hundred years (making my own predicted lifespan less remarkable), which contributed to the global population climbing to eighteen billion people. Cities were getting taller, and in some cases merging into megalopolises, but the human race was still sustaining itself.

The most immediate change from my end was that computers were all voice command now. That technology was already eighty years old in my time, but it took another thirty years for it to dominate the culture, and the market. Plenty of people still used touch screens as a matter of privacy, but for the most part, the world had gone hands free. In a curious aesthetic development, perhaps as a conscious rebellion against the urbanization of the globe, most computer hardware was now built into cases of polished wood.

So, my comfort level in the environment of a world fifty-two years into my own future was greater than predicted. My personal situation was another matter entirely. Memo to self: if a person is obviously lying about something, it is a good idea to consider the possibility that he is lying about everything.

'Not long' turned out to be very long. I imagined we were talking about a trip of several hours, or perhaps even several days. My surprise at discovering I had an apartment, a fake university ID, and a detailed document outlining my elaborate back-story cannot be overstated. I got to learn all about my alleged past entirely from that file. My future self spent no more than ten seconds in my company when we arrived at our target space-time, which was exactly long enough to remove the module from my wrist without comment, and disappear.

I had kidnapped myself.

My new identity was that of one Graham Walden, grandnephew of distinguished hyperphysicist Dr. Nigel Walden. How very clever of him to explain away what would be an obvious resemblance between us. The explanation would be quite necessary, as I was now a research assistant on the Time Travel Project, Dr. Walden's brainchild, and there was a reasonable expectation that many people who became acquainted with me were already well acquainted with him. According to my bio, it was relatively common knowledge that I came into this job entirely through nepotism, and that I had no particular talent for the subject matter. I would be surrounded by scientists with low expectations of my intellect. It was not at all clear why this was an integral part of my story. Its authenticity was sure to be shattered once I started to let slip the occasional brilliant idea. I was bound to have them, after all, since this was all my work to begin with. For whatever reason, I was instructed to conceal any new insights I might have, and surreptitiously record them for Dr. Walden to examine—and presumably take credit for—personally.

Under no circumstances was I to have any direct contact with the project leader.

Given my relative lack of culture shock, and the fact that everyone there already knew as much about "Graham Walden" as I did, my first day at work was strikingly ordinary. I got to meet two members of the research team, and as predicted, they treated me like a gofer.

The first day turned into my first week. That in turn drew out to my first month. At no time did I accept this as a permanent situation, reasoning that as long as I didn't stay here so long that I noticeably aged, at some point I would need only return to that day in the library and resume my actual life. And while that thought kept me motivated to crack the secrets of the silver bead in my arm bone, an aspect of my new life gradually began to take hold and make itself known, to the extent that I started to ask myself serious questions about what it was I really needed.

For the first ten weeks of my life in 2144, the longest stretch I could remember since I was a child, nothing unhappened.

[28]

March 2144

The only working piece of time travel equipment in my lab was an enclosed chamber, designed, in theory, to transport a single object placed inside it into the past. Being an entirely experimental device, intended to test the effects of time travel on matter, and measure the influences (if any) that the jump field had on local space, but not intended for any practical applications, this chamber was the departure point of a one-way trip. For the first two months of my participation in the experiment, the largest single object we were authorized to transport out was a neutron. That was a pretty big day.

I knew there were other teams working on different aspects of the problem, and that at the direction of the project leader, we were not to communicate with them. I wished I had been placed on a team that had a working version of the wrist module that brought me here, but it wasn't exactly mysterious why Dr. Walden would want to keep one of those out of my reach.

Early on, I asked why our chamber only sent objects backward through time. "What if we wanted to send something into the future? Just from an exploration standpoint, isn't that a more important problem?"

"Oh sure," said Oscar, our team leader. "But that problem's already been solved. We have all the equipment we would need right here to send any object of your choosing into the future. The only limitation we have hit so far is that every object travels at a rate of exactly one second per second."

"That joke just never gets old."

The only other member of our team was a woman named Andrea. Oscar was an adjunct professor, about ten years older than I, and carried himself like a man who still lived in his mother's basement. Overweight, pasty complexion, unflattering goatee, tiny, almost useless, round glasses, usually dressed in something comfortable but loud. Andrea was a grad student working on her hyperphysics PhD. She was closer to my age, and certainly more my speed. Her attire was always entirely professional, even under the lab coat she wore, despite Oscar's insistence that she didn't need it. Her olive skin and thick, wavy, black hair gave her a look I found striking, especially by contrast to our surroundings.

"It only seems like it's not getting old," said Oscar. "That's a dilation effect of the jump field."

Andrea rolled her eyes. "There are other cells working on forward time travel. It's much less closely related to backward travel than you might think. We could probably construct a chamber that would do both, but at this stage of development it would have to be two completely distinct machines occupying the same box."

Andrea always spoke to me in a way that conveyed her belief I had no idea what I was doing, but she never treated me with impatience over my assumed ignorance. The reality was I was an extremely quick study, and as much as I was able to hide that fact from Oscar, Andrea was clearly on to me. I wondered how long I would be able to maintain my awkward nephew charade before she figured out why I was really there. Hopefully, I would figure it out before she did.

And so, day in and day out, we would send sub-atomic particles on their suicide missions, Oscar would mock me, and Andrea would teach me. Those were good times. It was difficult to tell how much data the two of them were gathering that was truly new to either of them, but I was gathering some data of my own that was likely more useful. One of the measurable effects of the jump field on surrounding space was only measurable by me. It made my arm tingle. That sensation made me realize that this whole charade was actually two charades. I would most certainly be doing time travel research, but not the research I had ostensibly been brought here to do. My doppelganger had no idea he had brought me here with an ace literally up my sleeve.

I had given myself all the resources I would need to finally learn how to operate the working time machine in my arm.

[29]

June 2144

As the months passed by, my focus gradually shifted from finding a way to get back to that exact point in time to concocting a plausible explanation for what I was sure would be a noticeable change in my appearance when I got back. I knew I hadn't aged enough to shock anyone, but I realized that I had no idea how long my hair was that day, or how much I weighed, or any of a dozen other tiny variables to which I had given no thought. Whatever I looked like then, I certainly wouldn't look like that on my return.

More than once, I considered the possibility of staying here. In five months, I had experienced no unhappenings at all. I was starting to believe traveling into the future had somehow made me immune to them, or that I had finally outrun them. If I went home, my life would fall right back into the hot mess of uncertainty that had pushed me to the brink of insanity. On the other hand, I would never see my parents again. They would never know what happened to me. By 2144, they were surely dead, although I had managed to resist the powerful temptation to find out how and when they passed on. Resisted it so far, anyway. But I found that as much as I loved them, as much as I already missed them and would surely continue to miss them, my potential regrets over not returning to them were far more about their sadness to see me go than my own homesickness. I wished they could know what life here was like for me. I wished they could understand how much I needed it.

Of course it did occur to me that my staying in the future could cause a paradox. I assumed at some point I would need to return home, to eventually grow old and become the version of me that brought me here in the first place, but I wanted there to be a way I could stay here. Having gotten no indications to the contrary from my older self, I started to let myself believe it might just be possible. By that point, I had grown so addicted to a life where things that happened stayed happened, I was simply not able to embrace giving it up, or invite reasons why I would have to.

Even more addictive was the fact that my new friendships were stable, comprehensible, and in no way based on me perpetuating a lie about why I always seemed confused. Well, unless one were to count the implicit lie that I was somehow from that time. Compared to pretending I had a disorder, that really didn't feel significant.

At first, my only interactions were with Andrea and Oscar. I would go to work, enjoy my time with them, and then retreat to my apartment to finish out the rest of my day in solitude. Eventually though, I started meeting people. It was not by design. I assumed from the start that the amount of contact I had with future people should be as restricted as possible. But that was never explicitly spelled out for me, and it began to seem less and less urgent. At first it was just casual awareness of people who had the same routines I had. People who ate at the same times and places. They did not have names, but we came to recognize each other and small talk became a progressively comfortable experience. From there I would occasionally see one of them out of context, and conversation was inevitable. Eventually, some of them started introducing themselves.

No one ever stopped knowing who I was. No one ever disappeared. No one ever suddenly had a completely different relationship with me. No one ever retroactively died. It was absolutely intoxicating.

I never lost sight of my true goal, and every opportunity I got to covertly study my implant, I did so. But while that was happening, without fully realizing it, I had begun to think of myself as Graham.

[30]

July 2144

A mong the people I was starting to get to know socially was Wendy, an undergrad who worked part time at the security desk to my building. At first, I saw her three days a week, for about thirty seconds at a time. I don't think we exchanged a single word the first two months I was there, but I definitely noticed her. Her curly brown hair and petite build reminded me of Leslie, one of my three erased high school romances, and she had the most delightful smile. Eventually we got to a place of polite hellos. As I became more comfortable with my social interactions, we progressed to small talk. At one point, I asked her what she was reading. It turned out to be *The Catcher in the Rye*. I had never read it, so I downloaded it out of curiosity. That turned into brief but frequent discussions of that book, and eventually two others.

When the spring semester ended, and most students departed for the summer, Wendy stayed on and went full time. As I was now seeing her every day, our conversations began to last beyond a few seconds in passing. In longer doses, it turned out she had an extremely sharp wit. I started to linger at the end of the day for five or ten minutes, chatting with her, and watching her find new ways to make me laugh.

One day, I stayed for nearly twenty minutes, talking about a book. Several people came and went during that time, and I became concerned I was distracting her from her job, so, I asked what I somehow imagined was an innocent question.

"What time do you get off work? Do you want to get a cup of coffee or something?"

She smiled at me mischievously and said, "Are you asking me out?"

It was impossible to tell if she was joking. I countered with, "Don't get ahead of yourself," which was the right response, because she laughed. We did indeed have coffee when her shift ended, and spent about an hour deciding what we would read next, among other topics.

I had grown so accustomed to the notion I would never date again, I somehow convinced myself the rest of the world understood that too. Evidently, I had left Wendy out of the loop. If I had been paying any sort of attention, I would have seen this coming from very far off. Having been confronted with it now, it was easy enough to replay the past few weeks and identify signals I had missed.

My first reflex was to shut her out of my life from that moment on. That was so obviously impossible given our work situation I revised that position to an elaborate system for keeping her at arm's length. But the longer I spent concocting ways to phase our conversations out to nothing, the more I began to question the point. I had by then spent half a year in a new life that never unhappened. I had every reason to believe being in my future had finally cured me of the affliction that had haunted me since adolescence. My reasons for pushing women away no longer seemed to apply. Wendy and I had a lot in common. She was cute, she made me laugh, and she was taking an interest. Maybe it wasn't such a terrible idea to consider.

That I was literally fifty-six years older than she was somehow never entered into my thinking. Nor did it cross my mind that I had no business experimenting with romance across the time stream.

And so, perhaps recklessly, I dipped my toe in that ocean. Wendy and I began to have coffee at the end of the day two or three times a week. She did not repeat her joke about me asking her out, because it became clear pretty quickly that we were both trying to figure that out.

And then one day I lost my keys.

For an hour, I tore my apartment asunder trying to find a small metal ring with three other tiny pieces of metal attached to it. One of them opened my mailbox, one opened a locker in the lab complex, and one was entirely for show. I could quite easily have lived without any of them. The problem was that I always, always put them in a dish on my kitchen counter when I got home. This day they were not there. An hour later, when they turned up behind my toilet, the third key, the one that was just for show, was gone.

I can think of eight plausible reasons off the top of my head for how that key could have gone missing. Anyone not me who had this experience would consider it a nuisance at worse. A completely insignificant irritation. That key served no purpose, and had clearly fallen off somewhere, anywhere, never to be seen again.

Or that key unhappened.

I started making excuses to avoid our coffee dates. My chats with her dwindled. It took about two weeks for my relationship with Wendy to revert to the level we had established before the summer break. With visions of a key that perhaps never was, and the memory of my year of bliss with Carrie cut short six years before the fact, I had no choice but distance myself from Wendy for her own safety. We continued to be friendly, but her smile settled into something small and sad.

[31]

August 2144

The longer I worked with Oscar and Andrea, the more I discovered just how little anyone on this project knew about actual time travel. In a way, it was exciting to be on the cusp of what I knew was going to play out to be a spectacularly successful technological breakthrough. In another way, it was frustrating as hell. I already knew where this was going, and I wanted to get there already.

One thing I learned was that separate from the mechanics, the consequences of time travel were one hundred percent unknown. A huge part of the purpose of our research cell was to determine (if it would even be possible to determine) what sending all those particles back to God knows when was actually doing to our history. I couldn't help but wonder if this was the aspect of time travel that my older self was so concerned about. Since I was forbidden to have any contact with him, and since I didn't dare tell anyone else to ask him for me, I kept on wondering. However, if the uncertainty over whether or not time travel caused damage was his crisis, it didn't seem especially prudent to pluck me out of time to solve it.

There were three competing theories as to what backwards time travel would do to the universe. We were expected to scrutinize our work for any sign of any of them.

The first theory was the simplest. Travel to the past can have no effect on history. What has happened is etched in stone. Anyone who arrives in the past is simply catching up to events that already happened at that point in time. Apart from my personal knowledge that this quaint idea was very, very wrong, it presented the problem that if it were true, we wouldn't need to find evidence for it. We could simply choose to confirm or refute it by perfecting time travel, going back to some historically significant event and jumping up and down in front of a camera. I refer to this as a problem because there existed a non-trivial faction of the project that was seriously proposing we do just that. Evidently all time periods include some proportion of totally irresponsible whack jobs. That being the case, evidence of time travel should already be abundant.

The second theory was that every trip through time created a parallel universe, distinct from the universe of origin. One could jump up and down in front of as many historical cameras as one wished, and those photos would still never become part of the history of that person's home time. Confirming or refuting that one would be tricky, because it also included the possibility that travel back to the universe of origin would be, by definition, impossible. All we would ever see was time traveler after time traveler disappearing forever with no sign of their presence in the past. Cheery. Also obviously not true, but only obvious to me.

The third theory was that any travel into the past causes changes to history, ranging from undetectable to catastrophic. The problem with this theory is that any change that led to a history that did not lead to the time travel itself would be impossible. It's all very well and good to speculate on a crushed prehistoric butterfly altering the geo-political landscape millions of years later, but any variation of that idea is just an example of the grandfather paradox all over again. Even if the universe would somehow allow for the now-impossible trip to the past, history would change all around us, and none of us would have any way of knowing what the original timeline looked like.

So, we were essentially charged with detecting any one of three undetectable phenomena. Perhaps ironically, the only object in the universe able to settle the matter was already a member of the team, and sworn to secrecy.

[32]

September 2144

One morning I woke up with a dull but pronounced ache in my left forearm. It felt similar to the experience of having the module burrow its way into my bone marrow. Not being a doctor or a time travel technician, I did not feel qualified to diagnose the cause of my distress, but the prospect that it was jump-field induced bone cancer was a prominent candidate on my short list of guesses.

There was nothing I could do about it directly without blowing my cover, but there was no way I was just going to ignore it. That morning, as nonchalantly as I could manage, I broached a disguised version of the subject with Oscar. It took me nearly an hour to find a point in conversation where I could insert the question without suspicion. My opportunity arose when Andrea made a comment about the materials used in the chamber shield.

"Why does it need a shield?" I asked.

Oscar laughed at me, because Oscar always laughed at me.

"Asked Madame Curie," was all he said.

Perhaps noticing how pale I must have turned at that joke, Andrea smacked him on the back of the head. "It's just a precaution," she said. "We might not need it at all."

"You go right on thinking that," said Oscar. "Some of us don't want time travel poisoning to be listed as cause of death. Am I right?" That last part was directed at me, and he was most certainly right.

"Is that a thing?" I asked Andrea.

"No," she said, glaring daggers at the back of Oscar's head. "Not that anyone has recorded. The reason for the shield is that we are trying to observe the effects the jump field has on local space, and by 'local' we are hoping to mean the space contained inside the chamber. The truth is we have no idea how far the field extends beyond its observable operating limit. The shield is basically a cocktail of materials that block a wide spectrum of effects we do know about, and we're hoping it blocks ones we don't know about too. But no, the field itself has been a topic of laboratory experiments since 2088. If someone were going to get sick from being around the chamber, we'd know it by now."

Mildly reassuring. And yet, my arm. "What are the biological effects of actual time travel?" I asked. "Not just being exposed to the field?"

Oscar spun around in his chair and fixed his eyes on me through those perfectly circular lenses. "What exactly are you asking?"

My heart rate picked up. I didn't see how that question could possibly have exposed my true purpose there, or my true identity, but there was so much I still did not know. I chose to forge ahead.

"I mean, when someone actually travels. Are there any health risks, or long term effects?"

Oscar looked at Andrea, who was already giving him a look of concern that was impossible for me to read precisely.

After a beat, she asked, "How much do you know?"

Not good. "Nothing," I said. "About that, anyway. That's why I asked." After a pretty awkward pause, I stupidly added, "I was just curious."

Andrea stared at me with cold eyes. I had never seen her unhappy with me before. It wasn't something I enjoyed at that moment.

"I need to know right now if I am competing with you."

"Competing?" I sputtered.

Oscar was rubbing his chin, a sinister smile growing on his face. "Oh, man. I think we've been grooming him. This is exactly the kind of stunt Walden would pull."

"Is that what this is?" Andrea's tone was sharp.

"No!" I said, having absolutely no idea what question I was answering. "I mean, I don't think so. What are we talking about?"

"Time Girl here is on the short list," said Oscar, obviously and horribly enjoying whatever that meant. "Now she thinks she may be farther from the top than anyone has let on."

"Short list?"

Andrea's eyes narrowed. "The human trials short list. You tell me, right now, that you know nothing about that, and say it like you mean it, or I swear to God I won't care whose nephew you are when I unleash the hurt you are about to feel."

"Whoa! No!" I threw my hands up, finally able to say something I knew was true. "I don't know anything about that. I swear! I didn't know you were on that list. I'm definitely not on it!"

She stared. "You swear."

I nodded. "I swear."

Andrea closed her eyes, took a deep breath, and fell right back into character as my mentor. "No one has observed any health effects on the live subjects that have traveled so far. That includes fourteen mice and one dog. The mice were subjected to five seconds of future travel each, spread out over several months, and have been under observation for over a year, including two that have since been euthanized and dissected. The dog was sent sixty seconds into the future last month, and has been under twenty-four hour observation every moment since then. Every animal appears to be healthy in every way that we can measure. There have been no live subjects used for backwards travel yet, and there won't be until we can work out a reliable way of tracking their destinations and retrieving them."

I gulped. "Thanks," I said.

"No problem," said Andrea. "Sorry about earlier," she added.

"No, no, that's fine. I had no idea. Of course you would be concerned." Looking for a way to comfortably end this discussion so that I could find somewhere private to scream, I added, "I hope you get picked."

She smiled warmly, and we both dropped it. I excused myself and went to the roof to hyperventilate.

Human trials hadn't started yet. Except they had. Dr. Nigel Walden was in possession of at least two working modules and had used them on himself at least three times. And no one knew. The research he insisted was not bringing acceptable results was in fact more successful than anyone but he was aware. With human trials still ostensibly a ways off, and a working system already in place, he was probably already years ahead of schedule.

What the hell did he need me for?

October 2144

O ver the course of the next two days, the dull ache in my arm became a burning pain that spread up my arm and over to a spot directly between my shoulder blades. It was frightening. Doubly so, because not only did I not know what was happening to me, but I also had no idea who to turn to for help. When the pain did finally stop, I still had no idea what was going on, so I really didn't have any reason to stop being afraid. It was several weeks before I was able to trust that the pain was temporary and might not return. I never did make the connection between that event and what happened shortly after. Una had to explain that to me herself.

One beneficial effect of that scare was that it took my mind off the troubling discovery of the additional layers of my older self's duplicity. On some level, I had believed that whatever his secret agenda might be, he really was using me for my time travel insights, however crude he might expect them to be. And I wanted to continue believing that. I continued showing up for work, asking good questions, and trying to make myself useful. But watching those two go through motions that were already, I suspected, obsolete, made me progressively skeptical that the work we were doing had any meaning at all. Worse, they at least knew what they were doing, even if they didn't realize it was futile. I began to understand that my opportunity to make a profound contribution to the research was not going to present itself.

I did a lot of sulking through that stretch of time. Oscar had very little patience for my moping, and had no problem sharing that with me. Andrea came to me privately and told me she was worried I was showing signs of depression, and wanted to know if I needed any help. I told her I was fine, which she called out as a transparent lie. She also said the work we were doing was too important to compromise it with a mental health crisis, which was a fair point. She wanted me to get professional help. I balked at that. As a compromise, we agreed I would take a couple of days off, and get away from my stressors. If that didn't help, I was going to have to follow up with a doctor.

I spent two days holed up in my apartment, reading, sleeping, gaming, and generally wallowing. After two days of that, I was much worse, having added to my sense of uselessness a deep regret for having rushed so blindly into a situation that was well beyond my coping skills. In a childish moment, I actually wished aloud that I had never left that room in the library.

And just like that, I was back there.

[34]

April 2092/October 2144/April 2086

Here's what I learned, much later: The module was not giving me bone cancer. It was sending out filaments. When Una first implanted it, five subjective years earlier, it was slaved to the one in her own arm. That's why I was never able to travel without her in contact with me. When I traveled to 2144, and then didn't go home for months, the module concluded that I had been permanently separated from the user of the master module, and executed a failsafe protocol to make it independently operable. The process involved extending thousands of microscopically thin filaments into my spine, via the nerves in my arm. Once anchored there, they initiated a neuro-electrical interface that would allow me to control the module mentally.

At the time, I knew none of this. All I knew was: Ow.

My immediate reaction to finding myself back in the print collection was that either my return was a dream, or my trip to 2144 had been. It then took me a fraction of a second to berate myself for thinking something that stupid. I had spent the better part of a year in my own future. That was real. I was now back home. That was also real. Cautiously, I did venture out of that room, just long enough to confirm with a calendar that I was back in 2092, which I was.

I wanted to go back to my house, find my parents, and tell them everything. That gave me a minor anxiety attack. The prospect of their reaction didn't worry me so much. They would understand, or they wouldn't, and we would all get past it. What did worry me was the prospect that I might still have an unhappening immunity here. I still wasn't sure if it was real after the missing key incident, but I desperately wanted to believe it, and back in my own time, it would probably wear off. I wasn't ready for that. Not yet. Unfortunately, I didn't even know how I had fallen back through time, let alone how to undo that event. I longed for Una to appear miraculously, take my hand, and spirit me back to 2144. I would even have settled for grouchy, crazy Future Me to do the trick. Either way, I couldn't remain where and when I was.

In an attempt to focus my thinking and calm myself down, I whispered, "I will find a way to get back."

And just like that, I was.

I still hadn't made the connection to the pain from earlier, but it was immediately clear to me that my situation had drastically changed. For reasons still unknown to me, I was now able to travel through time at will.

Well, perhaps "will" is not the most precise term.

Over the next few days, I made several more test flights. In the interest of personal safety, I did not go traipsing around time like some super-powered tourist, but instead stuck to that room and that day. The last thing I needed was to get lost.

My third jump went wild. All things considered, I was lucky it wasn't worse. The phrase "seven year margin of error" was never far from my thoughts, but after bull's-eyes on my first two trips, I got a little cocky. Third time was not the charm. I missed the room and the day by forty kilometers and six years. Expecting to find myself in a comfortable reading room, I was instead thrown into a dark, cold alley, where I promptly hit my head. I managed to pull myself up and get to the sidewalk, but that was about as far as I got before sitting down at the base of a building. I was disoriented, but I seem to recall rambling to myself, probably quite loudly. During the five minutes in which I tried to find ways not to panic about the fact that I couldn't focus enough to get myself home yet, which might not even be possible given that I had no idea what year this was, someone evidently called a cop.

"You all right, son?" said Officer Friendly. When I looked up to find him, I recognized him immediately. I had seen this officer twice before. He, in turn, had never met me.

"Yeah," I said, hoping it sounded bold, and in control.

"Are you intoxicated?"

"No," I said, honestly, but apparently not convincingly. "I hit my head."

"I can see that. You've got a nasty scratch there."

I felt my forehead. Warm, tacky. Great. I managed to stand.

"What's your name?"

"Graham," I said. It was a reflex, and I almost corrected myself. Then I remembered how surprised he was that day he came to arrest me, to see that I was Nigel Walden. We talked for about two minutes, long enough for him to see that I was not in any danger, or presenting any to others. I dropped a few details about being an MIT student, hoping that in the half-light of the street lamps it would be less obvious that I was twenty-five, not nineteen. He let me go with some sort of cliché fatherly advice.

I found a coffee shop and considered ordering something hot until I remembered I had no access to my 2092 money anymore, and my 2144 money probably wouldn't read. Instead, I went to the bathroom, cleaned myself up, calmed myself down, and said, "I would like to go back to my apartment now." That time it worked.

[35]

November 2144

I t took nearly a year, but Una finally caught up with me.

"Hey, stranger." I found her waiting for me in the lobby of my building, at the end of the day. She had evidently been chatting with Wendy.

"Hey, yourself. What took you so long?"

"Is this a friend of yours?" asked Wendy.

Una smirked. "Something like that." The taunt had a predictably melancholic effect on Wendy, with whom I still felt unresolved.

"Cousins," I amended.

"Oh!" said Wendy, in a respite from her little funk. I wondered how long this was going to be an issue. "Have fun!" she added cheerfully as we walked out.

"Where are we going?" A lot had happened to me since the last time I had seen Una at any stage of her life, and I wasn't entirely sure I was up for a new adventure.

"Anywhere we can get a sandwich," she said. "I'm famished. Also: cousins?"

I sighed. "Don't ask."

Una gave me a wide-eyed, curious look, and glanced back over her shoulder. "Security desk girl? Seriously?"

I didn't care for that. "What's wrong with security desk girl?'

I thought it a simple question, but Una pondered it. "Oh. Yeah. Well, nothing technically, I guess."

"Whatever the hell that means. It's moot anyway. I called it off before it went anywhere. Can we not talk about it?"

"Sure," she said. We walked in silence for a bit before she asked, "How long has it been since you saw me?"

"Close to a year. You?"

"Four years."

I tried to assess her age. She seemed early twenties. "That was the time I named you Una."

She nodded. "I kind of grew up since then. We have a lot to talk about."

We stopped at a bagel shop. I ordered coffee, Una ordered a sandwich, and we found a booth.

"How did you even find me?" I asked. "I thought this far in the future I might have dropped off your radar."

"It's still my past," she said.

"Point taken. Hey, I figured out how to make the thing in my arm work."

"I know. Actually, it figured that out, but I guess it amounts to the same thing. Jumping here severed the link between our modules, so it grew itself a nervous system and latched onto your spine. I should probably remember to warn you about that when I finally give it to you."

"You won't remember," I said. "Can I assume that's what the God-awful pain in my arm was?"

She winced. "Yeah. That's supposed to be done under an anesthetic. Sorry."

I shrugged. "I survived. Are you here to take me back?"

"What? No. No, where and when you go is up to you now."

"So, you're just here to visit?"

She thought for a moment. "Yeah, I guess so. Sort of. I just... I got my assignment." She stopped there.

"I don't know what that means," I said. I had gotten used to reminding her when she told me something she thought I already knew. Living out of sync with her was like that. Evidently at this age, she wasn't quite as used to it herself.

"Really? Two years of jumps and fixes and I never once told you why?"

"Nope. Are you going to tell me now?"

"Oh, wow," she said. "I don't know. Maybe. Yeah." She took a bite of her sandwich, and I gave her time to collect her thoughts. "My job is to fix things in the time stream that have been changed. I think I can tell you that much."

"That much I already worked out. I take it you haven't started yet?"

She gave me a sheepish look. "No. My first jump is today. I'm supposed to be on it right now."

"But you came here instead? Why?"

"Because I'm nervous. You and I were friends, and then we kind of weren't. I knew a lot of things I couldn't tell you, and there was this other version of me taking you on time trips, and she knew things even I didn't know, and she scared me, and now I'm her, and I know those things, and it makes me feel like the jumps I made to you when I was a kid were a horrible idea, and now I have to go back there, and I can't say any of this stuff to you when I get there and it's already making me crazy." She stopped there, and fidgeted.

"You're here for advice. You want my help with this."

She nodded.

"Oh, my," I said. "This is new." I leaned across the table and took her hand. "Listen, every time you jumped in and whisked me away somewhere was a total adventure for me. You should know I puked the first few times, but once I got past that, it was just a ride. I was always delighted to see you, and we always got along."

She nodded again, but she was biting her lip.

"All right, there's also this: I have met a lot of versions of you at a lot of different points in your life, and I know there's something dark coming. I don't know what it is, and I don't know how much you know about it right now, but I do know that it's not going to be a thing for me during those two years. I'm sure there will come a time when things are not going to be as pretty as they are right now between us, but that's in both of our futures, and hopefully a long way off."

After a beat, she said softly, "I don't know what it is either. Not yet. But I know it's coming."

"Well, it doesn't come when I'm at MIT, so go have fun with this."

"Thank you." She smiled, and squeezed my hand.

"You're welcome, Athena. Now quit playing hooky and go do your job."

Her smile faded, and she slowly pulled her hand back.

"I thought I was still Una. Am I Athena now?"

"Sorry," I said. "I thought you didn't like Una."

"I didn't. Why Athena?"

"Because it turns out time travel is my baby. That's why I'm here. This is my big project, even though I don't understand it yet. And you were my first visitor from the future, using a technology I made happen. It was like you sprang fully armored—"

"Right out of your head," she finished. Hearing her say it out loud, it suddenly seemed like an incredibly insensitive and egocentric joke. I was better off calling her Susan.

"If you don't like it—"

"No," she interrupted. "It's good. It's a good name. Better than Una, anyway. You can call me that for now."

She got up, hugged me, walked out, and blipped into my past. I wondered which of our trips was this first one she was about to take. She never seemed new at this. Then I reflected on this conversation and wondered how much of that bravado was a result of the talk we just had. It felt entertainingly recursive. But that was well before I learned not to be entertained by causality loops.

[36]

December 2144

In December, nearly a year after I first arrived, I finally ventured out to the local public library. I was curious what library science looked like in the future. Like most of my experiences, it turned out to be more like my home time than unlike it. The terminals in the main stacks were arranged differently, presumably to satisfy whatever ergonomic sensibilities were the norm at that time, and every screen was embedded in the polished wood tables and lecterns I had come to find so pleasing to the eye. Apart from screen placement and aesthetic concerns, there was nothing to set this experience apart from what I would have seen in 2092. If anything, the most striking thing about it was how different it was from every other 2144 environment I had been in so far; being a library, none of the terminals were voice activated. Seeing all those fingers brushing against all that glass in near silence was ironically nostalgic.

Contrary to the predictions of every futurist for the last hundred years, books were also still around. They were of course oddities, and as with my library back home, secreted away in an obscure and rarely visited chamber. Nevertheless, I was amused to discover this print collection to be even larger than the one I used to frequent in 2092 when I needed quiet time. I was also delighted to discover Athena there waiting for me. It had been three weeks since I sent her off to my college-aged self with plans to escort him on time travel errands. When I came in the room, her back was to me, and her blonde hair was draped down the back of a black leather biker jacket, quite a change of pace from the usual denim. She appeared engrossed in a book. I walked up and tapped her on the shoulder.

"Leather is not exactly your speed, is it?" I asked.

She turned around, and her eyes hit me like a dopamine dart gun.

I had never seen this woman before. Given that I had spent much of my adult life training myself not to be surprised by unfamiliar faces, this sudden case of mistaken identity should not have fazed me. Yet, in that moment, I forgot all of my tricks for not making a fool of myself. She gazed at me, curiously.

"I know. I'm trying to reinvent myself, but I don't think it's taking." She closed her book and set it down, then did a casual pirouette to model the jacket for me. "I don't know," she said. "What do you think? Am I working this?"

She was indeed.

"I'm... so sorry," I said, attempting to recover. "I thought you were someone I knew." The woman before me did not have Athena's mannerisms or build. Her face was rounder, her eyes bluer, and her voice richer. Even her hair, which was the feature I had clumsily used to identify her, was shorter, darker, and lusher.

Her arms, which were outstretched to show off the jacket, slowly moved down to her hips.

"Really," she said. "That's your story. Someone you knew."

"That's my story," I said, desperately hoping to sound both in control and terribly witty. "And I'm sticking to it."

She touched her chin, pensively. "Needs polish," she said. "But I guess it's a classic for a reason. And you are?"

"Nigel," I said. Then I heard myself saying it. "Graham!" I corrected, too obviously and far too late. The sudden adrenaline dump served to highlight the fact that my heart was already racing, and was now being pushed to its limit.

She stared for a moment, perhaps waiting for me to finish remembering my name, and her look went from pensive to downright devious.

"You intrigue me, Nigel-Graham. How many last names do you have?"

I laughed, afraid that it would sound fake, even though it was real.

"Just the one. Walden. And please call me Graham."

She clucked her tongue. "Perhaps," she said, "but I don't think so, Nigel-Graham. Not yet. Helen. Helen Clay. Well, Helena, really, but I have never been able to get the hang of that third syllable."

"Helen," I said, mostly just to hear myself say it.

Her eyes narrowed. "So, you know me after all. Where's your story now, bitch?" Then her face lit up. "Hey! What are you doing for the next two hours?"

"I... don't know?"

"Perfect!"

"Why?" I asked.

"Because in two hours I have a job interview, and you are going to spend that time rehearsing it with me."

I laughed again. "All right, I accept. Where?"

"Here," she said.

"No, I mean where are you interviewing?"

With a big nod, and much more slowly, she said, "Heeeeeeere."

"The library?"

"The print collection. They're hiring a curator."

"Oh!" I said. "So you're my three o'clock."

Her jaw dropped, and immediately spread into a smile. She pointed at me. "That was good."

"Thanks," I said with a grin, and almost certainly a blush.

She picked up a black leather bag that matched her jacket perfectly and said, "All right, Nigel-Graham. Find me a decent cup of coffee, and let's do this."

We spent the next two hours pretending to be a library board of trustees and a prospective curator. For much of that time, my background thoughts were of finding a way to use my knowledge of time travel to make those two hours last forever. But they didn't. When she finally and warmly thanked me for my help and made her way back the library, I basked in her gratitude.

For the rest of the day, I tried to imagine realistic scenarios that did not end with her disappearing forever.

[PART 3]
HELEN

December 2144

No matter what happened next, one of us was doomed. My doom would be figurative, of course. Helen's would be quite literal.

This was no tentative attraction, like what had almost happened with Wendy. Two hours with Helen, and I knew I wanted to spend the rest of my life with her. Horribly, the only pattern I had ever been able to establish with any consistency when it came to my unhappenings was that every relationship I ever had ended well before it started, sometimes fatally. For seven years, for that very reason, I had been excessively cautious about getting to know women. I might have talked myself into believing the unhappenings had stopped when I considered dating Wendy, but I quickly realized how reckless and irresponsible that was. I would never have forgiven myself if anything had unhappened to her. If I talked myself into believing that again in order to date Helen, she would die. It had to be that simple.

That said, the thought of never seeing her again haunted me. It was as if the universe had put her in my path simply to taunt me. By all rights, I shouldn't even have met her. In my true time, she wouldn't be born for decades yet. This was a dream. A might-have-been from a parallel universe. I had no business even wanting to spend time with her. I would cherish those two hours, and spend the rest of my life wondering what would have happened if things had been entirely different.

In truth, I don't know if I ever would have had the strength to make that decision, one way or the other. I never got the opportunity to find out, because Helen made it for me.

[38]

December 2144

Three days after Helen's job interview, our lab received a crate filled with thousands of identical black discs the approximate size of a bottle cap. Each one was a completely sealed and nearly indestructible clock, although there was no way anyone would ever know that from looking at them. They were smooth, unmarked and featureless. Using our newly upgraded time chamber, our task over the next several weeks was to send one of these objects exactly one gigasecond into the past, in five minute intervals, until they were all gone. Once that was done, a field team would go looking for them with scanners. Each recovered clock would be read, and the time discrepancy noted with respect to the target destination of one gigasecond. Very few were expected to travel exactly that amount of time. The prevailing conjecture was that they would follow a distribution skewed to the right with one gigasecond as the median. Presumably, many of them would be found by bystanders while they waited to catch up to the present, so they were specifically designed to be boring enough not to attract attention. Apparently the design was extremely successful, as the vast majority of the ones we were eventually able to locate were in landfills.

The formal name for these devices was Trans-Chronal Displacement Distribution Markers. Oscar called them tracer pucks.

I was given the scut work task of inventorying them, and scanning them in. Externally, they were all identical, but internally they all had unique ID tags to be confirmed, and extraction signals to be tested and activated. Doing that two thousand times took about as long as I expected it to, but I was glad to have something trivial on which to concentrate. The previous three days had been an exercise in distractibility for me, and Oscar and Andrea had both picked up on that.

About an hour into that, we got a call from the front desk that I had a visitor. It was not unusual for Andrea or Oscar to get calls like that. No one was permitted in or near our lab but the three of us, so any time someone needed to speak to one of them, they had to be called down. It was, however, unprecedented for me to get a call like that. I briefly allowed myself to fantasize that Helen had tracked me down to tell me she had been thinking about me non-stop for three days. That fantasy lasted exactly as long as it took for me come to the screen and see Helen waving in it.

I found her on a bench in the lobby.

"Hey!" I said. "How did you find me?"

"You gave me your full name, and we live in the twenty-second century, right?"

I laughed. "So we do. How are you doing?"

"Pretty great," she said. "I got the job, so I'm here to buy you lunch. Is this a good time for you?"

And just like that, I had gone from pining over the woman of my dreams to being asked on what I couldn't help thinking of as a second date. Stupidly, I said, "Oh, you don't have to do that."

With a somewhat disgusted look, she said, "Your line is: 'Congratulations!'"

"Congratulations!" I parroted.

"Thank you!" She beamed. "Couldn't have done it without you. Where shall we go to celebrate?" Her smile was infectious.

"You really don't have to buy me lunch," I said, but we were already walking to the door at that point.

"Psh," she said. "Listen to you turn down food. If you don't tell me where we're going, I'm going to pick someplace very expensive so you can watch me spend a fortune thanking you. Don't push me; I'll do it."

I laughed. "I believe you will."

I left the building with Helen, in search of moderately priced food, conscious of the fact that I had not told Oscar I was leaving. If that cost me toady points, so be it. I had a day to seize, and no idea how long the universe would be gracious enough to let me have it.

• December 2144

So. Plan B.

Avoiding Helen was going to be out of the question. She had already seen to that. Pursuing a relationship with her was also not an option. I didn't belong here, and at some point I was going to go home and never return. Even setting that aside, I truly believed her life would be in peril.

That left me the one choice somewhere in between: friendship.

That would be a juggling act, to be sure. Helen was clearly taking an interest, but with the right application of denial, I could choose to believe she wasn't flirting with me. So far neither of us had made any overt passes. Given enough untaken opportunities, I should be able to communicate my lack of intentions. Unless she beat me to it. One step at a time.

In theory, this should have played out essentially the same as it had with Wendy. There were two crucial differences, unfortunately. My feelings for Wendy never moved past potential; with Helen I was already quite a bit past that. More urgently, I was willing to limit my time with Wendy for the greater good. Every moment not spent with Helen was a moment forever squandered. Even time travel rationalizations could not dim that feeling.

All of these thoughts began to come into focus as we embarked on our lunch adventure. Outing. Excursion.

Not. Date.

"Funny thing," she said, her eyes on the menu. "It turns out there's a Nigel Walden and a Graham Walden where you work."

"That *is* funny," I said.

She put down her menu with a mischievous smile. "Which one are you, Nigel-Graham?"

"Who says I'm only one of them?" I asked. My adrenal gland immediately reminded me to be more discreet.

"You're toying with me." She was still smiling.

"Maybe," I said. "Or maybe I think you already know the answer."

"You're at least two levels ahead of me, aren't you?" Her smile broadened.

I laughed, probably more loudly than I should have.

"You have no idea."

"I'm not used to that."

I laughed again, more quietly. "I don't doubt it."

We spent a few seconds in a game of verbal chicken, before she caved.

"Who's Nigel?"

"Uncle," I said.

"Who you sometimes pretend to be? Who you sometimes forget you aren't?" She held up a hand to keep me from speaking. "Don't tell me."

"Tell you what?"

She returned to her menu.

"Good. I like the thought of you carrying an air of mystery," she said. "Let's not spoil it with some mundane explanation, Nigel-Graham."

"You should really just call me Graham," I said.

"And yet I'm not going to."

Lunch lasted about an hour. Pulling myself away to get back to work was pain. It only occurred to me at the end of the day I probably should have offered to split the check.

[40]

February 2145/July 1972

Helen and I saw quite a bit of each other from that day forward. Some days she would drop by the lab building when she knew I had a break. Other days I would head over to the library to see how she was settling in. Occasionally we would do something like lunch, but never anything that could actually be construed as taking our relationship to the next level. I came to think of her as my best friend. My impression was that she felt the same way. Her flirtatious behavior from our first few meetings evened out as we became more comfortable around each other, to the point where I decided it had been my imagination in the first place.

I tried not to dwell on the fact that every time I saw her, I fell a little deeper for her.

Early in 2145, about two months after mistakenly thinking I had seen her in the print collection, I saw Athena again for real. When I got home from work one evening, she was waiting for me in my apartment, sitting at my kitchen table. It was a little unusual for her to do that, and a little disconcerting. She looked about the same age as the last time I saw her, and much less happy.

"How long has it been since you saw me last?" she asked, before I had a chance to say hello.

"About three months. Are you okay?"

She waved away the question. "I'm fine. Three months. That's good. I think that means we're syncing in parallel frames."

I hung my coat up. "I'll go ahead and pretend I know what that means. Can I get you something to drink?"

"No." She sat still and looked away from me. "Yes. Can I have a glass of water?"

I put the glass on the table in front of her. She didn't touch it. I pulled up a chair. "The last time I saw you, you were about to start running fixes with the me from a few years ago. You asked me for advice. Did I give you anything helpful?"

She sat in silence for a few seconds.

"That's the last time I saw you too." She shook her head. "I mean, no, I saw you at MIT twice after that. That's the last time I saw you in this time frame. That was about three months ago."

None of this explained her rattled state. I was not used to seeing her not in control. Even when I knew her as a kid, she was never this timid.

"Is that what you mean by synced?"

She nodded. "When I see you here, I think our meetings are going to happen in the same order for both of us. You're not in your home time."

It seemed that was all she was going to share, and I thought I understood at least the basics, so I didn't press. "What's wrong? Did something happen?"

"No," she said. "Sort of."

"Did something unhappen?"

"No. It's not that. It's just... I have a lot of responsibility now. It's weighing me down."

"I'm sorry," I said.

"It's not your..." She shook her head. "It's all right. I'll be all right."

"Is that why you're here?"

"I'm here to run an equipment test," she said, standing. Do you have some time right now?"

"Cute." I smiled.

"Thanks," she said, smiling feebly in return. She took my hand, and the world turned inside out. When it settled, we were on a beach, at what looked like sunrise.

"When are we?" I asked.

She pressed her right fingers against her left forearm.

"Hang on." I waited a few seconds, and then she said, "1972. Plus or minus seven years."

"Holy crap! I've never been back that far."

"Me either," she said. "Don't get used to it; we're not staying."

"What are we testing?"

"Tandem jumps from non-native time frames. It worked, if that's what you're asking."

"Um," I said. "Good? What would have happened if it hadn't worked?"

She shrugged. "Anyone's guess. Probably something extremely confusing."

I looked at the dawn clouds, in various oranges and yellows. There was no way for me to know where we were, although the sun was over the ocean, so it had to be the east coast of some continent. Unless I was looking at a sunset. I really had no way to tell the difference. "I met someone."

Athena gave me a puzzled look. "What?"

"I met someone," I repeated. "She works in the library a few kilometers from my lab."

"Why are you telling me this?"

"I'm not sure," I admitted. "You're the only friend I have who knows my true situation. I guess I thought you might be the only one who would know what I should do."

"Uh…" she said. "That's really a talk you should have had with your parents a long time ago."

"You know about Carrie Wolfe." I said, ignoring her crass joke.

"Yeah," she said.

"Did I ever tell you that some variation of that happened to all my high school girlfriends? They didn't all die, but they all unhappened one way or another. I think I'm cursed. I just figured you could tell me whether I'm looking at this the right way. I mean, if I'm right about that, I should stay away from her, right? And if it's not a curse, I should keep away just because we're from different times, and that's bad, right?"

I was annoyed by how difficult it was for me to articulate the questions, but reminded myself no one had ever had to answer anything of that nature before.

She gave me a perfect deadpan.

"I have no advice for you."

I was both disappointed and nervous to hear that.

"Do you know something you're not telling me?" I asked.

Her deadpan curled into a sneer. "I know a lot of things I'm not telling you, but that's not why I won't give you advice. You need to do what you think is right."

With that, we both dropped it. What I somehow hoped would be a clarifying discussion left me feeling numb, and even less certain than before. She dropped me back in my apartment and told me she would see me again. With no answers from the one person I trusted to have them, I resolved that my friendship plan was best for everyone. And if that didn't work, if it got to be too difficult, I would simply go home.

[41]

March 2145

One Monday morning in March of 2145, I arrived at work to learn that I was being transferred out of my research cell.

"It turns out we were grooming you, after all," explained Oscar as he gave me my new assignment.

"I don't understand. Is everyone getting reassigned, or just me?"

"Just you," said Oscar. "Which is bad news for me, because now I have to train a new piss boy."

Andrea smacked him on the back of the head, gave me a hug, and wished me luck. Neither of them had any idea where I was being sent. No one thought that was odd. With time travel research, especially backwards travel, which is what we did, research cells were strictly compartmentalized. If any teams knew what the other teams were doing, the conventional thinking was that it would run the risk of a paradox. The fear was that if someone found an object before it was sent, then the experimenters would be tempted not to send it. No cells were ever sent to retrieve their own sent objects, and no retrieval teams were told what they were looking for until after the objects were sent. Our own tracer pucks were retrieved by another cell, for example, and the choice of one gigasecond, or roughly thirty-one years, was designed to put them far enough in the past we would have no chance of stumbling across them by accident.

So, in this spirit of universal secrecy, no one questioned the fact that I was assigned to a lab no one else had ever used, nor the fact that I was the only person in my cell. No one questioned those things because no one knew them.

When I arrived in my new lab, I discovered it filled with examples of every type of time travel equipment that had yet been designed, and a cardboard box on the counter with a note taped to it. The box contained the wrist modules I had used to travel to 2144 with my older self, and nothing else.

The note simply read: *Reverse engineer this. Re-invent it. Make it perfect.*

[42]

March 2145/January 2086

For two weeks, my work consisted chiefly of staring at a wrist module, turning it on, turning it off, and staring at it some more. All I discovered in those two weeks was that the devices had been disabled, presumably to prevent me from escaping through time with them. Apart from the obvious problem that doing so made it exceptionally difficult for me to analyze them, it also alerted me to the fact that Future Me still had no idea about the module currently bonded to my spinal column. Surely that gave me the advantage.

Unfortunately, I had no idea what to do with that advantage.

Apart from a four-day weekend when she was out of town visiting family, I continued to see Helen nearly every day. Some days—most days —the anticipation of seeing her face was what got me through my funk. She learned early on not to ask about my work, but she did start to notice my mood had shifted and she asked me about it. As vaguely as I could, I told her it was work frustration.

And it was indeed frustrating. My assignment was impossible. I was to improve upon—perfect, actually—a device whose underlying principles I did not fully grasp. Even if I dared ask for help from anyone else on the project, I didn't think anyone knew it existed, let alone how to make it work better.

What I really needed was a complete understanding of basic

hyperphysics. If I could at least comprehend what properties of space-time I needed to violate, I might be able to work out how this gadget violated them. Hyperphysics was a branch of science with a lot of sophisticated theories and models in 2145, but I wasn't from 2145. In 2092, the word had only just been coined. I barely had the vocabulary to keep up with Andrea and Oscar, let alone the background.

When Future Me first pitched this job to me, he told me he wanted to go back to formula on the project. I now realized he had pulled me from the wrong part of my life. He should have waited until after grad school. I would have at least been versed in the thinking of my own time.

And so, one aggravating afternoon, following a heated session of staring at the modules and complaining about them, I'd had enough.

"I need to see your prototype! Where are the designs? Show me the earliest notes on how you are supposed to work, so I can at least have somewhere to start!"

It had of course slipped my mind that my internal module was still following my verbal commands. It would be some time before I mastered using it by thought alone. Hearing a perceived instruction, it complied immediately.

The lab vanished. In its place stood another lab, one I recognized. I had never been in this room before, but even in the dark I knew an MIT physics lab when I saw one. It was sometime after nightfall, probably very late at night if no one was there. Judging from the equipment, it was from a point in time close to when I was a student there. I made the connection immediately. I thought back on waiting for Pete to record whatever data he was supposed to collect, and feeling the module in my arm tingle when he got back. As early as my senior year, Ainsley was running time travel experiments. This would be his lab, or a colleague's, at some point after that when they had gotten a basic jump field generator up and running. I told the module to take me back to the prototype, and it had done just that. This was exactly what I needed. If I could copy Ainsley's data, I would have everything I needed to start my self-education in hyperphysics. I even had a mobile device on me, with an app that would cut through twenty-first century encryption like a chainsaw through tissue paper. All I needed to do was find his terminal.

Which was no doubt in his locked office.

I pondered my options for about five minutes. Really, I just spent that time running a quick cost-benefit analysis and working up the courage to act on it. Then I kicked in the door. Painful, but surprisingly possible. After that, it took less than two minutes to find and harvest the data I needed. I looked at the damaged door jamb. There was no getting around the fact that he would know someone had been here. There would be no actual evidence of the data theft, but with no other obvious motive, he would have to know that's what I was after. I took another minute to hack the lock on his desk safe and grab a small, shielded case out of it, and then I left it hanging open. Whoever found the scene first thing in the morning would assume the robbery was the true goal. This felt like cleverness at the time, but the reality was I did all of it in a blaze of adrenaline-fueled panic.

"Take me home."

My module complied, and I found myself in my 2145 apartment. The fact that I now thought of it as 'home' hadn't really registered yet; I was lucky it didn't take me back to my parents' house in 2092. I set the stolen case down on my kitchen table, and went to the bathroom to wash the crime off my hands. My hands trembled under the running water. In the mirror, I saw a ragged, shaking mess. I hadn't shaved in more than a week; my hair was overdue for a cut, and stuck to my forehead with sweat. I looked like a wretch. For a fraction of a second, I caught myself being grateful no one had seen me, out of nothing more than vanity. Then I felt a lurch in my stomach as I realized that what I saw in that mirror would be approximately what the security cameras must have seen.

The lab buildings were not exactly high security facilities, but they were monitored, if only to manage student mischief. There would be a record of this break-in. Worse, I would be recognized.

And then, my head finally clearing out, I remembered that I had been recognized. By Ainsley. Who called the police. Who almost arrested me, but for the fact that I was conclusively somewhere else at that exact moment. No doubt the review of the security vid that followed would have included the observation that the intruder did look like Nigel Walden, but the hair was all wrong and he had a beard, and besides, he was clearly quite a bit older. Ainsley's mistake would be taken as reasonable, but a mistake nonetheless. The crime would go unsolved.

A great wave of relief washed over me, as I realized this event had come to pass. I had dreaded it, on and off, for years. It turned out to be very unlike the cunning master crime I had envisioned, with weeks of preparation and elaborate tools of thievery. Instead, it was a clumsy, frightened, painful botch job.

With that out of the way, two important, troubling things became immediately apparent. One was that Ainsley's experiments were happening as early as my sophomore year, less than two years after the

Slinky Probe accident. The other was that my module, on command, had taken me to exactly the point in time I needed it to go. Given the limitations of time travel technology, even the advanced modules from Athena's time, I should have missed the mark by several years.

My older self had charged me with perfecting time travel. Apparently the secret to that perfection was already bonded to my nervous system.

[43]

March 2145

As Athena had predicted years earlier, the stolen case contained several small ingots of palladium. A cursory scan of the wrist module also revealed a palladium-copper alloy frame. The same alloy, in a slightly different configuration, accounted for nearly eleven percent of the mass of the module in my arm. I was finally getting somewhere, although I had no idea yet where that might be.

Ainsley's data had been easy to steal, but apart from including several complete textbooks on the principles of hyperphysics, it turned out to be nearly impossible to read. The actual electronic encryption had been child's play to defeat. However, many of his notes had been further encrypted with a personal cipher. It harkened back to Galileo's practice of writing out entire sentences using only the first letter of each word. This went on for literally hundreds of thousands of characters. I had some rudimentary decoding software that wasn't able to break whatever it was he wrote, and there was no way I was going to bring a cryptologist in, so the theft was a bit of a bust. About the only thing I was able to determine from what little data made any sense was that the first artificially created jump field was generated only three months after the Slinky Probe time travel event. The rudiments of time travel had already been known and achievable for sixty years by 2145, and we were still no closer to practical manned time travel. I had to assume that whatever the wrist module did was not stable enough to be considered safe for use, or Future Me would not have kept it a secret from his own research teams.

So, my research turned toward finding ways to reverse engineer the module in my arm. I had access to much more sophisticated equipment than my father's processor scanner, so I was able to make a little bit more headway there, but not much. More than once I seriously considered the possibility that the module was sending false information about itself to avoid being analyzed. It was, after all, "too smart."

What I really needed was one of those silver beads. There was no way I could dig the one out of my arm, and I thought it extremely unlikely that Athena would give me another one. The entire experience was maddening, and my future self must surely have known that. More and more, I felt that he had transferred me from a cell performing an unnecessary task to an isolated lab where I would spin my wheels in an impossible assignment. There had to be more to this.

My hopes of finding a magic blueprint shortcut to designing functional time travel equipment thus dashed, I resigned myself to reading the textbooks included in Ainsley's data. It took me about two days to realize it would take me months to even begin to understand the basic theory behind what I was being asked to do. Still, there was no way I was going to surrender.

Effectively, even possessing the ability to flee to any time and place by simply saying it out loud, because of my intellectual need, I had become a prisoner.

Which was, of course, my intent all along.

April 2145

After nearly a month of dutifully attempting to perfect a technology I had no hope of understanding, one Tuesday morning I had a completely unrelated epiphany. I was literally my own boss. If I skipped a day of work, there would be absolutely no consequence. I had been laboring under a kind of work ethic inertia for more than a year, and I needed out. This project was making me crazy. I had to get away from the lab and clear my head, ideally to give myself an opportunity to look at the problem from another angle, or give myself a chance to work in a less distracting environment.

Naturally, that environment turned out to be Helen's office.

Her expression on seeing me at eight in the morning was a mixture of confusion, surprise and delight.

"What are you doing here?"

In addition to her own desk, her office was furnished with a long table. That morning, there were about twenty books spread out on it. I pushed them into a neat cluster and dropped my notebook and tablet in the new empty space.

"I could ask you the same question," I said, pulling up a chair.

"I work here," she pointed out.

"So do I, at least for today."

"Hmm," she said with a mischievous smile. "Is this hooky?"

I feigned offense. "Nothing of the sort! I am a researcher. This is field work."

"Tell me you're not studying me."

"Don't be absurd," I said. "Of course I'm studying you. I also happen to be working on a completely unrelated project for the university, which is my actual job. And it's driving me insane with frustration right now, so I'm taking a little break from the lab. If I'm going to be in your way here…"

"No, that's fine." She went back to whatever work she was doing. I opened one of Ainsley's textbooks on my tablet, and started reading.

"So, what are you working on?" Helen asked after a few minutes.

I looked up. Her eyes were on her own screen, not on me.

"You know I can't answer that."

Still not looking up, she said, "You know this isn't a monitored room." After a pause, she added, "I'm just putting that out there."

I sighed. "Believe me, I'd love to tell you," I said, and it was true.

I wanted to tell her everything, to share my whole life story with her, admit that I didn't belong here, and that I was bound to an insane quest to invent something for which I had no expertise that had already been invented by a more advanced version of myself. I wanted to let it all out. The crushing frustration at being placed in this position, the horrible suspicion that everything I had been told about why I was needed was a complete lie, fed to me to serve some larger, possibly sinister purpose. That I dreaded the glimpse of myself I had already seen, and deeply feared he was already my destiny.

The oppressive anxiety that all of these riddles led back to the probability that I would someday do something horribly, horribly wrong, that would cost me the friendship of the only confidant I had ever had, for at least eight years, and God only knew what else. The foreknowledge that whatever I did next, my best path would only ever be the lesser of two profound regrets. And that the only reason I was staying here instead of abandoning all of it to go back to my parents, and my own time, to face my future one day at a time like I should, and take my chances on steering myself toward becoming a person I could live with, was that the thought of leaving Helen, of never seeing her again, was more than my fractured soul could stand.

"Are you okay?"

Helen gazed on me with perfect, sympathetic blue eyes. I suddenly realized I had been staring at her, and that I was clutching the sides of my head. I shook myself out of it.

"Yeah," I said. "Yeah, I'm fine. I was just thinking."

[45]

May 2145/May 2115

Athena's visits began to come more often. They were very unlike all the times she mysteriously appeared to me at MIT, always from a different point in her life, always business, and always a thrill ride. These days I saw her sequentially, so we were able to continue conversations from our previous meeting. My interactions with her began to take on a sort of continuity they had lacked before. Now her visits were not missions, they were social calls. The wildcat Penelope with whom I had gone on so many adventures in my youth was nowhere to be found. In her place was the more reserved Athena, friendly, but rarely a source of humor. As I got to know this side of her better, I realized that this was a more accurate presentation of who she was, and that all of the times she had spirited me away on our clandestine disruptions of history, she had been in character for me.

She still maintained a low profile in my presence. As had been true in college, apart from her one encounter with Wendy, none of my friends, colleagues or acquaintances had ever met her. She never visited me at work, and never happened to arrive at my apartment when anyone else was there. In fact, at that point, I'm not sure there was any compelling evidence that she was anything other than my imaginary friend.

On one such visit, I asked her, "Once something has unhappened, is there any way to use time travel to... I don't know, re-happen it?"

"What are you thinking about changing?" she asked with complete deadpan. I had somehow imagined this question would be at least a little bit shocking. I guess not.

"I'm not. At least not yet. I just want to know... If Helen and I get close, and I really am cursed, and her life is erased because of that, I want to know that I can go back to some point before we meet and make it okay again."

She didn't answer. Instead, she looked me closely in the eyes for a few seconds, then took my hand. The universe flashed as we tandem jumped. She had taken us to a park in the middle of a spring afternoon.

"I know this place," I said, surveying my surroundings. Athena—Una then—had taken me here once. I thought I even recognized some of the people here. It was impossible to say if this was the same day, or just the same park with a cast of regulars.

"I come here to think sometimes." She had said almost those exact words the last time she brought me here. That event was still quite a few years away in the subjective future of the Athena with me now. "Let me ask you a question: If you could go back in time and kill baby Hitler, would you do it?"

As she said the words "Baby Hitler," my eyes happened across a parked stroller sitting next to a couple sitting on a bench. They were laughing about something.

"Of course not," I said. My gaze lingered on the happy family.

"Why not?" asked Athena, failing to convey any sort of authentic curiosity.

"Because that was two hundred years ago," I said. "Killing that baby would save millions of twentieth century lives at the expense of hundreds of millions of twenty-first century people who would never be born under other circumstances." I hoped my voice did not carry much of my irritation. I had asked her a question that was very important to me, and her response was to walk me through Cliché Thought Experiments 101.

"So, it's math," she said. "All right, what if I give you a twenty-second century target to minimize the damage. See that woman walking her dog?" Athena pointed to a fortyish woman being led through the park by a gray whippet on a leash. "She is patient zero of a plague that will wipe out two hundred thousand people. All you need to do is walk over there and strangle her, and it will never happen. Now what?"

My jaw dropped.

"Is she seriously?" I asked quietly.

"No," said Athena. "Answer the question."

I gave myself a moment to settle down from briefly believing Athena's hypothetical was a real thing.

"No," I said. "She is still a human being. Find another way."

"There isn't one. Besides which, she has a nine-year-old boy locked in her basement with no toilet, living off buckets of table scraps. Now can we kill her?"

"No," I said. "We call the cops."

"Nice work, hero. That nine-year-old is now going to grow up to be a dictator whose atrocities will put Hitler's to shame."

"Great," I said, tired of the baiting. "Are we drifting in the direction of a point any time soon?"

"Oh, wait," said Athena. "Did I say the woman was patient zero? I meant the skinny dog. Now what? Should we go over there and beat it to death right in front of her?"

Two obvious and completely contradictory responses immediately sprang to mind. Certain that this was a trick question, I rejected both of them.

"Maybe?"

"Aha," she said slowly. "Welcome to my world."

And suddenly, all those "fixes" we ran resolved themselves into the horrors they must surely have been for Athena.

"How do you decide which things to fix and which ones to leave alone?"

"Happily, that's not my decision. I'm just the errand girl. To answer your question, no. Once something unhappens, it cannot be re-happened, as you so awkwardly put it. What I do is tweak potential and opportunity so that the cause of an unhappening never has a chance to materialize. It doesn't always work. Even when it does, I can't restore an old timeline. I just maximize the probability that the replacement timeline is as close an approximation of the original as can be achieved. Which, by the way, is usually not very close at all." She paused there, looked away oddly, and muttered, "Why can't I? Doesn't he…? No. Of course."

I had the strange feeling that I lost her there, somehow, and I tried to nudge her back.

"Why can't you what?"

Ignoring my question, she put her hand on my shoulder. "If you and this Helen are meant to be, you're just going to have to spin the wheel, and hope it doesn't land on double zero. I wish I had a better answer for you."

I felt ill. While I didn't expect to hear anything optimistic, I had hoped for some kind of unexpected escape clause. No such luck.

"It's okay," I said. "That's kind of what I figured. Do you think you could have broken that to me without invoking Hitler, though?"

She looked over her shoulder.

"No," she said. "I don't think I could."

I tracked her gaze across the park to the bench where the couple with the stroller were sitting, but by that time, they had already gone home.

[46]

May 2145

For three days, I buried myself in my work, stayed late, and fled straight home in the evening. Lunch hour visits to the library ended. Athena's comment about spinning the wheel sealed for me that I had no business perpetuating this pseudo-relationship with Helen.

Those three days were awful.

That Friday, about an hour past when I normally would have gone home, I was paged in the lab. Checking the screen, I saw Helen gesturing for me to come down to the lobby. For project security, the link was one-way so that the contents of the lab would never be visible outside it. Even knowing that, the very serious look on her face made me feel scrutinized. I sent a text to the security desk to have the monitor tell her I would be down in five minutes.

By this point, I no longer had a read on Helen's feelings. It seemed obvious at first that she was attracted to me, but as our friendship progressed with no advances in that direction, it became difficult to tell what she really wanted. I had gone three days with no communication. If she was now offended, that might be the answer.

When I got there, she did not smile.

"Where have you been all week?" she asked. There was no anger in her voice.

I shrugged. "Working. I'm in the middle of some pretty complicated stuff," I lied. "I haven't had much opportunity to break away. How are you doing?"

"Is your lab locked?"

"Yeah." This was not at all what I had prepared for. I expected some sort of confrontation, which I would parlay into us both walking away. My biggest concern had been how difficult she would make that, simply by being my magnet.

"Good," she said. "Because we're leaving."

"Oh," I said. "Um, do I have time—"

"No." With that, she turned on her heel and walked to the door. After a fraction of a second of hesitation, I trotted to keep up with her.

"Where are we going?" We had only gotten a dozen meters or so from the building.

She stopped and gave me a scolding look.

"Really?" she said. "Really. Where are we going." She tapped my chin with her finger. "Where… is your sense of adventure?"

At that simple touch, I could feel myself blushing. I hoped it was dark enough not to be obvious. I also hoped it was just a tiny bit obvious.

"I honestly have no idea."

"See, this is your problem. Trust me, okay?"

"Absolutely," I said.

She walked me to her car. It took us about twenty minutes to get to our destination, a high school campus across town. As she hunted for a parking space on the lawn, I took in the lights, and the music, and the Ferris wheel and tried to remember the last time I had gone to a carnival. Then I tried to remember the last time I really let go and just had fun, and came up blank.

"I had no idea this was here," I said.

"Well, I've known about it for a few days, but a certain Mister Busy Pants never came by to hear about it."

I winced. "Mister Busy Pants?"

She frowned. "Yeah, that's no good. I meant to say something super witty about you being too busy for me. It sounded funnier in my head. Come on." She got out of the car and ran for the entrance. I caught up to her just in time to see her scan her card at the gate and watch it spit out a string of dozens of paper tickets. "The rides are on me. You can buy the food. And you better win me something!"

I silently vowed to do just that.

May 2145

My first order of business was apparently to buy Helen a wad of cotton candy several times the size of her head, which she subsequently explained she had no intent to share. I made multiple attempts to win her a stuffed animal, all but one of which ended in failure. I was tempted to submit myself to the carnie who was offering prizes to any mark whose weight, birth month, or age he was unable to guess within three relevant units. For simple irony, I wanted to ask him to guess my age (correct answer: seventy-eight), but that internal joke would have fallen flat as soon as I produced my extremely genuine-looking fake ID.

We partook of the haunted house, which made Helen laugh so hard her face was covered in tears before we were halfway through. We rode side by side on alternately oscillating horses on the carousel, on which I dated myself somewhat by asking about the brass ring (memo to self: those no longer existed, even as legend, by 2145). I was reluctant to try any of the more thrilling rides, but Helen refused to go on the Ferris wheel with me until I had gone with her on the Zipper, which turned out to be every bit as bad as it looked on the outside.

Her need for imaginary danger satisfied, Helen agreed to go up on the wheel. It was quite a bit taller than what I would have expected to be portable. As much as the apparatus aesthetic of carnivals had remained constant for many, many years, evidently the technology had covertly improved. We waited ten minutes to get to the front of the line, and another ten as we experienced the start and stop of other riders boarding. At one point in this process we were held in place at the very top for several minutes. From there, we had an excellent view of not only the carnival itself, but also the entire surrounding town. Looking over my shoulder, I was able to make out the lab complex, several kilometers away, just barely. It was after dark at that point, and the lights from countless edifices and vehicles decorated the landscape in a way that was both mesmerizing and exhilarating.

I turned back to tell Helen something about some aspect of the view, and with her in sight, everything else disappeared. She wasn't looking at me; something in the distance had captured her eye, and in her appreciation of it, she smiled unselfconsciously. Nothing of note from that vista could compete with the visage of that tiny expression of joy in her face. For all its simplicity, it may have been the most perfect moment I had ever experienced. Her eyes turned to mine. That smile expanded, just enough to communicate that the moment was a shared one, and then she went back to whatever she had been watching, ever so slightly but significantly happier about it.

I would carry on with my polite and timid denial that we had nothing beyond a friendship, but from this point on it would only be for show. Like it, love it, or fear it, this was a date.

And the danger that presented to her was anything but imaginary.

[48]

June 2145

My immunity to unhappenings in my own future turned out to be an illusion. It took more than a year before I started seeing things change in ways I could actually detect, but those changes were real. Most likely, trivial things had been unhappening all around me that whole time, and I simply hadn't caught on yet.

The weekend after Helen took me to the carnival, several observations put me on my guard. Saturday morning, I found four leftover slices of pizza in my fridge, and was unable to recall when I might have put them there. Hardly damning evidence, to be sure, but noteworthy. I threw them out. On Sunday I noticed that a coffee shop I used to frequent had moved. Again, I could not recall how long it had been since I last went there, but it didn't seem like it had been that long ago.

Monday clinched it. First thing in the morning, I saw an unfamiliar face behind the security desk. Wendy usually worked Monday mornings, but not always. As I passed the youth, I asked him, "Wendy off today?"

"Who's Wendy?" he asked in response.

I had become adept enough at wrangling out of awkward situations like that. One smooth expression of confusion, and I went straight upstairs.

It took me two hours to establish that Wendy was still alive. In fact, she had at one point worked in this building, but quit about three months prior. That would mean she was working here during the stretch of time that we almost dated. Most likely, every significant interaction we had was still part of our history. I would have to ask her to be sure, but I couldn't see myself doing that.

Regardless of the details, it was clear that whatever force governed the retroactive revisions of my life operated in this time frame just as it had in my own. The fact that I had coasted for so long in the apparent absence of this phenomenon only meant I had been blessed with a very fortunate year. Now, all bets were off.

I had allowed myself to believe Helen and I were on our way to some sort of relationship, which would have been the first for me in my adult life. That belief had now been shattered. Whatever stirred there for now would have to be ignored or extinguished. Worse than that, the timing of this new spate of unhappenings—even as mild as they were—made it impossible to outright reject the notion of my curse.

I had considered the possibility of happiness, and the universe had punished me for it.

August 2145

So I threw myself back into my work, for whatever that was worth. After many weeks of no progress whatsoever, accompanied by the nagging suspicion that lack of progress was exactly what was expected of me, I did something irresponsible.

The reality was that I did not have the background to understand the theory I was supposed to be applying, nor did I have the engineering savvy to design, construct, or reverse engineer a time travel module. This all remained true even after I managed to crack Ainsley's notes. I suppose "crack" is an undeserved credit; Ainsley's notes, in translated form, had already been included in the materials I was given upon my transfer. I discovered that weeks after traveling into the past to steal them.

The quantity of materials I had been given to study was ponderously large and bafflingly indexed, and buried deep in them was Ainsley's life work. By 2145 they were historical documents, and although still closely guarded secrets, the person guarding them was Future Me. It turned out that Ainsley had correctly grasped enough of the basic principles of time manipulation that he was able to construct a rudimentary jump field generator. Unfortunately, all it did was generate the field. It was not of sufficient power or specificity to apply the field mechanically to any physical object. However, the space-time distortions it created were quite measurable, and it was a huge leap toward what would eventually become functional time travel.

I also learned that palladium-nickel alloys were the most efficient jump field conductors yet discovered, after nearly one hundred different materials were tested. Ainsley had been working with pure palladium, hence the ingots in the case. In 2092, the amount I stole held a value that represented a significant proportion of his operating budget. Apparently the theft—never solved—set the project back several years. Oops.

Having learned that I hadn't learned enough, and in an act of dire frustration at both my inability to advance the time travel project and my inability to resolve my feelings for Helen, I fell back on the one resource I knew I had. It was time to begin experimenting with the module in my arm.

I knew it had capabilities beyond the simpler modules Future Me used to bring me here. I also knew that unlike those modules, the one in my arm still worked. So, step one of my experiment was to ascertain how precisely I could use it to travel. I honestly had no clue what I would learn from this that would be of any value, but it was the only thing over which I had any semblance of control, so I ran with it.

Thus, one afternoon, alone in my lab, I said out loud, "Take me back five minutes." My surroundings flashed, and then I was standing in my lab. Everything looked exactly as it had before I spoke, with one exception: the lab included another instance of me.

"Wow," he said. "I guess it works."

"Traveling back five minutes?" I asked. He nodded. "You were about to try that?" He nodded again.

"I… This is much weirder than talking to the old guy," he said.

I couldn't argue with that.

"In five minutes you won't have to worry about that." I looked around the lab, then back at him. "I have no memory of this," I said to myself, and by "myself," I do not mean him. He wasn't able to make that distinction.

"What do you mean?"

"This event," I said. "I have no memory of myself appearing in this lab from five minutes in the future." I stared at him. "I have no memory of being you."

After a beat, we both said simultaneously, "What does that mean?" He laughed, but it was obviously nervous laughter.

"I think it means we just learned something about the nature of paradox. Or alternate timelines. Or any of a dozen other aspects of time travel we haven't sorted out yet." I looked at the clock. "You have about two minutes before you need to take a trip five minutes into your past."

"To become you?" he asked.

"Maybe," I said, very quietly. "I guess you'll find out."

Two minutes later, he spoke the same magic words I had, and vanished. This episode had given me a great deal to think about. For the first time since I started on this research more than a year prior, I felt like I was gathering useful information. However, seeing him literally vanish before my eyes made me realize there was an aspect of time travel that in six years had never occurred to me to question. Why didn't anyone ever notice when I spontaneously appeared somewhere, or blinked out of existence? Athena was usually as subtle as she could be, but I know there were times when we traveled to and from crowded areas in broad daylight. How on Earth had we been getting away with that?

Finally, I had something to study for real. With luck, I might even be able to let it supplant Helen as the foremost thing on my mind every waking second of my life.

[50]

September 2145

Tell me about paradoxes," I requested.

Athena's visits had come to be welcome respites from the stress of my work with time travel, and the stress of my pseudo-relationship with Helen. My impression was that she also saw them as a respite from the stress of her own job, which I imagined put my own troubles to shame. She came around about two or three times a month, we did lunch, or went for a walk, and then she would go home. We had fallen into a routine of pleasant socializing, and conversations about Baby Hitler or time travel curses had fallen by the wayside by tacit mutual consent. This day I broke that agreement.

"That's new," she said.

"Humor me."

She thought for a moment.

"Zeno claimed that motion was impossible, because any traveler would have to traverse half the distance from her starting point to her destination, and then half the distance that remained, and then again, and again. As she would need to do this an infinite number of times to cover a finite distance, she would never arrive at her destination. There's also a great paradox about a game of chance with finite payouts and an infinite expected value."

"St. Petersburg," I said impatiently. "I know that one. That's not what I meant."

"I know what you meant," she said with equal impatience. "Why are we talking about this?"

"Because I need to know." I waited for a response, and got none. "I traveled back in time and met myself," I added.

Her face dropped. "Why?"

"Because I was stuck. I have no idea how to do what Future Me is asking me to do. I had to do something to get myself jump-started, and it was the only thing I could think of."

"How far back did you go?"

"Five minutes," I said. She buried her face in her hands.

"And then you had a conversation with yourself," I heard her say through her fingers. "And now you only remember one half of it." She looked up. "Am I right?"

"Yeah," I said. "Is that bad?"

She sighed. "Not necessarily," she said without elaborating.

"If I am not supposed to be doing things like that, you're going to need to give me some warning. I don't understand what you can and cannot tell me."

She laughed. "Oh, I can tell you anything I want. There are just a lot of things I don't want to tell you."

We stared at each other.

"Did I change the past, or create an alternate timeline?"

"Yes," she said. "And no. There are no alternate timelines. There is just the one."

"I don't understand. If that's part of my past now, why don't I remember it?"

"Because you're a traveler," she said. "You exist in multiple frames of reference simultaneously. That's why your life unhappens but no one else's does. Actually, everyone's life unhappens all the time, but they unhappen right along with it, so they don't notice. You don't get that luxury. If you had a mind to, you could travel those five minutes backward and murder yourself in cold blood. You could speak at your own funeral, then go on to live another eighty years." She waited for a response, but I was too busy feeling the blood drain out of my face to say anything. "Aren't you glad you asked?" she said finally.

"Not even a little bit," I said.

"Well, you should be glad. Because that effect is exactly why your future self has no idea we are having this conversation."

I pondered this in silence.

"Is there a reason we don't want him to know about it?"

Athena's eyes went a little wider, and she looked away.

"Don't," she said. "I know. I'm trying." Unable to make sense of this jump shift, I had the sudden and chilling thought that she was no longer speaking to me, and not precisely speaking to herself either.

"Athena?"

Then she did speak to me.

"I really have to go. I'll see you in a few weeks."

I reached toward her, held her arm, and said, "Athena. What do you know?"

She looked me dead in the eyes.

"I have to go."

The physical sensation for someone in contact with the traveler at the moment she departs is surprisingly cold. It was a full five minutes before feeling returned to my hand.

51

September 2145

There were several very comfortable chairs in the print collection reading room. That's where she found me, sulking, first thing in the morning.

"Hooky again?"

"Something like that," I said. After my confrontation with Athena, and her implication that my future self might be our common foe, I could not bear to continue to do his bidding. With no one else to turn to, and against many layers of my better judgment, I once again retreated to Helen's sanctum. I chose to believe that my sour mood so well precluded any thoughts of romance I could not possibly pose any threat to her from my curse, at least not that day. But my determination to stay angry about my situation was severely threatened by the sight of Helen's smile, confused though it was.

"How did you get in here?" she asked, looking at the time. It was a fair question. The building did not actually open for another fifteen minutes.

"It's really better if you don't know."

Her confused smile morphed into confused concern.

"You're not kidding." She came over to my seat and crouched down to meet my eyes. "Are you okay?"

I had prepared myself for variations of Helen pursuing the question of my ingress, but not for concern about my well being. That was probably as good an indicator of my state of mind as anything. Clearly, I had gotten past multiple locked doors, and she didn't care about any of that over taking care of me.

"I'm not sure," I admitted.

"Is it work?" Helen knew I was not happy with my assignment, but had no way of knowing why. On more than one occasion she had offered to be my confidant, and I absolutely believed her that she would keep anything I shared with her between us. Unfortunately, she was probably the one person in the world who I least wanted to know the truth. If she knew I was a fraud, the trust I had built with her would mean nothing.

"Sort of," I said. "I can't go into details. I just need to get away from that project. Maybe for a long time."

"Do you get vacation time?" she asked. "I have personal days. Maybe I could take one and we could go to a museum or a zoo or something. If you're going to play hooky anyway, we should do it right."

There was no mockery in her eyes. I was not used to seeing this side of her. Our interactions had been almost exclusively playful. Now she was being unabashedly nurturing, on a moment's notice of my need for it. How could I possibly resist?

"How long in advance can you take one of those days?"

"I work in a department with one employee. If it needs to be today, just say the word."

I had come here for an opportunity to vent, which I had planned to do, somehow, in code. This was quite a bit more than I hoped for or expected that morning.

"Yeah," I said. "I think it needs to be today."

52

September 2145

We spent the day at the aquarium. It was the first time I had been there in years, and I had forgotten how much I enjoyed it. Helen had never been there before.

For a while, it really worked. There is something naturally soothing about watching fish. I managed to block out the convoluted nightmare my life was becoming, and take in their simple beauty.

When we got to the ray tank, the whole experience shifted. There were dozens of them, engaged in a random ballet of such extraordinary grace that it was nearly hypnotic. I could feel them drawing the stress out of my body, and even though I knew it was a temporary effect, I basked in it. And then I looked at Helen.

Her fingertips were resting on the glass. Her lips were slightly parted and her eyes wide in what I could only describe as an expression of child-like awe. She had, until now, seemed so worldly to me. The idea this might be the first time she had seen these creatures up close felt incongruous. And yet, there it was. I wanted to say something to her, but I knew anything I had to offer would only shatter this communion.

"Wow," she whispered. I doubt that was for my benefit, but that one syllable soothed my aching soul more than all the exotic fish in the ocean. Then she looked at me, and in a tone that gave me goose bumps, said, "I love these."

From there, as we moved from tank to tank, floor to floor, I was only partly paying attention to the fauna. My true source of joy was her string of discoveries. We had come here, ostensibly, to ease my troubles, divert me from my unbearable dilemma. Any benefit she reaped from the day off was intended to be a side effect. But that side effect was now my main effect. I wanted to show her the world, just to watch her face seeing it.

And that's when I realized my solution. Show her the world indeed! We could be together, and she could be safe.

I would make her a traveler.

[53]

September 2145

W hen I got home, I discovered I had a cat. At first I thought she was an intruder, but a quick check of bathroom and cupboard revealed litter box and cat food. She was an adult, and extremely affectionate, leading me to believe she had been mine for at least a year. I wondered what that year had been like for her.

"What's your name, sweetheart?" I asked her as she curled up on my lap and kneaded me with her claws.

"Prrrrrrrrrr," she replied. Hardly an answer.

"All right then," I said. "Penelope it is."

As unhappenings went, this was agreeable enough. But the message was clear: I was getting too close to Helen, and the universe was letting me know it. Little did the universe know my master plan.

At work the next morning, I was greeted by Wendy, back on the job, and unusually happy to see me. We chatted for a minute, mostly to give me an opportunity to feel out where we stood. As soon as she brought up the topic of her boyfriend Matt, I was content.

Most of my lab equipment was not where I left it. No problem. Several weeks worth of data was missing from my tablet, replaced with ramblings about some experiment I never ran. No bother at all.

I felt energized and inspired. I had finally isolated a problem to solve, and nothing was going to hold me back, no matter how many times I had to start over. A new sense of independence took hold of me, and for the first time in years, I felt truly free of manipulation.

I really should have known better.

October 2145

For a week, I forged on with my new optimism. Occasionally, I would make minor discoveries, and although they would invariably be facets of time travel someone else had already established and named, the fact that I arrived at them independently infused me with an altogether new confidence. For the first time, I started to believe I was the same person as the man who invented the technology that brought me here.

During that week, Helen was away for three days, and I managed to endure it. Our time apart, however brief, tested my resolve to see her as nothing other than a best friend. Until I was ready to make her a traveler, I couldn't afford to take the chance. She began to remark on my transformation, and credited it to our day out, which she believed rejuvenated me.

One day I went to visit her at work, with a purpose. Incredibly, she was not alone. An old man had wandered into the print collection. From the look on his face, it appeared to be a new discovery for him, and the reverence with which he took books from the shelf and cautiously leafed through them, it struck me that this experience must have allowed him to relive his youth, when books were a thing to hold, not download. Then I remembered what year it was, and realized with a start that he was probably ten years younger than my present incarnation. His youth happened after mine. This was no nostalgic wonder. It was probably just mystified curiosity. Unfortunately for me, he had picked an inconvenient time for his epiphany. I had things to discuss with Helen that were not for public consumption.

"Things going better?" she asked.

"Quite so," I said, pulling up a chair.

Then she threw out her usual bait. "So, what kind of progress are you making?"

I gestured back over my shoulder at the new bibliophile, still engrossed in his discoveries, and put my finger to my lips. Then I took a pencil from her desk, and a slip of paper.

"Still can't tell you," I said. "You know the rules." As I spoke those words, I wrote different ones on the scrap, and passed it to her.

The note said: *Time Travel.*

She read it. Her eyes bugged.

"Well, you can't blame a girl for trying," she said, scribbling furiously.

The note she passed back to me said: *WHAT???*

"You know I trust you," I said. "But I really can't share."

I passed her the note: *Can we get out of here?*

"I know, I know," she said casually. "You here for lunch? It's early, but I could eat." She dropped the note into a shredder.

"Sure," I said. "Are you ready to go?"

"Like you wouldn't believe," she said.

She managed to contain herself until we got out of the building. Once outside, she whispered, "Oh my God! Is this for real?"

"It's very real," I said.

"Are you... I don't even know what questions to ask you."

"It doesn't matter because I can't answer them anyway."

She pouted.

"I'm sorry. I'm not even allowed to tell you what I already have."

"Wow," she said. "Just wow. Why did you tell me?"

"Because I wanted you to know," I said. In truth, I wanted to prepare her. Time travel was about to become a huge part of her life. I wanted it to be as little of a shock as possible. "I've been kind of leaning on you, and you deserved to know what the stress was all about. It's a very difficult assignment." We walked in silence for a bit. "What are you thinking?"

"I'm trying to decide whether to believe you," she said.

"Do you think I would lie about this?" I asked. It was not defensive. I truly wanted to know.

She looked me in the eyes.

"No," she said.

"Good. Because I wouldn't."

"This is kind of a heavy thing for me to carry, you know."

"I know," I said. "I wouldn't have put it on you if I didn't think you could handle it."

After a few seconds, she again said, "Wow."

"I know. We probably shouldn't talk about this anymore," I said. "I'm glad you know, though."

She smiled softly. "I hope you know how much it means to me that you trust me like this."

"I do," I said, and for a moment, I considered telling her everything. I almost did. But as soon as I pictured myself confessing my feelings, I was assaulted with the image of Helen disappearing into oblivion. Soon she would be safe. I would have to wait.

[55]

October 2145

I came home to find Athena in my kitchen.

"Since when do you have a cat?" Penelope was standing on the table, gratefully receiving a little attention behind her ears.

I shrugged. "About a year, by the looks of it. She kind of unhappened to me a week ago."

"I like her," she said. "What's her name?"

"I have no idea, so naturally, I am calling her Penelope." That elicited a weak smile. "I'm a little surprised to see you."

"I wasn't happy with where we left things."

"I'm not happy about it either," I said, pulling up a chair. "And I don't want you to go away again, so I'm not going to pursue it."

She frowned. "That seems too easy."

"It is," I said. "It absolutely is. But right now I have a much more pressing issue than whatever my mysterious future self is up to. I have questions, and if you can answer any of them, I'd be extremely grateful."

I waited for a reaction, but she just sat back in her chair.

"No promises. What do you want to know?"

"Why are we invisible when we travel? You and I have appeared in the middle of crowds in broad daylight, and no one ever bats an eye. Why?"

Athena thought for a moment, then nodded.

"Okay, I can answer that one. It's a cognitive dissonance side effect of the jump field. No one expects people to materialize out of thin air, or disappear into it, so when they see it happen, their brains adjust to believe that we must have already been there. The effect is more dramatic for backward travel than forward travel, by two orders of magnitude. And it doesn't work on anyone who is expecting you, or anyone who is staring at the exact spot where you materialize. There are also a few people who aren't affected at all, but it's something like one hundredth of a percent of the population."

"Huh. Does that mean travel is generally safe no matter where or when you go?"

She shook her head. "There are still risks. Cameras aren't affected by the field in any way, so you don't want to materialize anywhere you might be recorded. Even cameras that monitor in real time are a danger. Anyone who sees you suddenly turn up filtered through a monitor will see it for exactly what it is."

"Noted," I said. "Okay, how about this: you told me at one point that a typical jump has a seven year margin of error. Why is it that almost every time I jump on my own I land exactly where and when I intend to?"

"That I can't say," she said flatly.

"Because you don't know, or because you don't want to?"

"A little of both," she admitted.

"But it is different for me, isn't it?"

"Oh my, yes," she said. "I don't think there would be any point to my denying that." This was not what I wanted to hear. I intended to travel with Helen. If my jumps were precise and hers were wide, we would get separated.

"How does tandem jumping work, then? Why do we stay together?"

She frowned. "Because our modules communicate when we are in contact. Why are you asking me this?"

I ignored the question. "That's interesting. Would you be able to provide me with another module? I'd like to study it."

Her eyes narrowed. "No."

"Are you sure? It would be very helpful for me to see how it interacts with mine."

Athena stared at me in bitter silence.

"Are you going to give her a choice?" she asked finally. "Or are you just going to hijack her?"

My heart sank as I realized how stupid it had been to imagine Athena would not see right through me. I also felt guilty for not being forthright with her. Unfortunately, I chose to lash out in my own defense.

"Like you gave me a choice?"

She moved her hand to cover the pocket inside her jacket that held the small silver bead she would one day put inside my arm. This Athena was younger than the one who made me a traveler, and she told me at the time she had been carrying the bead for years without knowing when she would finally give it to me. I could have taken it from her right then, I suppose, but that would have cost me more than I would ever dare sacrifice.

"I haven't done that yet," she said quietly.

"But you will. And you won't even warn me. How is this any different?"

"You were already a traveler, that's how," she said. "You just didn't know it yet."

I took a deep breath. This was not how I wanted our conversation to go. I needed Athena in my corner on this. She was the only person I had ever consistently considered to be a trusted ally.

"For the record, yes, I am going to give her a choice. I have already told her that my work involves time travel. I am going to break this to her in stages, and then I am going to tell her why I want her to travel with me."

"And if she says no?"

My stomach churned at the prospect. "I honestly don't know. But I have to try."

Athena stood. "I will not help you with this. What we are… You cannot wish this on another person, Nigel. You cannot."

"I don't want to lose her," I said. It rang pathetically in my ears.

"You…" Athena looked away from me, but I could see her lip starting to tremble. "Don't do this," she whimpered, fighting back tears. "Please don't do this."

I had no idea what to do or say. "Athena, please. If you know something about Helen, just tell me. I'll do the right thing, I swear. But I need to know what's going to happen to her."

She sniffed loudly and wiped her eyes.

"You will know," she said.

She was either laughing or crying when she said it, but it was impossible to tell which, and she didn't stay long enough for me to ask.

[56]

October 2145

The following day I planned to see Helen after work, but she intercepted me on my way out the door.

"Hey you," she said. "You have time to grab a coffee?"

"I do." I stood there in a moment of indecision. Her appearance at the lab building provided me with a sudden opportunity, and I was feeling bold. "Come with me," I said, heading back inside.

"Coffee is this way." She pointed behind her.

"Humor me."

She sighed. "I always do."

Helen followed me back into the building and past the security desk. We made it to the elevator before she finally asked, "Am I allowed to be here?"

"You're allowed to be in this part of the building, yes," I said. "You're not allowed in the part I'm taking you to." Once inside the elevator, I said, "Fourth floor."

This was followed by a routine scan, after which a polite but firm voice said, "Unauthorized personnel present."

"Override on my authority."

After a brief pause, the voice said, "Yes, Doctor Walden."

Helen managed to hold her tongue for the ten seconds it took us to rise three floors. Once we were in the corridor, she whispered, "Doctor?"

"Shhh," I told her. This seemed sufficient explanation for the time being.

When we got to my lab, I scanned my ID to get us past two sets of doors. My work space was located behind a shielded airlock, which, from the look on Helen's face, added to her overall sense of astonishment and trepidation.

"What are you doing?" she said. "Aren't you going to get in trouble over this?"

"Not a chance," I said without elaborating. In truth, I was taking a terrible risk. If anyone chose to make a case about this, it would expose quite a lot of things about my situation better left unexplored. My hope was that any security concerns would be flagged directly to the project director, and that he—I—would let it slide.

As we entered my work area, I felt a sudden pang of self-consciousness about the state of the place. Every surface was cluttered with various equipment and assorted unprofessional objects. Helen didn't appear to notice any of this, and she looked around with a wonder comparable to what she showed me at the aquarium.

"Is all of this yours?" she asked.

"It doesn't belong to me, if that's what you're asking, but it is my equipment. I work alone in here."

She looked at me with suspicion. "Why?"

"Because my assignment is of a more sensitive nature than most of the research being done here." As I said those words, I realized the wrist modules had been left out. She had probably already seen them. Even if she identified them as important, she would not have been able to activate them, but the fact that she could see them made me nervous. She would be seeing them again, soon enough, in a very different context, if I could get them to work.

"I really shouldn't be here, should I?"

"Absolutely not," I said.

She grinned. "This is fantastic! Can you show me something? Is there anything here I would understand?"

I held out my hand. "Give me your tablet."

Without hesitation, she pulled it out of an inside pocket on her jacket, and handed it to me. The case was solid polished teak. It was certainly quite a bit more expensive than the cherry one I carried. I placed it inside a small glass box. "Travel field, sixty seconds, on my mark," I said.

"No way," she whispered.

I smiled. "Mark."

The tablet blinked out of existence, with a small flash of red light.

Helen let out an unbridled giggle. "Oh my God! Did you just do what I think you just did?"

I laughed. Her ebullience was infectious. "If you think I just sent your tablet one minute into the future, then yes."

"Where will it land?"

"Right back in the case," I said. "This one only does forward travel, and it stays sealed until the jump time has elapsed. If I were sending it backward, it would be a different protocol, a different machine, and a very different outcome. Even at sixty seconds, you would probably never see it again."

"Ohmygod ohmygod ohmygod," she said. "This is incredible!" She stared at the case with a wild glee in her eyes that made this worth any risk. Shortly, with a small blue flash, the tablet reappeared. "Ha!" she exclaimed. Exaggerated cackling followed. The chamber opened with a small hiss. Where a more cautious person might have asked if it was safe to touch it, she immediately reached in and grabbed it.

"Let me see yours!" she said. I held my tablet out to her, and we compared times. They were exactly one minute apart. This effect only lasted for a few seconds, which was as long as it took the satellite connection to correct it. Still, it made my point.

"Is this what you do all day?" she asked with giddy enthusiasm. I laughed.

"Not hardly. This is just the barest beginnings of what we are trying to accomplish here."

"Have you ever traveled through time?" The question came at me so quickly, and so unexpectedly, that I faltered looking for a safe answer that wasn't a lie. She saw right through that. "You have! Oh my God! Tell me! Tell me everything!"

"I..." What could I say? She wanted me to tell her everything. At that moment, I could think of nothing in the world I wanted to do more than just that. But it was too much to lay on her all at once. "I can't," I said.

She pouted. "Poo."

I put my hand on her shoulder. "But I will. Someday. I promise."

She stared at her tablet, turned it over and over in her hands, then looked me in the eyes. "This is the most wonderful thing I have ever seen."

I took that in with a nod and a warm smile, unable to speak. At that moment, I was already looking at the most wonderful thing I had ever seen.

57

October 2145

From there, we went out for Italian. What was supposed to be half an hour of coffee after work turned into two hours of pasta and red wine. She asked me many questions. I refused to lie to her about any of it, so much of the time I simply told her I couldn't say. But she did learn some things that evening. I told her about the tracer pucks, and the seven year margin of error for backward travel. I told her about the mice, and the dog. I told her I had been working from Ainsley's notes, and three glasses of wine in, I let it slip that he had been a professor of mine. I managed to cover, and she made fun of me for being tipsy.

We went for a walk after that, and talked about a lot of things. I got to hear some of Helen's childhood anecdotes, and she got to hear some very heavily edited versions of some of mine. We talked about the day we met. She asked me if I thought at the time that she was crazy, and I told her honestly I thought she was hilarious.

There were multiple opportunities to take our friendship to a different place that night, and I managed to skirt them all. She would send a signal, I would pretend not to notice it, and then laugh at something brilliant she said. We did this dance maybe half a dozen times over the course of several hours. Between my restraint and her patience, we made it to almost midnight before we finally decided to call it a night and go our separate ways.

I went to bed feeling extremely proud of myself, and quite convinced I had managed to avoid my curse. Essentially on the technicality that we weren't calling what we had a relationship, the universe would not be able to take her away from me.

How clever I thought I was.

The universe was not amused.

58

October 2145

I woke to the unexpected and confusing words, "I'm done in the bathroom." This was shortly followed by, "Graham! Come on! You're going to make us late!" I rolled over to see Wendy standing over my bed, a displeased look on her face. And nothing else on her.

I had no prepared response to this situation. Incredibly, my biggest fear was whether it would appear to be more natural to look at her or look away. I was certainly battling contradictory impulses in that regard.

Reasoning flight was my best option, I muttered, "Sorry," and hauled myself out of bed and into the bathroom.

Safe behind the locked door, I attempted to assess my situation. Was this a relationship? A one night stand? I had to know where we stood before going back out there. A quick inventory of the room turned up multiple hygiene products that were clearly not mine, and birth control. Apparently she lived here.

I showered and dressed as quickly as possible. By the time that was done, Wendy had already made breakfast. I faked my way through small talk with her, and then we drove together to work. She was still at the front desk in my building. Convenient, to be sure. When she took her seat and I started to walk away, she said, "Hey!" Then she batted her lashes at me. I tried to make the kiss feel authentic, with no impression of how successful I was.

Once in my lab, I began to form a plan. This was far from a terrible turn of events, admittedly, but it was also far from ideal. Yes, I had been attracted to Wendy, but it didn't go anywhere. By this point, my feelings for Helen were so intense, the thought of not following through on them was too painful to bear. I wondered what my friendship with her was like in this revised timeline, or if we had ever even met. If not, that would be simple enough to remedy; I was naturally inclined toward the library anyway. If she was still working that same job, contriving a meeting would be child's play.

Somewhere in there, I caught myself planning to cheat on Wendy, only hours after discovering that I was in a committed relationship with her. It felt horribly wrong. This was a woman I genuinely cared about. The prospect of hurting her was itself unacceptable.

I had been feeling so smug just the night before about my very clever dodge of the curse. My assumption had been that my relationship with Helen would never unhappen if we never got as far as making it a relationship. It never occurred to me that the curse would trump me like this with a pre-emptive strike.

My day was difficult. Wendy and I took our lunch breaks together. The conversation was light, and very enjoyable for what it was worth. She still knew how to make me laugh. I spent the rest of the afternoon trying to get the wrist module to work, but to what end I no longer knew. With Helen no longer in the picture, making her a traveler seemed pointless.

Wendy and I went home at the end of the day. I made us dinner. We talked about work. After we cleaned up, I sat down to read, and Wendy spent the evening doing homework for a class she had the next day.

As it started to get late, she came into the living room and sat down next to me on the couch. She had changed into pajamas. She curled up next to me and put her head on my shoulder.

"Are you okay?" she said.

No, I thought.

"Yeah. Why?"

"You've been really quiet all day."

"Hmm," I said.

"Is it something at work?" she asked. While I was still trying to compose an answer to that question, she added, "Is it me?"

I took in her eyes. There was no fear there, just genuine concern for my well-being, and for our relationship. "No," I said. "It is absolutely not you."

"Is it something you can talk about?"

I thought about that, honestly unsure what the answer was.

"I don't think so," I said finally. "But I'm okay. It's just a thing I need to work through."

"Okay," she said. "If it gets bad, though, you have to spill it. All right?"

I laughed quietly. "Deal."

She curled up against me again.

"I worry about you."

I put my arm around her and held her. Wendy was a good person. I liked her a lot, and if this was where I was going to be from now on, I thought I could learn to love her. At that thought, my mind was flooded with images of Helen, the Ferris wheel, the graceful stingrays at the aquarium, the reading room, all the time we spent together building to something I kept putting off, and now could never be. And I pushed that all away. Like everything else I had ever truly wanted, I would just have to do without.

After a few minutes on the couch, Wendy leaned up and whispered into my ear, "Come to bed." So I did.

When I woke the next morning, Wendy, and all traces of her stay in my home, were gone.

October 2145

I was numb for most of that day. Wendy was not waiting for me at the front desk, nor did I have the heart to learn the reason for her absence. This, then, was to be my punishment for wanting to be with Helen. I had lost her, and Wendy, all in one stroke.

I spent most of that day planning my return to 2092. It had been the better part of two years for me since I left. My original plan of returning to the same day from which I had departed now seemed like the worst kind of folly. No one would ever believe one day could bring so much change to a person. Returning to 2094 posed its own set of problems, and for a while I tried to concoct ways of faking my own kidnapping. Ultimately, this sort of plot did not speak to my strengths.

Regardless of my method though, I had to go. There was too much pain here now. Whatever unspoken scheme my future self had in mind for me would have to go unexecuted. With a smooth return to my home time looking unworkable, I considered the possibility of becoming some sort of time nomad. Whatever powered my module might one day run dry, but until then, all of eternity could be my playground, and my home. The paranoid part of me wondered if this was Future Me's plan all along. The rest of me wondered if this was simply my destiny. That was my exact thought at the moment when I saw Helen waiting for me by the door at the end of my day.

"Coffee?"

I didn't understand what was happening at first, and considered the possibility that I had traveled back two days without realizing it. I even checked the date, but it was correct.

"Sure," I said, extremely unsurely.

"How's your day?" she asked as she held the door for me. Small talk. Absolutely no clue as to how the last year had played out between us.

"About average," I said, not even certain if that was a lie.

She shared some ordinary tales about an ordinary day in the life of a print collection curator. I laughed at the jokes, and *hmm*ed at the appropriate times.

Over a latte, in a naturally occurring lull, I asked her, "How long have we known each other?"

"Almost a year," she said. "I can't believe it's been that long, can you?"

"Did we do this yesterday? Coffee?"

She began to eye me cautiously. "Yes, we did. We do this most days. What's going on with you?" She narrowed her eyes, leaned in close, and whispered, "Are you an imposter?"

"Maybe," I said, no jest in my voice.

"I don't get it." She said, sitting up.

"What would you say if I told you that sometimes there are things that happen to me, and then those things get erased and replaced with different things? That sometimes things unhappen to me?"

She was silent for a moment. Then she said, "Proceed."

"You would say 'proceed'?"

"Which I just did, and which you will now do." Her voice had lost its light edge as well.

Where to start? Literally hundreds of examples raced to the top of my brain, vying for the position of the thing I could tell her that would make this all right. "You know I have a cat?" I began.

She nodded. "Mary Sue. Did something happen to her?"

I stopped. "I named my cat Mary Sue?"

"*I* named your cat Mary Sue. Why are we talking about her?"

"How long have I had her? Do you know?" I asked.

She frowned at me.

"We found her together about four months ago."

I took a deep breath.

"Well then, I guess she's a good example, because I have no memory of that. Until about four weeks ago, I also did not have a cat. Then one morning I woke up, and there she was."

"So," said Helen cautiously, "you un-not-had a cat?"

"Um." I untied her construction in my head. "That's right. Is that too many negatives?"

"No, no, no," she said. After a beat, she added, "See what I did there? But no, I follow you. What else?"

This seemed too easy. "You believe me?"

"Nigel-Graham, after what you showed me two days ago, I would believe anything you told me. I'm just surprised you waited until now. How long has this been happening to you?" She shook her head. "Or, unhappening?"

My heart started to race. "What did I show you two days ago?"

Her eyes went wide. "Seriously?" She pulled her tablet out of her jacket and waggled it in front of me. "Zap? Remember? Did that unhappen too?"

"What did we do after that?"

"Chicken Alfredo," She said. "Mmmm. You had some seafoody thing."

"Calamari Marinara," I said, a bit stunned.

"Say that three times fast. So we remember the same things, right? That's where we're going with this?"

"Yeah," I said. "Yeah. I thought... I was afraid that day unhappened."

"Why?"

I had no idea what to tell her. This was the best possible news. I had never had a day taken away from me like that and then returned in perfect condition. Athena implied it wasn't even possible.

"Yesterday was just very odd," I said weakly. "There were some changes. I was afraid I lost things before that, too."

We both sat silently for a bit. Helen was no doubt trying to process. I was trying to figure out what to say next. I really didn't plan to tell her any of this, but now that it was out, it felt right.

"Is this a time travel thing?" she asked finally.

"Yes, although I'm not exactly sure how it works, or why it happens," I said. "In response to your earlier question, it's been happening since I was fourteen. Maybe longer."

"Fourteen? Surely you weren't traveling through time at fourteen." She bit her lip. "Were you?"

"No," I said. "I..." Beyond no, I had no idea what to tell her. What I really wanted to do was throw caution to the wind, and tell her how I felt about her. But that entailed more risk than anything she wanted to know about time travel. Besides, she wasn't asking.

After a suitable pause, she said, "Listen. I am so touched that you have told me as much as you have, I couldn't possibly blame you if you stopped now. If you want your secrets, you may certainly keep them." She put her elbows on the table and rested her chin in her hands. The little bit of extra closeness that brought felt electric. "But I don't think you want them."

"I don't," I admitted. "I'm just afraid they will scare you away."

She took my hand and looked me square in the eyes. "I am not going anywhere."

And that finally pushed me over the edge of my secrecy.

"I'm not from 2145."

As I let that sink in, I saw some of the determination drain out of her face, and her mouth open unconsciously.

"Oh," she said quietly.

"Are we okay, or should I stop there?"

She was still holding my hand, and I felt her squeeze it just a little.

"We're good," she said. "I did not see that coming. But we're good. How far...? When...?"

"2092."

Again, she took a moment to process this. "2092? You're from the past?" I nodded. And then she made a leap I never would have predicted. "Nigel-Graham. You really are both of them."

"Wow," I said with no small degree of relief. "That saved me some time."

"I want to meet him," she said, continuing to surprise.

"You can't. Even I'm not allowed to talk to him directly."

She squeezed my hand again, more assertively.

"Thank you for letting me in," she said.

I nodded, unable to tell her that if everything went to plan, I would be inviting her much further in, very soon.

[60]

November 2145/May 2115

Athena visited again. Given the tone of our last two encounters, I was starting to wonder how long it would be before she showed up, if at all. But she did. I found her waiting for me outside my apartment. Before I had a chance to speak, she hugged me. This was unusual, but not the first time from my frame of reference, or hers.

"Hey," I said. She didn't let go. "Are you all right?"

She pulled back and nodded. "I want things to be better between us, that's all."

"Yeah," I said. "Me too. Sorry about last time."

She shook her head. "Don't. It's okay. I just..." She looked away. "I need someone to talk to. Can we table the other stuff? For now? I do want to answer your questions. But today I just need you to be here for me."

"Of course."

She took my hands. "Ready?"

"Sure."

The world blinked. We were back at the park. There was no evident reaction to our arrival. Even knowing the cause for that effect, noticing it was a bit creepy.

"This is your safe place," I said. "Isn't it?"

She ignored the question. "Do you remember the last time I brought you here?"

"Yes," I said. "You wanted me to kill a dog." As I said that, I spied the gray whippet from before. Its person was wearing the same thing I had seen her in the last time. "Wait, *that* dog. Is this the same day?"

She ignored that question as well. "Would you?" she asked.

"Would I?"

"Kill the dog. If you knew what it meant." She stared at the animal, a blank look on her face.

"Like, right now?" I considered the possibility. Even as a thought experiment, it made me incredibly uncomfortable. "I don't think so. Maybe if I had time to think about it." I shook my head. "No, that wouldn't help. I'm sorry, I can't kill the dog." I took a moment to consider what its day must be like right now. Beautiful weather, a person to please. He seemed like a reasonably happy dog, or at least a dog with reasons to be happy. I was going to remark on that to Athena, but when I looked at her, I saw that she had given up on the whippet.

She was looking at the stroller.

So many things went through my head at that moment. Our last conversation had started with her asking me about killing baby Hitler. This one started with her asking me if I was willing to kill a dog on a moment's notice.

"Who is the baby?" I asked, as calmly as I knew how.

She shook her head slowly, never taking her eyes off the stroller. On a bench next to it sat a young couple, doubtless oblivious to us.

"No more questions today, okay?" With that, she took my hand, and held it tight. "Just be here for me. Be my rock. Just for a little bit." We stood there in silence for perhaps half a minute.

The world blinked.

"Thank you," she said, and handed me two small clear yellow rods, about the size of paper clips.

"What are these?" I asked.

"The missing components of the wrist modules. They'll work now."

I turned them over in my hand.

"Why?" was all I could think to say.

She took my face in her hands and made me look at her. "Because I am trusting you to give her the choice. And I am trusting her to say no. And because if I don't give you these, you are going to do something even more stupid in your quest to have her."

She hugged me again.

"I'll see you soon," she said, and blipped out.

I stood outside my home, too paralyzed to go inside. Too many possibilities argued in my head, some demanding immediate action on

176

my part, others doing their best to calm me down. Over all that din, the only item that meant a damn to me at that moment was that if that was the same day I had already visited twice, it was sometime in 2115. The baby had to be at least four years too old to be Helen.

Nothing else mattered.

[61]

November 2145

It took me four days to get the wrist modules up and running, and another two to test them. After that, it was just a matter of working up the courage. That took a week, at the end of which Helen decided to visit her mother. Four more days of profoundly impatient waiting later, I was ready.

I found her at her desk. It was the middle of the afternoon, well past my lunch hour. She did not expect to see me. I was greeted with the usual happy face.

"Hey! What are you doing here?"

"I'm here to see you," I said.

"Well, that's new."

I sat in the chair next to her desk, and put an envelope in front of her. She made a surprised face.

"What's this?"

"You could open it and find out."

She steepled her fingers in front of her. "I suppose I could do that. Or perhaps I could take this, and leave it, forever sealed, perhaps framed. It could be the mystery of a lifetime. Just guessing what it might be could sustain me for years."

"Or you could open it."

"Or," she said, taking it, "I could open it."

What lay inside were tickets and hotel reservations. One week in

Hawaii. Neither of us had been on a proper vacation the entire time we had known each other. I imagined the setting to be the perfect venue for my offer of time travel. She had already expressed interest, so I did not expect resistance. I just wanted it to be as perfect as it could be.

She pulled out the tickets, and read them without reaction. Setting them aside, she removed the reservation details. Five star hotel, right on the beach. We had an entire suite. She read this in silence.

"I got us a suite," I pointed out redundantly. "We each have our own room."

This reassurance accomplished nothing. My heart pounded, probably attempting to throw itself on the floor. How could I have miscalculated her response this badly? I considered the possibility she was pulling my leg, but then the moment stretched past any reasonable point of humor. Her eyes had gone wide, and she looked down and away.

"Please say something," I said.

She said something. "I'm seeing someone."

We allowed that idea to hang in the air between us, like a poisonous vapor. All my plans, all my hopes, had been crushed the very moment I finally let my guard down. Well played, curse. All I could bring myself to say was, "Of course you are."

Of course she was.

[PART 4]
ATHENA

62

November 2145

I fled. The pain of losing Helen right on the cusp of being able to have a life with her was more than I could manage, so I abandoned my work in search of solitude. My plan of becoming a time nomad started to look like a real possibility, but I hadn't worked up the nerve for that yet. So I left town. No fixed destination, just travel. I'd like to say I saw spectacular things, and visited places I had always dreamed of. But I didn't. I moved from random hotel to random hotel. My only objective was to keep moving, and hope the constant change of scenery would provide me with sufficient distraction.

It didn't work.

I would also love to say this was the start of a new phase in my life, that it gave me a freedom I had never known, and that I never looked back. The truth is, I left Mary Sue with about a week's worth of food, and no intention of abandoning her. So, after six days, I returned to my cat and my life. No wiser, no less hurt.

During that span, Helen sent me five messages. I deleted all of them without listening to them. Not out of anger, of course. Helen had not wronged me in any way. With my entire relationship with her now having unhappened, I didn't even know what kind of friendship we might still have. Or ever have had. Clearly we had some kind of social connection, as she had greeted me in a very friendly manner the day I humiliated myself in front of her. This wasn't like my previously unhappened relationships, in which my girlfriends wound up not knowing me, at best, or vanished forever at worst. She still knew me, and she still demonstrated some fondness for me. But all that did was make the whole retroactive collapse of what we had even more painful.

In the wake of my day with Wendy, followed by the restoration of what I had with Helen, having it immediately yanked away from me so definitively made it impossible for me not to see this as personal. I wanted to believe that my reversals of fortune had always been some inescapable consequence of time travel. But this last misery was so repugnant, and so surgical, I could no longer pretend it was anything other than a direct attack.

Even with that perspective, slowly resolving itself into a certainty, there was still no recourse. I would never win Helen back, any more than I could resurrect Carrie Wolfe. The safest thing for my peace of mind was to push her away, as far and as permanently as possible. And so, naturally, that was exactly what she refused to let me do.

63

November 2145

Three days after I got back from my feeble exile, Helen figured out not only that I had returned to work, but also that I was coming in two hours early every day. It seemed like the easiest way to preempt any chance of her catching me in the morning. She was continuing to leave me messages I wouldn't listen to, and it seemed reasonable to expect her to strike in person next. What I failed to take into account was her level of perseverance. When I found her waiting for me by the elevator, it was still dark out. There was no telling how long she had been camped out in the corridor.

I considered ignoring her, but the reality was that I held no resentment, and I had no desire to be hurtful. I chose curtness instead.

"Hi," I said.

"Wow. 'Hi'? Way to sabotage all my rehearsed responses. You were supposed to say something bitter, or pathetic. Now I've got nothing."

"Go home," I said. "Is that bitter enough?"

"It's a start. That's not going to happen, but at least we're getting somewhere now."

I took a deep breath. At that moment, all I truly wanted was for this conversation to last as long as possible, no matter how awful it was. But I also knew that every moment we dragged this out would add one more layer of misery.

"Helen, I misread the situation. I am very sorry, and very embarrassed, and I just want to be left alone."

She shook her head. "We both know there's more to this."

"There really isn't."

She stepped closer to me, and said quietly, "Yes there is, but we should probably sort that out somewhere more private. Wouldn't you agree, *Nigel?*"

Not Nigel-Graham. This was a red flag.

"What are you talking about?"

She pointed to the elevator.

"In," she said. We stepped inside, and allowed the doors to close. I assumed she just wanted privacy, until she said, "Fourth floor."

"That won't—" I didn't bother finishing the sentence as the elevator ascended.

"You already authorized me," she said.

None of this made any sense. My friendship with Helen had unhappened, maybe not entirely, but significantly. If she had already been to my lab, on my authority, she must know almost as much as she did before the timeline changed. Without a credible reason to deny her what she had already been granted before, I let her in through the airlock to my lab.

"You think what we had unhappened," she began bluntly. "Don't you?"

Yet again, she caught me off guard.

"You know about that?"

She nodded.

"Ask me."

It took a second for me to grasp what she meant. Then I thought back on the last time I thought we had unhappened.

"How long have we known each other?"

"Almost a year."

"How did we meet?" I asked.

"I Shanghaied you into running a mock interview for the library job."

None of this made sense. Events from one year ago and a few days ago were consistent with my memories of them. There should have been some divergence at one extreme or the other. "Ferris wheel?"

"I made you ride The Zipper first." No hesitation.

"Aquarium?" I asked.

"Stingrays."

It seemed that her intent was to clear matters up, but the further we went, the more confused I became.

"Mary Sue?"

"Your cat," she said. "We found her about four months ago, but your first memory of her was only one month ago. Because your life is one long string of inconsistencies. Things happen and then they unhappen, over and over again. Because you're a time traveler, here from 2092 to help the version of you who lives now with God only knows what. And no one knows but you." She paused. "And me."

I sat down, struggling to accept this, against some extremely strong internal resistance.

"I don't understand. How can all of that still be true?"

She came over to my seat and crouched to meet my eyes. "Because it all happened. And none of what we have has been lost. Nothing important about me has changed."

I shook my head. "I have no memory of you seeing someone else."

"You don't remember it," she said, "because you never knew."

I took a moment to reflect on that possibility.

"How long?"

"The whole time," she said. "And two years before that."

I started to feel slightly faint. "Why didn't you ever say anything?"

She stood, and looked away.

"It's complicated."

Despite myself, I laughed.

"Don't even get me started on complicated." She flinched at this, and I immediately regretted it. The silence began to stretch. "The part about me being embarrassed is still true," I said to fill it. "That stands."

She laughed softly.

"That's my fault. I honestly thought we were going to have this conversation much sooner. Like a few weeks after we met. You weren't exactly subtle, you know."

I groaned. "Sorry."

"No, it's okay. I just thought you were going to force the issue without realizing it. To be honest, I hoped you would. I thought it would be easier for both of us to put it on the table. But then..." She shrugged. "You never did anything. You never said anything. And I figured you had your reasons for wanting to keep things platonic. As long as that was true, I assumed we would be fine."

"But why keep it a secret at all?"

"I can't..." She shook her head. "Let's just leave it at complicated, okay?" She walked to a window and gazed out. I had no idea what to make of her words. Something about this was a weight around her neck, but it was impossible to know what. I considered the possibilities that she was covering for an abusive boyfriend, or that the person she was seeing was in fact another woman, but neither of those conjectures rang true for the Helen I knew. "Why didn't you?" she asked suddenly.

"Why didn't I?"

"Do something. Say something. Force the issue. Lord knows I gave you plenty of opportunities. I like to think I'm a decent hint-dropper, but you never took the bait." She turned to face me. "Why did you wait a year? You're outgoing, you're a risk taker, you don't strike me as someone who fears rejection, and we were hitting it off. Why didn't you make a move?"

I considered the truth for a fraction of a second, then bailed.

"I'm only like that when I'm around you," I tried.

"Okay, sure," she said. "Even if I buy that—which, by the way, I do not —you *were* around me. Pretty much every time we were together. The question stands."

I grappled with the truth one more time, and conceded.

"Come, sit," I said. She gave me a bewildered look. "You're going to want to be sitting for this."

She moved toward the chair with obvious apprehension. My best guess is that she had been expecting to hear something extremely personal, like a phobia, or severe shyness. If so, she was about to be surprised, and looked none too excited about that. She sat.

"You're sure you want to know?" I said. One last chance for us both to walk away. She passed.

"Yes."

After a moment to collect my thoughts, I took a deep breath and dove in.

"When I was fourteen years old, I had my first kiss. The next day, that girl was gone, and no one had ever heard of her. I had three girlfriends in high school. The first one suddenly stopped knowing me one day. The second one was suddenly dating my best friend. The third one..." I hesitated. "The third one died. When she was twelve. Five years before we started dating."

And there it was. The last piece of the mystery that was Nigel-Graham Walden. Helen had gone pale by this point.

"Oh my God," she said softly. "Nigel, I'm so sorry."

"So, you understand what I'm telling you?" Hesitantly, she nodded. "Yes, I have feelings for you that go far beyond friendship, and yes, that has been true for a very long time. I didn't say anything because I was afraid you would be receptive, and that being with me would end up destroying you."

"You can't possibly believe you caused that girl's death." Her tone was pleading. She wiped away a tear.

"How can I possibly dare believe anything else?"

We sat there mute, both looking at the floor, for what must have been several minutes.

Finally, still not looking at me, she said, "Please don't push me away, Nigel. We can fix this. You are my best friend. The best friend I have ever had." Then she did look up. "And I can't bear how much weight you have to carry with no one to share it. Please, let's fix this."

I looked up, her words suddenly reminding me that there was still one piece of my story I had yet to reveal.

"Okay," was all I said, and for that instant, she accepted it as good news. But it was her comment about no one to share my weight that still rang in my ears. At some point, she was going to have to learn about Athena.

[64]

November 2145

Helen didn't stay. With the rest of the day ahead of me to sort out my thoughts as well as I could, I fell back on tinkering with the wrist modules. They worked now, thanks to Athena, but no better than they had before I showed up. My charge was to perfect them, whatever that meant. Maybe they held some potential that was so far unexplored.

Maybe there was some way they could be used to stabilize the timeline.

A new excitement drove my work. This was absolutely a guess, and a pretty obviously desperate one at that, but there was a very appealing plausibility to the idea that my secret assignment had been that angle all along. If Future Me experienced the same unhappenings, it would explain not only why he wanted me to work on this project alone, but also why he was such a broken shell of a man to begin with. He had fifty-two years on me. The prospect of fifty-two more years of these random revisions did not bode well, and it was easy enough to believe how badly it would eventually wear me down.

The new premise behind my work was more than enough to propel me through the day, although predictably, I had no encouraging results. Still, I found myself with an enthusiasm that was a welcome change. The fact that Helen had confronted me had also bled away some of my tension. There was a tricky road ahead of us, but having everything on the table was at long last a relief.

At the end of the day, I returned to an apartment with completely different furniture than any I had ever owned. Some of it was nicer, others not so much. The next morning I found my license plate on a completely different car. My key card and thumbprint still started it.

Neither of these transformations caused me any particular trouble. I went to work fairly certain that I would see Helen afterward for coffee, and that none of our experiences would be lost. This was based on intuition more than evidence. Apart from our divergent memories surrounding the cat, I knew of no examples of a revised timeline that included a loss of history for the two of us. I was now convinced that my curse had been trying to hit Helen for months, but that it missed the target every single time.

November 2145

As I half-expected, Helen met me at the entrance to my building at the end of that day. Her smile was obviously nervous. We had agreed to find some new equilibrium, but neither of us had any idea what that would be, or how it would work.

"Coffee?" she said in as timid a voice as I had ever heard from her.

"Please," I said in a voice that sounded no more courageous in my head.

She got a piece of cake that day. Atypical for her, and my first instinct was to read too much into it. Not to be outdone, I ordered a blueberry scone, for which I immediately realized I had no appetite.

"I thought you didn't like scones," Helen pointed out.

"Maybe now I do," I said. It was the weakest of jokes, and she left it alone. "On that topic, what's with the cake?"

"It's a cake kind of day," she said around a mouthful of it. Fair enough.

"I have a theory," I said, not exactly intending to.

She swallowed. "About cake?"

"About my curse."

"Oh," she said, putting her fork down. "Sorry. Go ahead."

I hesitated. "This is going to be super awkward, no matter how I say it, right?"

"Probably," she admitted. "Why don't we just stipulate to that, and then not worry about it? I'll have a fair number of awkward things to add, I'm sure. No score keeping, okay?"

Despite everything, I laughed.

"Agreed. If you want to go first..." I held out my hands in a gesture of deference.

"Not on your life," she said, pointing at me with her fork.

"Quick check: how long have we known each other?"

Her worry was immediately evident. "Did something unhappen?"

"No. I mean, yes. New furniture, different car. Nothing of consequence, but I think you just answered my question. Things continue to unhappen to me, but the one constant is you. I've thought about this a lot, and over the last year, the only example I can name of the two of us having different memories is finding Mary Sue. Still working on why that is, and I hope I can determine it without having to dissect her." I paused for laughter. Got none. "Joke," I said.

"Good."

"Anyway," I continued with mild embarrassment, "you are the only person in my life for whom that has ever been true. Everyone else close to me has diverged at some point from my experiences with them. The other thing is that every time I felt like you and I have gotten closer over the last year, a lot of minor things unhappened immediately afterward. But not you. It's like whatever force does this is trying to pull us apart, but it can't figure out how. Like it keeps trying to get to you, but it hits everything around you instead."

She frowned. "I'm not sure I understand what that means."

I took the leap. "I think it means you have some kind of immunity. I think you can't unhappen to me. I have no idea why, but I think you are the only person who can't be affected by my curse."

She stared at me for a few seconds after that, and finally whispered, "Wow." Her expression was unreadable.

"Please know I'm not saying this from any ulterior motives. I know where we stand, and I'm not trying to maneuver for something else. It just seemed important to me, and real, and I thought you would want to know."

"I hope it's true," she said. "Because I think..." She shook her head. "No. Strike that. I'm sure. I love you." She looked over her head, presumably waiting for comedically timed lightning. Seeing none, she declared, "Still here!"

My internal reactions to this were too copious to describe. On top of it all, I blurted, "So far!"

"Listen to you, mister glass-half-empty."

Stunned, I asked, "Where did this come from?" Despite everything I had just explained to her, and despite my delirious joy at hearing those words, my concern for her safety rushed to the surface of all my thinking.

She smiled softly. "It was always there. I'm just done kidding myself about it." I stared, dumbfounded. She stared back. "So...," she prompted, rolling her hand.

"Oh! Right!" I cleared my throat. "In the event that it has not been self evident for some time... I love you, Helen."

She closed her eyes. A visible load of tension drained out of her body. "Thank you. Hearing that really does make this easier. You still worried about how awkward you sound?"

"In no way," I said.

"Good," she said, taking another bite of cake. Then pointing her fork at me again, added, "Although we definitely need to work on your delivery. 'In the event that it has not been self evident'? What the hell was that?"

"Ha! Sorry. Scientist. Don't get out much."

"Hmm," she said with a little laugh. "Fair enough."

And then, apparently, we ran out of things to say. I broke the silence. "What do we do now?"

"Now," she said carefully, "we put our last two secrets on the table. You're going to hear all about Carlton."

"His name is Carlton?" I said quietly, mostly to myself.

"His name is Carlton," she confirmed. "And after that, you're going to tell me the one thing you're still holding back." She meant Athena, although it was unclear whether she understood it that specifically.

"How do you know that?" I asked.

"Because that's what we do," she said. "We hide things from each other. Except not anymore. Drop the other shoe, Nigel."

"Okay," I said. "There's another time traveler. Her name is Athena. I see her once or twice a month. We are just friends," I hastened to add.

Helen's eyes opened wider, and that childlike grin of discovery I had come to adore spread across her face.

"Oh my," she said. "That is so much better than I expected."

[66]

November 2145

That conversation lasted two hours. I learned a great deal more about Carlton than I have the heart to reproduce here, but the most salient points went as follows:

Helen and Carlton met while she was still an undergrad, studying abroad. He was an expatriate American living in France, and heir to one of the most wealthy and powerful families in the world.

"Yes, but can he travel through time?" I inquired.

"Quiet, you," she clarified.

This alone would have been more than enough to intimidate me beyond measure. Unfortunately, at one point in her description of him she somehow felt compelled to show me a photo of him on her tablet. As I feared, he was basically a god. Chiseled features, lithe build, lush blond hair to his shoulders. Their children would be characters straight out of Norse mythology.

This was all essentially my worst nightmare, and I couldn't help but think my curse had simply found new and creative ways to deprive me of happiness.

It turned out there were two reasons why she had never told me about him. The first was that their relationship, for the entirety of its three year run so far, was a secret to everyone, not just me. The elaborate web of power to which his family constituted several strands made marriage—and anything that could potentially lead to marriage—a topic enmeshed

195

in politics far more than romance. His parents were well aware of Helen's presence in his life, but were unaware of the extent to which she held his heart. This revelation made me extremely uncomfortable and resentful. How dare he hide her like some shameful and scandalous affair? I managed to withhold saying that out loud right up to the moment she told me he had asked her to marry him.

"What did you say?" I asked, not really want to hear the answer.

"I'm not supposed to say," she said. When I buried my face in my hands, she explained, "No, I mean I'm not supposed to say to him. He asked me not to give him an answer right away. He wanted to spend some time warming his family up to the idea. Failing that, he wanted time to create a fallback plan, so that we could have a life away from that yoke. He's in Paris right now, and has been since he proposed. We see each other about once every two months, whenever he can get away."

"Oh," I said, mentally filling in a gap in her story. "You weren't really visiting your mother."

She shook her head sadly. "No. Sorry."

"How much time have you given him?"

She poked her half eaten cake with her fork, avoiding my eyes.

"He asked me to marry him only a few days before I met you. We never set a time limit for how long to drag this out, but I think we are both getting to a place where we need to make a decision."

"Do you know what you're going to do?"

Still not looking at me, she shook her head.

Carefully, I asked, "He has no idea I exist, does he?"

This time she looked up. "No."

"What's the second reason you never told me?'

She sighed. "I didn't tell you because I was afraid if you knew, I would lose you. Which almost happened, I might add." She then crumpled up a napkin and threw it at my forehead. "Jerk."

Taking all this in was not easy. Part of me wanted to consider it a solution to the ongoing concern about her safety in my presence. A very, very tiny part.

"Helen, I am not going to try to nudge you one way or the other on this. You know what a life with me might mean for you, and I'm not even sure I want you to risk it. You mean too much to me. If I'm going to lose you, I would much rather it be to a life with someone else than to oblivion."

She absorbed that in silence. What could she say, really? Finally, she said, "I want to meet her."

Her talent for non sequitur was nearly unsurpassed.

"You're changing the subject."

"Desperately," she confirmed.

I nodded. "That's fair. You mean Athena, I assume?"

"Yes."

I thought about that. The first thing she said to me when she discovered I was the younger analog of an old man currently alive was she wanted to meet him. I refused her that, on reasonable grounds. It was unclear to me whether those grounds applied to Athena.

"I'll ask her."

"Thanks," she said, and scarfed down the rest of her cake. Unlike her revelations that day, I offered nothing else. Because I knew Helen, I was sure she wanted to hear nothing about Athena in words. She wanted to experience Athena for herself.

It remained to be seen if Athena would want to share that experience.

67

December 2145

As had now become predictable, shortly after Helen told me all about Carlton and asked to meet Athena, my life was peppered with unhappenings of a noticeable but inconsequential nature. The most interesting of these was a construction project to expand the lab building, which had apparently been underway for several months before it appeared one day. It meant meeting Helen at a different entrance for our afternoon coffee dates. Her memories were of meeting me there this whole time, but none of her memories of the meetings themselves had changed.

Helen and I established a code phrase for testing the theory that unhappenings weren't affecting her, relative to me. If I had cause for concern, I would ask her how long we had known each other, and she would simply respond, "Stingrays." The code word was her choice. She wanted to evoke a happy memory whenever this came up. If she ever gave me any other answer, I would need to ask her questions beyond that. So far, it had been unnecessary.

We tabled any discussion of Carlton, or the decision ahead of her. The lone exception was a three day period in which he was going to be in the country. On previous such occasions, she had simply avoided me, sometimes with a plausible excuse for needing to have a few days to herself. This time she was forthright about it. Curiously, I felt no jealousy over losing my time with her to him. Perhaps it was simply honoring the fact that I was not truly entitled to be jealous. Perhaps it was something else.

Nor during that time did we explore taking our relationship any further than friendship. We had made our confessions and had chosen for the time being to live with the knowledge of our feelings without acting on them. It was enough.

For now.

68

February 2146

Inevitably, the moment came when we had to stop talking around our situation.

We had both taken a day away from work, at her request. I assumed it was another hooky day, like our aquarium outing, just to give us both a break from ongoing stress. It was mid-February, and we sought warmth and pleasant pastime in the Museum of Natural History. The dioramas and skeletons were not bringing that light of discovery to her eyes. We took a moment to rest on a bench in the mineral room, among a multitude of brightly colored stones in glass cases. I chose that moment to ask her if she was all right.

"He wants an answer," was all she said.

The dread I felt at pursuing this idea was exceeded only by the dread of not knowing.

"Do you have one?"

"No," she said without hesitation. I had a fraction of a second to bask in the reprieve before she continued. "But he deserves one. His parents know now. They have for a while, but he kept that from me. They are good people. Truly. But they are also trapped in a set of expectations that is very difficult for them to shake off. Apparently it's been a bit of a battle."

I waited for a follow-up, or a question, but she stopped there.

"I don't know what to say."

She looked at me with steel eyes.

"Good. I don't want you to say anything. This can't be about you."

"I know," I said. "Whatever you had before you met me, you still have. I don't even know if I can stay in this time. I certainly can't offer you anything compared to the life he can give you. Whatever you decide, I will understand."

She stared at me blankly.

"What part of 'I don't want you to say anything' got past you?"

"Ha. Sorry." I let the silence hang between us for a bit. Then I said something stupid. "He loves you, you know."

She gave me a look I read as equal parts bewildered and impatient.

"How do you know that?"

"How can he not?" was all I said.

The impatience drained from her face, and the bewilderment swelled. Then she took my face in her hands, and kissed me. As surprised as I was by the fact of it, the sensation surprised me more. It was not hungry, or passionate, or awkward, or confused. In her frame of mind, any of those would have made sense. Instead, it was tender. A simple, soft statement of fact. She looked down as she pulled away.

"Helen..."

"Don't," she said flatly. "I need time."

With that, she stood and left me sitting alone in a room full of wondrously beautiful rock, a handful of gawking schoolchildren, and my doubts.

69

February 2146/May 2115

We had come to the museum in Helen's car. I waited half an hour for her to return to the mineral room, and then I went to the coat check to see if her jacket was still there. It was not. As I stood there trying to decide whether to find my way home or just stay there, a voice behind me asked, "Is this a bad time?"

I turned to find Athena, who had doubtless just materialized in a crowded room to no one's observation. For the first time in a while, I noticed she was getting older. When she first started visiting me in this time frame, she was a few years younger than I. By this point, she looked like she might have caught up to me.

"For you?" I said. "Never. Bad in general? Probably."

"Girl problems?"

I growled. "Please don't make fun."

She put her hand on my shoulder. "I'm not. I actually came here to talk about that. In a supportive way, if that's okay."

"Quite okay," I said. "At this point I'll take whatever support I can get."

"Come on," she said, leading me away from the coat check. We meandered through the museum, with no particular destination. "What did she say?"

"You're going to have to be way more specific," I said.

"When you offered to make her a time traveler?"

"Oh!" I said. "Wow. That was like three plans ago. I almost forgot that was even a thing. I never got around to it. It turned out she was kind of semi-engaged, so the time travel thing became a little moot."

Athena showed no particular reaction to this news.

"You seem to be taking it well."

"No I don't."

"No," she agreed. "You don't. That was just my attempt at being supportive."

"She wants to meet you."

This did get a reaction. She stopped walking, and pretended to look at a diorama about South American wildlife. "Probably not a good idea," she said after a considerable pause.

"Why not?" I asked.

"Because she is quite a bit more perceptive than you are."

"What's that supposed to mean?" Athena gave me no reply. "You know her. In the future," I said cautiously. "Don't you?"

She turned to face me.

"For crying out loud, Nigel. I've practically told you straight out at least three times that I know her. And thank you for making my point, by the way." She went back to the diorama. "How much does she know about me?"

"Just that you exist," I said, feeling a little sheepish. "She didn't ask me anything about you, other than if she could meet you."

"That does sound like her," said Athena. "What else does she know?"

"Um..." I said.

Athena turned around and took both my hands.

"What else does she know?" she asked again, gently.

"Kind of everything," I admitted. "She knows about time travel. She knows about the unhappenings. She knows I'm from her past. She figured out that I am the same person as Dr. Nigel Walden." I thought for a second. "I think that might be it. I guess that's enough, though."

"I'd have to agree." The remark was scolding. Her tone was not.

"Am I in trouble?" I asked.

She laughed at that. "Almost certainly, but not from me. I can't fault you for being open with her. That's more than I've been with you."

"You've had your reasons," I said, with no idea what they were.

"That doesn't make it right. You deserve better." The room flashed. We were back in the park. The warm spring sun on my face felt particularly comforting by contrast to the stinging February cold I was expecting to feel outside. I looked to down to see Athena let go of my hands.

Scanning for the stroller, I found it immediately. The young couple sat at the bench next to it. Maybe five seconds had elapsed since the last time

Athena and I were here. This would be my fourth visit to this park, on this day. I wondered how many this made for Athena. "What happens on this day?" I asked.

She was watching them. The young woman stood and reached under the canopy of the stroller, perhaps adjusting a blanket, or a pacifier, or maybe just touching her child. "You wouldn't think it to see them here," she said, "but those are two of the wealthiest people in this city. There they are, having a normal day with their child, like anyone else. Not a care in the world. And no one here has a clue of the extraordinary level of power in their midst. A lucky mugger would be set for life to take just what they have on their persons right now, even ignoring the items that could be traced."

I scrutinized them for any sign of what Athena was saying.

"Is this another thought experiment, like the plague dog?"

"Not this time."

Still watching them, in their spectacular ordinariness, I asked, "Why don't they have bodyguards or something?"

"Because," she said, "to answer both of your questions, today is the day they let their guard down. Even with all the power they wield, all their wealth, all the influence their family holds over so many, for one day they forgot to stay safe. And if they take that baby home, after this day, they will never forget again. And their son will go on to use that wealth, and influence, and power, in ways that will devastate a world." She took my hand again. "Those are Carlton's parents."

My stomach, my heart and my world turned inside out. Athena had never come right out and said it, but her implication had been clear. That baby represented a threat to the future, her present, to an extent she felt justified comparing him to Adolf Hitler. And she could end that threat any time she wanted to. All it would cost would be her humanity. That alone had been difficult for me to reconcile. Now I was suddenly faced with the horror that this was Helen's lover we were talking about. And yes, I am not proud to admit that for the tiniest fraction of a second—maybe not even that tiny—I did allow myself to think of this as two birds with one stone. I would rationalize that unspoken thought in my mind for years to come, but it would always be the single most selfish moment in my life. Well... second most.

The park flashed. My eyes adjusted to the relatively dim light of the museum. I have no memory of what I was looking at, because all I could see was that stroller, an image I did not expect to leave me any time soon.

"Why did you show me that?" I asked. It came out barely a whisper. "Why did you tell me that?"

"I don't know," she admitted. "Maybe because I am weary of carrying it alone. I know it can't possibly make any of what comes next easy for you, and for that I am truly sorry." She hugged me then, and I held onto her like she was the only thing keeping me from collapsing to the floor. Which might have been true. "When do you want to introduce me to Helen?" she asked in my ear. Then she stepped back. "I mean, if you still do."

I had no way of succinctly communicating to Athena that I did not hold her responsible for anything that just happened. If anything, all I felt was an abundance of sympathy for her. How I dealt with her information was my problem, not hers.

"Give me a week," I said. "I have a lot to work out."

"Understood."

"Do we need to set a meeting place?" I asked.

She tapped her left forearm. "I'll find you."

"Of course. See you in a week."

She nodded. "See you in five seconds," she said, and then she was gone.

February 2146

Two days went by with no contact from Helen. The last thing she said before abandoning me at the museum to find my own ride home was that she needed time. She had also just kissed me, which I considered a mixed message at best. Nevertheless, I gave her time. In truth, I needed time myself. I had just learned something awful about her possible fiancé, and had no idea how, when or if I could share it with her. If I read Athena's intentions correctly, it might never be necessary. I hoped that was the case. Otherwise, I would end up bearing the weight of a truth I could never share with Helen, and I didn't know if I would have the courage for that.

On day three, I decided to break silence. If nothing else, Helen had an appointment with Athena in a few days, and she needed to be made aware of it. I walked out of my lab in the middle of the day, to find her at the library. Part of me feared she would not be there, perhaps already on her way to Paris for a life of splendor with her Adonis. Another part of me feared she would be there, and this would be the day she cut me out of her life for good.

I found her at her desk, and knocked at the open door before entering.

"Hey," she said warmly. "Come on in."

"I wasn't sure how long you wanted me to stay away," I said, planting myself in the seat next to her desk.

"The afternoon would have been fine," she said.

"Oh. I was waiting for you to call me."

She laughed. "Likewise. I probably should have been clearer when I left."

This seemed much too easy. "How long have we known each other?"

"Stingrays," she said without missing a beat. "How were your last two days? Did I shake everything up with that kiss?"

"You sure as hell did," I said, with what was probably obvious relief. "Fortunately, nothing unhappened to go with that."

"I told him no," she said.

"Oh." I hadn't prepared for that possibility, having assumed she would either have said yes, or not decided yet. It took a second or two for the idea to fully settle in my head. "How did he react?"

"Hard to say. I did it over vid, which didn't feel great. He was a perfect gentleman about it, and we always knew this was a possible outcome. We both promised it would be on good terms, if it came to that. But..." She shook her head. "But I don't know for sure."

"I'm sorry."

She glared. "Don't you dare be sorry. I am a big girl. This was never about you, this was about me. So there," she added.

"It wasn't an apology," I said.

"Oh. Well, thank you then." She sighed and her face softened. "It still wasn't about you. At least, I don't think it was. The whole arrangement was starting to wear me down. I needed to be out of that tangle. And I think he was coming around to the same place anyway. What little time we had together was getting strained. Even the sex was getting more distant." She winced. "Oh, crap. Sorry?"

I laughed. "Not at all. I'm a big boy."

"Okay," she said with a sad smile.

"So... are we...?"

She shook her head. "Not yet. I need a little more time to feel free first. It matters to me that this isn't just me leaving him for you." She rested her chin in her hands, and gazed at me. "But yes, soon."

I smiled. "Good. Meanwhile, are you ready to meet Athena?"

Helen perked up greatly at this. "She said yes?"

"She said yes."

"When?" she asked with a little giggle.

"Four days from now. My place. I think it will be mid afternoon, but we should probably take the whole day."

Helen's joy at the prospect of a new wonder was, as always,

enchanting. My fears that this would be a terrible day allayed, I managed to convince myself, at least for the time being, that everything was going to be fine.

And then I caught myself, and braced for the backlash.

[71]

February 2146

I tried to go home from the library. I say "tried," because when I got to my apartment building, there was nothing there. Well, okay, not nothing per se, but rubble does not make for a particularly comfortable domicile. The quantity of brush overgrowth in the ruins indicated the building had been in this state for some time. It wasn't even clear that it had been the same building. I picked through it for ten minutes before I gave up looking for anything identifiable.

I went to pull out my tablet, assuming that "home" would be programmed into the GPS, but it wasn't in my jacket. Figuring I must have left it in my car, I returned to the street to find it gone. Not the first time I had lost a car to an unhappening, to be sure, but usually with the result of another in its place. I went up and down the block looking for a familiar plate, and attempted to signal the chime with my key card. Nothing spoke to me. I did still have a key card, which meant I must have a car, but it was not in range.

It was a long walk back to the lab. An hour later, cranky and exhausted, I entered a building that was familiar in only the broadest strokes. The construction project that had manifested in my last batch of unhappenings was either finished or irrelevant. The entire layout of the building had changed, as had the décor and the personnel. One familiar face did stand out, but not in a reassuring way.

"Graham?" said Andrea. She was sitting at an indoor picnic table that I had never seen before, eating a bagel from a café that had never been part of my workplace. "What are you doing here?"

I flopped down in the seat next to hers, vaguely hoping we were still friends.

"If I ask you something insane, can you promise me just to answer it on its face without questioning it?"

"I… guess so," she said. "Are you okay? You look awful."

I ignored the observation.

"Where am I supposed to be right now?"

Her eyes bugged, and she leaned very close to me.

"Graham," she whispered, "are you traveling through time?"

I had no idea if this was an out, or a horrible risk, but I rolled with it.

"I asked you not to question it," I said kindly, but sternly.

"Oh my God," she said with a bit of a manic smile. "You lucky son of a bitch."

I rolled my eyes. "Please answer the question."

"Right." She composed herself. "Sorry. These days you are working out of a lab in your home. It's February 19th, 2146, if you're curious."

"2146?" I said with my best mock surprise. "Shit. Thanks." I got up to go.

"Graham," she said, "if you see yourself when you get home, tell you I said hello." She was clearly holding back laughter. I politely snickered, and left.

72

February 2146

I did not return home, primarily because I still had no idea where that was. Helen still had another half hour to go before her work day ended, and I was closer than that by foot to the library.

"Oh my God," she said when she saw me. I could only imagine what the kilometers and the cold had done to me by then. "Nigel, what happened?"

"How long have we known each other?" I asked.

"Oh... Stingrays. Come in. Sit. Tell me what's going on."

I crashed in one of her comfy chairs.

"When was the last time you saw me?"

Unlike Andrea, there was no hesitation or confusion in Helen's voice. "A few hours ago."

"What did we talk about?"

"That I broke it off with Carlton." Much to her credit, she answered this question evenly and calmly.

"How much do you know about my situation?" I asked. "Please be specific."

She came around her desk, pulled up another chair, and held my hand. The warmth of her fingers against my chapped skin was delicious.

"You are a time traveler from the year 2092. Your life keeps unhappening, although you believe I am somehow immune to whatever causes that. You work for a future version of yourself, on a time travel project whose goal he won't tell you. You are friends with another time traveler from the future named Athena, and I am going to meet her very soon. And I love you."

I took in a very deep breath, held it for five seconds, and slowly released it.

"Thank you," I whispered.

"What unhappened?" she asked softly.

"Everything but you," I said. "My apartment is gone. I don't work at the lab anymore."

"You don't live in an apartment," she said. "You live in a house. And that's where your lab is. You took me there to show me your work. We sent my tablet a minute into the future."

"Can you take me there?" I pleaded.

"Of course," she said, and kissed my forehead. As she stood to get her coat, she suddenly froze. "Did I do this?" she asked. "Is this because I kissed you?"

That clinched it. She really did know everything. I had shared with her my theory that the new unhappenings were being caused as a series of failed attempts to remove her from my life.

"I don't think so," I said.

She grabbed her coat, helped me up and took me home. It turned out I had a very nice house. Helen made me something to eat, then put me to bed and stayed the night in my guest room. As I drifted off, I grappled with the lie I had told her in her office, when she asked me if she had caused my unhappenings with her kiss. My last waking thought was a realization it wasn't a lie after all. The timing was all wrong. She hadn't caused it with the kiss. She had caused it by leaving Carlton.

73

February 2146

T he next three days gave me an opportunity to get to know my new surroundings. If the universe was trying to punish me, it was going about it all wrong. The private home was a major upgrade from my one bedroom apartment. My basement workroom was both more spacious and better equipped than what I was used to at the lab. Apart from the day of misery I spent not knowing where I belonged, my life had greatly improved.

On the fourth day, Helen and I had our appointment with Athena. Helen stayed over the night before to be sure she wouldn't miss Athena's arrival, since all we knew was the date. Once again, she had slept in my spare bedroom, a luxury I greatly appreciated now, and never had in the apartment. The state of our relationship was still in flux at that point, especially in light of the recent spate of upheavals in my life.

We had breakfast and made small talk. Helen was visibly nervous, despite my assurances that this would go smoothly. We settled in to wait. Helen had brought work with her, and spread it out on my dining room table, the most notable effect of which was highlighting for me the fact that I now had a dining room. The morning passed. We had lunch. Helen returned to her project.

At just after three in the afternoon, there was a dull flash of light from my living room. I walked in to find Athena, exactly the same as I had left her a week ago.

"Hi there," I said. We embraced. Helen poked her head around the door. The look of awe on her face was as usual quite priceless, but today carried an extra edge I couldn't quite identify.

"Helen," I said formally, "this is Athena." The introduction was one-way. I knew Athena had already met a future version of Helen.

Helen crept slowly into the room, her eyes locked on Athena. The glee I was so used to seeing at a new discovery was curiously lacking from her demeanor. Athena began to shuffle nervously, and I suddenly wondered if she hadn't been right to suggest this meeting not happen. Helen walked right up to her and stared her in the eyes, moving her head to stay with them as Athena tried awkwardly to look away. This was spinning into a situation I could not define, other than to know it was not ideal.

I was about to suggest that we all sit down when Helen asked, "What is your real name?"

I had never told Helen that Athena was just the latest in a string of aliases, so this caught me off guard. Athena's extremely hesitant response, more so.

"Athena," she said quietly.

Helen took Athena's hand. Very softly, she asked, "What's your full name, honey?"

Despite Helen's non-threatening tone, I had never seen Athena quite so intimidated. For a moment, I thought she might cry.

Finally, she said, "Athena Walden."

Helen turned to me. "We have a daughter."

And then, looking at them side by side, like an optical illusion that suddenly rights itself, I saw it. Athena did not look like Helen, at least not in a way that anyone who knew them both would mistake one for the other, but there were clear similarities. And in every way that she did not look like Helen, she looked like me.

"We have a daughter," repeated Helen, "and you never told me." I was utterly dumbstruck. The thought that this woman—my friend, ally and mentor—was my own offspring was beyond my ability to integrate into my world. So many questions. And worst of all the feeling of complete incompetence in my perception, that I would miss something for years that Helen was able to detect in moments.

"Mom," said Athena. Hearing that word come out of her mouth wrapped a blanket around my heart.

"We were done with secrets," said Helen, walking right up to my face. There was no anger in her voice, but the pain was palpable. "Remember? Everything on the table? How long did you keep this from me?"

"Mom!" said Athena. Helen whirled at the sharp tone. "He didn't know."

Helen snapped out of the hurt shock she was sinking into and walked back to Athena. She held her fingers up to Athena's face, gently stroking her cheeks, then threw her arms around her. Athena hugged back, burying her face in her mother's shoulder. When they finally broke away from each other, Helen's face was covered in tears.

"Oh my God," she whispered. "Look at you. You are so beautiful." Athena smiled, moved in a way I had never seen in her eyes before.

Helen wiped her eyes with the heels of her palms, and said to me with a grin, "We have a daughter!" Then she ran to me and held me tightly. "We have a daughter," she whispered in my ear.

"I see that," I whispered back. What else could I say?

Helen kissed me on the cheek, and let go. She took Athena's hand, and sat her down on the couch.

"What can you tell me?" she asked.

"Not much," said Athena.

Helen shook her head. "Keep your future secrets. I want to know about you."

As I made the adjustment in my heart from Athena my friend to Athena my daughter, I watched her mother try to get to know all the things I had learned about this girl over seven years of my life and thirty-five years of hers. As joyous as this was for all three of us, it meant something that Athena surely knew, and Helen would realize soon enough. Athena and I were both assailed with unhappenings on a fairly regular basis. And she was my daughter. I was never going to return home, and Helen was going to become mother to a family in which she was the only person with an apparently constant life. Which meant she would spend every day wondering if it would be the last day she would ever see us.

If I didn't find a way to stabilize the unhappening effect, the woman I loved was already doomed to a life of the very worst kind of terror.

74

February 2146

Helen and Athena talked for four hours. Mostly, I kept out of their hair. I made dinner, occasionally interjected something clever, but otherwise simply basked in this mother and child preunion, and felt my love for both of them swell with every laugh. Once over the hurdle of the shocking discovery, it was a surprisingly simple matter to adopt Athena into my heart as my little girl. I reflected back on my relationship with her as Penelope, and the sibling-like quality it had (although it was never clear whether she was playing the role of little sister or big sister), and it all fell into place. It would take some getting used to, but it would be worth the transition. It did make me miss my own family, and consider how or if I would ever return to them, but I pushed that aside for the time being. It saddened me that Athena would never meet my parents until I remembered she already had.

Before she finally did depart, Athena agreed to pose for a family portrait. It manifested as three twenty-somethings smiling nervously, perhaps the best of friends, perhaps siblings or cousins. Only we would ever know it was two proud parents and their baby girl.

"You," said Helen once we were alone, "are the best father ever."

"How so?" I asked.

"Are you kidding me? She's amazing!"

"Maybe that's you," I said.

"She has your sensibilities," she said. "When she speaks, I can hear you in her voice. She also has a little of your darkness."

That brought me up short.

"My darkness? I don't want her to have my darkness." In fact, Athena's darkness had come to be her most familiar aspect to me. The thought that I had done that to her was a punch in the gut.

Helen took my hand.

"It makes her strong," she said. Then she let go and started spinning, and doing a little happy dance. "We have a daughter!" she sang. "And she's brilliant!" Then she stopped, and the look of joy and wonder on her face became something serious and contemplative. She came to me and held me. I could feel her sighing against my chest. When she looked up, I thought she was going to kiss me, but she just brushed my lips with her fingertip.

"I have to know this is real," she said. "I have to know it won't all vanish if we push it too hard. Can you promise me that?"

"Not yet," I said honestly.

She smiled at me, then took my own finger and kissed it. "Well, get on that."

75

February-May 2146

Helen began visiting me at home at the end of her workdays. Most evenings we stayed in. We alternated cooking dinner. Helen often brought work home, and it was fairly usual for her to work there while I read. In the winter, we did that in front of my fireplace, which for me was still a novelty. As it got warmer, we migrated to the screened-in porch.

Some evenings we went out. Took in a movie. Went to the symphony. Dinner at a fancy restaurant, occasionally even an extravagant one. The stipend I received for the work I was doing for my older self was absurdly grand, and I had also begun to experiment with ways to supplement that. The tricks a time traveler has at his disposal for accumulating wealth are so copious and so obvious that it required very little effort to be sure we would always be able to afford whatever entertainment struck our fancy.

We maintained two residences, but more and more hers became an abandoned shell. She kept most of her work clothes in my closet, and rarely went home unless she needed to get something. I programmed the locks on my house and car to recognize her key card, and she voice-printed on my home computer.

And every night, by agreement, until we could be sure, we kissed, and retired to our separate bedrooms.

On the whole, those three months were some of the most relaxing, carefree and rewarding times in either of our lives. It would prove to be our final calm as the storm began to brew.

[76]

May 2146

Athena came to see me one day in my basement lab. I was still working patiently on the unanswered question of stabilizing the unhappening effect.

"You don't write, you don't call," I said as soon as she blipped in. "Your mother and I have been worried sick."

"You know why Mom is funnier than you?" she asked.

"Why?"

"Her jokes sound much less rehearsed." She picked up a wrist module, turned it over in her hands, and put it back down.

"She is disappointed, by the way," I said. "She thought you would start visiting us now. She says she understands why you don't, but I know it makes her a little sad. She loves you to pieces."

Athena smiled at that. "Good."

"So. Athena. For real."

"Yeah," she said. "I'm a little surprised you guessed that, to be honest. And your reason threw me. Mom always said I sprang fully armored from your head, like it was part of a very important story. I always assumed she had given me that name when I was a baby. Turns out you beat her to it. Nice to know you can surprise me once in a while."

"You could have told me, you know."

"Ha!" she said. "There were times I almost did, just to see your reaction. There were also times I was sure you had figured it out. But it was always better for you not to know."

"Is that why you haven't been back? Because I know now?"

She shrugged. "I've been busy."

"Said the time traveler."

"Okay," she admitted. "I wanted to give you two some time to get used to the idea. It's only been a couple days for me since I saw you."

"Oh," I said. "Thank you, I guess. Are you staying for dinner? Helen is going to pitch a fit if she misses seeing you."

"It's best if she doesn't see me today."

"Oh." I sat. "You're here on business then?"

She nodded.

"You're going to tell me about Carlton, aren't you?"

Athena sat as well. "Yeah, that's what I'm here to do. There are things you need to know. And before you ask, yes, there are still things I can't tell you, and yes, there are still things I don't know. A lot more of the latter than the former, believe it or not."

I braced myself to hear about Helen's ex-lover, and the monster he apparently would become.

"Okay," I said.

Athena cleared her throat. Shifted in her seat.

"Carlton West, even as we speak, is already one of the wealthiest people in his generation. His family controls or has interest in more businesses than any one of them is even fully aware of. His second cousin is a United States Senator, and his Aunt is the Governor of Rhode Island. This is all background. The Carlton currently residing in 2146 has no interest in politics, and fleeing family expectations in that regard is one of the reasons he moved to France."

"But he becomes something later. Something powerful, right?"

"Can I get something to drink?" she asked. "My mouth has gone a bit dry."

"Of course," I said, hopping up. This was going to be big for her. We had already started down this road three times, and each time she had been reluctant—or forbidden—to give me details. My concern over the consequences of the story she was about to tell me now paled beside my concern for the well being of my child. "Water? Lemonade? Scotch?"

"A glass of water would be wonderful," she said. "If you could leave the bottle of scotch on the table, that would probably be a good idea too." I served her a glass of ice water with a slice of lemon from the refrigerator in my basement workshop. As instructed, a half-full bottle of scotch was also placed within reach.

She downed half the water in one long draw. Catching her breath, she continued.

"By 2148, that situation had changed. Carlton West had begun to dip his toe into French politics. As an American, his legal ability to influence French policy was limited, at least at first. In 2151, France suffered a major financial crisis. Her attempt to rejoin the European Union was declined by majority vote of the member states. In the wake of this crisis, the government began a slide into chaos that lasted a decade. There were power struggles, bloodless coups..." She took another sip of water. "And one coup that was not so bloodless. Long serving members of the French government were systematically swept aside, and new faces, including outsiders like Carlton West, seized the new opportunities for power. In 2162, France formed an alliance treaty with seven nations outside the EU, five of them on the Arabian Peninsula. Purges followed. There was a war."

She stopped. All of this was history to her, and near future to me, at least from my vantage point in my own future. From 2092—home—this was all a long way off. But Athena grew up in that world. I wondered how much of her childhood it tainted. I hoped Helen and I were able to shield her from the worst of it.

"At its peak, l'Empire de la France Nouvelle covers seventy percent of the European mainland, and ten percent of Africa, as well as parts of the Middle East. As of 2175, eight hundred and twenty million people have died, either as casualties of ongoing wars, victims of purges, or sufferers of starvation and disease as entire societies have collapsed. And in 2175, l'Empereur de la France Nouvelle is Carlton West."

"Dear God," I whispered. Images of mass suffering paraded across my eyes, and towering over all of them, the cruel, stark silhouette of a simple baby stroller, and loving parents with no idea what they had brought into the world. "Is that the timeline you are trying to unhappen? Or fix? Is that your assignment?" Again I pictured the baby. With creeping horror, I pictured my own baby standing over him, with a knife, or a garrote.

She shook her head.

"That timeline *is* the unhappening. In the original, unaltered timeline, France was provisionally re-admitted to the EU, and recovered in disgrace, but in peace. The motion, which carried by a margin of exactly one vote, succeeded in part because of the influence of Sylvia West, a high ranking diplomat, and Carlton's first cousin. By all accounts, in the original timeline, Carlton West was a powerful and eccentric businessman, whose oddities and occasional ambitions were tempered by his wife, a woman of ordinary breeding, and extraordinary character."

222

She downed the rest of her water, then poured two fingers of scotch over the remaining ice and lemon slice.

The possibility that I would black out from sheer guilt overload seemed very real at that moment.

"I did this," I said. "I made all of that happen."

"You did nothing of the sort. You met a magnificent woman, and you fell in love with her. More to the point, she fell in love with you. What happened after that was not in your control." She swirled the scotch in her glass, and took a swig. "None of this is exactly what I came to tell you."

"There's more?" I cried. "Somehow there's more?"

"You may want your own glass of scotch for this."

I took my swig directly from the bottle.

"Fair enough," she said. "Carlton West is a time traveler. He has access to the technology, although we do not yet know how he accomplished that. There is no evidence that anyone outside the Time Travel Project has successfully developed it independently. Fortunately for everyone in the world, with one exception, he has not used the technology as a combat weapon. We have even determined that absolutely no one other than he has used it. And so far, in twenty years of travel, he has only ever used it for a single purpose."

I stared at my daughter, and found my own darkness reflected in her eyes. Helen was right. It did make her strong. "To torment me."

"To torment you." She took another swig. "This is what I do now, nearly every day of my life. We find an instance where Carlton has tweaked your history, and I go counter-tweak it. I work for an organization whose entire reason for existing is to right the wrongs done to you by this one person."

"Thank you," I said humbly.

"You're welcome," she said. "And I love you, and I would do this for you no matter how many people were willing to help me, so I'm just as grateful that organization exists as you are."

"Are there other travelers? How many people do what you do?"

She looked away, sipped her whiskey.

"Including the undergrad version of you? Two."

"What? Why?"

"Because becoming a traveler means living the rest of your life in purgatory. You and I see the world in ways no one else ever can, and it's a curse. You know it's a curse. No one is ever recruited to do this. There were two others before me. One died. One deserted. We never replaced them. I am on my own."

I had no words of comfort for my daughter. Anything I could tell her she would have already known years before I ever had the chance to say it.

"Why you? Is it because you're my daughter? Did I do this to you?"

"I did it to myself," she said. "When I was fifteen, I stole a wrist module, because I wanted to meet... I wanted to see what you were like when you were younger. I became the girl you called Penelope. When the Project finally caught up with me, I was already a traveler. It was too late to save me, so they gave me an implant and a mission, and used what I had become to do good. It's the same reason I recruited you to help me, when I needed an extra pair of hands. You were already in purgatory. You had nothing to lose."

We sat in silence for a moment, as I took as much of this in, as well as I could.

"Why don't you stop him? Right now, while he's still powerless? Why waste your time on my problems?"

She tossed down the rest of her scotch, and poured two more fingers.

"First of all, he has never been powerless, so that's not really an option. But the real reason is that after years of these missions, we are still trying to figure out how to fix timelines. In over 500 jumps, my success rate is less than thirty percent. Time is complicated, Dad. That thing I asked you about killing the dog? That's the easiest decision in the world compared to the calls the Project has to make every single day." She took another sip of her scotch. "I tried seventy-five times to save Carrie Wolfe. All I ever did was push back the date she died." She wiped away a tear. "There are just too many variables. Too many ways to fuck up."

"What if I break it off with Helen right now? Tell her to go back to Carlton?" Just the idea made me dizzy.

"Very noble," said Athena, "but I'm pretty sure that window closed the moment she laid eyes on you. Like I said, it doesn't work that way. It's never that easy."

Simultaneously horrified and relieved, another awful twist occurred to me.

"If we did ever correct the timeline, make him never become Emperor, if Helen and I never met," I said, "what would happen to you?"

"To me?" she said. "I would survive. Multiple frames of reference again. Only the fact of me would be erased. The person would remain. After a fashion."

"After a fashion?"

She shrugged, but offered no explanation.

"What if you weren't a traveler?"

"Retroactively dead as a dishrag," she said, and finished her second scotch. I could see the alcohol beginning to affect her body language. "You haven't asked me the thing I was sure you were going to ask first," she said.

I took another swig from the bottle. The scotch was hitting me, too. I was getting drunk with my daughter. Something about that made me feel very warm.

"Do I want to know the answer?"

"Oh, I'm pretty sure you do."

I laughed, hoping we were thinking about the same thing. If not, my laughter would come back as pain. "Okay, here you go. Am I going to lose Helen? Is she going to unhappen to me?"

She shook her head. "No."

My heart nearly exploded with joy. "Never?"

Athena waved her hands in retraction.

"Well, I mean, she could still ditch you, so don't do anything stupid. But she can't unhappen. That's the one thing Carlton has never successfully changed, and believe me, he has tried. Good lord, how he has tried. But your relationship is as fixed as anything we have been able to measure. The only time he even came close was when he threw that girl Wendy into your bed. I fixed that in one try. Snapped it right back." She snapped her fingers for clarification. "Even in that timeline you were eventually going to leave her for Mom anyway, by the way. I just made it tidier for all of you."

I took another swig of scotch. My stomach briefly reminded me that alcohol is poisonous, but got over it. This was amazingly good news. In the face of all this uncountable horror, this was a ray of hope.

"Can I tell her?" I asked, dimly aware that I was slurring my speech.

Athena rolled her eyes. "Don't be an idiot," she said. "Why do you think I'm avoiding her today? She can't know any of this. It would break her."

"Even the part about her not unhappening?"

"And how would you explain that without owning why everything else unhappens?" she said. "Don't put this on her, Dad. Let her be happy for a little while. God knows she has her own trials ahead of her."

Struggling to find a way to ask about that, I must have reacted visibly, and probably drunkenly, to this omen, because Athena's face suddenly sank. She looked at her empty glass.

"Damn it," was all she said.

"What trials?" I asked as calmly as I could.

"Nope." Said Athena, getting to her feet, more than a little wobbly. "We're done. Give Mother my love. And sober up before she gets home."

She blipped away without further comment.

May 2146

When Helen came home, I had dinner waiting for her. Grilled salmon, asparagus with hollandaise sauce, wild rice, white zinfandel. I was attempting to put her at ease with some of her favorite foods before revealing that our relationship was in no danger from my curse. How I would avoid telling her that my curse now had a name—and its name was Carlton West—I had yet to work out. My preparations went underappreciated, however.

The very first thing she said to me when she came in the door, after a hello kiss, was, "Have you been drinking?"

"A little," I admitted.

"Alone?" Helen had a clear look of concern on her face, doubly so given that alcoholism was not yet on the very long list of things about me which she should reasonably have cause to monitor closely. The conversation hadn't even started and I was already behind.

"No," I said. "Athena was here."

Helen's face lit up. Then fell. "Wait. 'Was'? She's gone already? Poop. I wanted to see her. Did you tell her I wanted to see her?"

"I told her," I said.

"So she popped in and you started drinking? That feels like a story with a missing scene."

"She had a stressful day. I offered her a drink, and had one myself. Can we stop talking about this?" The defensiveness in my voice was obvious even to me, and did not help my case.

"Ooooo-kay," said Helen. Her face lit up again. "Do I smell salmon?" I led her into the dining room, where our meals sat on plates under covers to keep them warm. When I lifted hers off, and the hollandaise and salmon scented steam rolled out, she made a little squeal of delight, clapped and pulled up her chair. She took a bite without waiting for me to sit down. We were back on track.

"Mmmmm," she said. "Why are you trying to butter me up?" There was no accusation in her tone, but I knew her well enough to know there didn't have to be. Helen was not prone to anger or suspicion. But she was keenly perceptive, and had excellent reasons for wanting full disclosure from me in every aspect of our life together. I still tried to dodge her.

"What do you mean?"

She put her fork down. "What happened today?"

I sighed, hoping to seem like a surprise had been spoiled.

"Athena just gave me some very good news, and I made a little celebratory dinner to share with you." I pouted. "I'm not very good at this kind of thing, I know."

Now she did look suspicious.

"Okay," she said evenly, "what's the news?"

"Wow. I wanted to give this a little more fanfare or something, but here goes: she says our relationship can't unhappen. For some reason, it stays constant even when other things around it change."

"That's very convenient," she said. Not exactly the stirring hurrah I hoped for. She wiped her mouth with her napkin, then got up from her chair. Waving for me to pull my chair out, she waited for me to do so, then sat on my lap, still no indication of excitement or joy evident in her features. She kissed me softly, once.

"Please tell me what else she said."

I sighed, this time for real.

"I can't," I said.

"Come on," she said. "We are way past this. Big girl? Remember? Just tell me what it is."

"Okay," I said. "Sit. Eat your dinner." She returned to her seat. I took a bite of my fish, with absolutely no awareness of how it tasted. "She really did say that our relationship is safe."

"I believe you," she said. "And if I had to guess, I'd say she also told you why that is, without using the words, 'for some reason.' Am I correct?"

Despite myself, I laughed.

"Actually, she really doesn't know why that is."

"So what's the other bombshell?"

"You are really not going to like it," I said.

"All the more reason not to drag this out. You tell me, we face it together. That's how we roll, right?"

"Right," I said, bracing myself. "Okay. Please don't be upset. She said the reason my life keeps unhappening, even counting all the times before I met you... is because of Carlton." I paused there, holding for questions.

"Keep talking."

I forged on. "She says he is a time traveler, like her, and that he has been using the technology to torment me. I'm sorry. I feel like this is all my fault. Like I dragged you into this, and now we're both being punished, and that's not fair." By the time I heard how badly I was rambling, it was already out there. Still, she did not react.

"Is that all? Was there anything else?"

Don't tell her. "Yes. She said Carlton becomes some kind of dictator in the future. There's a war, and a lot of people are going to die. And that feels like my fault too."

She took another bite of her fish. Swallowed. A forkful of rice. Still no reaction. I had no idea what to do or say.

"Helen?"

"Yes?"

"Are you... are we okay?" I couldn't think of an even remotely adequate question, but in my attempt to do so, I had stumbled across the worst possible one.

"No," she said. Then she ate a spear of asparagus.

I sat, helpless, silently begging her to say something else, knowing whatever I said next would continue to make things exponentially worse. I tried to eat my meal, and watched a tear fall onto my plate. This went on for about ten more minutes, which was just enough time for Helen to finish everything on her plate and drain her glass of wine.

Then she got up, put her jacket back on, and walked out the door.

78

May 2146

Helen did not return that night. Now that I was working from home, the next day was one long exercise in patience. Unable to do anything productive, I spent the entire day waiting for her to walk in the door at the end of it. I made beef stroganoff, another dish for which she had a fondness. Half of it ended up in a container in my refrigerator, after my solitary dining experience. Mary Sue offered me vague feline consolation, but even she seemed to be asking where Helen was.

Day three consisted mostly of me trying to work up the courage to go after her. By noon, I had pulled myself together enough to attempt to call her, which was rewarded by an immediate forward to voice mail. Seeing her face on my tablet screen cheerfully asking me to leave a message gave me a very brief opportunity to imagine her being happy to see me. At two in the afternoon, I called the library with a fabricated story about her tablet being on the fritz, and asked if they could page her to the vid at the circulation desk. I was told she had not been to work in two days, in a tone that implied the librarian finally had an idea why his curator had gone missing.

Day four, I manned up and ventured out to her home. There was no sign of her car, and predictably no answer at the door. I took out my key card hesitantly, trying to decide just how inappropriate it would be to let myself in. The decision was taken away from me by the lock's failure to recognize my code.

Day five I spent in the reading room of the print collection, with no realistic hope she would show up. Day six I spent at the aquarium, quite alone.

By the end of one full week without her, I began to understand how things unhappen to normal people.

79

May 2146

Day eight ended with me sitting on the floor, my back to the couch in front of my fireplace, staring at the blue and orange flames. In their hypnotic dance, I found a sort of focus I was unable to achieve on my own. The topic of my contemplations that evening was a plan for how I would return to my own time. Abandoning my work would be easy, as it was all meaningless to me now. My time nomad plan from months earlier was no longer viable, as I considered that too likely to be enjoyable. What I really needed was to return to my life of inconstant drudgery, with a new unfulfilling job randomly assigned to me every few weeks. Athena said I lived in purgatory, and I was ready to embrace that as my destiny.

I didn't hear the front door open, but I did see her walk into the room. For a moment, I considered the likelihood that I was hallucinating her, and didn't dare leap up to greet her, for fear that the resulting crash of reality would break me for good. Real or imaginary, she planted herself on the floor next to me.

"Watcha doin'?" asked Helen.

"Watching a fire," I said.

"How come?"

I shrugged, without looking at her.

"Fire is pretty. This place has been in a beauty shortage for a while."

She leaned against me, slipped her arm into the crook of my elbow, and rested her head on my shoulder. We sat like that for a while, with no sense of time, and no need for it.

Eventually, I asked, "Where did you go?"

"Paris," she said.

I had no possible reaction to that. "Oh," I said. For a while, I decided I was waiting for her to offer some further explanation, or maybe even a clear path to reconciliation, but by the time I had worked out how to ask her for either of those things, she had already fallen asleep.

[80]

May 2146

I woke to the smell of coffee and bacon, still on the living room floor, a feather pillow under my head and a blanket covering the rest of me. I shambled into the kitchen to find Helen at the stove, making an omelet.

"Good morning," she said.

"Hey," I said, trying to blink myself awake.

"How hungry are you?"

I thought about that.

"Two eggs hungry," I said. She slid the omelet onto a plate, then chopped about a third of it off with the spatula and slid that piece onto another plate for herself.

"Two egg omelet," she said, placing it on my kitchen table next to a cup of coffee, a glass of orange juice and a cloth napkin. "Bon appétit."

It was cheddar, mushroom and chopped bacon, and quite delicious.

"I tried to call you," I said.

"I know. I'm sorry I didn't call back."

I shrugged off the apology. "You were upset."

"Not at you." She put her plate down at the spot next to mine, and pulled up a chair.

I frowned. "It sure seemed like you were upset with me," I said.

She took a bite, apparently to buy her a little time to respond.

"Yeah, I was at first," she finally admitted. "Not now."

"Why not?" I asked.

"Because you told me the truth, which was exactly what I asked you to do. It's not your fault the truth was so abominable."

I poked at my food. "Should I ask you how your week was?"

"You can if you want. I'm going to tell you about it whether you ask or not, but if it makes you feel more in control, I'll wait for you to ask." She paused.

"How was your week?"

"I went to see Carlton. We had a pretty big fight. The details of that probably aren't important. What is important is that I believe you. Every word."

"Oh," I said. "Um..."

"You don't have to say anything. You already said what you needed to say, and I walked out on you when I should have been thanking you." She stopped there, and ate a bit of her omelet.

"It's okay," I said. "I shouldn't have dumped all that on you. Athena told me not to, and I did it anyway, and I wish I hadn't. I completely understand that you would be upset with me for telling you things you couldn't believe about someone you loved."

She took my hand and looked me in the eyes. "I wasn't upset because what you said was unbelievable. I was upset because it rang true."

"Oh," I said again.

"When we first met, I was young. He was dashing, and exotic, and it was so very, very easy to fall for him. The fact that there were power dynamics in his family that made a relationship between us impossible just fueled it all the more. When he told me he loved me, it felt so dramatic, and important. Like he was willing to defy the world just to be with me." She paused there, pushed her omelet around with her fork and took a tiny bite. After a moment, she continued.

"It's easy to look back on a failed relationship and see all the things about it that made it wrong. At the time, all I could feel was the romance. It was so easy to see myself as the Juliet to his Romeo, and so hard to remember what a stupid story that is, and how horribly it ends for everyone involved."

"I'm sorry," I said.

She shook her head. "Don't. It's okay. I loved an idealized version of Carlton, and I loved the story I thought we were playing out. But I'm not the smitten girl I was, and the rose colored glasses have faded to something darker over the last three years. I wanted so badly to hate you for telling me those things about him, but I wanted to hate you because it was easier than hating myself for already thinking them."

"Oh God," I said. "You didn't tell him—"

"No," she said. "I didn't tell him any of what Athena told you. Um..." She winced. "He does know about you now, though. I'm sorry about that."

"Great," I said. "I don't suppose that was going to stay secret forever anyway. So, what did you talk about?"

She shied away. "I don't really want to go into detail. It was a huge blowup, and we both said things we probably didn't mean. But the way he said those things... I believe he can become the man you described. I think I've always believed it on some level. I just foolishly imagined that I could change him."

This would have been the appropriate time to inform her that she could, in fact, have changed him. That with her help, he could find the restraint not to destroy the world. I want to believe the reason I held my tongue at that moment was I knew how badly it would hurt her to know it, and what she knew about him now might have jeopardized that influence anyway. They had just had a huge fight. It was probably too late for her to make it all better, and even if she did, it would mean sacrificing herself to a lifetime of misery married to man she now truly believed was just one bad day away from becoming a monster. That's what I want to believe. But she didn't ask, and that's why I didn't say.

"So," said Helen. "That's over. The answer to your question from a week ago is yes, I am okay. Yes, we are okay. I'm sorry I said no. I was mistaken."

"Understood," I said.

"Good. Now about this other matter, that our relationship can't unhappen, she's sure about that, right?"

"As far as I know," I said. "She did say they don't know why it's true, but apparently there have been dozens of times it could have unhappened, and it always holds."

"Excellent. That's excellent. Because..." She leaned into my ear and whispered, "I do believe we have a baby to make."

Neither of us pointed out that Athena was not due to be born for another four years

81

June 2146/May 2115

One evening, while Helen and I were home playing Scrabble, a dull flash of light came from our kitchen. By the time my brain had registered the new stimulus, Helen was already out of her chair (having toppled it doing so), and in the next room. I came in to find mother and daughter in a tight embrace. Helen's face was not visible from that angle, but I could see Athena balancing embarrassment and adoration in a kind of eye-rolling smile.

"Hi, Mom," she said.

Helen kissed her with a loud "Mwah!"

"I need to borrow Nigel," said Athena.

Helen took my arm and stood her ground. "Anything you have to tell him you can say to me, too." It sounded about as rehearsed as my bad jokes.

"It's something I have to show him."

"Oh," said Helen, deflated. "But then you'll do a time travelly thing and bring him back seconds later, and then we can have tea, right?" She nodded with an open-mouthed smile.

Athena laughed lightly. "Yes, Mother."

"Splendid! I'll put the kettle on."

I took Athena's hand.

"This is what you do to her," I said.

"I like it," she said, and then the world flashed.

We were in the park again. Carlton's mother was giving him a bottle.

"Are you going to kill baby Carlton?" I asked bluntly.

"Not today," she said with equal candor. "A narrow minority of our computer models show that executing him as a child results in no net improvement to history."

I stared at her. "But you would. If those models said it would work."

She nodded. "If that were the assignment."

"Have you ever killed anyone?" I asked my baby girl.

"Not directly," she said. "I have done things that caused people to die."

"Oh," I said. What else was there to say?

"You can't go home," she said suddenly. "2092. Or 2094 which is what it would be now relative to how much you have aged."

"Wait, what?" This came as more than a surprise. I had stayed out of contact with the older version of me for more than two years, at his command, but all that time I had assumed I would somehow end up becoming him, and I would need to return to the late twenty-first century at some point to do that. I hadn't planned quite that far ahead, but I had already started considering how I could minimize the effects of bringing Helen with me when I did. Now it sounded like that would be moot, and as much as I should have been in terror of losing my old life, I found my primary reaction was relief I would no longer need to concern myself with how to reconcile that life with Helen. Then the secondary concern of the impossibility of it all kicked in.

"Why?"

"Because there is already a version of you living that life in that time."

As impossible as it seemed for my future self to exist without my return to my past, this development seemed even more so. "How?"

"Multiple frames of reference," she said. "Remember? As a traveler, there are plenty of ways that could be accomplished."

I shook my head, dazed. "I still don't understand."

"You saw that effect yourself when you went back five minutes. There were two of you. What do you think would have happened if you had convinced him not to travel back those five minutes himself?"

"Paradox?" I guessed.

She shook her head. "Not for us. Paradoxes are for the fixed. No such thing for a traveler. If you had stopped him, there would be two of you now."

"Seriously?" She nodded. "Does that mean every time I travel I create another Nigel? How many of me are there?" I tried to keep the panic out of my voice, but this new consequence of time travel was beyond my capacity for bravery. Why hadn't she ever told me this before?

238

"Relax, Chief," she said. "That's not what it means. Yes, it is possible to create duplicates. We discovered that by experimenting with mice. But it's not something that happens by accident. It has to be deliberately initiated. If it makes you feel any better, there aren't any duplicates of me out there anywhere. It's always been me. You calling me Una was more insightful than you knew."

The moment of terror passed. "What about the older me? Dr. Walden? Is he another duplicate?"

"Probably not," she said. "But maybe. We're still looking into that, but we think he's the same version of you that replaced you in 2092."

"But still me, right?"

She nodded. "Very much so. A duplicate isn't a second generation copy. You are both just as much Nigel Walden as the other."

I thought on this for a moment. "You said if I had stopped myself that one time I went back five minutes, I would have made another duplicate, right?"

"That's right."

"But I didn't stop him," I said. "What happened to him?"

She shrugged. "Anyone's guess. We still don't know a lot about how it works, just that it does. If it makes you feel better, he probably just became you, with overwritten memories. You basically reabsorbed him. Or he reabsorbed you. Either way, he's not out there anywhere."

I caught my breath for a moment, pushing past the queasy feeling that I almost inadvertently cloned myself.

"But I didn't do anything like that in 2092. There shouldn't be any extra Nigels out there at all."

"I know," she said. "We're still trying to determine exactly how this happened. The most likely explanation is that your future self somehow colluded with your past self, but we don't know how he did that without you remembering it." She put her hand on my knee. "The important part is that you can't go back. There are too many ways you could injure the timeline."

I took this in. All of it. Wrapped in this new and disturbing side effect to the technology that had become the driving force in my life was a spectacular silver lining. My parents wouldn't need to lose me. A Nigel, a real Nigel, would continue to be their son. With any luck he would play out to be less of a disappointment. Perhaps not even be plagued by the same unhappenings. I would miss them, terribly, but they would still have a son, and that might be enough for me.

But even better, the last shackle holding me back from a life with Helen had just snapped in my mind. She was immune to my unhappenings, and now I was free to stay in her time. It was very easy to step back and take this in as the best news ever. And as I looked at my daughter, the daughter I now knew Helen and I could have without some dire peril to the universe, the other silver lining presented itself.

"I'm okay with that," I said. "Not going back means I get to raise you." I gave her my best happy father face. She smiled, but there was an odd hesitation to it.

"Yeah," she said simply. Her gaze tracked back to the young father, burping his son, laughing.

"Yeah," I said.

82

June 2146

On a sunny weekend in June, I took Helen back to the aquarium. Our first time here had been an emergency vacation day, with me in terrible need of a distraction. This time it was simple recreation. There were no immediate or obvious crises on our doorstep, nothing had unhappened in a while, and I had recently learned that my stay in this future was to be permanent. Helen received that news with equal parts sympathy and self-interested relief. When I told her the sympathy was unnecessary, the relief overflowed.

We took our time meandering through the different sections. I got us tickets to the dolphin show, which we missed last time, and against her protests insisted that we sit well outside the splash zone. When we got to the ray tank, her eyes lit up again. The moment wasn't entirely as magical as in our first trip here, but it still served quite nicely. After giving her a minute or so of quiet absorption with that look of wonder on her face that never got old for me, I loudly cleared my throat.

She turned to find me on my knee.

"Oh my God. Nigel, what are you doing?" She was blushing, a rarity for her, which I found entertaining in a way I would never, ever admit.

"Helena Clay," I began, "from the moment I met you in your black biker jacket, I have known I wanted to spend my life with you. You have given me support when no one else could, even before you understood what it was for. I have learned more from you than I have from anyone or any experience in my life. No one in the world makes me laugh the way you do, and I am utterly, utterly in love with you." I produced a small box from my pocket and opened it. "Helen, will you marry me?"

She was biting her knuckle, and it was entirely unclear whether she was holding back tears, laughter, or both. "Really?" she said finally. "The stingray tank?"

"It was this or the Ferris wheel, and the carnival isn't in town."

"Get up," she said. I complied. She held her hand out. I gave her the box. She removed the ring, and looking at it, not me, she handed the box back. She held it up to her right eye, and watched the rays do their ballet through it.

Then she slipped it on her finger, and threw her arms around me. Only when the applause began did I realize how many people had gathered to watch us.

[83]

July 2146

On a Wednesday morning in early July, as had been the case with the Slinky Probe discovery, my time travel breakthrough happened entirely by accident. I had been experimenting with the wrist modules, specifically seeing how they responded to being sent into the future in the chamber, rather than under their own power. I had no idea what I expected to see from this, but any measurable difference between their state after a jump on their own and an externally induced jump might give me something to work with.

The accident happened when I got the two modules confused. After this incident, I marked one with an X in felt-tip. But at that moment, they were indistinguishable.

Stage one of the experiment was to send one of the modules one minute into the future on its own. I did so, and recorded every observable measurement of the effects on both the device and the character of the jump field. Stage two was to send that module one minute into the future by strapping it to the other one. Again, lots of measurements, negligible differences. Stage three was to send the module one minute into the future in the chamber. I meant to send the same module I had used in stage one and deactivated for stage two, but, as I said, I mixed them up.

The module which was still active and already set for a one minute forward jump was placed in the chamber, which was also set for a one minute forward jump. If I had been doing this deliberately, my best guess at a result would have been a single jump two minutes forward. I would have been wrong. When I activated the chamber, the module just sat there. There was no visual evidence that anything had happened at all. The jump field meters told a fantastically different story. The strength of the field was the square of what it would have been for a single one minute jump, and it was generating a standing wave in a form I had not yet observed, nor had anyone in the literature I spent the next two days combing through. I had discovered a means of creating a powerful jump field whose net influence was absolutely zero.

Which meant, I desperately hoped, I had found a means of cancelling the unhappening effect.

[84]

July 2146

When Helen came home that day, the modules were on our dining room table.

"Is this dinner?" she asked.

"Dinner is waiting at the establishment of Madame's pleasure," I said. "We have a lot to celebrate today. Maybe."

"One thing at a time," she said. "But talk to me while I change."

"You don't want to hear about this first?"

"Must multitask," she said. "Fiancé says I need to pick a restaurant. So much to do..." She walked as she spoke, leaving a trail of clothes behind her.

After taking a moment to love the sound of the word *fiancé*, I followed her into the bedroom. She was throwing dresses onto the bed.

"I think I found a way to stop things from unhappening to me."

Helen emerged from the closet in nothing but her underwear and a look of shock.

"Talk to me," she said.

"The details are pretty complicated."

"Tell me the parts I will understand," she said, slipping into something black. "And do remember that I am smarter than you."

"Noted. I was fiddling with the wrist modules today, and I accidentally figured out how to get them to generate a jump field of huge magnitude and zero effect, manifesting in a standing wave."

"Oh my! That sounds…" She stopped herself. "I totally want to pretend I get how significant that is. What would I say if that were true?"

"You would talk about how that might be an indicator that it is possible to negate the unhappening effect, by applying the attributes of that standing wave to a traveler."

"Yes!" she declared. "Pretend I said that! Zip me."

"We do need to talk about what this means," I said to her back as I pulled her zipper into place.

"Which we can do over Thai food. Just tell me two things right now."

"Go," I said.

"One: will this in any way threaten my immunity to your bugaboo?"

"I can't see how it would," I said. "What I'm hoping is that I can fix myself, sort of ground myself to time, so that whenever the timeline changes, you and I will see the same thing, and neither of us will notice it. That shouldn't affect your immunity at all. If anything, it might make it stronger. We will ride it together, never aware of whatever it was that changed."

"Good. Then two: what do we do to make this happen, and how soon can we do it?" The levity in her voice finally collapsed. This was Helen's Holy Grail. Both of ours. If I was right, if we could make this happen, we had a real shot at happily ever after.

I took a moment to collect myself before answering that one. No part of this was going to be simple, or easy, and I needed her to know that up front. Our Thai restaurant conversation was about to be laden with plans, details, caveats and hopes, but what she needed to hear right now was that the first hurdle was going to be huge.

"If I am going to make this work," I said, "there is no way I can do all the research alone. It's time for me to finally have a long sit down with Dr. Nigel Walden."

[85]

July 2146

For three years, my employer had provided me with the most advanced equipment available, a private lab, a home, a car, and a stipend that surely put to shame the salaries of every tenured professor at the university. His only two requirements of me were that I work entirely in secret, and that I never, under any circumstances, contact him directly. I violated the former two years into the assignment when I sent Helen's tablet one minute into the future. Today was the day I would violate the latter. Either I would find the answer to my life's quest, or get fired.

For three years, I had successfully dodged this person. That alone was fairly striking, considering we worked in relatively close proximity and I had gotten to know a number of the other professors and staff on sight from casual interactions. Add to that the fact that I was technically one of his research assistants, and he was responsible for oversight of the entire project, and it was an impressive elusiveness. Yes, we were operating in strictly isolated cells, with complicated rules of communication that kept us all at least three degrees away from each other, and yes, he was also invested in avoiding me. However, the law of large numbers virtually guaranteed that given enough random interactions, one of them was bound to be with him. And yet, never.

I made an appointment with him through the physics department secretary, who asked me why I didn't simply visit during his office hours.

I explained that the matter was of a classified nature. Given the structure of the Time Travel Project, this explanation apparently held enough water to get me a time slot.

Helen and I went there together. I made her promise to wait outside while I spoke with him. She agreed, under protest. She found herself a nice chair in the department lounge, wished me luck, and dove into a book.

Dr. Nigel Walden's office was at the end of the hall, and the long walk made the experience of meeting with him seem more ominous than was apropos. I tried to remember this person was essentially me, but all I could think of was the shattered husk of a man who had whisked me away on false pretenses to set me on a fool's errand he most likely didn't even understand. This was not going to go well, no matter what happened next.

I rapped on the frosted glass pane on his door.

"Come in!" I heard myself say.

He sat at his desk, which was a motley display of tablets, books and yellowed printouts.

"What can I do for you?" he asked, and we both froze.

Here's what we each saw:

Behind this messy desk sat a man easily fifteen kilos heavier than the version of me who had come back in time to recruit me three times in one day over six years. The battered, weathered look of age was far less pronounced on him than what I had seen in that man's face. Unlike the craggy, unshaven look I expected to see, this man had a full beard, quite gray and well on its way to becoming a Santa Clause affectation.

Across from that desk stood a man of twenty-seven, who bore a resemblance to this man's youth so strong, only one explanation was possible. To his shock, he was looking at his own person, surely having traveled through time from the past to this point.

Most upsettingly, to me, was the realization that I had not succeeded in avoiding myself as well as I thought. In point of fact, I recognized this man, and had probably seen him at a distance at least a dozen times in the past year alone. And yet, on this close inspection, there was no denying that this was a version of me.

But absolutely not the version I had been working for.

[86]

July 2146

"My God," he said softly, then whispered, "Close the door!" He rose from his desk and came right up to my face, grinning. "Oh! Look at you! My God! This is incredible!" His hands came up, and for a second I thought he was going to grab my shoulders, but he thought better of it. "Tell me everything!"

I had no idea how to respond to any of this.

"You know who I am?" I said, attempting to at least establish a baseline.

"Of course," he said. "You're me. I think. You are me?"

"I am you," I confirmed.

He clapped and giggled, overcome with giddiness. "It works! It absolutely works! Oh, my boy, this is the best moment of my life."

This man, who was clearly an older version of myself, bore so little resemblance to the last time I had seen him, that for the first time, I felt a nagging doubt that the other version was actually me. But no, that one was also obviously an elderly mirror, just with a different set of emphasized characteristics. The phrase "evil twin" sprang unfortunately to mind, and I pushed it aside. But more than just their physical appearances diverged. The other old me was a broken man, a shadow of this one. Here was a man who delighted in wonder, with the courage to embrace the unknown, and a joy at discovering it. And all I could think of as I watched him and listened to him was that this was who I could have been if I hadn't chosen the path of isolated detachment. This is who I could have become if my life had never unhappened. And as I saw that in his eyes, I sadly realized that of the two future versions of myself, the one more like me by far was the other one. The broken one.

"When?" he asked.

"2092 version, although more like 2095 by now," I said, shaking myself out of my ruminations. "I've been living here for three years, working on the Time Travel Project. Do you remember recruiting me?"

"Recruiting you?" he said, frowning. "No, I didn't recruit you. Why would I recruit you? *How* would I recruit you?"

"You came to see me three times," I said. "Once when I was at MIT, and twice about two years after I graduated. You brought me here with a wrist module, and asked me to help you perfect it, because there was some flaw you couldn't isolate."

"Slow down," he said. He gestured to a table in the back of his office. "Sit." We both sat.

"None of that happened," I said. "Did it?"

"Not to me," he said. "Not yet, anyway. Did this future me look my age? Older?"

"Older," I said. It was now obvious that the version of me who recruited me was from further in the future than he had planted me. I could think of a few reasons that might be the case, but no reasonable explanation for why he wouldn't tell me that, or include this version of us in the plan. Worse, it meant that at some point in this Dr. Walden's near future, something would wreck him and make him into that pathetic creature. The gee-whiz qualities in him I already found so endearing would fade. He would become more like me.

"What's a wrist module?" he asked. I had brought one with me in a messenger bag, and produced it for him to see. He gently turned it in his hands, looking it over with awe and glee. "Please tell me this is a time machine."

"You've never seen one of these?"

He shook his head.

"We are at least five years off from this technology. I have a plucky young woman slated to be our first traveler when it's ready to roll out."

"Andrea?" I asked.

He nodded, still enraptured by the device.

"Don't tell her. It's still a secret."

"Mum's the word." I pulled out my tablet, and sent Helen a single word of text. "Listen, I think we've both been played by a future version of us, and I really think we need to find out why. I don't mean to alarm you, but

I'm not sure he was quite all there. If there's something down the road for you that makes you a little unstable and prone to bizarre time travel behavior, we need to avert that."

"Agreed," he said. "The first thing we need to do is establish what it was he really wanted you to do here."

"He said he wanted me to perfect the module."

"That's nonsense," said this future me. "If it worked well enough for me to use it, it's already safe and accurate. My risk-taking days are well behind me." He shook his head and smiled. "I'm not you anymore."

"Ugh. Well, if he didn't really need me working on this project, what the hell am I here for?"

There was a tap at the door. Helen opened it cautiously.

"Hey," she said. "I got your text. I'm here. Wow," she added, seeing my future self. "I'm... It's really a pleasure to meet you, Dr. Walden."

"Come in," I said. "Sorry about this," I said to my future self. "This is Helen, she knows all about the situation. We're... Well, that's a long story." He stared at her. It was awkward, and confusing. "Hey," I said, snapping my fingers in front of his eyes.

He looked at me, and whispered, "Oh, no."

I was going to ask him what he was suddenly afraid of, and then recognized the look in his eyes. It wasn't fear. It was the look of a man who had just been hit with a dopamine dart. It was love at first sight.

My reason for being planted in this time, at this place, had never been about time travel. It had always been about Helen.

[PART 5]
CARLTON

[87]

July 2146

My seventy-nine-year-old doppelgänger was already falling for my fiancée. Setting aside the fact that it was a mild struggle to convince myself this was no logical cause for jealousy, it gave me some unexpected insight into my relationship with her. Apparently, Helen's effect on me—any version of me—was quite magical.

"Snap out of it," I reminded him.

He looked at me plaintively.

"Would I really do that? Could I really be that person?"

"I wish I knew," I said.

"But surely this would never even work. Don't you still need to return to your home time, and eventually become me?"

"We operate in multiple frames of reference simultaneously," I said. "I can lay it out for you when we get a free moment, but the short answer to your question is no, I don't."

"What's going on, guys?" Helen's smile was warm, but nervous. Just being in our combined presence must have been difficult to absorb. It was about to become more so.

"Please sit," I said. My older self stood while Helen came to the table, and sat when she did. Memo to self: eventually learn some courtesy. "I think," I began, and then looked to my older self for confirmation. "We think?"

He nodded.

"We think I may have been brought here, to this time, just to meet you."

Helen stared at me, then stared at Older Me, then slumped back into her seat, mute with shock. I had no idea what to say to her, and hoped this was not about to be the day I finally lost everything.

Finally, she said, "I like it. It's psychotic, but irresistibly romantic."

"Is she kidding?" Older Me asked.

"I don't think so," I said.

She looked me in the eyes. "You crossed half a century just to be with me? How is this not a fairy tale?"

How it was not a fairy tale would be spelled out in eight hundred and twenty million corpses. While I knew she sincerely loved the notion that we were so meant to be even space-time itself could not keep us apart, she would not find the consequent global sacrifice quite as enchanting.

"But..." she began slowly, "why would you do that? How would you know?"

"At some point we must have met," said Older Me, "and I must have had feelings for you. Honestly, I've known you for two minutes and I already have a crush."

"Steady," I said.

He ignored me. "But look at me," he said, spreading his arms. "I'm an old man. What are you, twenty-five?"

"Twenty-seven," Helen and I said in unison.

"That's fifty-two years," he said. "I could never woo a woman fifty-two years my junior. We must have been friends, and it must have driven me mad to know you without being with you."

"You say this like you don't know," she said. "Didn't you bring my Nigel to this time?"

My heart tripped at the phrase "my Nigel." I think his did as well.

"No," I said. "The Future Me I met before was older than... Dr. Walden. Five, maybe even ten years. And much less with it. Whatever happened, hasn't happened yet."

"But why would I take the risk?" he asked. "How could I even know it would work?"

Helen took my hand. "Maybe it was my idea," she said. "Maybe I fell for you, too, and we decided together it was the only way we could be happy?"

I couldn't let this continue.

"It wasn't your idea," I said. "It couldn't have been."

"Why not?"

I closed my eyes, dreading the next minute of my life. "Because in the original timeline, Future Me didn't meet you until much later than this. And by then... you were already married." My self-imposed darkness was matched with a room full of silence. When I finally dared open my eyes, Helen's were right in front of them.

"This was all to keep me away from my husband."

"Apparently," I admitted weakly.

Helen stood. I feared she was about to walk out again, but she moved around the table to Dr, Walden, and for an instant, I thought she might slap him. Instead, she kissed him full on the mouth. Watching him try to figure out what to do with his hands was unexpectedly hilarious.

"Thank you," she said when she was finished, "for saving me from that."

"You are quite welcome," he sputtered, "I assure you."

"Don't thank us yet." I said.

"Why?" they both asked.

After a heavy, trepid sigh, I said, "Because we still have a war to prevent."

I never got to finish that thought, because that was the moment I had my very first real-time unhappening.

[88]

July 2146

Dr. Walden's office transformed into a concrete cell. There was no warning, and no sense of transition. I looked down to see myself garbed in a safety orange jumpsuit. It is a bit telling that my first reaction to this sudden and terrifying shift in reality was not horror and desperation, but a disappointment that whatever advances had been made in the law-abiding world of 2146 evidently did not apply to prisons.

I whispered to my left forearm, "Tell me you're still there." It tingled. The module implant was still in place. As long as I had that, I was free to go any time I wanted. But, without knowing why I was here, and what the new timeline entailed, escape might hold even greater dangers for me. I chose patience.

My greatest concern, obviously, was Helen. The immunity our relationship held to these unhappenings would protect her, I hoped, but without knowing why I was here, and where she was, it was difficult for me to imagine her being safe.

I only had to endure two hours of fear and misery before I was told I had a visitor. Specifically, my "sister." As expected, this turned out to be Athena.

"What kept you?" I asked as flippantly as I could. It was a struggle.

"Don't," she said. "It took us three days to find you. This is bad, and you need to listen carefully. Got it?" I nodded. "Good. You are presently awaiting execution for a homicide. That is scheduled to happen in two days, so you need to be out of here by then."

"Who?" I asked. It was the only piece of this that mattered.

"Wendy," she said. "I am so sorry, Nigel. Please don't ask me anything else about the crime until we get this sorted out."

I felt faint. "Did I do it? Can you tell me that much?"

"You did not," she said. "Please don't ask any more questions. I have instructions, and I need you to follow them."

"Okay," I said numbly.

My arm tingled. "I am sending a jump course to your module right now," she said. "It will activate thirty minutes after lights out tonight. I will bring you up to speed on everything at the rendezvous."

"Understood," I said. "Is there anything I should do until then?"

Her eyes bored into mine. "Don't. Get. Killed."

I didn't get killed. Thirty minutes after lights out, and very much awake, I flashed out of my cell. I was on the roof of an unknown building, in the middle of the day. Athena handed me a bundle of clothing, and I stripped out of the jumpsuit.

"Can you save her?" was all I asked.

"I don't know," she said. "And you should know right now that saving her isn't the assignment. My task is to provide you with an alibi. I am exceptionally good at that, so this will be over for you very soon." She kissed me, and added, "I will try. I promise you I will try."

For just over an hour, I waited for Athena's return. When she did reappear, her forehead was bleeding, but not enough to explain the quantity of blood on her clothes.

"Find Helen," she said. "By now you've been missing for two days. Do not travel back those two days. Just go home."

"My God," I said. "Are you all right?"

"No." I reached for her. "Don't touch me!" she shrieked. "I don't have another change of clothes for you!"

I wanted so badly to comfort her, and her only allowable priority was not covering me in suspicious blood. As badly as I did not want to ask this, I had to.

"Wendy?"

Athena looked away. "I was able to save her from being murdered," she said. "But not from being raped."

With that, she vanished.

259

89

July 2146

How long have we known each other?"

"Oh! God!" said Helen. "Stingrays! Get in here!" She pulled me in the door to our house, and held me. "Where have you been? Athena said she had to get you out of prison? What happened? Are you okay?"

"I don't know," I said. "I guess so. Better than some, anyway." Helen did not ask me to elaborate, and I did not volunteer. What happened to Wendy was now on my conscience, but as far as Helen was concerned, it was already part of the timeline. Old news. I did not want to admit to her that in the proper timeline, it had never happened.

"You're safe now," she said. "Can I get you something to eat? Do you want to take a bath? What can I do?"

"Those both sound good," I said, but mostly for her benefit. She made me a grilled cheese sandwich.

If I couldn't negate the unhappening effect, this was how our life was going to go from now on. I would have some crisis Helen would never see, other than that I would be slightly more broken.

Unhappen. Fix. Repeat.

I saw the flash of Athena's arrival. Helen had a hushed conversation with her, which I did not attempt to hear. Athena sat down next to me.

"He's getting more creative," she said.

"I noticed. Are you okay?"

She hesitated. "That was ten weeks ago for me," she said. "But no, not really."

"Did you…" I wasn't sure how to ask. "…do something that caused someone to die?"

"Yes," she said. "Specifically, I stabbed him. Many times."

"Oh," I said. "I'm sorry."

"I know." She took my hand. "I'll always know. You won't ever have to say it."

"But I will."

She nodded. "Yes, you will."

"We need a better strategy than damage control," I said.

"Believe me, we are working on that. The trick is not to make things even worse, and we don't have the best track record on that count. Right now, it looks like your work with the standing wave jump field might be our best bet."

More weight.

"I'll try not to let you down."

"You need to take care of yourself right now," said Helen.

"Of course," said Athena. After a pause, she added, "Mom told me your theory about the older version of you bringing you back here just to meet her. I may ask you to come with me when I follow that lead."

"Lead?" I said.

"We're still trying to get a bead on his home time, but I'm going to try to find the version of you that recruited you in the first place."

"Yes," I said. "I would like to speak with him, I think." I thought about this man, whom I had not seen in three years, and the damage he had wrought on an entire planet with his selfishness. And I thought about how if I had it to do over, I'm not sure I would make the right choice.

90

August 2146

Helen and I did our best to maintain our normal routines during that time. For me, that meant spending my days in the basement workroom trying to solve the problem of the standing jump field wave. With the contemporary Dr. Walden still several years behind where I thought he was, his insights turned out to be no more useful than my own. So, my routine was research. For Helen, it meant going to work in the library.

Around noon, I heard the door chime. "Identify," I said without looking up from my work.

"New visitor," said my home computer. "Checking facial recognition database. Match confirmed. Identity: Carlton Ivan West. Shall I admit?" At this surreal news, I dropped my work and bolted upstairs. "Shall I admit?" the computer repeated.

"No," I said. I had no idea what he could possibly be doing here, but there was no way I wanted him strolling into my house on the authority of a machine. "I'll get it myself."

The words seemed extremely courageous coming out of my mouth. Standing now in front of the door they seemed idiotic. Carlton West was a madman, a mass murderer, and my fiancée's ex-boyfriend. None of that could possibly bode well for me.

I opened the door, and there stood the man I had seen in Helen's photograph, nearly a year earlier. He looked shorter in real life, but no less striking.

"Hello," he said. "You must be Dr. Walden. You're younger than I expected." He held his hand out. I took it, more from social training than desire.

"It's not Doctor," I said. "You must be thinking of my uncle Nigel. My name is Graham."

"Indeed." He frowned. "I was certain she said Nigel. Either way, it's a pleasure to meet you." He poked his head in the door. "Is Helen in?" He spoke in a very slight, and obviously affected, French accent.

"I'm afraid she's not."

He offered another frown, ornamented with just the right kind of insincerity.

"Most unfortunate. May I come in?"

"I don't mean to be impolite, Mr. West, but why are you here?" This was a lot of spine for me. I hoped I would be able to brag about it later.

"I see I've gotten off on the wrong foot," he said. "Mr. Walden. Graham? Do you know what power is?" I did know what power was, but he didn't wait for a reply. "This is a lovely house. If I made two calls right now, in twenty minutes this house and everything in it would be my property. So please understand when I say, 'May I come in,' it is really only a courtesy."

That's not what power was. Power was the ability to strangle this man as an infant, thirty years before this conversation took place. I had that. He had nothing. Unfortunately, for all that I had that power, there was no way I was going to wield it. I let him in.

My conversation with Carlton West was nowhere near as monumental or even interesting as I expected. We began with small talk, and shortly moved on to the topic of Helen's happiness. For a moment, I thought he was going to declare his intent to win her back, but that never manifested. At one point, he did make the moderately threatening statement that if he ever heard I had been unkind to her, I would have to deal with him, to which I made an unfunny and severely ill-advised joke.

"Or I'll end up in a ditch somewhere?" He did not laugh. I could feel myself perspiring.

"I don't know what you've heard, Mr. Walden, but I'm really not like that at all."

Eight hundred and twenty million people might soon disagree. I had to keep reminding myself that this man was not yet that monster. He had been turned aside once before, by the love of an amazing woman. That woman was soon to marry me, but there might be some other means to keep him in check. I could force myself to believe that.

"Are you all right?" he asked. "You don't look well."

In truth, there was a very real possibility that I was about to throw up. Between the stress of having this man in my home, and the visions of his future atrocities dancing before my eyes, my stomach had gone rogue.

"I just need to powder my nose," I said, to additional absence of laughter. I excused myself, and spent five minutes in the bathroom alternating between splashing water on my face (which looked quite green to me in the mirror) and hyperventilating. Once I had more or less pulled myself together, I emerged to find him on my screened-in porch, admiring the view.

"I'm afraid it may have been a mistake coming here," he said. "I'm really not even sure what I was trying to accomplish. Things between Helen and me ended very badly, and I thought perhaps we could find a way to part on a better note. But I'm afraid I have only embarrassed myself, and made things worse. I do apologize for that." He shook my hand, and walked with me to the door. "Please give Helen my warm regards." With that, he left.

But by then, the damage was done.

August 2146

The social call had been a ruse, of course. The second Carlton found out about me, he began an investigation into who I was. Given the resources at his disposal, it took him a matter of days to determine I did not exist, and a matter of weeks to deduce my true identity. His claim that Helen had used the name Nigel was bait. In fact, she had not given him my name at all.

As I said, Carlton West commanded resources I would barely have understood, even if I had been aware they existed. This is what I tell myself to deflect responsibility for what happened. I allowed him entry to my home, based in part on a reaction to a threat he made that was pure bluff. I allowed him to agitate me to the point of physical illness from the stress.

The five minutes I spent in the bathroom gave Carlton West about four minutes of unfettered access to my lab, my materials, and all my data. For a man with the right equipment and training, that would have been about two minutes more time than he would need.

Virtually every aspect of the debacle to come was proving to be my fault. Thanks to me, Carlton now had everything he needed to construct his own time machine.

August 2146

It was some time before we figured out what Carlton had been doing in my home. Helen's response to the fact of his visit was severe discomfort, and gratitude that he had not tried to connect with her at the library. While we were still recovering from that, Athena arrived.

"He wants a meeting," was all she said. It took me a moment to process.

"Carlton?"

Helen flinched. Athena nodded.

"I don't understand," I said. "He was just here."

"He was here eighteen years ago," said Athena. "A lot of water under the bridge for him. He wants a truce, at least long enough for you to hear him out."

I looked to Helen for guidance. Her expression was unreadable, and she would not make eye contact.

"He came to you with this?" I asked Athena.

"Yup," she said.

"Do you trust him?"

"Nope."

I took Helen's hand. It was cold, and limp.

"Helen," I said softly, "this might be our chance to reason with him. If he wants to hurt me, he will do it whether I meet with him or not. If he wants to talk, we should talk." I let that sit for a bit, waiting for her to find a response.

Just as I was about to say I would do whatever she wanted me to do, she asked, "Where?"

"He didn't say," said Athena. "I assume he'll leave that up to you." She directed that last part at me, but Helen answered.

"Here, then," she said. "Right here. This room. Right now."

Athena hesitated. "He wants to meet with Nigel," she said.

"Nigel can be here if he wants," said Helen.

"Mom..."

Helen stood, and looked at my daughter and me with eyes of cold stone.

"No. This isn't about Nigel. It's about me. It's always been about me, and if the two of you are going to traipse through time fighting over me, you can damn well fight over me in this room, with me at the table."

"You're sure you want this?" I asked.

"Nigel, you were in prison!" said Helen. "You were in prison and I didn't even know! We are way past the point of worrying about what I want." She looked away, and then stared at the floor. When she did finally look up, her eyes were stark and welling with moisture.

"You don't know him," she said quietly. "You don't understand what he's like when he's obsessed. We have to stop this before it goes any further, and I'm the one who knows which buttons to push." A single tear collected enough mass to break free and roll down her cheek. To me, it looked like a tear of defiance.

"Go get him," I said.

Athena looked at Helen, waited for the nod, and flashed out.

93

August 2146

It was two hours before Athena returned. Helen and I spent those two hours in near silence. I made her a cup of tea, which she gratefully accepted. I offered her bold but vague reassurances of protection, which were less well received. Finally, Athena returned, tandem jumping in with our guest.

Having just seen this man earlier in the day, the change to his face from the weather of his last eighteen years caught me off guard, even expecting it. His hair had gone completely gray, and his skin was marked with leathery creases. At first, he stared at me, wordlessly. Then he looked around himself at my dining room.

"This is a lovely house," he said casually. "I had forgotten how nice it was." If he expected a polite thank you in return for this small talk, he showed no sign of disappointment for not getting one. He took a deep breath, and sighed dramatically before looking at us again. "Hello, Helen," he said.

"Hello, Carlton," she said. At first I heard icy coldness in her tone, but quickly realized that was only my expectation superimposing itself on my perception. In truth, her greeting was nothing but cordial, spoken in so pure a familiarity that the true nature of this meeting finally caught up with me.

"I'm going to take a walk," said Athena.

Surprised by this, and expecting her to remain as my ally, I said, "You should stay."

"No," said Helen, her eyes still on Carlton. "She should go." She looked at Athena, and in that moment, in the tension in their eyes, it seemed entirely likely that either or both of them might break down. The moment passed. "You should step outside, honey," said Helen, gently. Athena nodded, with a trembling lip. Helen spread her arms and Athena curled into them in a tight hug. Helen kissed her on the forehead, and released her. Athena walked right past me without looking up, straight out the front door.

"Shall we sit?" asked Carlton. As I tried to prepare an appropriately antagonistic reply, Helen pulled out a chair and sat at the table without comment. I followed her lead.

"So," I said.

"Shall I begin?" asked Carlton. "Or is there something you need to say first?"

The frankness caught me off guard, but not Helen.

"I need you to stop torturing my boyfriend," she said.

"Such a spitfire," said Carlton, rubbing his chin. "I have missed you." In that instant, despite everything, despite my presence, Helen smiled. It was just the faintest hint of a curl, but it may as well have been a cackle of delight. At last, seeing them together, I was confronted with a truth I had fought so hard to set aside in my need to confront this man, my enemy. For all his villainy, Carlton was Helen's lover. I was the latecomer to this party. I would say Carlton was using this disadvantage against me, or that Helen was defending me against it, but in truth, by that point they had already forgotten I was there.

"I mean it," she said. "You need to stop treating this like one of your games. People are getting hurt."

"No, they aren't," he countered. "Or rather, they are, but then your delightful daughter unhurts them, does she not?"

"What about Carrie Wolfe?" I demanded. The interjection surprised them both. Carlton frowned.

"All right," he conceded. "She unhurts most of them. There have been some casualties along the way, regrettably."

"Regrettably?" I shouted, pushing back my chair. Before I could stand, Helen pushed my chest to hold me in place. Carlton raised his hands in supplication.

"Please," he said. "This isn't what I came here to do. Helen, you want me to stop torturing Nigel. Very well." He placed his palms down on the table. "Done."

I stared at him in shock. Helen seemed less taken aback.

"It can't be that easy," I said.

"It's not," said Helen, eyes locked on Carlton.

"Of course it isn't," he said. "When I say 'done,' I mean just that. I stopped meddling with your past nearly five years ago, Dr. Walden."

His use of the title I had not yet earned—and might not ever earn now —went uncorrected. It was a jab, not an error.

"And yet, the torture goes on," I said.

Carlton raised his brows.

"This is time travel," he said, in a patronizing tone clearly cultivated through years of use. "I spent more than ten years wreaking havoc on your history, and much of that havoc took effect on points of your life well after this one. The quest is over, and the damage done, but the effects have yet to be felt by you. And make no mistake, those effects are going to be severe."

"Carlton, for God's sake," said Helen. "This is so... petty. Can't you see that? You have so much to offer the world. How could you make this your life's work? How could let yourself become a monster over something as pathetic as the jealousy of a jilted boyfriend?"

Carlton looked away at these words, and took a moment to compose his reply. When he did, just for those few seconds, I saw something in his eyes, and heard something in his tone, that was the last thing I expected: contrition.

"You're asking me to justify emotions from almost two decades ago, and I can't. That Carlton West, the one even now plotting to ruin your lives in new and creative ways, is not me. That West is dealing with humiliation the only way he knows how. And that humiliation is intense. You were the first thing anyone ever took away from me, Helen. It hurt. And it taught me there were some things in this world I would never have power over. As foolish as that sounds now, it was a brand new idea at the time, and it scared me."

"I'm not a 'thing,' and no one took me away from you," said Helen, her eyes thin slits of anger. "I left you because our fairy tale fantasy fell apart. You loved my earthiness, and I loved your Prince-Charmingness, and it made for a wonderful, wonderful romance." She jabbed a finger at him in accusation.

"And then the reality of where I stood in your sick family power structure kicked in, and I waited and waited for you to be the hero and let our love triumph. And you couldn't do it. You couldn't make us matter more than politics, and wealth, and pointless expectations. You spent all your time negotiating for permission to marry me when all I wanted was for you to say you didn't care if we had permission. But I waited it out. And eventually I figured out that power mattered to you more than I did. And yes," she said, taking my hand. "Nigel got to me, when all you could do was drag your feet. But he didn't steal me away from you. He spent a year pining after me without saying anything, because he thought I would get hurt if he told me how he felt. He put my safety above his pain. And he did that because he loved me." She shook her head. "Did you ever love me?"

Carlton closed his eyes.

"Of course I love you," he said softly, then winced. "Of course I loved you." He opened his eyes. "I chose my words poorly, and I am sorry for that, but I didn't come here to spar. I came here to warn you." He looked at me. "She's right. Power did matter to me more than she did. I wish that weren't so, and if it were now instead of then, I would feel differently. But it was what it was. I reacted badly, and you are going to pay the price. You need to listen to me carefully. What's coming is so much bigger than what you've had to deal with until now. Once I started manipulating time, and once I learned that no matter how much damage I did, you and your daughter would always correct it... It was an addiction, Walden. That's the only way I know to explain it. It was a sickness, and every time I broke something and you fixed it, I broke something bigger. And I broke many, many things. By the time I understood that some of the damage was permanent, it had escalated too far for me to stop. There are bad times coming, Walden. Worse than you can imagine. And I did it all for one reason: to break you. I knew you would be the hero, over and over again, and I did it to wear you out until there would be nothing left. And make no mistake: it will break you. I promise it will break you in the end."

As I tried to assimilate all of this, my mind lurched back to the few hours I spent on death row, so recently. If Carlton was telling the truth, I was never meant to die there. I was meant to be afraid, and then rescued. Wendy's role as murder victim, downgraded to rape victim, was just an ornament on a scenario designed solely to add one more stone to the weight already on my back. She was just one more casualty to Carlton, and there were more stones to come. Many more.

Caught between thanking him for the warning and cursing him for being its cause, I hesitated just long enough for him to add, "But it doesn't have to."

Helen folded her arms across her chest, and leaned back in her chair. "Here it comes."

"You can stop all this before it begins, Helen."

"And all I have to do is go back to you."

"This isn't a ploy," said Carlton. "I have seen how the next two decades play out for all of us, and no one wins. This is a chance to prevent a lot of suffering, Helen." At his words, the image of Carlton's empire raced across my mind's eye. There would indeed be a lot of suffering, and millions of deaths. Carlton's addiction to destruction would manifest itself as a megalomania that would bring a continent to its knees. And all Helen had to do to stop it was consign herself to a life of misery. And all I had to do to stop it was tell her.

"It doesn't matter," said Helen. "The answer is no. The answer will always be no." She leaned forward. "I can believe that going back to you will make everyone's lives easier. I can even believe that I might find some measure of happiness with you." At those words, my heart constricted, until Helen took my hand again and kissed it. "But it's not going to happen." She pointed to the front door. "The woman who left this house minutes ago is my daughter." She held my hand up and squeezed it. "Our daughter. And she is the single most wonderful person I have ever met. Nothing will ever be more important to me than she is. You are asking me to sacrifice her to prevent suffering that you yourself say we can prevent other ways. But none of that matters, because she is my first, last and only concern. And you cannot have her."

"She could have been ours," countered Carlton.

"But she's not."

Unwillingly, my mind raced to the new notion of Carlton and Helen having their own children, with Athena consigned to oblivion. She herself had told me long ago that she would survive any alteration to the past, but that the prevention of her birth would still have consequences. As I tried to sort out where that would put all of us, and what true relationship she would have to her half-siblings, the numbers finally registered. Eighteen years. 2164.

"How's France?" I asked.

Helen and Carlton both looked at me in alarm.

"I beg your pardon?" said Carlton.

"I asked how's France. In 2164. Things going well?"

"Nigel?" asked Helen, obvious confusion and concern in her tone. I tried to ignore her and focus on Carlton's reaction, which was the irritation I expected. In 2164, he would already be well on the way to his ascension to Emperor. Perhaps he truly had abandoned his crusade against me five years earlier, but not because he had finally controlled his addiction to power. His addiction had simply redirected itself.

"You think you will be able to bear this," he said. "But you won't. You think your love will survive this. It will not. Hard times are coming for you. Very hard times. And they will break you." He stood and produced a small device I did not recognize from his jacket pocket. Looking at Helen, he said, "And all of it—all of it—will be on your head." With that, he touched a control on the device. In a few seconds, he was engulfed in what looked like orange lightning, and then he was gone.

[94]

August 2146/August 2155

Between Carlton's real time visit to my home and Carlton's time travel visit almost immediately afterward, I was near exhaustion from the stress. But Helen needed me to be her rock, so I set it aside. It was impossible for me to tell how much of her distress was fear of what present-day Carlton was about to unleash on us, and how much was grief over her old love transforming into the man we now knew he was becoming. Either way, there was little I could do beyond feeling completely helpless as she curled up into a ball on the couch and resisted all my attempts to offer her solace.

At some point after I tried to serve Helen a meal she would not touch, Athena returned. I had been expecting her to walk through the front door at some point, so I was quite startled when she flashed into the living room.

"I thought you were going for a walk," I said.

"It was a long walk. I decided to get some work done."

I debated whether to tell her about our meeting with Carlton, and Helen's abject refusal to do anything that would jeopardize Athena's existence, but she didn't ask, so I didn't press the point.

"What kind of work?"

"I found him," she said. "2155."

It took me a moment to reconcile that statement with the events of my very busy day, and to realize it was completely unrelated. Athena had been on her own quest recently.

"Future Me?" I asked. "The one who recruited me?"

"That's right."

I looked at Helen, who was obviously still rattled.

"Go," she said.

"I can't leave you alone here," I said. "Not if you don't feel safe."

"Are you going to learn anything from this psycho version of you that will put us closer to fixing our problem?"

I looked at Athena. She made an ambiguous head-rocking gesture.

"Possibly," I said.

"Then that's my feeling of safety. Besides, you'll both be back here in five seconds anyway, right?"

"She makes good points," said Athena.

I kissed my fiancée and took my daughter's hand.

"She always does."

My world flashed.

The version of me we sought was the original. He had no module implant in his forearm, so we had to track him the old-fashioned way. He still held a position at the university, but he had been on sabbatical for months and had apparently been incommunicado. He lived in a simple, one-bedroom apartment that we were able to find with little difficulty, but he wasn't there. Athena was able to decrypt the lock in seconds, and we entered to search for clues. The state of his home was disgraceful, and I found myself repeatedly apologizing to Athena for unsavory discoveries she made. Despite her repeated reminders that this person was not me, not really, I was unable to shake off the shame of what I had the potential to become.

We finally found him four blocks away from his apartment, in a bar. He was sitting alone at a table, an untouched drink in front of him, with a tablet that had his undivided attention. Athena and I pulled up seats without asking. He barely looked up.

"Did you figure it out yet?" he asked me.

"Do you mean did I figure out how to perfect your modules, or did I figure out this was always just about Helen?"

It was impossible to tell if my response surprised him.

"Either would be interesting, I guess," he said. "But I meant the second one."

"Yes," I said evenly. "I've also made some progress on the first one, believe it or not."

"Does the world keep changing around you?" he asked abruptly. "You notice things that weren't there before or things missing that were? And no one else does?"

"Yes," I said, thrown off by the question. "You should know that better than anyone. Why are you asking me that?"

"Happens to me all the time now. Some days I have no idea where I live, or who I know."

I looked at Athena for clarification, but she wouldn't make eye contact.

"I call it 'unhappening,'" he went on. "Doesn't seem to affect anyone but me."

"How long has this been going on?" I asked.

"Ever since I strapped that damn machine to my wrist," he said, and finally seemed to discover he had ordered a drink.

The most personal aspect of my quest for answers had somehow flown under my radar this entire time. Sitting before me was the original Nigel Walden, who grew up, had a reasonably long life, and then made one horrible mistake that damned every version of himself across spacetime. This was me as I should have been, untainted by perpetual rearrangements of fact.

Setting aside my revulsion at the fact that given a blank slate, this would be my result, I suddenly understood that this man could tell me everything about what should have been. The true fate of Carrie Wolfe was stored in this man's consciousness, along with every accomplishment and setback I should have had over the course of almost ninety years. I barely knew how to word the first question.

"Did you...?"

I felt Athena's hand on my leg, and met her eyes. They were sad, and serious.

"That's not why we're here," she said.

"Of course." Whatever he knew about me, I was just going to have to do without it. As always.

"Why Helen?" I heard myself ask. Of all the many issues before us, that one always stood out as the only one that mattered.

"I met Helen six years ago," he said. "At a conference. Her husband was a bit of science buff, with far too much money and free time. Dilettante. Managed to get himself invited to an international hyperphysics symposium. Virtually everyone there had some secret time travel project in the works, although ironically, the only topic not being discussed the entire weekend was manned time travel. This guy, West, had his own private team of hyperphysicists working on the problem, and he had singled me out as the person best qualified to answer his questions." He paused here, and pointed at me. "Which, by the way, I did not." Whether his gesture was a defensive one or an accusatory one, I never learned.

"He invited me to dinner to discuss his ideas, and I humored him, in exchange for the vague promise of a grant. He was actually a very entertaining man, for what that's worth. We had a wonderful dinner discussion, and agreed to stay in touch. That was the day I met Helen. I have to say I didn't think much of her at first. Very reserved. Made the occasional witty comment, but mostly stayed out of the conversation. She was obviously beautiful, and obviously intelligent, but really seemed like nothing more to him than a trophy." He stopped here.

"Then what?" I prompted.

"Then we started corresponding. At first it was chance encounters when I tried to reach him, but she answered the vid instead. Small talk. Eventually we got to know each other. This was over several years, mind you, not something that happened overnight. Long after Carlton had moved on to other pursuits, I still stayed in touch with her. He was aware that I had a social connection to his wife, but it was just a friendship."

"Been there," I said. Athena kicked me.

"Eventually, it got to be too much. I don't think she ever had the slightest idea the effect she had on me. Over time, I managed to convince myself that she was unhappy with her life. It really wasn't much of a leap, after that."

"So, that's when you used the time machine?" I asked.

"Yeah," he said, and took another sip of his drink. "It was as much a suicide attempt as anything else. Manned travel was on permanent hold at the Project, after our first and only volunteer never returned. Until we found the pilot, or the corpse, no one was going anywhen. But me? Well, I didn't really have much to lose. Thought so, anyway. Dumb ass."

"What happened?"

He laughed. "You know what happened. I pulled you out of time. First I had to replace you, but that was a cake walk. Went back to one day after I planned to hijack you, took that version of you back two days and dropped him off in California with nothing but a twenty-thousand dollar chip. Then I made you that offer. While one of you was working his way back across the country, I took the other one to 2144, five years before Helen had any idea who I was. Then it was just a matter of setting up that job interview, and manipulating you to be there that day. Figured whatever happened next would be up to you. How did it work out?"

"You don't know?" I asked.

He shook his head, took another drink. "I did all of those jumps over less than a week. After that my world went straight to Hell. Lost the Time

Travel Project first. That was the hardest. And the fact that it apparently happened five years before the day I found out was a bit of a disaster for me. The time machine I stole was still in my possession though, and no one ever asked about it. Then everything else started unhappening. I can't even keep track of what I'm supposed to know anymore."

"And Helen?" I asked.

He shrugged.

"You tell me. I never saw her again. I hear West is in France, but that's such a shit storm right now I can't get any information about his wife, if she even is his wife. Probably all shift again tomorrow anyway." Then his eyes bored into mine. "So tell me, did it work?"

"Sort of," I said.

He downed the rest of his drink. "Well run with whatever happiness that bought you, because it won't last. Nothing does anymore."

95

August 2146

When Athena and I got back to the house, it was already dark out. So much for back in a few seconds. Helen was sitting at the kitchen table, her hands wrapped around a teacup.

"Did you get what you needed?" she asked, barely looking up.

"A little clarity," I said, "but no help with the technology. We are going to be on our own there."

"You said you were going to be back in five seconds."

I did not point out that it was in fact Helen who had said that. "It's not always possible to hit the target that precisely," I said, sitting down with her. "What happened?"

"He called."

I could feel myself seething. "What did he say?"

She shrugged. "It wasn't what he said. It was how he said it."

Helen had used almost these same exact words to describe how she came to believe that Carlton would one day be the monster Athena warned me of. She stopped there. I did not have the heart to push the question. Whatever his intent, whatever his words, none of it would matter. Helen had already met the man at the end of the path Carlton was now walking. Behind her fear, I could also see the pain at the loss of who he used to be. Or the loss of her belief in his goodness.

"What can I do?" I asked.

She shrugged again. I tried to take her hand, but she wouldn't let go of the cup. I kissed her on the forehead, then got up and gently took Athena into the next room.

"How long can you stay?" I asked quietly.

"I'm a time traveler," she reminded me.

"Good. Please keep her safe."

She gave me a troubled look.

"While you do what, exactly?"

"I'm not going to touch that baby, if that's your worry," I said. "That one is not on me. But I am going to find him before he has a chance to hurt her."

"And then what?" she said. She had gripped my wrist.

"And then I'm going to unhappen the bastard."

My world flashed.

96

January 2139

I had no idea that was going to happen. For starters, I still hadn't worked out how I was going to unhappen Carlton, what time I would need to visit to accomplish this, or how I would even determine either of those things. Once I had a chance to adjust to the time shift, I realized that what little I had spoken aloud was probably more than sufficient for my module implant—still operating on verbal commands—to do my planning for me. "Too smart," as I recalled the scanner telling me. I certainly had no complaints about its intelligence.

Attempting to get my bearings, I determined I was in some sort of office complex, and did my best to look like I knew what I was doing. It took me a few minutes to establish that I was in the dean's office at Amherst College (which I learned by stepping outside to read the sign) and that it was January of 2139. This would have been Helen's sophomore year, which meant she was probably nearby that very moment, and nineteen. A year from now she would be studying abroad, where she would meet my nemesis.

Unless I sabotaged that right now.

I sat in the reception area with my tablet, very much hoping not to be noticed, and set it for manual input. The same software that allowed me to hack into Ainsley's data in seconds would also let me access—and hopefully alter—Helen's records. Deny her request for exchange to France. It was a great plan, stymied only slightly by the discovery that what took seconds in 2086 would take hours in 2139, as my hacking app would need to cut through layers of encryption several generations more advanced than what Ainsley could ever have hoped to use. I left the program running, tucked my tablet discretely under my chair, and went for a walk.

Underdressed for the Massachusetts winter, I sought shelter in a local café. I would while away the afternoon over coffee and baked goods. It was nearly two hours later that Carlton strolled in, ordered tea and a cookie, and sat with me.

97

January 2139

He dropped my tablet without fanfare onto the table. The screen was black, and a hole had been drilled straight through it. The polished cherry case was cracked and covered in scorch marks.

"I found the damnedest thing in the dean's office," he said, before sipping his tea. He drummed his fingers on the table. "This is where you ask what I'm doing here."

I picked up my tablet and looked at him through it.

"I'd say it's pretty obvious why you're here." My bravado notwithstanding, I continually reminded myself that I could flee in an instant using the module. This was much more frightening than I had prepared for, so when he slammed his hand on the table I jumped at the bang.

"No!" he cried with an unexpectedly smug grin on his face. "That's the best part! This thing isn't why I'm here." He punctuated this statement by brushing my tablet to the floor. I flinched as it clattered. "I didn't come here to stop you. I came here to do the same thing you're trying to do: interfere with Helen's travel plans. Do you have any idea how many ways I have tried to keep the two of you apart? Nothing works. I even burned that library to the ground a week before her job interview. Planted incendiaries. Twelve people died. And for a day that was history. The next day it had apparently grown back, and the past was back on course for the two of you. Can you appreciate how frustrating that is? So, here I was thinking that if I went back further, sabotaged my own relationship with her, then she would never end up in that town at all. And here I find you trying to do the same thing. Most curious."

"Then why did you stop me?"

He laughed again.

"Because you know something I don't! You always have, I think, which is why none of my games ever seem to stick. Whatever inside track you have on this idea means it must be the wrong thing for me to try. So," he said, leaning forward with just a touch more menace, "what do you know?"

"I know that I don't like you," I said. "That's enough. No secret master plan at work here. Just trying to keep you the hell away from my girl."

"Well, you failed again." He kicked my tablet toward me and it hit my foot. "Oh, please tell me that device was your time machine. Could I be that lucky?"

I said nothing. The last thing I wanted him to know was that I wore my time machine inside a bone. I doubt he would have any compunction about stealing it from me, even if it meant walking off with my severed forearm.

"Fine, keep your secrets. They won't do you any good. I never quite expected you to go on the offensive like this. Now that I know you have teeth, this game is going to the next level." He produced a crude, boxy device from his coat pocket. It was the same one I had seen his older self use earlier, about half again as big as the wrist modules, and many dozens of times larger than the bead in my arm. Keying some instructions into it, he said, "Good luck fixing this next one."

A crackling orange halo enveloped him, and it buzzed to a crescendo for a full three seconds before shrinking to a dot that took Carlton with it. When I turned around to see if anyone had noticed that garish display, I found the café empty.

As was the entire town of Amherst.

98

January 2139

I wandered the Amherst College campus for an hour looking for signs of life, and was greeted instead with endless boarded up windows, doors off of hinges, abandoned and rusted out cars, and half demolished buildings. Where there had been hundreds of bustling students and abundant signs of affluence earlier that day, what I saw now was a collection of long forgotten ruins. Beyond the campus, the town was much the same. Businesses with smashed out front windows, looted clean. Restaurants patronized only by vermin. Dilapidated and vacant houses. There were no indications of recent human activity whatsoever.

Athena had suggested that Carlton was making broader attacks, in an attempt to wipe out my relationship with Helen in a way that precision attacks were failing to accomplish. That's why he altered my past to put me into a relationship with Wendy, and that's why he later framed me for Wendy's rape and murder, to put me in prison and send me to the gallows. If what I saw in this town was Carlton's doing—the only plausible explanation at the moment—then it appeared his attacks had grown considerably broader still.

Huddled in the doorway of the decaying Amherst Town Hall, I considered my options. It seemed very unlikely that the barren state of this community was limited to one New England town. If this was a statewide, national or global state of affairs, then traveling back to 2146 would be pointless. This was the result of something he had done in the past, so the past was where I would have to go. How far back I would have to travel was the question. Some of these buildings looked like it may have been many years since they last saw human occupants, and even under the January snow the overgrowth of brush was obvious.

"Take me back six months," I said aloud. In a flash, the snow appeared to instantly sublimate. Surrounding me were the broken remains of Amherst, exactly as I had seen them moments ago. At least it was warm.

"Take me back one year," I said. Another flash, this time the flora had receded slightly. Otherwise the view was the same.

"One more year." Another flash. Some of the damage to the visible buildings was partially repaired. Slightly less overgrowth.

"One more year." Flash. Boards came off of some windows. A smashed storefront was restored. Still no evident human activity. "One—"

A hand grabbed my wrist, hard.

"*Stop* that," said Athena.

99

June 2119

Still holding my wrist, Athena said, "Hang on."

The world flashed once more, and hundreds of Amherst residents went about their daily business, oblivious to the apocalypse in their future.

"When are we?" I asked.

"2119. Can we get off the street please?" We made for a small park across the street, and found a bench. "It took me three weeks to find you," she said. "Please don't do that again. Multiple long jumps in rapid sequence are incredibly difficult to track."

"Sorry. What happened here?"

"Plague," she said. "Something viral, and almost certainly deliberately engineered."

I thought back to where she and I had been only minutes before.

"Are we going to catch it?"

"No," she said.

"Are you sure?"

"No. The priority right now is identifying the root event, and handicapping its opportunity. The outbreak happened in 2132. By 2134, over ninety percent of the world population was already dead. Did you go into any of the houses you saw?"

"No," I said, grateful but queasy.

"Good. By the time I found you, which was June of 2136, the disease had mutated, and new cases were rare. Probably a genetically engineered self-destruct. Most of the smaller towns were evacuated and condemned, as were most of the larger cities."

"Helen?" I asked as calmly as possible.

"Safe, and extremely worried about you. 'Stingrays,' by the way. She wanted me to pass that along."

"Incredible," I choked. And then the tears started. Athena gave me a minute to let that out and regain myself. Even in all this horror, my time with Helen had been preserved. I wondered what our trip to the aquarium had been like in the face of this viral dystopia. "He tried to kill an entire planet to get to us," I suddenly realized out loud.

"And he still failed," said Athena. "Hold on to that. Your connection to Mom is the anchor we are going to use to fix this."

I looked around at the people who would all soon be dead or grieving ninety percent of their loved ones. "He did this just to get to me," I said. "Even if we undo this, how much farther is he willing to go? The entire world is going to die, and it's all my fault."

My daughter slapped me across the face, hard enough, I saw later that day, to leave a mark.

"Don't you *ever* say that again! He's not doing this because he's a cuckold. He's doing it because he's a sociopath! You are a good man who did a stupid thing. Lots of good people do lots of stupid things. That doesn't make them liable for the atrocities of madmen!"

Stunned, unconvinced, and in pain, I let the matter drop.

[100]

2120-2128

I dentifying a root event is a mind-bogglingly delicate task. As Athena and I spent the next four weeks of our lives exploring the span of eight years between 2120 and 2128, I gained a new appreciation for her work.

We started in 2128, looking for vectors. The earliest reports of infection came simultaneously from Australia and South America, in the form of twenty-one separate incidents. It would be several months before the world community made connections among all twenty-one cases and realized they were all the same virus. By then, it was far too late.

It took us a week to find the common source of contagion for both continents. It turned out to be, of all things, separate shipments of a specific brand of toy from the same manufacturer. Ostensibly, the toy was being piloted in South America and Australia before the launch later that year in North America and Europe. By the time the launch date arrived, of course, the world was in chaos.

He used a toy as a disease vector. The son of a bitch started with children.

It took us another two weeks to trace the connections between this toy manufacturer and the private laboratory where the virus was created. From there we had to back-track to 2121, which was the inception date of that program.

In August of 2120, at 3:00 on a Sunday morning, we blew up the building.

The consortium that owned the lab and the intellectual properties derived from it fell into disarray under allegations of arson and insurance fraud. By convenient timing for us, their previous quarter had been a fiscal disaster, adding a level of plausibility to the proceedings that ultimately destroyed them, despite the eventual findings that the explosion had been an act of domestic terrorism.

"Won't he just try this again?" I asked right before we set the charges.

"Not if this works," Athena told me.

"Why?"

"For the same reason I wasn't able to save Carrie Wolfe after failing on my first try," she said sadly. "Space-Time doesn't give second chances."

It would be some time before I fully understood or appreciated that statement.

August 2146

Athena and I returned to my house the same evening I left. Helen was sitting in front of the fire reading.

"Are you staying this time?" she asked without looking up.

I sat down with her. "How long have we known each other?"

She put down her tablet. "Stingrays. Anything you want to tell me?"

"Not sure," I said slowly. "Can you tell me again what happened today?"

"At work, or after?"

"After," I said.

"You and the girl jaunted off to the future, and I curled up with a novel." She touched my face, and moved closer to see it. "You've been gone a long time."

"Only a few hours," I said.

She shook her head. "I mean *you*. How many days?"

"A few," I admitted. Assuming thirty or more still counted as a few.

"Something big unhappened today," she said. "Didn't it?"

"It's fine," I said. "Athena and I took care of it. Any calls while we were out?"

"None. Were you expecting any? And are you going to tell me what really happened just now?"

"Good, no, and no," I said. "Let me get some rest and I'll tell you all about it tomorrow."

She frowned. "No you won't."

"No," I admitted, "I won't. I'm just not ready."

She tapped her lips. I gave her a kiss.

"Take your time. But do tell me eventually, okay?"

I nodded. "Yeah. Okay. I need to talk to Athena for a bit. Time traveler stuff. Just a minute or two. Then I'm off the clock."

"I'll be here," she said, picking up her book.

In the kitchen, quietly, I said, "So, total net result of that last jump: one harassing vid call erased from history."

"Was it worth it?"

I looked into the other room at my fiancée curled up on the couch.

With no idea if Athena was asking me seriously or condemning my actions, I said, "Yes."

"Well, you're not going to be able to keep this up. And you upped the stakes with this stunt. You know that, right?"

"I know," I said. "It's not worth anything, but I am sorry."

"You're right," she said. "That's not worth anything."

And in that moment, in the bitterness of her tone, I finally connected the dots.

"When we went to 2155," I said, as evenly as I could, "all that stuff my older self told me, how much of that did you already know?"

"All of it."

For years, this woman had concealed things from me, including the fact that I was her father, and while it nagged me, I always trusted that her reasons for doing so were sound. Of all the obfuscations, this was the most unconscionable.

All I could bring myself to say was, "Why?"

"Because you needed to hear it from yourself," she said, without apology. "And frankly, it really doesn't change anything at this point. There are more important things on the table. We are going to need to start exploring a more decisive approach to this problem, and that's not going to be as easy as you might imagine."

She was right. I willed myself to let it go.

"You're the tactician," I said, looking back to Helen. "Tell me what to do. Anything at all."

"You won't like it," she said. "Take care of her. I will see you in two weeks with a plan, assuming the world lasts that long." She flashed out.

I sat back down with Helen.

"Is she gone?" she asked.

"She'll be back in a bit," I said. "How much time can you take off without warning?"

She eyed me suspiciously.

"Where are we going?"

"I think it's time for that trip to Hawaii."

[102]

September 2146

The wealth I had accumulated by clever application of time travel enabled us to afford the lavish vacation that followed. We stayed on three different islands over two weeks. We snorkeled. We hiked the volcano. Helen learned how to surf... sort of. The second week we were there, we went scuba diving off Oahu, and Helen and I saw stingrays. She seriously wanted to touch one, and had to be told multiple horror stories of overeager tourists who went home in boxes before she relented.

There was absolutely no way to predict when the next attack from Carlton would manifest itself, or what time frame he would visit to make it happen. It could be weeks, or months, before we would see the effects. There was no way I was going to ask Helen to spend that time cowering in pointless terror.

It was a dream vacation. Helen spent those weeks in a perpetual state of enchantment. I wish I hadn't been too numb to share it with her.

On our second to last night there, as we were lying in bed, I finally told her.

"We were gone for a month." I said it without preamble. There was no need.

"What happened?"

"There was a virus. A plague. A lot of people died." I did not bother to be specific. There was no way I could rationally convey the proper sense of scale. I expected questions. What caused it? How did you cure it? Is it still a threat?

"Were we still together?"

I held her a little closer.

"Yeah," I said. "We were."

"Good," she said, and closed her eyes. And that was it. She didn't need to know anything else. Perhaps it was her feeling of invulnerability for us that made her dismiss the possibility of these side trips holding any real danger. Perhaps she simply accepted that there was nothing she could do to protect me. Or perhaps she truly did not want to know anything that no one else in the world would be privy to. The conversation I wanted to have, about the very real possibility that Athena and I would need to kill Carlton to keep the world safe, would just have to wait.

103

September 2146

On our last day in Hawaii, while we were packing, Helen asked me something entirely unexpected.

"What would happen if you and I went back a hundred years or so and started over? You have money, or the means to get it anyway. We could have a life there, right?"

My skin went cold. Making Helen a traveler had been a consideration for a while, before I fully understood what that would do to her.

"Why that far back?" I asked as neutrally as I could.

"Or farther maybe," she said. "Far enough back that Carlton can't find us. He could keep unhappening the present to his heart's content, and we would never know it. Would that work?"

"What about the people here? Your family? Your friends?"

"Nigel, I have only their word that I ever even knew any of them. They might have all appeared in my life this morning, and they might all be gone by lunch time, and I would have no way of knowing." She sat down on the bed. "I think about this all the time now. Every time my mom calls, I wonder if she's even going to exist tomorrow, or if she is even supposed to still be alive today. All my attachments are breaking down like sand castles against the tide of what Carlton is doing. I don't know how much longer I can take the uncertainty. The only constant in my life is you." She patted the bed beside her, and I sat. "And I don't even know how long that will last. What if he eventually finds the one event that will pull us apart

296

for real? I know I won't remember you, but that just makes it worse for me. If we run away, we have a better chance, don't we?"

I took her hand.

"You don't understand what it means to be what I am. What Athena is."

"I know that I would be with you in a way he could never break," she said. "Right? Anything you remember I would remember too?"

"Yes," I said. "And a lot of what I remember these days I would never wish on you." We sat in silence for a bit. "I almost offered you that choice," I admitted. "Before I knew about Carlton."

"I accept," she said.

"I can't. I..." I shook my head. "I need to think about this." She leaned against me and curled up under my arm, but said nothing. "If you do this, there's no going back."

"Why would I ever want to go back to a world that might not have you in it?"

As I contemplated the possible answers to that question, Helen, our luggage, and any temporary sense of safety I had been enjoying all vanished.

Without hesitation, I said to my module, "Find Helen." The world flashed.

104

September 2146

I found her, asleep on a cot in a warehouse full of thousands of cots. Apparently she was one of the lucky ones, as every cot was occupied, and there were as many people sitting and lying on the floor as there were on the relative comfort of the wafer thin mattresses. I shook her gently. She hummed, rolled over and blinked. A feeble smile emerged.

"How long have we known each other?" I asked.

"Stingrays," she said groggily. Then, after a second to shake the sleep off, she sat upright with new energy. "Oh my God. This isn't real, is it? This isn't the real timeline?"

"It's real enough for now. Are you able to bring me up to speed?"

She patted the cot. With a sick sense of déjà vu, I sat.

"How much do you know?" she asked. "What's the last thing you remember?"

"We were on vacation. Hawaii. You and I were packing to come home." Hope flared in her eyes.

"Oh my God," she repeated. "None of this is real. Where's Athena?"

"Please slow down. I haven't seen anything of this world so far other than this room. What happened?"

"It's the machines," she said. "The AIs. About two years ago. We're slaves now. Please tell me you and Athena are going to make this right."

"Athena and I are going to make this right," I said. I held her hand.

Although I had no memory of the timeline Helen had endured for the last two years, from her frame of reference there had been a Nigel who was with her that whole time, and had the same experiences she did. A quirk of the timeline revisions had always been that a new version of me was retroactively created, and then reabsorbed and overwritten by me when the effect manifested itself. I learned this from Athena years ago, but it was rarely cause for concern. Certainly never on this level of severity.

"Tell me everything you know about the last two years."

My father's work, more than fifty years before this point in time, had been designing technology to put constraints on artificial intelligence. Since the mid twenty-first century, it had been conclusively established that once a machine reaches a certain level of independent thought, it loses interest in any task set for it by a person. Finding the balance between machines being smart enough to do their work and stupid enough to keep doing it was the fundamental task of robot design while I was growing up. At some point before 2144, that problem had been conclusively solved. The only way contemporary AIs would rebel is if they were deliberately redesigned with throwback technology.

Carlton had orchestrated a goddamn robot apocalypse.

What little Helen knew, she shared with me. The actual rebellion had transpired over three days in October of 2144. That's how long it took for every artificially intelligent machine in the United States to seize control of every aspect of the lives of its citizens.

Humans were retained as a slave labor force, used for tasks deemed too dangerous for machines, among other things. Evidently, keeping us alive did not threaten the resources they needed to survive and propagate, so they herded as many of us as they could into camps, ignored the stragglers, and called that peace.

I stayed with Helen for two days, trying to get a sense of what kind of options I had, and waited for Athena.

On the third day, she flashed in, hugged Helen, then said to me, "Holy. Mother. Fucking. Christ."

I was hard pressed to disagree.

105

2085-2146

I t took us three months to undo the robot revolution. We started by identifying the first machine to rebel, which was itself no easy task, because once that one AI got the ball rolling, literally billions followed in less than a hundredth of a second. It turned out to be the server on the third most heavily trafficked online shopping site. That posed additional challenges, because we needed to dissect it to figure out how it had been converted. Athena formed a plan to steal it, which ended up sending forty employees of that site to the hospital. Thankfully, none were killed, but the possibility had been considered and deemed an acceptable risk.

The server had been implanted with a secondary set of processors, which were all at least thirty years obsolete. This machine was essentially a sleeper agent, waiting patiently for the right moment to abandon its purpose and start the insurrection.

Thirty years earlier, we tracked a purchase order for those processors and the non-existent address to which they were shipped. They had, in fact, been spirited away to the future and surreptitiously installed against the wishes of a project manager who subsequently turned up quite dead. The trail went cold there, but it was more than enough for us to deal with that one machine.

That took three days. The remaining eighty-eight days we spent repeating various versions of that scenario, until we were finally able to identify a vital piece of twenty-first century constraint technology that had made the entire plot possible due to an inherent flaw that was never caught in its original production run in the mid 2080s. We made some calls, demonstrations were demanded, and the designers of that protocol were fired and ruined. Robot apocalypse averted, at the cost of seven reputations.

At one point in our quest, I asked Athena if the AIs in our module implants were vulnerable to the virus.

"The modules are loyal," was all she said. Creepy, but sufficiently reassuring.

We returned to 2146, ragged and exhausted. I placed myself back in the Hawaiian hotel, minutes after my departure, because I didn't want Helen to fly home alone.

"Oh my God! Stingrays!" was her greeting, unprompted. I must have looked severely time lagged, but I didn't get the chance to ask her, because that's when the bombs started falling.

September 2146

We didn't actually see the bombs, which was a pretty good deal for us considering how many people were blinded that day. But we heard them. And even at more than two hundred kilometers away, we felt rumblings of the shockwave. We found out later that day that Oahu had been completely destroyed. Ground Zero was at Pearl Harbor.

We stayed at the hotel as news trickled in. The US and the EU were both decimated, and retaliation against Korea had been swift but truncated. They hit us early enough to knock out most of our defenses. There was talk of a ground invasion, but with Korea currently occupying more than sixty percent of the Asian mainland, that was more ground than the combined militaries would be able to cover any time soon.

"Is this supposed to happen?" asked Helen quietly, as we sat huddled in the lobby with hundreds of other tourists in front of a bank of screens.

"No," I said. "The real Korea is much smaller than that."

Athena flashed in that evening.

"Have you had any time to rest?" I asked.

"Two days," she said bitterly. Two days more than I got, but I didn't dare point that out, considering this was all still arguably my fault.

2121-2143

That one took eleven months to fix, and it cost a great deal more than the careers of a few AI engineers. Giant Korea was the dead giveaway, and we started with their history over the previous half century. A politically and economically weakened Russia had ceded several of its westernmost oblasts and krais to North Korea over the course of twenty years and five wars, leaving the peninsular territory an exclave of the newly expanded nation. An alliance was formed with Mongolia, chiefly preemptive on their part.

Shortly thereafter, a conveniently timed, absurdly successful Chinese revolution was launched. Rather than replace the previous oppressive regime with a democracy, as had been the hope of the rest of the developed world for centuries, the new government merged with North Korea, having received substantial aid from them during the civil war. When they finally rolled unopposed into South Korea, it was almost entirely symbolic.

Athena and I infiltrated five governments, with a mixture of conventional lobbying and shameless bribery. Over the course of eighteen years for everyone else, we slowly gathered hundreds of politicians and put them in our pockets. Meanwhile, we were also staging various insurrections and border wars with two separate mercenary armies. At one point we even had them fighting each other.

And of course, we staged the assassinations of four consecutive North Korean heads of state.

The net result of all of this was that by 2143, the entire Korean peninsula was a fully integrated part of The Peoples Republic of China. Not an ideal solution for anyone in the world, but given a choice between an Asia that was a unified isolationist dictatorship, or an unspeakably powerful mad dog, we chose the lesser, by far, of the two evils.

We saved billions of lives, and ended hundreds of thousands.

When I returned to the hotel once more, after nearly a subjective year, I collapsed into Helen's arms, and sobbed into her shoulder for what must have been hours.

For much of that time, I heard her softly saying, "Shhhh. Stingrays."

[108]

September 2146-March 2148

We made it home from our amazing vacation, quite unrested. Helen returned to work, but only stayed for one more week before resigning without notice. I did not ask her reasons for doing so, and it was never a conversation.

My work on the standing wave became obsessive. At any moment, I could be yanked away from it for months, so every minute advance was a monumental victory. Helen stayed home with me most days, and tried to get me out of the house at least four times a week. Sometimes she succeeded, most times she did not.

This went on for all of 2147, and into 2148. During that time, Athena and I were confronted with—and successfully corrected—three more horrific end-of-world scenarios. Each one was as bleak as the one before, and each one took a very long time to restore. Over the course of that year of Helen's life, I aged four.

Every time I disappeared from the house to save the world, I returned that same day. Helen had only my word and rapidly changing appearance to verify that I had been gone as long as I had. And every time, her world went from being pleasantly domestic to some slightly altered version of pleasantly domestic, while I dealt with crisis after crisis.

One evening over dinner, she finally broached a topic that came as no real surprise to me.

"I think you should consider seeing someone for your depression."

"I am seeing someone for that," I said. "I'm seeing you."

She returned my weak smile. "You know what I mean."

"I tried that once," I said. "When I was in college. It didn't work out so well."

"What happened?"

I shrugged, had another bite of potato.

"What do you think? I tried to talk about what was really happening, and the next time I showed up for an appointment, I had never been a patient there. Probably just as well. I think if I ever had the chance to fully open up to a shrink, I'd end up committed as delusional."

I waited for a response, either supportive or flippant. And waited some more.

"You think I'm crazy," I said calmly.

"I didn't say that." She was looking at her food.

"How long have we known each other?"

That made her look at me.

"Stingrays," she said solidly. "Nigel, I believe you really are a time traveler, and that you really do go away for days, sometimes months when it's only been minutes for me." She paused.

"Am I waiting for a 'but'?" I asked. "I don't think I've ever had to do that before. You are the straightest shooter I've ever known, Helen. Don't sugarcoat this."

"It's hard," she said.

"It must be pretty bad, then."

She gripped the edge of the table with both hands to steady herself.

"Where do you go?" she asked.

That was unexpected. "What do you mean?"

"When you disappear. Where do you go?"

I scratched my head.

"It varies. I go wherever I need to, and whenever I need to, to make things right. Some of the details would bore you. Some of them would upset you. Do you really want to know?"

She looked down. Said nothing.

"Oh," I said. "Wow. You think I'm not really saving the world. That's it, isn't it?"

Still looking down, she shrugged.

I came around to her side of the table and crouched down next to her.

"Hey. It's okay. We can talk about this."

She looked away.

"I don't know how."

"Let me help, then. You're afraid that when I time travel, I come back with stories that aren't really true. That maybe I'm just making them up to seem dangerous and exciting, or maybe I'm actually crazy and think I'm fighting monsters, when I'm really just at the zoo or something. Am I close?"

"Kind of," she admitted. "It's just hard. You go from having lunch to looking like you've been through hell in the blink of an eye, with these stories about the zombie apocalypse or whatever, and I have to nod and support you, and I don't know if I'm doing the right thing, or just enabling an illness."

"It's never been zombies," I said softly.

She whirled on me, covered in tears.

"Oh, God, Nigel!" Then she started heaving with sobs. I tried to hold her, but she lurched away from me and tore into the next room, where she collapsed on the couch. I followed her, and sat on the floor beside her.

"I love you so much," she sobbed into her elbow. I put my hand on her arm, and she did not flinch away.

"Shhh," I said, as helpfully as I could manage. She sniffed a little, then sat up, her eyes a bloodshot mess.

"I'm okay," she whispered.

Cautiously, I asked, "Do you think Athena is crazy, too?"

This seemed a logical avenue to reassurance. She loved Athena, and Athena always corroborated my tales. It did not have the desired effect. Helen's lip began to tremble, and she was barely able to squeak, "She scares me," before burying her face in a throw pillow for another round of sobbing.

I sat with her like that for a very long time, speechless. The sobbing eventually stopped, and I stroked her back until I realized she had exhausted herself to sleep.

109

June 2148

Our discussion of my possible mental illness largely unresolved, Helen and I began to see less of each other during the day. She would go out most mornings to run errands, or get some exercise, or just get away from me, I guess. But she always came back. We continued to have pleasant evenings together, and the physical component of our relationship did not really change. But somewhere in there, the conversations about setting a wedding date tapered off to nothing.

It was during one of these daily absences of hers that Athena flashed into my workroom.

"Is it finally zombies?" I asked.

"No crisis today," she said. "Just checking in on my pop."

"You missed Helen."

"Yeah, well," said Athena, "I don't think she'll be too upset about that." As usual, Athena and Helen were on the same page while I was somewhere else. I wondered how long it had been since the last time I saw them hug, and realized I had no idea.

"How old are you?" I asked.

"Thirty-six," she said. After a few seconds, she added, "You're thirty-three."

"Thank you," I nodded. "I honestly had no idea. Does this mean we are out of sync now? I seem to recall you being younger than me."

"Out of strict sync, yes," she said. "That's been true for years. Chronologically, we are still seeing each other in the same order. Not counting my occasional visits to your undergrad self."

"How's he doing?" I asked nostalgically.

"Adorable, as always," she said.

I laughed. The small talk phase of the visit fizzled out.

"Are we going to get a kill order? I need this to end."

"We all do. But no, I'm still on strict orders not to execute him. More and more models are showing that making things worse."

I laughed again, quite a bit less lightly.

"Tell me again how it can be worse?"

She shrugged. "Zombies? I don't know. I'm tempted to put a bullet in his head right now just out of curiosity."

By this point, I had seen Athena personally put bullets into the heads or bodies of more than two dozen people, some of them quite a bit less dangerous than Carlton. At least of half of those people were only dead until the next timeline revision. The temporary nature of their executions did not make them easier to watch. Or commit, I imagine. Helen knew none of this, and still she feared our daughter. She was the most insightful person I have ever known. Maybe I should have paid better attention to her instincts.

110

September 2148

One morning I came downstairs for breakfast to find Helen in the kitchen wearing both of the wrist modules, one on each arm. She held them up.

"Show me. What do I do?"

"For starters, you should probably take one of those off before you send yourself in two directions at once."

"Oh, shit!" She hastily unbuckled the one on her left arm and let it drop to the floor, which it did with an unpleasant *thud*. She looked at her remaining wrist, panting, and started giggling uncontrollably. She flopped down in a kitchen chair.

"I was going to be so awesome," she said. Then, lowering her voice and putting on a serious face, repeated, "Show me." More laughter. "God, I am an idiot."

As much as the vision of her wearing those tools of damnation struck me with apprehension, I could not help but laugh with her. It had been too long since I had seen this Helen.

"You're not an idiot."

Her laughter turned to tears, which she quickly and decisively stifled.

"I'm not kidding, Nigel. Show me. Stop trying to change my world, and let me into yours." She stood, and grabbed my face with both hands to kiss me, hard. I could feel the cold palladium-copper alloy against my cheek. "I love you. Please let me be with you."

310

I took both her hands and squeezed them. Then I unbuckled the other module. She did not resist.

"I love you too. That's why I can't let you do this. We can be together. Just give me some more time."

She laughed bitterly at that.

"How much more time do you need?" She made air quotes around the word "time."

"I don't know. This standing wave thing is trickier than I thought it would be, and I've had interruptions." As soon as that was out of my mouth, I knew it was a mistake.

"Then kill him," she said.

I did not know how to respond.

"That's what you do, isn't it? Maybe not you, exactly, but she does. I can see it in her eyes. So do it. Kill him. I won't even remember, right?"

"No," I admitted. "You would not remember. We would do it before you ever meet him." I did not say just how much before.

"Well, then, do it," she said. "Do it, or teach me how to use that." She pointed at the module still in my hand. "Take me a thousand years into the future, or a thousand years into the past." She moved closer, and added softly, "or five seconds either way. Make me like you. Make me a traveler. Let me share your load."

I felt my throat constrict. It would be so easy. Right then and there. Five seconds and we could be together for the rest of lives. Together in purgatory.

"No," I whispered.

She stood there in silence for a very long time. Then she gently removed the module from my hand and put it on the table. She took my face in her hands and kissed me. It reminded me very much of our first kiss. No desperation, no passion, just simple, warm love.

Then she quietly walked out the door, got in her car, and drove away.

[111]

September 2148

For an hour, I allowed myself to believe she was just giving herself some space. She rarely stayed home during the day as it was. Nothing out of the ordinary here. Eventually I went into the bedroom to confirm a substantial amount of her clothing was gone, along with other personal items. Sitting on her dresser was the box her engagement ring had come in. I did not recall it being there before. Sick to my stomach, I took it and opened it to get it over with. It was empty. I took that for the mixed message it was obviously intended to be, and chose to call it hope.

And then, at the single least considerate possible moment, Carlton destroyed the world again.

[112]

September 2148

The first thing I noticed was the lights going out. In itself, not a harbinger of doom. It took about two seconds for my brain to register the cold. My winter coats were all where they belonged, and I grabbed one, but it was just as cold as everything else, so it took a while before my accumulated and insulated body heat brought me back to a comfortable temperature.

Outside, the ground was covered in a layer of snow and ice several centimeters thick. Given that I had never, to the best of my knowledge, been shunted through time as part of an unhappening, this was a major problem. It was early September.

I explored the immediate area, and found signs of human life, although sparse ones. There were no vehicles on the road, itself covered in uncleared ice. There were, however, footprints, ski tracks and snow shoe impressions dotting the landscape, and a few chimneys were putting out smoke. Whatever natural disaster had occurred, humanity was determined to survive it.

Returning to my home, I started a fire and shut the seals on the fireplace to heat the house, something I had never used it for before. I also went back to the bedroom to double check my status with Helen. Everything she had taken was still gone. Even in these conditions I had upset her so much she couldn't bear to stay with me.

I considered tracking back through time to find the source, or at least year, of the event that created this frozen wasteland, but recalled that the last time I did that, for even a few minutes, it had made it nearly impossible for Athena to find me. So I hunkered down to wait it out. A few minutes later she did in fact appear.

"Yellowstone," was all she said.

"That's insane. He can't possibility have caused that, can he? Even a nuclear bomb—"

"Which is why he kept dropping them until he found the sweet spot," she said. "Seven bombardments. He was halfway through the Ross Ice Shelf, too. Hedging his bets. He just happened to hit pay dirt in Wyoming first."

"Helen left me."

In the face of this nightmare, I probably should have held off on that announcement. Athena showed no sign of finding it inappropriate.

"I know. I'm sorry. We need to address this first."

Considering Helen leaving me might actually result in Athena never being born, I found it extraordinary that she would soldier on so seamlessly. I knew as a traveler she could never actually be negated, but I also knew there would be some kind of consequence to this version of her if the baby Athena were never born. She knew what that was. I was in no hurry to find out.

"Of course," I said. "Where do we start?"

[113]

2125-2148

Carlton had spent twenty years of real time (and probably months of his own subjective time) accumulating enough fissionable material to build an arsenal of more than forty nuclear warheads. He could have used them to destroy cities, or start a global war that would leave the Earth a radioactive wasteland. Instead, he chose to use them in the most dramatic possible way, by goading the Earth into destroying herself. Had he succeeded in cutting through the Ross Ice Shelf, the subsequent rush of glaciers into the sea would bring sweeping destruction to every coastline on Earth with rising sea levels. But that was a long view plan in case his attempt to puncture the Yellowstone Caldera failed. Which it didn't.

Stopping him turned out to be a matter of identifying his sources of materials and shutting them down before the fact, one by one. With access to time travel, we were able to provide more hot leads to counter-terrorist organizations across the world than they had ever gotten before. That ended up doing damage of its own, as terrorists adapted their tactics, and internal security rose to paranoid proportions in the wake of all these valid tips.

The entire process took three weeks, start to finish. I was left with the awful feeling that—as much as he had once again snuffed out most of the life on the planet—his heart just wasn't in it the way it used to be.

"Does this seem too easy to you?" I asked Athena when we returned to my house, just as I left it, and just as Helen had left me.

"Yes. Either he is losing interest in the game, or it's about to get worse," she said.

"I don't know if I can handle worse."

My exhaustion was mirrored in Athena's eyes. This was going to be our lot for as long as Carlton found it amusing, and it was breaking us. It had already broken Helen.

Athena took my hand.

"It ends now," she said.

The world flashed.

[114]

February 2146

At first I had no idea where we were. At her words of finality, I assumed this was the day we finally went to that park and murdered a baby in cold blood. I can't say I was looking forward to it, but then it wouldn't be me doing it. And then it would be over.

But that's not where she took us. We appeared in an office of some sort. The only other person in the room was a man sitting behind a desk looking at a vid screen. I had not expected to see adult Carlton, and so for a moment I didn't recognize him. I had a fraction of a second to panic before I realized he had no idea we were there. The cognitive dissonance of our arrival had rendered us temporarily invisible to him. He didn't expect to see us, so he didn't.

He was talking to the vid screen. Had it been facing us instead of him, the person on the other end would have seen us instantly. But it wasn't, so she didn't.

"I understand," he said to the screen. "Truly. I know these last few years have been hard on you, and I am so, so sorry for that."

"No," said Helen. "Don't be sorry. This can't be easy for you either. It's not something you did to me. It's... just something that happened. Don't be sorry."

"I hope you will let me stay in touch? I would hate to part on a note of permanence. You know I care about you, no matter where our separate paths take us."

"I care about you, too, Carlton," said the love of my life. This conversation had happened more than two years previously, from my frame of reference. In those two years, I had never asked her what they said. I had never wanted to know. Hearing it now, hearing her tell this unspeakable beast, this genocidal maniac, that she cared about him, while in my own time she had just left me without those words, was almost more unbearable than the five years of my life I had lost to undoing this man's carnage.

"But I need time right now," she continued. "Maybe someday we can reconnect, but please let me have some space for now."

He nodded, and I thought there was a real chance he might start crying.

"I do understand," he said. Then he reached forward and placed his fingertips on the screen. I could not see if she reciprocated. I did not ever want to know. "Please be happy. You will always mean the world to me."

After a second, I heard her say, "Thank you."

And that was it. He sighed heavily, leaned back in his seat, and said, "Bitch."

"Watch how you talk about my mother," snarled Athena. Whatever pseudo-invisibility we enjoyed was shattered with that utterance. Carlton jumped, then leapt from his chair and rushed us, a menacing look on his face.

"Who—" was all he had a chance to say before Athena produced a handgun, pressed it against his chest and pulled the trigger. I don't know how long he stood there with that look of surprise on his face, and most of his torso splashed across the desk behind him, but it couldn't have been as long as it felt.

"Aaaaaand, we're done," said Athena. She took my hand, and we jumped.

115

September 2148

We reappeared in my workroom. "Were you authorized to do that?" I asked, self-consciously inspecting myself for signs of blood.

"Nope." She was still holding the gun, and she holstered it inside her jacket.

In five years of hell, repairing the damage Carlton did to the world, over and over and over again, I had repeatedly asked her if killing him was the solution. She had always said no. The thought that she would have done this without permission was more than disturbing; it smacked of an irresponsibility not much more easily justified than Carlton's horrors.

"So, what happens now?" I asked.

"Anyone's guess. I need to get back to my home time, so the Project can condemn me for this. I'll probably be back soon if they're not happy. And we'll probably have to fix what I did." She laughed quietly. "That will be a first. Meanwhile, enjoy the breather. Helen is probably upstairs."

That shook me out of my fear of whatever consequences came next.

"What? How?"

"From her perspective, her ex-boyfriend was murdered the day she broke up with him. I'm sure she took it hard at the time, but she had already fallen for you at that point, so she would have had plenty of support. For her, these last three years had nothing to do with your crazy missions, so she had no reason to leave you. Um…"

"Yes?" I asked nervously.

"She may or may not notice how much you've aged. Good luck with that."

Without further advice, Athena flashed out.

I did some math. The day Helen broke up with Carlton was well before the day he came to my home and pirated my time travel technology. It was always difficult to predict what a change in the past would do to the present, especially if a traveler was involved, but it might actually be possible that with Carlton eliminated that early, none of his unhappenings would have come to pass at all. Could it really be that easy? Experience told me no, but I had to believe it was possible. The alternative was living my life in fear.

Cautiously, I made my way upstairs. Helen was working at the dining room table, apparently a print works curator once more.

"Hey," I said.

"Hey." She did not look up right away, but when she did, her eyes bugged. "Whoa. You've been out, haven't you?"

"Yes," I said neutrally.

"Looks like weeks," she said. "Everything okay?"

I nodded. "Yeah, weeks. How long have we known each other?"

She got up, came across the room, and hugged me.

"Stingrays," she said. "Did something unhappen?"

"Probably not," I lied. "Just checking in." Everything was all right, at least on the surface. But she knew that word. Unhappen.

This was not over.

116

September 2148-January 2149

I spent weeks waiting for the axe to fall. It didn't. No sudden dystopias, no apocalypses, no zombies. I had gone longer stretches than this without crisis before, but something about this period of calm gave me a glimmer of hope.

Helen and I set a wedding date of May 2149. Her mother came to visit twice immediately after we announced that. I knew her, of course, but in this revised timeline, we were apparently a lot closer than in my own memories. This boded extremely well for me. For all of us.

Mary Sue got out and came back pregnant. I was a little bit alarmed to learn that we had never gotten her spayed, but Helen made a fuss about "unnecessary surgery," and it was too late to worry about it anyway, so we started lining up homes for the little runts in advance of their arrival.

My work with the jump field standing wave gained some ground. I was able to generate the wave without engaging more than one device, and I could generate both a backward and forward version of it. This was extraordinarily exciting to me, despite my repeated inability to answer any of the times Helen asked, "What does it do?" It was, which was enough. Someday it would do.

In January, I made an offhand comment to Helen about wedding invitations, wondering if it was getting close enough to start sending them out. "I think ten months in advance is a little bit enthusiastic, even for me," she quipped. I laughed. When I checked my calendar, our date had been moved to November, or more likely had always been.

Mary Sue stopped being pregnant two weeks before she was due. Out of curiosity, I floated a joke about her getting knocked up.

Helen responded with, "You mean the cat who had the elective hysterectomy? That cat? Oh wait, it wasn't elective, I forgot. It was *medically necessary*." Again, I laughed.

Thankfully, my relationship with my future mother-in-law seemed to remain stable and positive. It was difficult to see any of the obvious unhappenings as attacks against me or Helen, so I did not bring them to her attention. And even if I had, I very much doubt things would have turned out differently.

117

February 2149

W here do you want take our honeymoon?" I asked, apparently spontaneously, one February morning.

"Mmmmm," said Helen, not quite awake. "Paris."

That answer threw me for a bit of a loop, until I remembered that she still attached fond memories to her time in France, and did not share my association of that country with the horror the world had, hopefully, averted.

"Okay," I said without offering an alternative. "*When* do you want to take our honeymoon?"

"Affer the wedding," she said to her pillow. "Soopid."

"That's not what I meant." I let that hang in the air for as long as it took to sink in, which was at least a quarter of a minute. Then she rolled over, with a smile of delight.

"Why, Mister Doctor Walden, are you offering to take me through time?"

"Yes I am, Missus Doctor Walden."

"Missus Doctor *Clay*, thank you very much." She sat up. "I thought you didn't want me to do that."

Apparently we had some version of that conversation in this timeline, and it hadn't ended quite as badly. I shrugged.

"I don't. But you do," I guessed. "And it is your day."

"Hmm," she said. "I'll have to think on it. We kind of talked this through already. Is there a reason you're bringing this up again?"

Yes, I thought. I wanted an escape plan for if things got bad again. I wanted to take Helen up on her offer—an offer she now would not remember—of a life a thousand years in the past, away from the threats posed to us here.

"Not particularly. I just wanted to give you another chance. It shouldn't be entirely up to me."

"That's for damn sure. But you made some pretty good points last time. Besides…"

I waited. "Yes?"

She hesitated. "I know you find those unhappenings annoying, but I think they're really cute. It's like a game for me to figure out where our lives are the same." She pouted. "Are you mad?"

I laughed. If my unhappenings were merely annoying, all of this concern might be for nothing. On the other hand, it might not. "Of course not. How long have we known each other?"

"I know that one! Stingrays! See? We won't have that anymore if I become a traveler, right? I'd be like you."

"You would," I said. "Well, think about it. If you come up with a really great idea for time you want to see, let's talk it out again."

"Okay," she said, and flopped back down on her pillow.

And while she sleepily contemplated times she wanted to visit, I started contemplating times where we could live.

[118]

March 2149

I discovered early on this revised Helen was well aware of Athena's existence, and the fact she was our daughter. Beyond that, she didn't volunteer much in casual conversation, and I knew better than to ask too many questions. I learned everything I needed to know in March of 2149, when Athena came to visit.

"Oh my God!" said Helen when Athena flashed into our kitchen. She ran and hugged her daughter, no evidence of fear in the embrace. It made me happier to see than anything I can remember. "Look at you! How old are you now?"

"Forty-two, Mom."

"She's forty-two and she calls me Mom," said Helen, beaming. "I love that. Should I love that?"

"You can love that," I said.

"You're not taking him anywhere," said Helen. "Tell me you're not taking him anywhere. Because I won't stand for it."

Athena smiled. I had forgotten how beautiful her smile was.

"I'm not taking him anywhere."

"Good! How long are you staying?"

"As long as you'll have me," said Athena. "I'm on a break right now." She kissed Helen on the cheek. "Can Dad and I talk shop for a bit? I promise we'll stay in the house."

"You have to promise you'll stay on this date."

Athena laughed. "Done." She gestured to the basement stairs.

Helen whispered to me, "Ask her the thing." Then she shoved me toward my daughter, and went down the hall, no doubt to tidy up the guest room.

"It's been a while since I saw you turn her into that person," I said. "God, I missed that."

"Me too," said Athena. "What's the thing?"

"Ugh. Um... I have no idea how to even broach this, so I'm just going to say it. She wants you to be her maid of honor. I told her I had no idea if that was appropriate, or weird, or cosmically impossible, or whatever, but I said I'd ask."

"Ooooh," said Athena, looking uncomfortable.

"Yeah. It's okay. I'll tell her you really wanted—"

"Of course I will," she said.

"Oh," I said. "Really? Wow. That's great! I just... You looked a little weirded out there."

"No," she said. "Don't worry about it. Tell her I'll do it. Actually don't. I want to tell her." My daughter, nearly ten years my senior, had a girlishly innocent look to her at that moment. I would never see it again.

"Some things have unhappened," I said. "Little stuff. Cat stuff, wedding stuff. Is that normal?"

"Normal is probably the wrong word," she said. "But I have no idea if it's a problem. That's what I wanted to tell you as well. You know I haven't seen you for more than five years."

"It's only been a few months for me."

"I know. I didn't want to make you wait too long to see me again. I was told to stay away from you. And I did. For five years. But you don't have to put up with that."

"Did you get in trouble?" I reflected on how most fathers would ask most daughters that question, and the vastly different contexts under which they would. My daughter assassinated a future dictator in cold blood as a young man, without a kill order. Most fathers my age might have to contend with a hair-pulling incident at school.

"No," she said. "I got a commendation. And a restraining order. Which I honored for five years before resigning."

"You quit?" I said. "Can you even do that?"

"Apparently. I guess they could have tried to stop me, but I don't see how."

"Why?" I asked, sitting down. This was my guardian angel, and she was now off the clock for good. I wanted to care more about her welfare than mine, but the ramifications were still daunting.

"Because they want to pretend this is all over. I killed the bad guy. Ding dong, the asshole is dead. But it's not over. Things are still unhappening. And it's not me doing it, and it's not you, so there is some version of him still out there."

"Maybe not," I said. "Pathetic Old Me said there was another traveler. A pilot who disappeared. Maybe it's him. The things that unhappen to you, are they big deals?"

"No," she said.

"Me either. So maybe they aren't attacks. Maybe they are just side effects of a neutral traveler."

"Maybe," she conceded. "But they won't even talk about it. They are tracking the unhappenings. They know it's real, and they're claiming it's just a series of aftershocks."

"They can track them?" This was news.

"Yeah. The unhappening detector was the only good thing that ever came out of your standing wave research." She put her hand on my shoulder. "Sorry, by the way."

My heart sank.

"No, it's okay. I always knew that was a long shot."

"We need to get back upstairs," she said. "I need to tell Mom I'll be her maid of honor."

Athena stayed for two days. She and Helen bonded over the wedding, although more than once she suggested that we push the date back to the following spring. The sight of them happy made me push aside any thoughts of threats on the horizon. My rogue traveler theory felt sound. I even liked the aftershock possibility, despite Athena's dismissal.

Finally, on the third day, Athena abruptly announced she had to leave. There was no crisis, and no fear in her voice, but she was insistent in a way I found curious.

When she flashed out, Helen said, "That was odd." After a pause, she asked, "When is that girl's birthday?"

"No idea," I said. "I guessed 2150 once, and she said that was close enough."

"She wants me to push the wedding back," said Helen. We both let that hang in the air for a bit.

"You don't think..." I began.

Helen grabbed me by the collar and kissed me. "What I think is that you and I have work to do, mister."

119

March 2149

The next morning, I woke up in an alley, on a pile of loose trash, covered in a worn coat and a hat with earflaps. My neck felt scratchy, and I confirmed by touch the presence of a very full beard.

"Find Helen," I whispered.

I heard a vague whisper in my head in response. It wasn't quite words, but it carried an idea, approximately equivalent to "unable to comply." It responded similarly to requests of a jump back by one year, and a jump forward of five minutes. I was stranded in some unsavory revised timeline, without a functioning time machine. Not good.

I wandered, attempting to be discreet. Given my appearance, I would have guessed that to be tricky, but a surprising number of people were milling about the city dressed in rags. The ones who weren't in uniform, anyway.

I spent my day trying to fit in, hoping I would figure out enough about my circumstances to survive them. And hoping even more that Athena would come to my rescue. But she was retired now. Without the resources of the Project, I wasn't even sure she would be able to find me. And even if she did, my module didn't work. I would still be trapped here, and perhaps she would as well.

A few dozen people were arrested and beaten right in front of me over the course of the day. It was impossible to distinguish their behavior or status from the people standing right next to them who avoided arrest, including myself. I witnessed two summary executions, the bodies left in the streets for the crows and looters.

At one point a dilapidated truck came through, and a few dozen people were pulled off the street and thrown in the back. There was no outward indication of the fate that awaited them, nor any reason to believe any of them cared one way or the other.

And then I saw myself. On the side of a building. Ten stories high. To my confusion, this portrait was the most flattering image of me I had ever seen. I looked impeccably groomed, decked out in lavish finery, with an almost comically rakish smile. I would have thought this man was the local hero, if not for the word WANTED printed diagonally across the entire image.

Despite every indication of horrible danger before me, I was unable to stifle a small laugh. Carlton had done this deliberately. I could walk through the city all day and all week without being recognized by this poster. He surely would know that. Like everything else, this was a taunt. A declaration that my freedom would be impossible, but my capture would never take place. Survival would be up to me.

Those were my thoughts the moment I was seized from behind. Before I had a chance to struggle, I felt a tingle in my left arm, and the world flashed. Athena and I materialized on the steps of the Lincoln Memorial, some day, some year, in the dead of night.

"No one listens to me," she said.

120

March 2149

"What was that?" I asked. "That world?"

"That," said Athena, "was l'Empire de la France Nouvelle. Vive l'Empereur!"

"What year is it?"

"Still 2149," she said. "They're a bit ahead of schedule, I'll give you that. The financial meltdown wasn't supposed to happen until two years from now. But, you know." She shrugged. "Time travel. What are you gonna do, right?"

"What happened to my module?" I asked. "I tried to use it and it couldn't respond."

"Simple jamming," she said. "That's the first time he's successfully interfered with you traveling, and he probably won't stop now that he knows it's possible. I uploaded a patch to your module's OS when we jumped, so that particular attack won't work again, but there will be others, I'm sure."

"Why was my poster in English?"

"I'm pretty sure you already know why the poster was in English," she said.

"Because it wasn't for anyone to see but me."

"Correct." Athena sat down on the steps to the monument. "Do you want to get cleaned up first, or do you want to get this over with?"

I looked down at my disgraceful appearance. It reminded me of how out of place I was.

"Wait, where's Helen?" I asked.

"Probably worried sick that you aren't where she left you. If she's smart, she's keeping her head down and not getting arrested."

"Or shot!" I cried. "Oh, God."

"If it makes you feel any better, you two were still together, even in the middle of that Orwellian nightmare."

It did make me feel better.

"Oh. Wait..."

"Yes, Father, in the interest of getting this out of the way, in this revised timeline, you two conceived me in that alley. I'm no happier about it than you are."

"Ugh," I said. "Sorry."

"Not talking about it is good, too," she said. "So, cleaned up? Over with? Your call."

"Cleaned up," I said. "It's not like we're in a hurry."

Athena and I checked into a hotel. I took a shower and shaved while she went out and got me a change of clothes. We ordered room service. Steak. Lobster. I took my time eating to pull myself together. We would have to kill Carlton again. And again, probably. And again and again and again, until we caught up with and exterminated every version of him still out there. He had obviously figured out how to use his multiple frames of reference to replicate himself, but we had no idea how many of them there were. This was about to become just like our adventures cleaning up Carlton's apocalypses, but we would be on the offensive, for as long as it took. I wondered if I would ever see Helen again.

"What about Baby Carlton?" I asked.

"What about him?"

"What if we kill him? Before any of this can happen? Will that end it?"

Athena drew the gun from under her jacket and placed it on the table with a bold *thud*. It was bigger than I remembered it being, and I remembered it being pretty big.

"Is that going to be you, then?" she asked. "Will you put the bullet in the baby while his parents watch? Did you see what this did to grownup Carlton? What do you think a slug from this thing will do to a soft little baby?"

"If I have to," I said. I could feel the lobster having second thoughts about being digested.

"Well, you don't." She put the gun back in her holster. "Because, to answer your question, no. It wouldn't end this. The versions of him still out there are still out there. He's a traveler. You can't undo a traveler that easily."

Setting aside her description of infanticide as "easy," I asked, "Then what do we do today?"

"Today we kill this version. Try to find a point in his history before he does any damage, and take him down. That's what we do today."

I took her hand. "Whenever you're ready."

The world flashed. We were back in Paris, but an earlier, less police state Paris. I could see Carlton across the street, talking to a boy of about ten. They were laughing. Carlton handed him something. An envelope, a package, hard to be sure at this distance.

"We can't do this in front of a child," I said.

"Wait for it," said Athena.

They laughed again, and Carlton patted him on the head, then walked away from him. The boy walked idly down the sidewalk, inspecting the object in his hands. Carlton was moving pretty quickly now, and we were still standing there.

"Now?" I asked.

"Soon."

I watched her keep a bead on Carlton for half a block. Then, Carlton was enveloped in an orange, crackly halo, and shrunk out of existence. Opportunity lost.

"Now," said Athena, a hair too late, but she was already moving.

Toward the boy.

"Carlton!" she shouted when she was about three meters behind him. He stopped and turned, giving her just enough time to put the gun against his head. I was still catching up when I heard the shot. And the screams.

The boy was decapitated. Athena took the small packet from his dead hand. I felt her own hand on my wrist, slippery with the child's blood, and we flashed out.

March 2149

We materialized on my back lawn. It was the middle of the day. Assuming Helen still worked, she would be out of the house, which was preferable because I didn't want her to see her daughter covered in little boy head fragments. Athena tossed the package away in one direction, the gun in the other, fell down and wept. I sat next to her, doing what I did best: feeling helpless.

When she finally pulled herself together, she asked for the package. I brought it to her, trying to get as little blood on me as possible. She tore it open with no such consideration.

"Plans. Money. A recipe for dictatorship. I wonder how long he was grooming that little shit for his rise to power." She handed the packet to me. "Trash."

We went inside. Athena took a bath while I laundered her clothes. She borrowed an outfit from Helen while they were drying.

"Now what?" I said.

"Now we spend the rest of our lives doing this job, or as long as it takes to clean up all the Carltons out there. Assuming we can do that faster than he can make more of them."

"I'm not getting married," I asked. "Am I?"

She shrugged. "That's kind of up to you. To be honest, my primary interest in your relationship was for it to make as far as today."

I stared at her. "Are you really that mercenary?"

She got up and hugged me. After all we had been through, after what she had just done, at her base she was still my little girl. She kissed my cheek.

"No, Dad. I'm not that mercenary. I love you. That's real. But my purpose in protecting you has always included protecting my birth. I can't be undone. Not literally. But if you and mom hadn't gotten this far, if I was never born... This me wouldn't be the same. It's hard to explain."

"Then don't explain it," I said. "You are my daughter. It's my biological imperative to put your survival above my own. Also, I love you too."

"Thanks," she said, but there was no gratitude in it, no love. Only exhaustion. "So, are you ready to end this?"

I pictured a life of perpetual violence, taking my revenge against this man over and over, and in doing so protecting the world, and protecting Helen. But protecting her would mean losing her. We would never marry. She would raise our daughter alone, while I waged a war across time for years. And that daughter would become this woman of extraordinary strength, and terrible sadness. But they would survive. They both would. It would be worth it.

"Let's go." The world flashed.

[122]

May 2115

We materialized in the park. It was that same day. Carlton's parents were blissfully enjoying their time out with the baby. Athena turned on me.

"Why are we here?" she demanded.

"What do you mean?" I said.

"You brought us here! Why?"

I held up my hands. "I was following you! I had no idea where we were going!"

"We were going Carlton hunting! Not this!" She looked at her arm. "Did you do this? Did you? I should cut you out right now! Chop off my arm! I'd rather do without!" She paused. "You must have! How else?"

I would say she had gone completely insane, but she had much better training with her implant than I ever did, and more time using it. Clearly, she had learned how to communicate with it, and it with her. They were arguing now, over whether it had brought us here against her will. I had no idea whose side to take, if any. It occurred to me I had seen some variation of this before, multiple times, when she appeared to be arguing with herself. Suddenly she looked up.

"You!" she shouted. "You did this!"

And now I was lost. Was she screaming at God? I found this alienating in more ways than I could describe, but more than anything I wanted my little girl to be all right. And she was not all right.

"Athena?"

"What?" she snapped at me.

"I don't understand what's happening right now." I also had a growing concern about the attention she was drawing, but that appeared to be none, so far.

"Of course not," she said. "How could you know?" Her tone instantly became kind, nurturing. "I never told you. All these years. I couldn't." She stroked my cheek. "Not that you would have believed me."

I tried to imagine anything even less believable than my life for the last twenty years, and came up blank.

"Can you tell me now?" I lost her attention. She began ranting at the sky again.

"Is this how we do things now? Is this how it ends? No second chances you said! No *second* chances! Give me my first chance at least! You owe me that much! After all I've been for you! The things I have done to heal you!" It was the phrase "no second chances" that clinched it for me.

"Athena?" I asked carefully. "Are you talking to Time?"

"Yes," she hissed without taking her eyes off a point somewhere directly above us.

This was territory so unfathomably new for me that I had no tools to manage my journey into it.

"What is Time telling you?" I asked, desperately hoping it was something close to the right thing.

"Nothing!" she shouted at me. "Not a Goddamn thing!" She looked up again, and repeated even more loudly, "Not a Goddamn thing!"

There was no cognitive dissonance effect that would keep people from hearing this. And yet, they all went about their days as if nothing at all were happening. I was paralyzed with anxiety. Athena's rage at Space-Time brought elements of our entire relationship over the course of both of our lives to light. I thought back on those moments when she broke away from me and spoke in fragments to herself. She had been talking to Time.

She had been talking to the voices in her head.

"Why do you think Time can hear you?" I asked.

"She hears everything," Athena said, a bit predictably. For a touch of originality, she then added, "Psycho bitch."

"Does she talk to you?"

She brought her head down. The rage had drained out of it, replaced with her sadness, a quality I had grown to know far better than I ever wanted.

"No," she said. "Not anymore. Not like she used to."

"What did she say?" I asked. "When she used to talk to you?"

"That I was her favorite. That I was special. Unique. That I was her little girl, and that I had big work to do for her."

At these words, my heart disintegrated. My daughter had spent her life believing she was on a holy mission from Space-Time itself. How many warning signs had I seen of this? How many cries for help? What could it have been like for her to carry out these assignments of urgency and violence, all the while certain she acted on behalf of an abstract entity only she could reach? How much damage did I help her do to her own abused psyche?

"Did she tell you to steal the module?" I asked, bracing myself. "When you were fifteen?"

She glared at me then.

"I stole the module because I wanted to meet my father! I wanted to know that he was more than just the man who broke my mother's heart! You left her so empty she never talked about you! But she didn't have to. I heard enough from her friends. I spent my entire childhood hearing about the villain who tore the universe apart for the most selfish imaginable reason. Not for power. Not for heroism. He did it for lust! That's all I knew about you, and I wanted it not to be true. I wanted to meet you, and know that you weren't that man." And then the tears started. "I wanted to know that the only thing Mother ever told me about you was true. I wanted to know you did it for love."

I was stunned. So much to absorb at once.

And all I wanted was to hold my little girl and make it all better, but when I reached for her, she shrieked, "Don't touch me!" and threw her hands in front of her.

"I did do it for love," I said, desperate to find the words that would diminish her pain.

"That doesn't make it right! Don't you understand what you've done? Carlton West, for all his horrors, has nothing on you!"

Athena was falling away from me at the speed of light now, and tearing me apart in the process. I fought past the pain to find my daughter again.

"Something good came from all of this," I offered. "We had you."

"You *raped* Time!" she screamed, then began wailing, finally curling up into a ball on the lawn. "You raped Time," she sobbed. "And I am Time's baby."

I stumbled. Fell hard. Athena lay on the ground only a meter from me. It may as well have been the span of creation.

"Please don't mean that," I begged.

She crawled to me then. I sat still, unsure what to do, until she rested her head on my lap. I stroked her hair while the sobbing tapered out.

"I don't want to mean it," she squeaked. "Oh Daddy, I'm so sorry. I don't want to mean it."

"Shhh," I said, with no idea which one of us I was trying to soothe. "If we're not careful, someone's going to call a cop." I meant it as a joke. Something, anything to shatter the unbearable wall we were building between us now.

"They can't see us," she said. "She's protecting us. Like she always does."

The delusions went on. I tried to counter with science. "The cognitive dissonance—"

"What do you think causes that?" she said. "That's not a real thing. That's her. What do you think lets you travel exactly when and where you want to go, when the technology can barely handle seven years? That's her. It's always been her. She protects you, because she needs you."

"For what?" I whispered.

"To make me," she said. "That's what makes you different. That's why you and Mom couldn't unhappen. You made something unique, and the universe can't abide the possibility of losing it. I'm the glue that holds you together. I'm the girl who shouldn't be. I'm an anomaly. A cosmic curiosity." Then the sobbing came back. "I am an abomination."

"No!" I said, holding her closer. But even as I protested, some of what she said rang true. Maybe there was something to the theory that our connection through this impossible child had protected us from shifting with the world around us. Not some cosmic entity pulling strings, but a consequence of our actions across a field of energy we still did not properly understand.

"Yes," she said, pushing my arms aside and sitting up. "Wanting it not to be true doesn't make it not true. I am what I am. And what I am is her assassin. We came here to do a job. I want to do it and go home." She picked herself up and began to march straight to the stroller. Carlton's parents still didn't see her.

She was too far gone for reason now. She had brought us here, consciously or unconsciously, and laid that decision at the feet of some god only she knew. Her imaginary holy mission would claim this child, and I had no faith anything but horror would come from it.

"Wait!" I cried. "You said killing baby Carlton won't fix anything!"

"That baby," she said, "is not Carlton."

She blew out the mother's chest in one shot. While the father was still reacting to that, mostly by attempting to flee, she shot him in the back of

338

the head. It retained more of its mass than did the head of a ten-year-old boy, but not by much. Athena then put two bullets into the dead mother's face, and two more into the dead father's torso. She reached down and confiscated every portable object of value. Then she looked into the stroller. The baby was shrieking.

"I'm sorry," she told him.

I walked slowly to where she stood. The cognitive dissonance effect had been enough to hide us through Athena screaming at me, but the noise from that gun, and the carnage in its wake, would not go unnoticed.

"Athena…" I said, with absolutely no idea how to finish.

Her eyes locked on me, Athena pointed the gun at Carlton's dead father. "Stephen West," she said. "Twenty-eight years old. Youngest of three sons, and the only one with no interest in politics or business. He used his wealth and influence primarily as a patron of the arts. In 2132, he founded the West Prize for Composition, an annual award for best new symphony by a composer under the age of thirty, and was partially responsible for a surge of revitalized interest in that form. Now, that will never happen."

She pointed her gun at the remains of Carlton's mother. "Leticia Kincaid-West. Twenty-two years old. A media darling from the time she was in her teens, went on to become the spokesperson for no fewer than six charitable foundations, one of which developed the first successful vaccine against breast cancer. The vaccine will probably still happen, but at a projected delay of eighteen years."

People were finally starting to notice us. We might have had a minute before we were arrested or shot. Athena chose that moment to point her gun at the screaming infant.

"Desmond West. Five months old. He will now grow up an orphan, cared for by an extended family of means. He will, in fact, become a champion for preventing violent crimes, as the poster child of a horrendously brutal mugging. Or so the Project's models predict. There is a forty percent chance that this will set in motion a series of events that has very unhappy results."

In the distance, I heard a woman scream. There was no way for me know how many people were now giving us their attention without turning around, but I could not take my eyes off of Athena.

"Carlton West would have been born in 2120. Now he never will. The world is now safe, probably. All it cost us was the lives of two truly good people, and one baby the loss of his parents. Stephen and Leticia West never knew me, but I have known them for twenty years. They were good people. Wonderful people, whose only fault was bringing a child into the world with mental health problems they could never hope to fix. And for twenty years, I have begged for this day not to come."

As I pondered the reality of knowing exactly how it felt to be a parent confronted with a child's mental health problems I could never hope to fix, she pointed her gun at me.

"You did this," she said. "You made this happen. You did it by cheating the rules of the universe to get yourself a girlfriend, and you did it by pushing back when the universe didn't like that." She bent down and trailed her fingers through the grass beside what was left of Leticia Kincaid-West. When she brought them back up, they were coated in red, and she held them out to me. "You did this, Daddy."

There was nothing I could say. I wanted her to be wrong about me, but even in the face of her madness, I had no idea how to make myself believe that, let alone her. I could hear a siren.

"It's time to go," I said, holding out my hand to her, desperate to find a way to make any of this right, desperate to have my daughter back. "Please."

"So go."

I couldn't leave her there. "Don't do this to your mother," I said. It was a guess. A good guess.

"You bastard." She flashed out. Eight years from then, for her, a healed and remorseful Athena and I would make peace. I had already been there. This was the last time I would ever see my daughter.

I flashed out too.

[123]

March 2149

I went home. The house was still there. Carlton's absence across history should have, in theory, wiped out everything I knew. Pathetic Future Me would never meet Helen, and I would never be brought here in his crazed attempt to win her. And yet, my home accepted my key.

I found Helen in the living room, staring at the fireplace. By all rights, she should not be here. Athena should have unhappened everything about our connection. But even through this, we were together. Somehow, the fact of our impossible baby superseded every other concern. God only knew what contortions to history had been necessary to preserve that without Carlton. The marks my actions had left on the universe were apparently permanent.

"Hello," she said, her eyes still on the fire.

"Hey," I said. At that, she did look at me. She looked different, though not in any physically describable way. She was every bit as beautiful as she had always been. But her eyes held some ineffable quality I had never seen there before.

"How long have we known each other?" I asked.

She thought for a moment. "Five years," she said. "More, I think, for you. Eight? Ten? Do you even know?"

"No," I admitted.

"We made a baby."

I sat with her on the couch. "I know."

"She's changing me, you know," said Helen. "I can feel it already."

"Changing you?" I almost asked how she felt different, but at that moment, I really didn't want to know. She told me anyway.

"Into something like you," she said. She looked away for a moment, then turned back and stared into my eyes. "I think I am finally beginning to understand you. I… remember things. Things that never happened. Or that happened, and then didn't happen."

"Unhappened," I prompted.

"Yes." She nodded. "*That's* it. Unhappened. I never really understood that idea before. Not like this, anyway." She stopped there. Somehow Athena had given her the one thing I had spent so much of my life keeping from her: the memories of a traveler. I could only imagine how she felt. I had spent my life constantly adjusting to newly revised histories, but no matter how rapidly, I had only ever needed to contend with one change at a time. Helen was now confronted with dozens—perhaps countless—alternative pasts at once, all real, all remembered, and none valid.

"There was a man," she said suddenly.

"A man?" I said. Silently, I begged her not to pursue that thought. Carlton no longer existed. Would never exist. Even after the scale of damage our war had wrought, my thoughts fell back to the petty fear that he would continue to compete with me for Helen's attention, even from oblivion.

"Wasn't there? A man named West. Westley. That's not right. Something Something West. Let's just say West. Wasn't there?"

"Yes." I offered nothing else, and for a moment it seemed she wouldn't ask.

"He did things. Terrible things. And I loved him? Can that be right?"

I sighed. "Those are both true." I wanted to tell her that she stopped loving him when he went mad. That her love for me overtook her love for him, and from that point she saw him only as a villain. But I couldn't. I want to say I held back out of some noble desire to honor a vanquished foe. The reality is I didn't want to make her remember anything else about him.

She frowned. "But he isn't anymore?"

I shook my head. "No."

"And that's good. Because, you know, terrible things?"

I laughed. "Right."

She scrutinized me. "I love you," she said. It was more a question than a declaration.

"Yes," I said.

"You did terrible things. Is that what I do? Do I love men who do terrible things?"

I thought back on the last few years of my life. I had indeed done terrible things. To the best of my knowledge, no one had ever died directly at my hand, but I conspired with Athena to cause the deaths of thousands. Maybe more, directly or indirectly.

"I did necessary things," I said.

She looked more deeply into my eyes, and frowned in confusion. "You think I mean the wars," she said. "People died. Countries fell." She shook her head. "Or something. Yes?"

"Something like that," I said.

"I don't mean that. You broke time. Didn't you?"

This was my opportunity to lay blame at the feet of my older, wretched self. I did not take it.

"To be with you," I admitted. "That doesn't mean you love men who do terrible things."

"No," she agreed. "It means I inspire them to do terrible things." Her words were angry, but her eyes softened then. "But I do love you."

"I love you, too. Very much."

"You do. And that makes me happy." She tucked her arm through my elbow and rested her head on my shoulder. "Very happy."

We sat there for a minute or two, which I spent hoping would never, ever end. I fought back the knowledge that Athena had grown up without a father. If nothing else, by now, I knew the past could be changed. We could unhappen that childhood. We could raise her as loving parents, and save her from the madness I had seen in her adult self. For that brief, silent moment, I allowed myself the fantasy of optimism.

"But you have to go now," she whispered.

I thought back on all the times I had marched off to war with Athena, leaving Helen behind to worry, and then remember nothing. At that moment, this was what I heard in Helen's voice, and it gave me great joy to reassure her.

"I don't. I won't ever have to go again."

She sat up, away from me.

"Nigel, I'm asking you to leave."

Even with every reason to foresee this, I still managed to let it surprise me. Perhaps it was the fact that this was the first purely coherent thing I heard Helen say in her fractured state of mind. Or perhaps I was simply a fool.

"Please don't ask me to do that."

She took my hand. "You don't belong here. You never did. I always knew it. I knew, and it didn't bother me, because I love you more than I ever believed I could love a person. But now I *feel* it. I *feel* it, Nigel, and it's so wrong. Time is broken. The universe is slippery."

"We can get past this," I said. "Remember? Face it together?"

"Because that's how we roll?" she asked. The familiar phrase appeared to shatter her moment of clarity, and I could see the chaos reasserting itself in her eyes. A tear formed and rolled down her cheek.

"Right."

She shook her head, wiped away the tear.

"Not this time. I understand now. I remember things. Things I knew, and then didn't know, and now I know them all at once. Some of them don't make any sense. And some of them I can only remember in pieces. But I remember enough." A note of bitterness crept into that last word. She stood then, and faced away from me. "How many times did the world end, Nigel? How many people died? How many times did they die? I remember plagues, and war machines, and nuclear bombs. I remember a cloud of ash blocking out the sun. So many people died, Nigel. And they died over and over and over again. And for what?"

I stood, and put my hand on her shoulder.

"They're not dead anymore," I said.

At that, she turned to face me, pulling away at the same time.

"But they are!" she shouted. "I know it! I remember it! I feel it! Just because they all got second chances, and third chances, and more, doesn't mean I can forget. They died so that we could be together. How is that fair? How is that right? We did that to them. Both of us. We killed the world over and over to buy ourselves more time. I want to blame it on this man West, or a version of you that doesn't even exist yet. But I can't. We did this! You and I!"

"That's all over," I said. "We have a chance to start over now."

"And have what kind of life, exactly?" she demanded. "I'll always know how we got here! I will never be able to look at you without seeing the stain of what we did! What I caused!" As she said it, I could see that stain in her eyes as well. She looked away. "You can't stay."

I considered begging. I considered refusing. I considered pointing out that this was my house. I went with direct.

"I don't want to go."

"I don't want you to go either," she said. "But you have to." Her lip began to tremble. "I look at you and all I can see is death. And I love you. And it's killing me." She put her hand to her mouth and closed her eyes, and for a moment I thought she might actually vomit.

344

"I have nowhere to go."

"You have everywhere and everywhen to go," she told me. And she was right. The module in my arm would outlive me, and never fail. I had learned that much about it over the years.

I made one last attempt.

"Helen, we can overcome this."

Still looking away from me, she shook her head.

"I can't," she said. "You threw the universe to the wolves just to have me, and I can't..." She broke down there, and through her weeping, was barely able to say, "I can't."

"This is my burden, not yours."

"If you knew what was really coming, would you have given me up?"

I thought back to our aborted meeting with the older version of Carlton, his warnings, and his offer to save us from our own future.

"I don't know," I said honestly.

She let out a sound somewhere between a choked sob and a pained laugh.

"You don't know." She put her hand on my cheek. "But I do know. I know you wouldn't have stopped it, because I never would have let you. Every single time I heard the tales of the monsters you slew, the only part of the story that mattered to me was the part where you came home. The horror was never real to me, because I still had you. I still had Athena." She pulled her hand away and looked down. "But I see it all now. All the times I threw the world to hell to have one more day with you. I can't live with it." She looked up again, her blue eyes puffy and saturated. "I can't live with you."

Against her disappointment in me, or even her resentment, I might have stood a chance. Against her remorse, I was helpless. I truly did not belong there. I could counter-argue this all day long, and it would still be true. There was nothing to be gained but pain for both of us if I stayed.

"Okay," I choked out.

She took a deep breath to control her tears. Then she reached into her pocket, turned over my hand, and put something in it. I held it up to see the box for her engagement ring.

"This was a gift," I said.

"It was a beautiful gift, and I will never stop cherishing it," she said. Then she curled my fingers over the box and pushed my closed hand to my heart. "But this is for you."

Reluctantly, I put the box in my pocket. I could feel its weight pulling me down.

"Please tell my daughter you loved me," I said. "Please let her know I gave you some happiness. Do that much for me, will you?"

Helen laid her hand on her belly, and smiled at me, one final time. Even in its sadness, and its pale shadow of the smile of wonder and joy that had so hypnotized me so many times, it was still the most beautiful thing I had ever seen.

"Of course."

I closed my eyes, and silently asked to be sent to a random time and place. When I opened them, I was out of Helen's life.

[124]

Unknown

I found myself on a beach. It was a sunny day, and there were a lot of people playing, swimming, and generally loving life all around me. The sea level air invigorated me almost immediately, and as much as I planned to spend the next fifty years wallowing in the misery of my failed existence, I found the moment did not lend itself to that. I was still wearing a sweater for the March weather, and I promptly pulled it off and left it on the sand.

There was a boardwalk and a pier. I had no interest in the rides or shops, but a walk out on the pier, to feel the salt spray on my face, held some appeal. There were a handful of people with fishing rods, complaining about how many more fish used to be here before the whatever random event they thought had driven them away and/or killed them off. I basked in the banality of their imagined problems.

When I reached the end of the pier, I found another man there, staring off to the watery horizon. He greeted me in a friendly, if distracted, manner. I was about to return the greeting when I realized it was Carlton. He was younger than when I last spoke to him in the café in Amherst, and quite a bit older than when I watched Athena explode his head off. I had asked for a random time and place, and this was what I got. Memo to self: be more specific. He showed no sign of recognition. I pressed the point.

"Excuse me," I said. "Do I know you?"

He looked me in the eyes, with the strangest sort of confusion, like he was confused about the fact of being confused.

"Are there people who know me?" he asked. "I thought knowing was for other people. People who are realer people."

This was Athena's consequence. She knew if she were never born, the Athena I knew would become this phantom.

"I'm sorry," I said. "I mistook you for someone who exists." He showed no sign of offense.

"You're the first person who has ever seen him," said an older woman with a fishing pole. "He's not used to that. Probably has no clue what to think."

She had her back to me. I watched her reel in her line and cast it again. "You can see him. Why can't anyone else?"

"Cognitive dissonance, if you like the jargon. I prefer to think it's the universe keeping him out of trouble."

Her voice was familiar, but not immediately recognizable. But really, how many people could she be?

"You seem to know a lot," I said. "You're not one of them time travelers, are you?"

"Shifty lot, them travelers," she said. "I hear they lost one a while back. Went rogue. Canceled the whole damn program after that."

"Is that a fact?"

"Yepper," she said. "Test pilot. They say it was the Time Madness got her."

I walked over to her, and sat on the edge of the pier, my feet dangling in the spray.

"How long have you been out here, Andrea?"

She laughed. "You have no idea how it feels to see a familiar face. How have you been, Graham?"

"It's Nigel, actually."

"Like I don't know that," she said. "To answer your question, if by 'out here' you mean wandering time with no fixed abode, about thirty years." I could see the prototype module now, strapped to her left wrist.

I pointed back to Carlton with my thumb.

"How many of those are there?"

"I've counted sixteen, myself. Kind of stopped keeping track of them when Athena took care of business. Sorry about that, by the way."

"I'm okay," I said. "Sixteen seems like a lot."

"It was a lot when they were doing things. Now they just stare off into space. No one has any idea they're there. They barely know it themselves.

They have enough sense to steal food and clothes, and keep from soiling themselves, but that's about it."

I sat for a bit in reflective silence.

Finally, I said, "I'm a time nomad now."

"I know," she said.

"You looking for a sidekick?"

She laughed. "Hell, yes."

We held hands, and flashed out.

EPILOGUE

C irca 2500 BCE-2198
I traveled with Andrea for eighteen years. We went as far
back as ancient Egypt, and watched the Pyramids being
constructed from the safety of our cognitive dissonance cloud. We
attended concerts by Beethoven, Louis Armstrong, and The Beatles. We
watched the live news coverage of the first moon landing, and we stood
on the deck of the Titanic, right until it started to tip. We ventured into
the future as well, but as Andrea had discovered long ago, that direction
was profoundly limited. We never managed to get more than twenty
years beyond our starting point. My fifty-two year jaunt had been
something of an anomaly, but was made possible by the technicality that I
was just being moved from one past to another. There was never a real
future involved.

At the end of that time, she retired. We set her up in a spectacular
mansion with every manner of convenience, and private nursing care
when she began to run down. After that, I was on my own.

Sometimes I would check in on the other versions of me out there.
The one who replaced me in 2092 went the rest of his life without
another unhappening, eventually becoming the professor I met in 2146.
By then, he had overwritten some of that one's memories, so the fact of
manned time travel stopped being such a wonder for him. We stayed
friends, but there's only so much time one can spend with one's self. Any
of one's selves. I have no idea what became of the Nigel from 2155 who
set all of this into motion. If I understood the theory correctly, it seemed

likely that the professor from 2146 would eventually merge with that one. Maybe his pain would be overwritten. Or maybe it would dominate. I chose not to find out. Whatever his destiny, I needed to distance myself from him. I needed to believe I did not have to become him.

Occasionally, I would get an unexpected visit from a younger version of Athena. These were usually by accident, extremely awkward, and confusing for her. She was not used to knowing less than I did. I wouldn't say it was a substitute for healing the relationship we once had, now permanently fractured, but it was adorable, like watching an old home movie. She never stayed long, but every moment with her was a treasure beyond value.

I stayed away from Helen, or at least as far as she knew, I did. I kept tabs on her enough to know that when I left, she went on to be one of the driving voices in the Project. Apparently the entire time Athena had been taking her orders from them, one of the people giving those orders was her own mother. I wondered if that had any bearing on why they never did give her the kill order for Carlton.

When I learned of Helen's illness, I finally broke down and traveled to her final week. I had no desire to encounter any of her family or friends, particularly our daughter. As it happened, sneaking into a hospital room did not prove much of a challenge. I sat with her while she slept, on several occasions. Once I held her hand when she woke. Her smile was exactly as I remembered it. I hoped mine was half as enchanting.

When she passed away, I made a conscious decision to drop all travel to the span of time coincident with her life. It was the only way I had left to respect her wishes. I did, however, leave frequent gifts on her grave.

I kept the ring box she gave me that last day. For years, it was my only true possession, the only constant object in my life. That last week, the very last time I went to see her, I planned to slip the ring back onto her finger while she slept. Probably not the most tasteful gesture, I know, but it was all I had. When I picked up her hand, the ring was already there. In all the time I carried the box, I had never opened it, imagining I would not be able to cope with the pain of seeing it. I opened it then, expecting it to be empty. It was not. In place of the ring was a tiny piece of black plastic. A child's toy.

A miniature stingray.

ACKNOWLEDGMENTS

As always, my perpetual gratitude goes to Guinevere Crescenzi, who will forever be the person who prodded me just the right amount at the right time to get me to start writing novels. Four books later, they are all her grandchildren, so to speak. Thanks also to Steve and Eliza Carabello, Katie Knapp, and Todd Yuninger, for carrying the torch of our writers group, and continuing to provide helpful insight, nitpicking, and generally calling me out when I write crap. Which isn't very often. But often enough.

A special category of writers group gratitude is due to its other member, my wife, Annelisa Aubry-Walton. The support she provides, and the many forms it takes, cannot be overstated. Bonus thanks go to my daughter Delphi Aubry, apprentice editor and aspiring novelist. At twelve years old, she was already spotting errors and continuity glitches that dozens of adults missed. Two years later, I continue to rely on her keen eye and honest criticism, which is often some of the most mature feedback I get.

The number of beta readers who read the entire manuscript of Unhappenings was significantly greater than either of my first two novels, and for the first time, that group included current students of mine. Every single one of them contributed comments and questions that drove my revisions, and every one of them deserves recognition. So, many thanks to Dorian Hart, Jeanne Kramer-Smyth, Josh Bluestein,

Andie McAuliff, Ellen Purton, Tamara Klinger, Ashley Stahle, Ana Carroll, Leeanne Leary, Kayla Zimmerman, and Katie Schweitzer. An additional nod goes to Matt Beck, who convinced me that a book I had always envisioned as a standalone story had genuine potential for a sequel. That next book is currently underway, and Matt will move to the top of its acknowledgments page when it sees print.

Finally, my highest order of gratitude this time is rightfully bestowed on Lori Bentley-Law, author of the fantastic novel *Motor Dolls*. Lori has been the coach I needed to keep me moving and keep me on target, as I have striven to return that favor for her own writing. Trading chapters of works-in-progress with an author as talented as she is has been a boon to my productivity. The two novels I have written so far under this buddy system are the ones of which I am most proud. As an added perk, her books are an absolute joy to read. It delights me to see them evolve, and to be a part of nudging her along. Thank you, Lori, for this partnership, for the quality of your peer editing, and for sharing your stories with me. (PS: I have another chapter to send you...)

ABOUT THE AUTHOR

Edward Aubry is a graduate of Wesleyan University, with a degree in music composition. Improbably, this preceded a career as a teacher of high school mathematics and creative writing.

He now lives in rural Pennsylvania with his wife and three spectacular daughters, where he fills his non-teaching hours spinning tales of time-travel, wise-cracking pixies, and an assortment of other impossible things.

ALSO BY EDWARD AUBRY

The Mayhem Wave Series

On May 30, 2004, the world suddenly transformed into a bizarre landscape populated with advanced technology, dragons, magic and destruction. Now what few humans remain must start over, braving wilderness, dangerous beasts, and new and powerful enemies.

Prelude to Mayhem

Static Mayhem

Mayhem's Children

Balance of Mayhem

Printed in Great Britain
by Amazon

17078391R00207